UNFORGIVEN

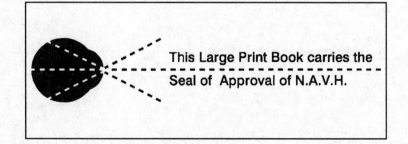

This Large Print Book carries the
Seal of Approval of N.A.V.H.

THE HORSEMEN TRILOGY

Unforgiven

Mary Balogh

THORNDIKE PRESS
A part of Gale, Cengage Learning

GALE
CENGAGE Learning·

Farmington Hills, Mich • San Francisco • New York • Waterville, Maine
Meriden, Conn • Mason, Ohio • Chicago

GALE
CENGAGE Learning®

LIBRARY OF CONGRESS CATALOGING-IN-PUBLICATION DATA

Names: Balogh, Mary, author.
Title: Unforgiven / by Mary Balogh.
Description: Large print edition. | Waterville, Maine : Thorndike Press, 2016. | Series: The horsemen trilogy | Series: Thorndike Press large print historical fiction
Identifiers: LCCN 2016021336 | ISBN 9781410489241 (hardcover) | ISBN 1410489248 (hardcover)
Subjects: LCSH: First loves—Fiction. | Large type books. | GSAFD: Love stories. | Regency fiction.
Classification: LCC PR6052.A465 U54 2016b | DDC 823/.914—dc23
LC record available at https://lccn.loc.gov/2016021336

Published in 2016 by arrangement with New American Library, an imprint of Penguin Publishing Group, a division of Penguin Random House LLC

UNFORGIVEN

1

"I am for bed," Nathaniel Gascoigne said, yawning hugely as he lifted his brandy glass and noted with a look of faint regret that it was empty. "Now, if only I had legs to take me outsh— outside and carry me home. . . ."

"And if only you could remember where home is," Eden Wendell, Baron Pelham, said dryly. "You are foxed, Nat. We are all foxed. Have another drink."

Kenneth Woodfall, Earl of Haverford, raised his glass, which still contained an inch of brandy, and looked at the other two, who were sprawled inelegantly in two chairs on either side of the fire. He himself was propped against the mantel, to one side of it. "A toast," he said.

"A toast," Mr. Gascoigne repeated and then swore quite profanely as his glass drew level with his eye again. "Nothing to toast *with,* Ken."

Kenneth waited politely while his friend lurched to his feet, crossed unsteadily to the sideboard, and returned with a much-depleted decanter of brandy. He poured some into each of their glasses, succeeding with marvelous skill in not spilling any.

"A toast," Kenneth said again. "To being foxed."

"To being foxed," the other two repeated solemnly, and they all drank deeply to their own inebriation.

"And to being free and merry," Lord Pelham said, lifting his glass again, "and *alive*."

"And alive," Kenneth repeated.

"In spite of Old Boney," Mr. Gascoigne added. "Devil take it." They toasted the freedom they had each bought after Waterloo with the sale of their commissions in a cavalry regiment. They toasted the merriment that had followed their arrival in London. And they toasted their survival of years of fighting against Napoleon Bonaparte, first in Spain and Portugal and then in Belgium. Mr. Gascoigne added, "It don't seem the same without old Rex here with us."

"May he rest in peace," Lord Pelham said, and they all lapsed into reverent silence.

Kenneth would have sat down if the nearest empty chair had not been some distance from the fire or if he could have been quite sure that his legs would carry him that far. He had progressed beyond the comfortable stage of inebriation. He had probably arrived there hours ago. They had drunk more than was good for them during dinner at White's. They had drunk at the theater, both during the intervals and in the green room afterward. They had drunk in Louise's parlor before going upstairs with three of Louise's girls who had sat with them there. They had drunk at Sandford's card party, which they had joined after leaving Louise's. And they had drunk here in Eden's rooms — because it was too early to go home to bed, they had all agreed.

"Rex was the wise one," Kenneth said, setting his half-empty glass down carefully on the mantel. He looked ahead with an inward grimace at the size of the headache he would be nursing when he woke up some time around noon or later. It was something he — and his friends — had been doing with increasing regularity for weeks now. All in the cause of freedom and merriment.

"Eh?" Mr. Gascoigne yawned loudly. "To take himself off to Stratton Park when he had sworn to spend the winter here with us, enjoying himself?"

"There is nothing for him at Stratton but

respectability and work and endless dull-ness," Lord Pelham said, loosening his already loosened cravat. "We promised ourselves a winter of self-indulgence."

Yes, they had. And they had spent the autumn indulging themselves with every entertainment, excess, and debauchery that had presented itself. They expected even better of the winter: parties and balls, respectable entertainments to balance the less respectable ones. Ladies to ogle and flirt with as well as lightskirts to bed. Parson's mousetrap to avoid.

Kenneth hiccuped. "Rex was the wise one," he said again. "Unalloyed pleasure can grow tedious."

"You need another drink, Ken," Mr. Gascoigne said with some alarm, reaching for the decanter, which he had set beside his chair. "You are beginning to spout heresy."

But Kenneth shook his head. It never paid to think when one was drunk, but he was doing it anyway. They had talked endlessly, the four of them, about what they would do when the wars were over. They had talked about it at a time when it had seemed very probable that they would not survive at all. They had been close friends for years. Indeed, one fellow officer had even dubbed them the Four Horsemen of the Apocalypse

10

for their daring and often reckless exploits in battle. They had dreamed of going home to England, selling out, going to London, and giving themselves up to enjoyment. Nothing but enjoyment — mindless, unalloyed pleasure.

Rex had been the first to see that enjoyment for its own sake did not satisfy forever or even for very long — certainly not for a full autumn *and* winter. Rex Adams, Viscount Rawleigh, had gone home to his estate in Kent. He was settling in to life after war, life after survival.

"Ken is starting to sound like Rex," Lord Pelham said, holding his head with one hand. "Devil take it, but someone should stop the room from spinning. And someone should stop *him.* He will be talking about going home to Cornwall next. Cornwall! The back of beyond. Don't do it, Ken, old boy. You would die of boredom in a fortnight."

"Don't put ideas in his head," Mr. Gascoigne said. "We need you, Ken, old chap. Though we don't need your damned looks to turn the eyes of even the whores away from us. Do we, Ede? On second thought, we would be wise to let you go. Go home, Ken. Shoo! Go home to Cornwall. We will write to tell you about all the gorgeous look-

11

ers who come to town for Christmas."

"And fawn all over us," Lord Pelham added, grinning and then grimacing. "We are heroes, you know."

Kenneth grinned too. His friends were not such bad lookers themselves, though they were somewhat the worse for wear at the moment, sprawled as they were in their chairs, deep in their cups. Of course, in Spain they had always accused him of having the unfair advantage of being blond and thus more attractive than they to the Spanish ladies.

He had not given serious thought to going home, though he supposed he would have to, eventually. Dunbarton Hall in Cornwall had been his for seven years, since the death of his father, though he had not been there for longer than eight years. Even when wounds had brought him back to England six years ago, he had avoided going home. When he had left, he had vowed to himself that he would never go back.

"We should all go there," he said. "Come with me. Christmas in the country and all that." He lifted his glass to his lips and frowned when he saw his empty hand.

Mr. Gascoigne groaned.

"Country misses and all that?" Lord Pelham said, waggling his eyebrows.

"And country matrons and country squires," Mr. Gascoigne said. "And country morals. Don't do it, Ken. I take back what I said. We will put up with your damned handsome exterior, won't we, Ede? We will compete for the ladies with our superior charm — and Ede's blue eyes. A man can look like a gargoyle and the ladies don't notice, if he has blue eyes."

There was no reason why he should not go back, Kenneth thought. Eight years was a long time. Everything would have changed. Every*one* would have changed. He was a different person. He was no longer an earnest and idealistic young man with romantic dreams. The very thought was amusing. God, but he wished he had not drunk so much. And he wished he had not gone to Louise's — again. He was getting sick of casual beddings. And sick of endless drinking and gaming. It was funny really — for years the life he had lived for the past few months had been his dream of heaven on earth.

"I mean it," he said. "Come to Dunbarton for Christmas." He remembered Christmases as the merriest of times at Dunbarton, the house overflowing with guests, the days filled with parties — and the grand ball on the day following Christmas.

Mr. Gascoigne groaned again.

His mother would be delighted, Kenneth thought. She spent most of her time now in Norfolk at Ainsleigh's. Viscount Ainsleigh was married to Helen, Kenneth's sister. His mother would love to come to Dunbarton. She had written to him more than once asking him when he intended returning there, and when he intended choosing a bride. Ainsleigh and Helen and their children would come too, though Helen might not be too eager about it, he supposed. There were armies of relatives who would come, despite the rather short notice. He would invite some himself. He would give his mother carte blanche to invite others as she saw fit.

No, there was really no need to avoid going back to Dunbarton. Was there? He frowned and thought of one reason. But she would be eight years older than eighteen by now. The devil — he frowned in concentration over the arithmetic. Six-and-twenty? It was hard to imagine. She would be married with a parcel of children. *That* was hard to imagine too. He reached out to take his glass from the mantel — of course, he had set it down there — and drained its contents. He grimaced.

"He means it, Nat," Lord Pelham said.

"He is going."

"He means it, Ede," Mr. Gascoigne agreed. "Tonight he means it — or do I mean this morning? Deuce take it, what time *is* it? Tomorrow — or do I mean today? — he will change his mind. Sobriety always brings sanity. Think of all he will miss if he goes to Cornwall."

"Hangovers," Kenneth said.

"He will miss hangovers," Lord Pelham said. "They do not have hangovers in Cornwall, Nat."

"They do not have *liquor* in Cornwall, Ede," Mr. Gascoigne said.

"Smugglers," Kenneth said. "Where do you think all the best smuggled liquor lands? I'll tell you. Cornwall, my fine lads." But he did not particularly want to think about smugglers. Or about hangovers, for that matter. "I am going. For Christmas. Are you coming?"

"Not me, Ken," Lord Pelham said. "I have wild oats yet to sow."

"And I have to find a bed," Mr. Gascoigne muttered. "Preferably my own. Cornwall is too far away, Ken."

He would go on his own, then, Kenneth decided. After all, Rex had gone alone to Stratton when they had all refused to accompany him. It was time he went home.

15

High time. It seemed rather typical of him, though, that the decision should be made impetuously, while he was too drunk to think straight at all. There were all sorts of reasons why he should not go. No, there were not. Dunbarton was his. It was home. And *she* was six-and-twenty and married with a parcel of children. Had someone told him that?

"Come along, Nat," he said, taking the risk of pushing his shoulder free of the mantel. "Let us see if we can weave our way home together. Rex has probably been in bed for hours already and will wake with the dawn — and with a clear head, the lucky devil."

Both his friends winced visibly. Mr. Gascoigne stood up and appeared rather surprised that his legs held him, even if they did so rather unsteadily.

Yes, Rex was the wise one, Kenneth thought. It was time to go home. Home to bed and home to Dunbarton.

It was a beautiful day for early December: crisply chill, it was true, but bright and sunny, nevertheless. The sun sparkled off the surface of the sea like thousands of diamonds, and the wind that so often whipped across the water to buffet the land

and knife through its inhabitants was a mere gentle breeze today.

The lady who sat at the top of the steep cliff, almost at its edge, in a slight grassy hollow of land that hid her from the road behind, clasped her arms about her knees and drew in deep breaths of the salt air. She felt soothed and invigorated both at the same time.

Everything was about to change, but surely for the better. How could it be otherwise when she had thought herself beyond the age of marriage just two days ago — she was six-and-twenty years old — and was now awaiting the arrival of her future husband? She had told herself for the past several years that she had no wish to marry, that she was happy to live at Penwith Manor with her widowed mother, enjoying a freedom that most women never knew. But the freedom was illusory, and she had always known it. For longer than a year she had lived with insecurity and ignored it because there had been nothing she could do about it. She was a mere woman after all.

Penwith Manor had belonged to her father and to his father before him and so on back through six generations. But on her father's death, it — and his baronet's title — had passed to a distant cousin. In the fourteen months since her father's death, she had continued to live there with her mother, but they had both been fully aware that Sir Edwin Baillie might at any moment wish to take up residence there himself or else sell it or lease it. What would become of them then? Where would they go? What would they do? Sir Edwin would probably not turn them out destitute, but they might have to move to a very small home with a correspondingly small income. It had not been a pleasant prospect.

But now Sir Edwin had made his decision and had written a lengthy letter to Lady Hayes to announce his intention of taking a bride so that he might produce sons to secure his inheritance and to care for his own mother and three sisters in the event of his untimely passing. His intention was to solve two problems at once by marrying his third cousin once removed, Miss Moira Hayes. He would come to Penwith Manor within the week to make his offer and to arrange for their wedding in the spring.

Miss Moira Hayes, he had seemed to assume, would be only too happy to accept his offer. And after the initial shock, the initial indignation over his taking her meek compliance for granted, Moira had had to admit that she *was* happy. Or if not exactly happy, then at least content. Accepting would be the sensible thing to do. She was six-and-twenty and living in precarious circumstances. She had met Sir Edwin Baillie once, soon after Papa's death when he had come with his mother to inspect his new property. She had found him dull and somewhat pompous, but he was young — not much older than five-and-thirty at a guess — and respectable and passably good-looking even if not handsome. Besides, Moira told herself, looks were in no way important, especially to an aging spinster who had long outlived any dreams of romance or romantic love.

She rested her chin on her knees and smiled rather ruefully down at the sea below the cliffs. Oh, yes, she had long outlived dreams. But then, so much had changed since her childhood, since her girlhood. So much had changed outside herself, within herself. She was now very ordinary, very dull, very respectable. She laughed softly. Yet she had never outlived the habit of going off by herself, though a respectable female had no business being alone outside her own home. This had always been a favorite spot. But it was a long time since she had last been here. She was not sure

19

what had drawn her here today. Had she come to say good-bye to dreams? It was a somber thought.

But it need not be a depressing one. Marriage with Sir Edwin would doubtless bring no real happiness with it, but then, it probably would bring no great unhappiness either. Marriage would be what she made of it. Sir Edwin wanted children — sons. Well, so did she. Just two days ago, she had thought even that dream impossible.

She tensed suddenly as a dog barked somewhere behind her. She tightened her hold on her knees, and her toes clenched inside her half boots. But it was not a stray. Someone gave it a sharp command and it fell silent. She listened attentively for a few moments, but she could hear nothing except the sea and the breeze and the gulls overhead. They had gone, the man and the dog. She relaxed again.

But just as she did so, something caught at the edge of her vision, and she knew that she had been discovered, that someone else had found this spot, that her peace had been shattered. She felt mortified at being caught sitting on the grass like a girl, hugging her knees. She turned her head sharply.

The sun was behind him. She had the impression of a tall, broad-shouldered man dressed fashionably in a many-caped great-coat with a tall beaver hat and black top boots. He had arrived earlier than expected, she thought. He would certainly not approve of finding his future bride thus, alone and unchaperoned. How had he known she was here? She was more than three miles from home. Perhaps his dog had alerted him. Where was the dog?

Those thoughts flashed through her mind in the mere fraction of a second and were gone. Almost instantly she knew that he was not Sir Edwin Baillie. And in the same instant she knew who he was, even though she could not see his face clearly and had not set eyes on him for longer than eight years.

She was not sure afterward how long they stayed thus, staring at each other, she sitting on the grass with her arms about her knees, he standing above the hollow, against the skyline. It might have been minutes, but was probably only seconds.

"Hello, Moira," he said at last.

Kenneth had come to Cornwall alone, apart from his valet and his coachman and his dog. He had been unable to persuade Eden and Nat to come with him. They had been unable to persuade him to change his mind, even though his decision to come had been made when he was deeply inebriated. But then, he often acted on impulse. There was a restlessness in him that had never quite been put to rest since his sudden decision to leave home and buy himself a commission in the cavalry.

He was coming home for Christmas. His mother, Ainsleigh and Helen, numerous other family members, and some friends of his mother's were coming after him. Eden and Nat might come in the spring, they had said, if he was still here in the spring. Perhaps Rex would come too.

It had been a mad decision. Winter was not the best time to travel into such a remote part of the country. But the weather was kind to him as he journeyed west, and despite himself, he felt his spirits rise as the landscape became more familiar. For the last two days he rode, with only Nelson for company, leaving his carriage and his servants and baggage to follow him at a slower pace. He wondered by how many days his letter to Mrs. Whiteman, the housekeeper at Dunbarton, had preceded him. Not by many, at a guess. He could imagine the sort of consternation he had caused belowstairs. However, they need not worry. He was used to rough living and no one else would arrive for another two weeks.

He rode frequently in sight of the sea along a road that never took him any great distance from the edge of high cliffs except when it dipped down into river valleys and up the other side after passing through fishing villages and allowing him glimpses of golden beaches and stone quays and bobbing fishing boats.

How could he ever have thought that he would never come back?

The next dip in the road, he knew at last, would give him a view down into the village of Tawmouth. Not that he would go down there on this particular occasion. Dunbarton was on this side of the valley, no more than three or four miles inland. There was sudden elation at the thought. And memories crowded in on him — memories of his boyhood, of people he had known, places he had frequented. One of the latter must be close by.

Nostalgia caught at his stomach and knotted it. He unconsciously slowed his horse's pace. It had been one of his favorite places, that hollow. It had been a quiet, secluded place, where one could sit unobserved on the grass, alone with the elements and with one's dreams. Alone with *her.* Yes, they had met there sometimes. But he would no longer allow memories of her to color all his memories of home. He had had a happy boyhood.

He would have ridden on by if Nelson had not barked, his head toward the hollow. Was someone there? Quite unreasonably, Kenneth felt offended at the thought.

"Sit, Nelson," he commanded before his dog could dash away to investigate.

Nelson sat and gazed upward with intelligent eyes, waiting for further orders. Without realizing it, Kenneth saw, he had drawn to a complete stop. His horse lowered its head to crop at the grass. How familiar it all looked. As if the eight years and longer had never been.

He dismounted, left his horse to graze unfettered and Nelson to wait for the command to be revoked, and walked silently toward the lip of the hollow. He hoped there was no one there. He did not feel like being sociable — yet.

His first instinct was to duck hastily out of sight. There *was* someone there — a stranger dressed neatly but rather drably in gray cloak and bonnet. She was sitting with knees drawn up, her arms clasped about them. But he did not move, and his gaze sharpened on her. Although she was clearly a woman and he could not see her face around the brim of her bonnet, it was perhaps the girlish posture that alerted him. Suddenly he could hear his heart beating in his ears. She turned her head sharply toward him and the sun shone full on her face.

Her plain clothing and the passage of years made her look noticeably older, as did the way her very dark hair was dressed beneath the bonnet. It was parted in the center and combed smoothly down over her ears. But she still had her long, oval face, like that of a Renaissance Madonna, and her large dark eyes. She was not pretty — she never had been. But hers was the sort of face that one might see in a crowd and look back at for a lengthier gaze.

If for a moment he imagined he was seeing a mirage, it was for a mere moment. If his imagination had conjured up her image here in this place, it would have been the image of a barefoot girl with a flimsy light-colored dress and hair released from its pins and falling wild and tangled down her back. It would not have been this image of neat, almost drab respectability. No, she was real. And eight years older.

They had been staring at each other, he realized finally. He did not know for how long.

"Hello, Moira," he said.

2

He should not have called her by her given name, he thought too late, but he did not know her other name.

"Kenneth," she said so quietly that he saw her lips move more than he heard the sound of his name. He also saw her swallow. "I did not know you were coming home."

"I sold out a few months ago," he said.

"Did you?" she said. "Yes, I knew. It was spoken of in the village. Such things are talked about, you know."

She had stood up, though she had not moved toward him. She was still very slender. He had forgotten how tall she was. He had always admired the way she held her shoulders back and her head high, disdaining to stoop or try to diminish her height even after she'd grown taller than most men. He had liked the way she had grown to within a few inches of his own height. Although there was a pleasantly protective

26

feeling about being close to women who did not reach even to his shoulder — and that was most women — he did not really enjoy having to look so far down to them.

"I trust you are well," he said.

"Yes," she said. "Thank you."

Why was she here? he wondered. Had she made it so thoroughly her own private haven during the past eight years that memory of his being here with her had been eradicated from her mind? Not that they had been here often together. Or anywhere else for that matter. But there had been such stealth and such guilt involved in their meetings that they had seemed many. Why was she alone? It was not at all proper for her to be without any companion, even a maid.

"And Sir Basil and Lady Hayes?" he asked stiffly. He was reminded that her family and his had been estranged for several generations, that they had had no social dealings with one another for all of that time. He had once hoped, with the youthful idealism that had clung to him almost until he left home, that his generation — and hers — would bring about a reconciliation. But the enmity had only been made worse.

"Papa died over a year ago," she said.

"Ah," he said. "I am sorry." He had not heard. But then, he had heard very little from Dunbarton. His mother no longer lived here and he had not kept up a correspondence with any of his former neighbors. With his steward he had exchanged only business news.

"Mama is well," she said.

"And —" He paused. The name would have changed. He spoke reluctantly. "Sir Sean Hayes?" His lips tightened at the thought of Sean Hayes.

"My brother never succeeded to the title," she said. "He died a few months before Papa. He was killed at the Battle of Toulouse."

He grimaced. He had not heard that either. Sean Hayes, the same age as himself, had gone away just before him. His father had purchased a commission for him in a foot regiment, presumably because he could not afford anything more glamorous. Sean Hayes, once his closest friend, at the end his bitterest enemy — dead?

"I am sorry," he said.

"Are you?" The question was quietly, coolly asked. Her dark eyes, looking directly back into his, held no discernible expression, but he could feel her dislike, her hostility. Eight years had not changed that, then. But she had suffered the loss of both her father and her brother in that time. And she and her mother . . .

"Your husband?" he asked.

"I am not yet married," she said. "I am about to be betrothed to Sir Edwin Baillie, a cousin who inherited the title and estate from Papa."

She was not married? Had no one been able to tame her, then? And yet she looked tame. She looked different — and the same. More different than the same. Why was she now marrying this cousin? For convenience's sake? Was there any affection involved in the match? But it was not his concern. She was not his concern. Eight years was a very long time. A lifetime.

"It seems," he said, "that I have come home in time to offer my congratulations."

"Thank you," she said.

He realized something suddenly. He looked back toward the road to confirm what he already knew. "How did you come here?" he asked. "There is no carriage and no horse except my own."

"I walked," she said.

And yet Penwith Manor was several miles away, down in the valley and inland a couple of miles. Had she not changed after all, then, despite appearances?

"Allow me to escort you home," he said. "You may ride my horse." He wondered what manner of man Sir Edwin Baillie was, allowing her to roam alone through the countryside. But perhaps he did not know she was alone. Perhaps he did not know *her,* poor man.

"I will walk home — alone, thank you, my lord," she said.

Yes. It had been foolish of him to offer. How would it have looked if he had suddenly appeared in Tawmouth for the first time in longer than eight years with Moira Hayes, betrothed of Penwith's owner, upon his horse? And if he had taken her all the way to Penwith when no one from his family had set foot on the property for longer than any living person could remember?

He must remember that there was a feud between Penwith and Dunbarton and that it would be a foolish expenditure of energy to try to end it. He no longer wanted to end it, though if he had thought of it in the past few days he would have thought it ridiculous to keep alive a feud that had started with his great-grandfather and hers. He did not want to tangle with Moira Hayes again. And he could see that the feeling was mutual.

He nodded curtly and touched the brim of his hat. "As you wish," he said. "Good day to you, Miss Hayes."

She said nothing and stayed where she

was as he made his way back to the road and mounted his horse. Nelson scrambled to his feet with a hopeful *woof* and was given the nod of release. Kenneth turned inland to ride along the top of the hillside, leaving the main road before it dipped into the valley and through the village of Taw mouth. The sun was still shining, he saw, looking upward in some surprise. It was his imagination that the day had clouded over. He was feeling out of sorts, his mind and his emotions in some sort of turmoil. He resented the feeling. He had been enjoying his homecoming.

It was understandable, he supposed. There had been something between them, powerful feelings, which in his naïveté he had called love. She had been his first — and his only — love, though he had been sexually educated during his years at Oxford. Really, there had been little to it — one chance meeting, a few planned ones, all of them bringing him feelings of guilt because he should not have been meeting either a Hayes or a young lady alone. He and Sean had been meeting and playing together and fighting each other for years, of course, but that had seemed different. It was the very guilt over Moira that had excited him and convinced him that it was love he felt for her. He realized that now. It was understandable that seeing her again should discompose him somewhat, he supposed, though he would not have expected it. He was a different man now: hardened to life, cynical of romantic sentiment.

He looked down into the wooded valley below him, at the river that wound its way toward the sea. Soon now he would see Dunbarton. He was not sorry he had come. On the contrary, he was feeling a pleased anticipation that amounted almost to excitement. How Eden and Nat would tease him if they could know.

And then suddenly there it was. It could always take a person by surprise, even someone who had lived there for much of his life. One moment one was riding along a plateau that stretched into the distance with much of a sameness, and the next one was looking down into a hollow, into a wooded parkland that appeared very green in contrast to the rest of the hillside. And in the middle of it all stood Dunbarton Hall, a large and imposing granite mansion built around three sides of a quadrangle. A high wrought-iron fence and gates made up the fourth side.

"We are home, Nelson," Kenneth said, his temporary irritation forgotten. It *was* home, too, and it was his. It was all his. For the first time in seven years, the reality of it struck him. Dunbarton was his.

Nelson barked and raced ahead down the driveway toward the house.

Moira stood for many minutes gazing not out to sea but at the bare skyline about the hollow. She had heard the sound of hoof-beats receding into the distance but did not quite trust to her aloneness.

She had not thought of him with hatred for a long time. Not even when Sean had been killed. Not really. There had been too much terrible, raw grief to be dealt with. After that, and after the loss of her father a mere few months later, there had been too much else to think of, too many practicalities of the present to be worried over. Life had changed so drastically that there had been no room in her memory for the rather confused passions of girlhood. Or for the heedless girl she had been.

She should have expected him to return, of course. She should somehow have prepared herself — though there had seemed nothing really to prepare herself *for.* But ever since word had reached Tawmouth that he had sold his commission and was back in England, the conversations at tea and after church and at evening gatherings had inevitably included the topic that fascinated them all: Would he come home to Dunbarton? But even if the people of Tawmouth had not been too genteel to place wagers, there would have been little point in doing so. Everyone would have wagered in favor of his coming. Except for Moira. She had not really expected him to come. He had said he would never return, and she had believed him.

How foolish of her. Of course he had come. He was the Earl of Haverford, owner of Dunbarton, lord and master of almost the whole of this corner of Cornwall. How could he resist coming back to exert his authority? He had liked power before he left. He had had eight years of practice in wielding it and she did not doubt he had done so with ruthless efficiency. There had been an air of cold command about him just now.

The force of the bitterness and hatred she felt had taken her quite by surprise. She breathed in deeply, imposing calm on herself. He had every right to come back. Just as she had every right to avoid him at every turn. The Hayes family and the Woodfall family had become experts at avoiding each other over the generations. It was a pity that

she had had to learn the hard way to con-
form to family rules.

Throughout their conversation she had
not seen his face clearly because of the sun's
angle behind him, but she had seen enough
of him to know that he was magnificently
built — as a very young man he had been
handsome beyond words to describe but
perhaps a little too slender for his height —
and strong and healthy. She did not doubt
that his face still had its aquiline, aristocratic
beauty. Beneath his hat she had been able
to see the gleam of his very blond hair. He
had come home looking even more splendid
than he had looked when he went away.

And Sean was in his grave somewhere in
southern France. She had not been bitter.
Grief-stricken, yes, but not bitter. Soldiers
fought, and soldiers died. Sean had been a
soldier, an infantry lieutenant, and he had
died in battle.

But she was bitter now. And cold with
hatred. Sean would never have become a
soldier if it had not been for *him.* He had
really had no alternative . . . She was cold.
She looked up at the sky and was surprised
to see that the sun was still shining.

She must not hate him. She would not do
so. Hatred was too strong an emotion. She
had no wish to be pulled back into the past.

She had no wish to experience again the extreme passions of the girl she had been. She had grown up since then. She was a different person. *He* was doubtless a different person. She must forget about him, as far as that was possible when he was going to be living within a few miles of Penwith. Would he stay long? she wondered. It did not matter. She had her own life to live and it was about to be yet another new life, one that would bring her further respectability. And fulfillment. She thought deliberately about the children she could now hope for.

She climbed out of the hollow and looked cautiously about her, but of course there was no one in sight. Only then did she wonder why he had come here to the hollow instead of riding on past. He could not have seen her from the road. Why had he stopped here? And why had she chosen today of all days to come here herself? She could not remember the last time she had been here. It was a horribly unfortunate coincidence. Or perhaps not so unfortunate. Perhaps if she had merely heard of his having come, she would have dreaded seeing him for the first time. That ordeal was over now at least.

She set off homeward, walking briskly. She should not have sat for so long when it was

December, no matter how pleasant the day. She felt so very cold.

The people of Tawmouth and its surrounding properties had not been so blessed with exciting events in many a long year. One could not count the passing of poor Sir Basil Hayes fourteen months before as an exciting event, after all, Miss Pitt told the Reverend and Mrs. Finley-Evans in hushed and pious tones when she took tea with them and Mrs. Meeson and Mrs. and Miss Penallen.

No sooner had everyone recovered from the news that the Earl of Haverford had arrived at Dunbarton Hall so unexpectedly that Mrs. Whiteman, his lordship's housekeeper, had scarcely had a day's notice of it herself, than word followed that his lordship's mother, the Countess of Haverford, was expected for Christmas as well as a whole host of houseguests. Mothers with marriageable daughters began to dream of eligible male guests. Mothers with marriageable sons did the like for female guests.

The gentlemen began to call upon his lordship. The ladies waited in breathless anticipation for him to return the calls. After all, as Mrs. Trevellas commented to Mrs. Lincoln and Mrs. Finley-Evans, one could get little satisfaction from one's menfolk. All *they* had come back from Dunbarton with was word that his lordship had indeed fought at Waterloo and that he had seen the Duke of Wellington with his own eyes. As if *that* could be considered interesting news, though it was said that his grace was a fine figure of a man.

"Nothing," she concluded, having worked herself into a passion of indignation, "about how his lordship *looks.* Or about how he *dresses.* Mr. Trevellas, if you please, could not even remember what his lordship wore even though he conversed with him for all of half an hour."

The other ladies shook their heads in sympathetic disbelief.

When the gentlemen were not discussing what each of them had learned about the earl's war experiences and the ladies were not wondering if he was as handsome now as he had been as a boy, all of them were speculating on what Christmas might have in store for them by way of entertainment. With the old earl there had always been the tradition of the Christmas ball at Dunbarton.

"And with the earl before him," Miss Pitt added. She was one of the few among them who could remember the present earl's grandfather. "He was a handsome man too," she added with a sigh.

"And perhaps there will be some Christmas entertainment at Penwith, too, this year," Mrs. Meeson said when she took tea with Mrs. Trevellas, "with Sir Edwin Baillie expected daily."

Sir Edwin Baillie had slipped down on the roster of exciting events anticipated in Tawmouth, though he had headed the list before the earl's sudden appearance. But his arrival at Penwith was still eagerly anticipated and speculation was rife on the purpose of his visit at this particular time of year. Would he offer for dear Miss Hayes? And would Miss Hayes accept if he did? They had all been deeply shocked when she had refused Mr. Deverall four years before. But then, everyone knew that Miss Hayes had a mind of her own and could sometimes be just a little too independent for her own good.

Some of the ladies turned to Mrs. Harriet Lincoln for her opinion since she was a particular friend of Miss Hayes. But Mrs. Lincoln would say only that if Sir Edwin did indeed make an offer and if Moira Hayes accepted it, then doubtless they would all hear about it soon enough.

There was another question that consumed the curiosity of everyone. What would happen between Penwith and Dunbarton when Sir Edwin Baillie arrived? Would the feud continue for yet another generation?

All these topics of conversation had to be avoided, of course, whenever Lady Hayes or Moira Hayes was part of the company. Then the weather and everyone's health were discussed in long-familiar detail.

"Poor Miss Hayes," Miss Pitt commented on one occasion when that young lady was not present. "And Lady Hayes too, I daresay. If the feud is to continue, they will not be able to attend the Christmas ball at Dunbarton. If there is a ball, of course."

"There will certainly be a ball," Mrs. Finley-Evans said firmly. "The Reverend Finley-Evans has agreed to speak to his lordship about it."

"Poor Miss Hayes," Miss Pitt said.

Sir Edwin Baillie came alone to Penwith Manor one week and one day after the Earl of Haverford returned to Dunbarton Hall. Sir Edwin took tea with Lady Hayes and Moira in the sitting room before retiring to the master suite — Lady Hayes had vacated it in deference to the new master — to supervise the unpacking of his bags. He never allowed anyone, even his valet, to perform the task without him, he explained. But apart from that brief explanation, he spent the half hour of tea apologizing to Lady Hayes for the absence of his mother, who of course would have accompanied him on such an important occasion — he inclined his head in Moira's direction — had it not been for the fact that she was suffering from a slight winter chill. It was not a severe attack, Lady Hayes would be relieved to know, but as a precautionary measure he had insisted that she remain at home. Thirty miles of travel might well have been permanently injurious to the delicate health of a lady.

Lady Hayes assured him that he had made a wise decision and had shown admirable devotion as a son. She would write the next morning to inquire after Cousin Gertrude's health. She trusted that the Misses Baillie were all in good health?

The Misses Baillie were indeed, it seemed, though Annabelle, the youngest, had suffered from earache a mere few weeks earlier after going out in the carriage on a particularly windy day. They would all be waiting anxiously for word that their brother had arrived safely at Penwith Manor. All had advised him against traveling such a distance during December, but such had been his

41

eagerness to bring about a happy settlement of his affairs — another bow in Moira's direction — that he had taken the risk of traversing winter roads. His mother, of course, had understood and had urged him not to stay at home merely on account of her health. If he was a devoted son — a bow to Lady Hayes — then he had merely learned from a devoted mother.

Moira watched him and listened to him without participating to any active degree in the conversation, but then, an occasional word or smile of encouragement was all Sir Edwin needed to keep the conversation in happy progress. At least, Moira thought, she would have a husband for whom family was a high priority. She might have done worse.

During dinner Sir Edwin announced his intention of remaining at Penwith Manor until after Christmas, although it would be a severe disappointment to both himself on the one hand and his mother and sisters on the other to be separated for the holiday. But it was time he became more familiar with the property he had inherited on Sir Basil Hayes's demise, if Lady Hayes and Miss Hayes would excuse such plain speaking — a separate bow to each — and called upon his neighbors so that they might become acquainted with the new baronet of

Penwith. And of course he would delight in the opportunity of giving his company during the Christmas celebrations to his two relatives — yet another bow — one of whom he hoped would have formed a closer relationship to him by the morrow. He smiled almost coquettishly at Moira.

In the drawing room after dinner, Sir Edwin asked Moira to play the pianoforte for her dear mama's entertainment and his own. He loved nothing better, it seemed, than listening to a recital on the pianoforte performed by a lady of taste and refinement. After Moira had started to play, he raised his voice and explained to Lady Hayes that all three of his sisters were accomplished on the pianoforte, though Cecily's talents lay more in her voice, whose sweetness she had inherited from their mother. Miss Hayes's performance was commendable though it might be found, if put to the test, that Christobel's touch was lighter. Nevertheless, Lady Hayes must be proud of her daughter.

Yes, Lady Hayes was.

And he, too, Sir Edwin assured her, leaning toward her and inclining his head in an elegant half bow, would be proud of Miss Hayes when he had a right to be proud and not merely delighted by her display of musical talent. By then, of course — he smiled conspiratorially — she would no longer be Miss Hayes but would have been elevated to a superior rank.

Sir Edwin retired to bed at a respectable hour, having bowed over the ladies' hands and assured them that the following day was surely to be the most important day — and perhaps the happiest — of his life.

It would be the most important day of hers too, Moira thought after she had retired and throughout a largely sleepless night. She doubted it would be the happiest. She did not want to marry Sir Edwin. He was even more pompous and dull and fussy than she remembered. When she had met him the first time, of course, she had not been looking at him as a prospective husband. She feared that living with him for the rest of a lifetime would be a severe trial. And his mother, she recalled, was in many ways similar to him. But sometimes in life, one's choices were cut to almost none at all. If she had only herself to consider, perhaps there would still be some choice. But there was Mama to think about and so there was no point in thinking in terms of choices. She fixed her mind on her future children.

She ate breakfast the next morning with a

determinedly calm and cheerful aspect. She really had no viable alternative than to accept the offer that was about to be made, she told herself yet again. She and her mother had no independent means. At the age of six-and-twenty she had no other matrimonial prospects. It would be thoroughly irresponsible, both for her mother's sake and her own, to refuse Sir Edwin Baillie. And his faults, though many, were at least not vices. She could be faced with having to accept a gambler or a drinker or a womanizer or all three. Sir Edwin was without a doubt thoroughly respectable.

And so, when he presented himself to her, after a great deal of pomp and ceremony and bowing and smirking, in the morning room when morning was almost over, she quietly accepted the marriage offer, which he was sure would not surprise her but which he was consoled into believing would gratify her. She allowed her newly betrothed to pronounce himself the happiest of men and to kiss her hand, though he apologized profusely for allowing happiness to drive him to such levity.

The wedding, he informed Lady Hayes and Moira over luncheon, although personal inclination would urge him to have it solemnized tomorrow or even — he smiled at his own playfulness, surely excusable in a newly successful lover — today, would take place later in the spring, when his mother's health could be expected to be more robust and when the weather would be more clement for the long, thirty-mile journey she and his sisters would be required to make. In the meanwhile he would do himself the honor of remaining at Penwith Manor until Christmas was over and would then return home in order to see that his affairs were in order prior to the permanent move to Penwith to claim his bride.

Moira breathed a silent sigh of relief. She would have a few more months in which to prepare herself for the new life that was to be hers. Her mother touched her hand on the table and smiled at her. Sir Edwin expressed his pleasure at this sign of happiness in his future mother-in-law for the good fortune of her daughter. Moira knew that her mother understood, and that she realized as well as her daughter did that the sacrifice must be made. Though it was unfair to think of her approaching marriage in terms of sacrifice. It would be no worse than the vast majority of marriages that were solemnized every single day, and it would be considerably better than many.

3

Sir Edwin introduced another topic of conversation before luncheon was over, one that animated him even more than that of his own wedding. In questioning the butler about the neighbors of sufficiently elevated rank that they merited a call from him during his stay at Penwith Manor, he had discovered an extraordinary fact. Doubtless Lady Hayes and Miss Hayes were already aware of it, since apparently it had occurred all of a week earlier. The Earl of Haverford had returned to Dunbarton Hall to take up his residence there.

"Yes, Cousin Edwin," Lady Hayes assured him, "we have heard. But —"

But Sir Edwin scarcely paused for breath. He smiled at the ladies. "It is a conceivable truth that less generous, more petty-minded gentlemen than myself might resent the fact that I no longer outrank everyone else in the neighborhood, ma'am," he said, "but I must pronounce myself deeply gratified to be given this chance to claim the Earl of Haverford as a neighbor. And as an acquaintance, of course. Was his lordship not a war hero? A major in one of the finer regiments? One can only assume that he would have reached the rank of general had the wars continued for a year or so longer. I must regret even more deeply than I did yesterday that ill health prevented my dear mother from accompanying me here. But she will be happy for my sake, and for yours, ma'am. And yours, Miss Hayes. She has a generous heart."

"But Cousin Edwin —" Lady Hayes tried again.

Moira knew it was hopeless. It had been a wretched week. Not a word had been spoken at Penwith about the Earl of Haverford after her first abrupt announcement of his return when she had come back from her walk that day. Not a word had been spoken about him during any of the visits they had paid any of their neighbors during the week or during any of the visits paid them. And yet she — and surely her mother too — had been fully aware that conversation when they were not present must center about nothing else. Dunbarton had been without its master for seven years, after all. It was almost a relief to hear Sir Edwin finally speak openly on the forbidden topic.

"I intend to leave my card at Dunbarton today, before I call upon anyone else," Sir Edwin said. "It is, of course, a fitting courtesy that I wait first upon the Earl of Haverford. It would be quite unexceptionable of his lordship to receive my card and refuse my admittance today, but I must congratulate myself on the hope, ma'am, that he will receive in person the baronet of Penwith. His lordship, after all, will be happy to discover that there is someone of such elevated rank nearby with whom he might consort on terms of near equality. He has perhaps been informed that only ladies still reside at Penwith, though of course even one of those ladies bears a title." He bowed his head to Lady Hayes. "And the other will do so within the next few months." He smiled at Moira. "What an extraordinary coincidence it is that has brought both of us into Cornwall at the same time. I will call today, this afternoon. Miss Hayes, will you do me the honor of accompanying me?"

Moira had been accepting his plans with resignation, even with some approval. Doubtless it would be best if there were some civility between the two men, who would, after all, be quite close neighbors. But she took instant alarm at the suggestion that she be personally involved in that civility. She looked at her mother, who was sitting straight backed and unsmiling on her chair.

"We do not visit at Dunbarton, sir," Moira said. "There have never been any social dealings between our two families."

"Indeed, Miss Hayes?" Sir Edwin said. "You amaze me. Is his lordship quite so high in the instep, then? One does not expect it of the aristocracy, especially when one is oneself of superior rank, but it is perhaps understandable. I shall demonstrate my worthiness to be an acquaintance of the Earl of Haverford. I shall apprise him of the fact that my mother was a Grafton of Hugglesbury. The Graftons, as you surely are aware, have the purest of bloodlines, ma'am," he assured Lady Hayes, "and can trace themselves back to a brave knight who fought at the elbow of William the Conqueror himself."

"There was an unfortunate incident several generations back," Moira explained. "My great-grandfather and the present earl's great-grandfather were both involved in smuggling, which flourished on the coast here at that time."

"Dear me," Sir Edwin said, looking genuinely shocked. Moira wondered with an unexpected flash of amusement if he had never sipped wine that had come into the country via the back door, so to speak, without the customary duty having been paid on it. She wondered if his mother and his sisters had never drunk tea that had arrived in their teapot by similar shady and circuitous routes. But even if they had, and even if he knew it, he doubtless would not consider that he had been involved in any way with smuggling. Most people did not.

"The Earl of Haverford acted more in the way of a sponsor and purchaser of smuggled goods than in an active capacity," Moira continued, "while my ancestor was the leader of the smugglers. He went out at night with his face blackened, I daresay, and a pistol in his belt — and a cutlass between his teeth." She avoided her mother's reproachful glance.

"I had not realized that there was such a blemish on the Hayes's baronetcy," Sir Edwin said, clearly distressed. "Smugglers? Pistols and cutlasses? I beg you never to disclose these facts to my mother, Miss Hayes. They would send her into a decline and perhaps even bring on fatal heart palpitations."

"When the coast guard caught my great-grandfather," Moira said, "and dragged him before the nearest magistrate — the Earl of Haverford — the earl sentenced him to seven years in transportation. He was carried off to the hulks."

Sir Edwin sighed with noticeable relief. "It is bad, but it might have been worse," he said. "If you had had a hanging in your family past, Miss Hayes . . ." He shuddered.

Moira felt unaccountably amused — and vindicated. Sir Edwin had made no reference to the dreadful hypocrisy of the Earl of Haverford. "He returned after the seven years," Moira said, "doubtless coarsened and hardened by his experiences. He lived for twenty more years as a visible embarrassment to his neighbor. There has been an estrangement between the two families ever since." Almost but not quite total. It would have been better if it had remained total.

"It is ever the way," Sir Edwin said, "for wrongdoers to resent those who in all justice reprove and chastise them. It distresses me that ladies of delicacy and refinement" — he bowed first to Lady Hayes and then to Moira — "should have been left alone to suffer the consequences of such villainy. But that time is past. I am here now to both protect and rescue you. Although I will never besmirch my mother's ears with this story of villainy, I feel confident in asserting that if she knew, she would advise me to the course of action that I shall take. I shall call upon the Earl of Haverford this afternoon, as planned, and I shall apologize most sincerely for my forebear's actions and for his neglecting to humble himself and his family before the present earl's forebear by taking himself away and living out his life in quiet obscurity."

Moira was feeling a strange mingling of embarrassment, outrage, humor — and anxiety.

"My dear Cousin Edwin," Lady Hayes said faintly, one hand over her mouth.

But Sir Edwin raised a staying hand. "You need not thank me, ma'am," he said. "As the present baronet of Penwith Manor, I have inherited not only a title and property, but also responsibility for the actions of all the baronets who have gone before me. And for the protection of their womenfolk." He bowed to Lady Hayes. "I shall attempt to effect a reconciliation in this matter, ma'am, and I feel confident that his lordship will honor me for my humility and for my assumption of all the blame for what happened long ago."

Moira stared at him in silent incredulity.

There was no longer anything funny about this. What would the Earl of Haverford *think* of them? And she despised herself for caring.

"Contrary to general belief," Sir Edwin continued, "pride need not be lost in humility. I shall lose no pride in making my apologies to his lordship. You must not fear it, ladies. You will accompany me, Miss Hayes."

"I beg you will excuse me, sir," she said hastily. "It would perhaps be more proper for you to call alone since the Earl of Haverford is himself alone at Dunbarton."

"It is said," Lady Hayes added, "that the countess, his mother, is also coming to Dunbarton with other houseguests for Christmas, but I have not heard of their having arrived yet, sir." It was surprising what one heard in a country neighborhood even when everyone was careful to avoid certain topics in one's hearing. "He is undoubtedly alone at Dunbarton. Moira was to accompany me to tea in Tawmouth this afternoon."

But Sir Edwin was not to be deterred. "It will be entirely proper for Miss Hayes to accompany me," he said, "as my newly betrothed. It will be seen as a superior mark of courtesy in me to present you first in that capacity, Miss Hayes, to his lordship since he is, beyond any doubt, the social leader of this community. And it is entirely appropriate that you be present for the reconciliation of your family with his lordship's. You will be able to lift your head high, Miss Hayes, after having had to keep it bowed in shame throughout your life. It would appear that some good angel has brought me here at this particular time. I can only conclude that my mother has aided and abetted that angel by insisting that I travel here rather than stay home to comfort her through the trial of her slight chill."

Lady Hayes said no more. She only glanced at her daughter with a helpless, half-apologetic look. Her mother, Moira remembered, had once been a vocal advocate of ending a feud that had begun so long ago. She had come from Ireland to marry Moira's father and had expected that she would live a full and happy social life. She had not enjoyed finding that she must avoid all entertainments that were to include the Countess of Haverford and her family. But that had been before the feud had been updated, of course. Perhaps, Moira thought belatedly, she should have mentioned those facts to Sir Edwin too. Undoubtedly she should have.

But she said nothing more. She did not

argue further. Sir Edwin Baillie, Moira suspected uneasily, was a man with whom it was going to be difficult — perhaps impossible — to argue, merely because he heard only what he wished to hear and made assumptions to which he held fast as unassailable truths. It seemed that she was to make an afternoon call with him at Dunbarton. She dreaded to think of what awaited them there. She could only hope, she supposed, that the Earl of Haverford would be from home or that he would refuse to receive them.

But Sir Edwin Baillie, she thought, was not a man to be put off easily once he had set his mind upon a certain course of action. If the visit was not successfully made today, then it would be made tomorrow or the next day. On the whole, it would be better to get it over with today so that perhaps she could sleep tonight, having known the worst humiliation of her life. Surely it would be the worst.

She had not set eyes on the Earl of Haverford for over a week. She had hoped that she might never do so again. But it was a forlorn hope, of course. She had the uneasy suspicion that he had returned to Dunbarton to stay, and it appeared that Sir Edwin Baillie intended to make his permanent home at Penwith. Even if the families remained estranged, she and Kenneth were bound to meet again.

She wished he had not come back. She even found herself wishing for one rash moment that it were he, and not Sean, who . . . but no. She shook off the horrifying thought. No, she could never wish such a thing even in exchange for Sean's life. She never could, no matter who he was or what he had done — or what further embarrassment he was now unwittingly to cause her. She remembered how through the years she had waited for every scrap of news that had filtered through to Dunbarton — how she had waited with dread, how she had despised herself for both the waiting and the dread. She remembered how she had felt when news had come six years ago that the severity of wounds sustained in Portugal had sent him back to England — but not to Dunbarton. Surely a soldier was sent back to England only when he was permanently maimed or not expected to survive, she had thought. She had waited in agony for more news, all the time telling herself that really she did not care at all.

She remembered the letter that had come from the War Office about Sean. Oh, no, she could never wish what she had just almost wished. Never.

She just wished he had not come back. And that Sir Edwin Baillie had not come to Penwith. She wished she could simply return to the rather dull spinster's life she had been living until a few weeks before.

Kenneth had just returned from a few hours spent with his steward riding about some of the outlying farms of his estate. He was changing from slightly muddy clothes — the previous two days had been wet — and was just starting to warm up when his valet answered a knock on his dressing room door. Two visitors were awaiting his lordship in the downstairs salon.

His lordship sighed inwardly. In the nine days since his return to Dunbarton it seemed that he had done little else but visit and be visited. It had been pleasant to become reacquainted with old friends and neighbors, to meet a few new neighbors, but sometimes he wished he could have more time to himself. The situation could only worsen during the coming week as his mother and sister and his other houseguests began to arrive. Still, he looked forward to having the house full, to learning the new role of host.

He tried to think as he descended the

staircase a few minutes later of someone in the neighborhood who had not yet called upon him. He could think of no one. But he had already returned most of those calls. The second round must be starting, then. He sighed. Whoever it was might at least have waited until after his mother's arrival.

He did not recognize the man who stood in the middle of the salon, one hand behind his back, the other fingering the fob on his watch chain. The man's shirt points, stiffly starched, were almost piercing his cheeks. His brown hair was combed upward to stand an inch or two above his head. Was it to bring him to more of an equality in height with his companion, Kenneth wondered, turning his eyes on her. She was definitely the taller of the two and was doing nothing to conceal the fact. She held her chin high, a look of proud defiance on her face as if he had challenged her in some way. She was dressed as she had been on the day of his arrival. Moira Hayes was masquerading as a demure lady and doing a very poor job of it. What the devil was she doing in his salon?

But he hid his surprise and bowed to them both. The man was smiling and bowing in return, for all the world as if he were making his obeisance to Prinny or even to the mad king himself. Moira Hayes stood stiff and tall and did not even attempt the curtsy that good manners dictated.

"Sir?" he said. "Miss Hayes?"

The man introduced himself as Sir Edwin Baillie, baronet of Penwith Manor since the unfortunate passing of Sir Basil Hayes and in the absence of any surviving direct male issue. Moira, Kenneth noticed without looking directly at her, did not wince at this summary dismissal of her father and her brother. Sir Edwin Baillie was also related, through his mother, to the Graftons of Hugglesbury, whoever the devil they might be. Sir Edwin looked keenly at his host, clearly expecting a start of amazement at this news. Kenneth raised his eyebrows. So this was the man Moira was to marry? Why had she come here?

"And Miss Hayes you have addressed correctly indeed, my lord," Sir Edwin said with another deep bow. "But you will deem it the proper courtesy in me to announce to you before I do so to anyone else — except for Lady Hayes, her dear mama, of course — that Miss Hayes has done me the signal honor today of agreeing to become Lady Baillie in the near future."

This time she did wince, not quite imperceptibly. Kenneth turned his eyes on her.

Her face was already set into its look of proud disdain again, but one thing was perfectly obvious to him. This was not a match involving any affection on her part. And who could blame her? The man was clearly a pompous ass. She was probably squirming in embarrassment behind that aloof mask. Good.

"My good wishes, Miss Hayes," he said. "And my congratulations to you, sir. Do please have a seat, Miss Hayes. I shall ring for tea."

She sat on the chair closest to her, her back ramrod straight, her hands resting one in the other in her lap. For all the tautness of her posture, she succeeded somehow in looking graceful, Kenneth thought.

"That is extremely civil of you, my lord," Sir Edwin said and cleared his throat somewhat theatrically. "Especially under the circumstances."

The devil, Kenneth thought. She must have *told* Baillie. Confession time to precede the official betrothal? A few clandestine meetings. A few kisses. Had she confessed the kisses? But it appeared that the circumstances referred to were other than the ones that had leapt to his mind. It appeared that it was extremely civil of him to receive the great-granddaughter of the man his own great-grandfather had been obliged to sentence to seven years in transportation. It was extraordinarily civil of him to offer her a seat and tea.

For one moment when Kenneth looked at her, startled, their eyes met. She lowered her own hastily. He felt a strong urge to shout with laughter. It seemed inappropriate, however.

"As the new baronet of Penwith Manor," Sir Edwin continued, "I must of course assume responsibility for all the actions of my predecessors, my lord. Though personally blameless, I would nevertheless humbly beg your pardon for the distress caused your ancestor by being forced to impose justice on one of his closest neighbors. I would ask your pardon on Lady Hayes's account and on Miss Hayes's account, though you would undoubtedly agree with me that women cannot be blamed for the perfidies of their menfolk. However, both Lady Hayes and Miss Hayes have been saddened by the estrangement that has existed between the two families for several generations."

Moira bit her lip and her nostrils flared very slightly. Kenneth wondered if her betrothed realized that she was angry and guessed that he did not. *Women cannot be blamed for the perfidies of their menfolk.*

Could they be blamed for their own? Had she told Baillie only about their great-grandparents? Not about eight years ago? He half smiled at her lowered glance.

"I think it unnecessary, sir," he said, "for you to ask pardon for something that did not concern you in any way. I think it unnecessary for me to pardon what did not concern me and what happened so far in the past that it is beyond living memory. But if it will make you more comfortable, then I am perfectly willing to agree that the past be both forgiven and forgotten."

"You are more than generous, my lord," Sir Edwin said. "But I have ever found that members of the aristocracy are characterized by their generosity of spirit."

Good Lord. And Moira was going to *marry* this? Kenneth glanced at her again. She looked a little white about the nostrils and mouth. She was still furious. He could not resist fanning the flames.

"And if it is true that you have been distressed by the estrangement, Miss Hayes," he said, "then allow me to assure you that all is forgiven. I bear no grudges. You will be welcome to call here at any time with Lady Hayes or with Sir Edwin."

She had matured, he thought a moment later. Her temper did not break as he knew it was on the brink of doing. She looked him very directly in the eye — he doubted that her betrothed could see the venom there — and spoke coolly.

"You are too kind, my lord," she said. "You forgive me? I am overwhelmed."

Sir Edwin Baillie, as expected, did not recognize either anger or sarcasm, even when they rose up in a curled fist and punched him between the eyes. He smirked and bowed, first to Moira and then to his host.

"And I am overwhelmed," he said, "with this happy outcome of my gesture of humility. My dear mother always taught me, my lord, as I am sure your dear mother has taught you, that humility and pride go hand in hand, that displaying the first does not force one to forfeit the second, but on the contrary merely strengthens it."

"Indeed," Kenneth said. He gestured the footman who had appeared bearing the tea tray to set it down before Moira. "Miss Hayes, will you pour?"

Sir Edwin Baillie apparently believed that the new amity between families that had been estranged for generations was ample excuse for extending his visit beyond the half-hour limit that good manners dictated. It was Moira who finally got to her feet after forty minutes, doing so hastily but quite decisively when her lover paused to draw breath during a lengthy description of the superior education he had secured for his sisters at great expense to himself.

Kenneth saw them to the door and watched as Baillie handed his betrothed inside his carriage and insisted on wrapping a blanket carefully about her legs before following her inside and wrapping another about his own. He was convinced, he explained to his host, that most winter chills were taken from careless travel habits. One could not be too careful.

He would, Kenneth supposed as he watched the carriage drive out of the courtyard, be obliged to return the call. He had never been inside Penwith Manor. He had sneaked into the park numerous times as a boy, just as Sean Hayes had sneaked into the park at Dunbarton, but neither of them had entered the other's house. And now Moira Hayes had been to Dunbarton. Times were changing indeed.

He was not sure he wanted to be on visiting terms with her. He was very sure that he wanted no intimacy of social relations with her future husband. But it seemed that he had little choice except to leave Dunbarton. And he did not believe he would do that. He had discovered something during the past nine days. He had discovered a direction for his life. He had lived by his wits and by the skin of his teeth for eight years. He had thought himself restless and eager for further adventures after he had sold his commission. But he had merely been restless for home.

It was just a pity that home was so close to Penwith and that she was to marry the owner of Penwith. And it was a pity that, after all, the past was not completely dead, not completely forgiven or forgotten, no matter what words had been exchanged here within the past hour.

His mother had indeed invited some friends to Dunbarton, friends who significantly had a young daughter, the Honorable Miss Juliana Wishart. His mother had even mentioned the girl by name in a letter she had written to him. Paving the way. Playing matchmaker with little attempt at subtlety. What had surprised him about the realization was his lack of alarm. He was, he realized, willing to look the girl over. He had come home to Dunbarton, all his wild oats sown. He wanted to stay here. But if he stayed, perhaps it would be as well to go the whole distance into settling. Perhaps it really was time to take a wife.

Moira Hayes, he thought as he returned to the relative warmth of the indoors, had listened to an offer from that oaf today and had accepted. She was to be a married woman and perhaps soon he would be a married man. They would be neighbors and on visiting terms, though not to any familiar degree, it was to be hoped. Well, he thought grimly, it was a reality he must and would grow accustomed to. One thing he had learned during his eight years with the Peninsular army was that one could grow accustomed to almost anything.

And familiarity, it was said, bred — perhaps not contempt, but indifference. They would grow indifferent to each other and would perhaps forget about the dislike, the hostility.

4

The Countess of Haverford arrived at Dunbarton Hall a few days after Sir Edwin Baillie had called there with his betrothed. With her came her daughter and her daughter's husband, Viscount Ainsleigh, and their two young children. The whole of Tawmouth and its surrounding area knew of the fact before the next day had passed. And of course there were still the other houseguests expected daily.

There seemed no end to the excitement the month of December was bringing to this quiet corner of Cornwall. For even before the countess's arrival, word had spread that Sir Edwin Baillie of Penwith had called upon the Earl of Haverford — *and had been received.* He and Miss Hayes had even been invited to take tea. And his lordship had been the first to be told of the betrothal of Sir Edwin and Miss Hayes.

"It is all too, too gratifying," Miss Pitt

said, wiping a tear from the corner of one eye with a serviceable cotton handkerchief.

And it was, too. For not only was their Miss Hayes to be settled comfortably, and not only was the long-standing feud between Dunbarton and Penwith at an end, but also everyone was free to talk about the topics dearest to their heart when in company with the ladies from Penwith.

And when in Sir Edwin's company too, of course. He made himself very agreeable. Indeed, it was he who was first to mention — and even to expand at considerable length upon — the call he had made on his lordship, the handsome apology he had made for past embarrassments, and the gracious manner in which his lordship had granted pardon to both himself as the new baronet of Penwith and Miss Hayes as a direct descendant of the original — he paused for a delicate cough — offender. Humility, Sir Edwin explained, was not at odds with pride but rather complemented it. His mother, in her wisdom — she had been a Grafton of Hugglesbury, of course — had taught him that when he was a mere lad.

Mrs. Finley-Evans commended Sir Edwin on his wisdom and on his courage. Miss Pitt congratulated Miss Hayes on the happy end to an unfortunate past. Mrs. Harriet Lincoln, Moira's closest friend, tapped her on the arm and spoke softly beneath the level of the conversation proceeding around them.

"Poor Moira," she said. "You are going to need a great deal of patience, my dear."

Moira did not believe Harriet was referring to the reconciliation that had been effected at Dunbarton a few days before.

Speculation about a Christmas ball at Dunbarton increased. But on the whole, though they discussed it endlessly, everyone agreed that it was a virtual certainty. How else would his lordship keep his houseguests entertained? And there was such a splendid ballroom at Dunbarton. Mrs. Trevellas wondered if there would be any waltzes at a Dunbarton ball, but her hearers dismissed the notion out of hand. Two waltzes had been included among the dances at one of the Tawmouth assemblies earlier in the year and had scandalized the Reverend Finley-Evans, among others. The intimacy of a man dancing exclusively with one woman, his one hand at her waist, the other holding his partner's while *her* free hand rested on his shoulder had so shocked Miss Pitt that her niece had found it necessary to revive her with the aid of Mrs. Finley-Evans's vinaigrette. Sir Edwin Baillie had only *heard* of the dance, but what he had heard was quite enough to convince him that he would devote all his energies to having his mother and his sisters and — with a bow to Moira — his betrothed protected from its pernicious influence.

No, one could not imagine her ladyship allowing the scandalous dance even if his lordship, being a young man, might have brought home some newfangled ideas from Spain and France. Everyone knew that the Spanish and the French were in possession of looser morals than the English.

Moira had no opinion to offer on the matter. She did not care if there were waltzes or not at the Dunbarton ball — if there were a Dunbarton ball. She hoped not. And she fervently hoped that if there were, no invitation would be sent to Penwith. She hoped that the Earl of Haverford would not continue the association that Sir Edwin had tried to begin. She hoped he would ignore them, even if doing so would be thoroughly bad mannered.

But any hope Moira might have had that the earl would dismiss Sir Edwin's visit as a mere impertinence was dashed when he returned the call one afternoon soon after three ladies, who had shared a carriage from Tawmouth, had taken their leave. He came alone and sent up his card to the drawing room, where Sir Edwin was in the middle of congratulating the ladies on the superior conversation of their acquaintances.

"Ah," he said to the butler, "bring his lordship up, and do not keep him waiting. And have another tea tray sent. You will be gratified, ma'am" — he bowed to Lady Hayes — "to be able to take your true place in society at last. You will find that his lordship has quite distinguished manners."

Since his lordship was already in the doorway and heard this high praise of himself, Moira winced inwardly. One haughty eyebrow rose above the level of the other, she saw, but he bowed courteously enough to her mother, after whose health he inquired, and to her. Her mother, she noticed, was quite flustered. He took the chair offered after the ladies had first seated themselves and proceeded to answer the detailed and impertinently personal questions Sir Edwin asked about his mother and his sister and his nephew and niece.

"Yes indeed," he agreed to Sir Edwin's suggestion, "my sister made a very eligible match. My parents approved the wisdom of her choice."

His rather light gray eyes — Moira had never quite understood how they could be both pale and penetrating, but they always had been both, and frequently cold too — met Moira's and held them for a few moments. There had been a definite message in his words, she realized, quite beyond their stated meaning. She stiffened with anger. A match between Lady Helen Woodfall and Sean Hayes would have been quite ineligible, he had said in all but words, and certainly not approved by his parents.

Moira lifted her chin and told him just as clearly and just as silently that on that point at least they were in thorough agreement. There was a gleam of understanding in his eyes before he looked away to deal with Sir Edwin's next question. How dared he, she thought, her pulse thundering with fury. For the message must be as clear to Mama as it was to her. Mama had remarked only this morning that perhaps Sir Edwin should have been told that the enmity between the two families rested not solely upon what had happened several generations ago. Yet Mama did not know the half of it.

He continued to converse with Sir Edwin just as if he found the occasion and the conversation quite to his liking. He behaved with perfect good breeding and was dressed with perfect good taste. And of course he was even more handsome than he had been eight years ago, if that were possible. Tall, powerfully muscled in all the right places, blond, handsome featured, he also exuded an air of confident command that gave him an almost irresistible aura of masculinity — and of arrogance. How pleased he must be to come here to lord it over all of them, to demonstrate his own superiority in every conceivable way to Sir Edwin Baillie.

It took Moira a full fifteen minutes to realize how much she was seething with resentment and hatred. By then it was too late to compose herself, to convince herself that the past was dead. It was *Sean* who was dead, not the past. This would not do, she told herself. This would not do at all.

The earl rose to take his leave well within the accepted limit of time; even in that, his manners were impeccable. He bowed to the ladies and inclined his head to Sir Edwin. "A card will be delivered within the next few days," he said, "inviting you all to the ball to be held at Dunbarton Hall on the evening following Christmas. It is my hope that you will attend."

Sir Edwin was effusive in his thanks and in his assurances that his lordship's guest list would indeed be enhanced by the presence of the baronet of Penwith. Lady Hayes merely curtsied and Moira could guess at the determination her mother must feel never to cross the threshold of Dunbarton Hall. Moira did not feel that any reply was necessary. She did not have her mother's freedom. Indeed, she despised herself for the little flutter of excitement caused by the idea of attending a grand ball. The Tawmouth assemblies, she was sure, could not compare in splendor to what was planned at Dunbarton.

"Miss Hayes," the Earl of Haverford said, "perhaps you would be good enough to reserve a waltz for me — with the permission of your betrothed, of course."

Moira's betrothed was quite overwhelmed by the honor to be paid his future bride and gave the requested permission with a gracious bow. Though it was only fitting, he supposed aloud, since they were to be neighbors and Dunbarton and Penwith were without any doubt the largest and most influential properties in this particular part of Cornwall.

"Thank you, my lord," Moira said quietly and turned her anger inward on her thumping heart and weakened knees. She had watched those waltzes at the assembly, though she had never participated. And she had not shared in the censure heaped on the dance by the more staid, elderly elements in the neighborhood. She had thought it the most heavenly, most romantic dance ever invented. She had dreamed of dancing it and had laughed at herself for still being capable of such girlish dreams at her age.

Well, now it seemed that she was to dance the waltz. At the Dunbarton ball. With the Earl of Haverford. His cold eyes held hers as he inclined his head again. She half smiled at him. But she knew he understood that the smile was not one of pleasure or gratitude but was one of self-mockery. He had asked and she had accepted — because they disliked each other but could not seem to resist challenging each other.

"My mother has always declared," Sir Edwin said when he was again alone with the ladies, "that one should judge nothing on reputation alone, but should first observe for oneself. I see now that I have unfairly judged the waltz. If his lordship is willing to include it in the musical program for the ball at Dunbarton, then it must be unexceptionable. His own mama is to be present, after all. My dear Miss Hayes — if you will pardon the familiarity of such an address — I hope you understand fully the honor his lordship is according me in soliciting your hand for a waltz at his ball. We will be not only neighbors and acquaintances, you will see — we will be friends. And all because I was willing to humble myself. My dear ma'am" — he bowed to Lady Hayes — "I congratulate you."

Lady Hayes merely looked at her daughter and lifted her eyebrows.

"What was that, dear?" The Countess of Haverford, seated at the small escritoire in the library at Dunbarton, held her quill pen poised above one of the elegant cards in which she had been writing when her son had entered the room a few moments before. Viscountess Ainsleigh was seated beside her, holding a list of names, most of which had been crossed through.

His mother's expression told Kenneth that she had not so much failed to hear as disbelieved what she had heard. He repeated what he had just told her.

"You will include an invitation to Lady and Miss Hayes and to Sir Edwin Baillie at Penwith Manor, if you would be so good, Mama," he said.

"That is what I thought you said," the countess admitted. "Is it wise, dear? Perhaps you have forgotten —"

"No, of course I have not, Mama," he said. "I have forgotten nothing. But Sir Basil Hayes is dead, as is Papa, and the new owner of Penwith Manor is but a distant relative. He has, moreover, called upon me here. He is betrothed to Miss Hayes."

"He called on you?" the countess said with a frown. "And you received him, Kenneth? It is to be hoped that at least he came alone."

"Miss Hayes came with him," he said. "And I received them. It is time that old quarrel was put to rest, Mama." His sister, he had not failed to notice, had turned rigid as well as pale.

"It is not entirely an *old* quarrel, Kenneth," she said, her voice quite brittle. "There were fairly recent victims of it, if you will remember."

"It is best forgotten," he said.

"Forgotten." She laughed and then looked back at her list. "Did you know he was dead? Did you know he had been killed?"

"Yes," he said quietly.

"One might say, if one wished to be unkind," their mother said sharply, "that he deserved his fate and that he might have have come to a worse end than a hero's death. But what can one expect of a Hayes?"

"Pray do not distress yourself, Mama,"

Helen said. She looked up at her brother again. "I would rather not see Moira Hayes here, Kenneth. Or Lady Hayes either. For Mama's sake."

"I have already invited them," he said. "I called upon them this afternoon. It would have been uncivil not to return Sir Edwin Baillie's call, and unacceptable bad manners to omit them from the guest list for the ball after I had called."

"I wonder," his sister said rather sharply, "if civility was your only motive, Kenneth. You fancied her once upon a time. Do not imagine that I did not know."

"Helen," the countess said curtly, "we have work to do. Add Sir Edwin Baillie to the list and the ladies at Penwith."

"If they know anything of good taste," Helen said, "they will decline the invitation. But I daresay they know nothing of good taste."

Helen was not by nature spiteful, Kenneth thought. There was an unmistakable affection between her and Ainsleigh and she openly loved their children. But clearly she carried about her own demons from the past. He had never known quite what her feelings for Sean Hayes had been — love or infatuation or neither. Sean had been a charmer and for reasons of his own had turned that charm briefly on Helen. She had denied afterward that she had willingly agreed to elope with him and had seemed quite resigned to being sent away to an aunt. She had married Ainsleigh within the year. Her true feelings for Sean had remained her secret. Yet she had asked a few minutes ago if he knew that Sean was dead. How much had that death meant to her? And how had she learned of it?

"We cannot count upon their refusing," he said. "Sir Edwin Baillie seems determined upon being civil and neighborly, and Miss Hayes is to be his wife. We will all be civil to them when they attend the ball. This is a new era, and I choose to begin it in a wholly new manner. I do not wish to have neighbors living a scant three miles away whose very existence must be ignored. I will not have my children and theirs forced to make the difficult decision of whether to obey their parents or to strike up clandestine friendships. There has been enough of that."

The countess raised her eyebrows.

"Sean Hayes is dead," he said, "as is Sir Basil Hayes. Sir Edwin Baillie is of a different stamp altogether."

His mother was dipping her quill pen rather determinedly into the inkwell when he left the room and closed the door behind him. What, he wondered, had possessed him to ask Moira Hayes to reserve a set of waltzes for him? He wanted nothing more to do with her than was necessary. He certainly did not want to touch her. She had been dressed very demurely this afternoon. She had even been wearing a cap, which for some reason had irritated him. She had conducted herself with quiet decorum and had succeeded in looking dignified even during the worst of the pomposities and impertinences of her betrothed. And yet he had felt, contrary to all surface appearance, that there was a passionate femininity leashed just behind the veneer of gentility. He might have been wrong. He very probably was. She was a twenty-six-year-old spinster, about to make a very proper and dull marriage with a pompous ass. Of course, there had been her hidden anger and the strange silent communications that had occurred between them. They had been real enough.

He did not want to touch her. He did not want to risk unleashing what he was not even sure was there. Or perhaps, he thought in some astonishment, what was leashed was not so much in her as in himself. If it was so, then he need not worry. He was long accustomed to discipline, to self-control.

He was to waltz with her. He wondered if she knew the steps and found himself hoping that she did not. It was far too intimate a dance to perform with someone who knew the steps — and someone one was afraid to touch.

When Moira delivered baskets of Christmas baking to some of the poorer families in Tawmouth on the day before Christmas, she went alone, with only a maid for company. The outing gave her a much-needed feeling of freedom despite the fact that Sir Edwin had insisted upon both the maid and the carriage in which they rode to the village. He was too busy writing Christmas letters to his mother and each of his sisters to accompany her himself, for which dereliction of duty he apologized profusely. Lady Hayes was busy with the cook and the Christmas puddings.

It was rather a lovely day, Moira thought, even though the fishermen were predicting snow within the next few days. The blue sky was dotted with fluffy clouds, which allowed the occasional sunny interval. The breeze was fresh and brisk but not unduly cold or fierce for the time of year. It would have been the perfect day for a walk to the village along the valley. Alas, for her betrothed's sense of propriety, she was forced to ride, all cooped up inside the carriage with a hot brick at her feet and a blanket over her legs. She wondered if she would ever be allowed to walk anywhere again after their marriage. The half-humorous thought nevertheless brought a twinge of alarm. While not by any means a harsh man, Sir Edwin was almost impossible to defy.

The maid had a married sister in Tawmouth and was more than pleased to pay her a visit on Miss Hayes's suggestion after all the baskets had been delivered. Moira intended calling upon Harriet Lincoln and perhaps persuading her to look about the shops. But the temptation of the outdoors was just too strong. Like a truant schoolboy, she hurried along the street that would take her to the seawall, a waist-high granite structure that marked the end of the valley road and protected the unwary pedestrian from the long drop to the beach below. She braced her hands on top of the wall and drew in deep breaths of the bracing sea air.

Beneath her, the golden beach stretched away to either side. A few fishermen worked at the boats moored against the long stone quay away off to the right, but there was an inviting air of solitude about the beach. The tide was out. A few gulls screamed and wheeled overhead. She should turn and make her way back to Harriet's, Moira thought. But she walked instead to the only gap in the wall. Beyond it a flight of steps descended sharply against the side of the wall to the beach.

Normally, she would not have hesitated. Must she do so now merely because she knew that Sir Edwin Baillie would disapprove? He would more than disapprove. He would doubtless deliver a lengthy lecture that would feature his mother's early teaching. He would remind her, after many verbal tokens of his respect and regard, of what she owed her position as a lady and as the betrothed of the baronet of Penwith. Was she to bow to his will for the rest of her life? Was she to retain not even a modicum of independence, of self-respect? This was Cornwall. It was hardly improper to walk alone on a deserted beach at Tawmouth. And so she would say with calm firmness if he should somehow discover the truth. For the truth was, of course, that she was already halfway down the steps.

She had always loved the beach, both as a playground and as a place where dreams could be allowed to take flight. She had come here a great deal with Sean. Their parents had been somewhat indulgent, allowing them more freedom of movement than many children had. They had built sand castles, gathered seashells, paddled in the water, chased each other while shrieking with laughter or frustration or plain exuberance. And sometimes, beyond the jutting headland that hid the deeper cove beyond from the village and the quay, they had come across Kenneth, and he and Sean would exchange insults until they began to play together — smugglers and pirates, games involving sword fights with lengths of driftwood brought up by the tide, and scrambles up the cliff face. Moira had always been sent away to search the pools or to keep watch or simply to behave herself. She had often suspected that those meetings were deliberate, that the two boys had planned them.

As a child she had adored Kenneth, the handsome blond boy from Dunbarton, whom they were strictly forbidden to so much as acknowledge. She had used to watch him while he played with Sean, imagining him turning to her and inviting her to play, *wanting* her to play. He never had. He had been unaware of her existence, a mere girl. Until much later, that was.

Later, after he had been away at school for a few years, during one of his holidays, she had met him there alone. She could no longer remember where Sean had been. She knew that she had left her governess in the village, doing some shopping for her mother. She had rounded the headland into the cove and he had been there, sitting on a rock, apparently dreaming. He had looked at her without recognition at first but with definite appreciation. Then recognition had been there too. And he had smiled. At her. For the first time ever.

Foolish girl. Oh, foolish young girl that she had been to be so beguiled by male beauty and charm. She had been so very *flattered.* She had fallen mindlessly in love.

She strolled toward the cove now, remembering. So many memories. They made her feel old, dull. She had not really expected life to come to this, an aging woman about to contract a marriage of convenience with a man she had to make a conscious effort even to tolerate. But no, it was not so much that she was an aging woman as that she was a mature woman who had learned that the reality of life and the dream of life one had when young were, more often than not, poles apart. Life was not so dreadful now. She was not destitute. She was not abused. She was not —

She stopped suddenly, rooted to the spot

with alarm as a huge black dog came loping out from beyond the jutting cliff. Its pace increased to a gallop when it saw her, and it came charging in her direction, barking ferociously. She had always been terrified of dogs. This one was more monster than dog. If she had been capable of any movement at all, she would have turned and fled in blind panic. But even the instinct for survival could not set her in motion.

5

"Nelson!" The word of sharp command was perfectly audible above the barking. It could have proceeded only from the throat of a man accustomed to making himself heard above far more deafening noises.

The dog's pace decreased to a lope again, and he circled about Moira, his bark considerably less ferocious.

"Sit!" the same voice commanded and Nelson sat, his tongue lolling from his mouth as he panted and gazed at Moira with unblinking eyes.

She held her teeth clamped firmly together, as if only by doing so could she keep herself from disintegrating into several pieces. She kept her eyes on the dog although her brain had begun to tell her to whom that voice belonged — as if she had conjured him with her wayward memory. Her brain was also reminding her that she was quite alone, without even the respectable presence of a maid — just as she had been during that first meeting with him up on the cliffs.

"He would not have attacked." Two black top boots had come into view as well as the lower part of a greatcoat. "Not without my command."

She raised her eyes. He was standing a few feet off, his hands clasped behind him. He was quite alone, as she was. "Not without your command?" she said. "But with it, he would have torn me to pieces?"

"He would have restrained you with sufficient force to prevent you from attacking me," he said, his faint smile succeeding only in making him appear haughtier than usual.

"I must be thankful," she said, "that he is well enough trained not to attack first and look for your command second."

"He would not have got out of Spain," he said. "I made the mistake of feeding him there once when he was just one of scores of abject strays. He attached himself to me after that with flattering devotion. But I set certain conditions to his remaining with me. He has never attacked without my permission. But he has saved my life more than once."

"I shudder to think," she said, "what became of those from whom he saved you."

"I would not tell you if you asked," he said. "You would not wish to know."

She was feeling angry at her own paralyzed fear and at the fact that he had witnessed it. "And do you think it fair, my lord," she asked, "to allow such a war-hardened beast to run loose about an unsuspecting nation?"

"Why, Miss Hayes," he said, and there was definite hauteur in his voice now and perhaps annoyance too, "the nation is full of thousands of such beasts, most of them two-legged and most of them ignored and unwanted by a country for whose honor and freedom they fought through hell. Fortunately, most of them, like Nelson here, know a thing or two about discipline and obedience to commands."

Nelson had decided that he had sat for long enough. He approached Moira and pushed his nose against her gloved hand.

"Are you still afraid of dogs, Moira?" the Earl of Haverford asked when she drew back her hand. "Even when they come to apologize and make friends?"

"No, of course not." She patted the dog's head and felt enormously proud of herself. He had always had a dog with him as a boy. She had always cringed from it even though the one she remembered had been a friendly little mutt, which had liked to jump up on

90

her and lick her face.

Nelson was gazing up at her with intelligent eyes and was nudging at her hand for more petting. She smoothed her hand between his ears. She felt embarrassed and tongue-tied. She wanted to escape. Should she just bid him a good morning and walk on? Or walk back the way she had come? She should have made some observation about the weather, she thought when the silence had stretched a little too long, but doing so now would seem awkward. *Why* had she given in to temptation and come down onto the beach?

"Why are you walking here alone, Moira?" he asked.

Indignation wiped away embarrassment. She looked up at him. It was enough that she had Sir Edwin to give her such reminders of her status as a lady. She had been forced to ride down the valley swathed in blankets and hot bricks inside a closed carriage, with a maid for company. "Because I choose to do so," she said. "Why are you walking here alone, my lord?"

"Because I have a houseful of guests in need of entertainment," he said. "And because today the Christmas festivities are beginning in earnest and my educated guess is that I will not have a single moment to

91

myself that is not stolen for the next week or so. Because I remembered that Nelson needed exercise and judged that none of my guests, especially the ladies, would wish to accompany us. They are all terrified of him. Foolish, are they not?"

Perhaps, she thought, those same lady guests would be wise to be fearful of *him.* Although he spoke with a half smile on his lips, as if he were making a joke, there was something dangerous about him, a certain coldness about his eyes. He had changed, she thought. He was not the Kenneth she had known. This was a man who had faced death and had seen death and had inflicted death and had become, perhaps, indifferent to it. This was a man who had commanded other men and who, she did not doubt, had made himself feared. And yet even as a boy he had liked to go off alone sometimes. Sean would not have met him otherwise. *She* would not have met him. But his eyes had been soft and dreamy in those days.

She looked back down at Nelson and patted him some more. "I have been busy with Christmas preparations," she said, "and with receiving callers relative to my betrothal. I have been accustoming myself to the presence of a stranger at Penwith — a stranger who is also the owner and master there, and my betrothed. I came to Taw-mouth this morning to deliver Christmas baskets. I needed a little time to myself. Do you know how tedious it is always to be trailed by a maid?"

"I believe," he said, "it is for your safety."

She had an alarming feeling of déjà vu. She had asked him the same question once before. And he had answered with the same words — *before kissing her.* Her eyes widened.

"Am I not safe with you, then?" she asked.

His expression was controlled, his eyes cool. But they lowered to focus quite unmistakably on her mouth for a few moments. "You are quite safe," he said.

No, she was not. "I must return to Taw-mouth," she said abruptly, "and my maid and carriage."

He raised both eyebrows. "I shall not offer to escort you, Miss Hayes," he said, "but I will swear not to report your little truancy to Sir Edwin Baillie. My guess is that he would be less than pleased."

She opened her mouth to make a sharp retort about caring nothing for pleasing her betrothed. But she *was* betrothed to him and owed him her loyalty.

"Good day to you, my lord," she said, and turned to make her way back along the beach to the seawall. The Earl of Haverford and Nelson stayed where they were or went back into the cove. She did not look back to see which.

She had the uncomfortable and quite mistaken feeling that something intimate had passed between them, that it had been a guilty and clandestine meeting, something to be kept from Sir Edwin — and even her mother — at all costs. He had looked at her mouth and she had looked at his. . . .

There were just too many kissing boughs at Dunbarton. Or to be more accurate, since kissing boughs were at least clearly visible and therefore possible to avoid half of the time, there were too many sprigs of mistletoe stuck up in all sorts of unexpected places, and too many females lying in wait for unsuspecting gentlemen to alight beneath them. Though one or two of the ladies — the younger, prettier ones — were volubly and quite insincerely complaining of the reverse.

Kenneth had kissed every female in the house, with the exception of the servants, at least once before Christmas Day was out. He had kissed giggling cousins and simpering aunts and coy great-aunts. He had kissed his puckering niece. He had kissed a blushing Miss Juliana Wishart. He had kissed her three times in all, in fact, though not once by his own designing.

She was extremely pretty, with hair as blond as his own, with wide blue eyes, and trembling rosebud lips. She was enticingly rounded and fashionably and expensively clad. She was good-natured and smiled frequently. She was compliant and eligible — and her parents, Baron and Lady Hockingsford, were downright eager. The pursuit was on, and everyone at Dunbarton, from his mother on down, appeared to be aiding and abetting the courtship.

She was seventeen years old. She was the veriest infant. He could not force his eyes to see her as anything more. Kissing her was very like kissing his niece — but potentially far more dangerous. One did not kiss a seventeen-year-old young miss three times, even beneath the mistletoe, without raising expectations and arousing speculation.

Having kissed Miss Wishart three times, Kenneth felt uneasily as if some declaration had been made — or should be made. The girl had sat beside him in the earl's pew at church and had ridden home in his carriage with his mother and hers, and with him, of course. She had been seated beside him for Christmas dinner and had been his partner at cards afterward before being a member of his team at charades. One of his aunts had even referred to her as "your Miss Wishart, Kenneth, dear."

His Miss Wishart?

He had been quite prepared to look the girl over, to consider her as a possible candidate for wife. But having looked, he had rejected. He could not imagine living with the girl for the rest of a lifetime, making a companion of her. And he could no more think of having marital relations with her than he could think of doing so with his niece or any other child. His mother had suggested that the Christmas ball might be a suitable occasion on which to announce his betrothal. Most of his family members and most of his neighbors would be in attendance. Spring would be a wonderful time for the wedding. He should suggest spending an hour of the afternoon before the ball with Lord Hockingsford, she had added.

"Lady Hockingsford has been my close friend since we made our comeout together," she said. "This is something we have hoped for and even dared plan ever since Juliana was born. You can make us both very happy and proud."

He had been thirteen when Juliana Wishart was born, Kenneth thought — only four years younger than she was now. He had been at school already. He felt horribly trapped and pressured, but he would not marry merely to please his mother and her particular friend. He would not marry at all — yet. He was not ready for such a step. At the ball, he decided, he was going to have to steer clear of Miss Wishart after the opening set, which somehow, he had discovered, he was to dance with her. He must dance with all his female guests and with all his female neighbors. He was already engaged to waltz with Moira Hayes, he remembered.

And he remembered, too, his regret at having solicited her hand for the set, his reluctance to touch her. He remembered his unexpected meeting with her on the beach and the flood of memories encountering her there of all places had brought to mind. Of course, those memories had not depended upon his coming face-to-face with her. He had walked about the cove long before she came into sight and had even stood still there, remembering. Remembering meeting her there for the first time alone and realizing that she had grown from a child he had scarcely noticed into a tall, willowy, darkly alluring young woman. He had only recently begun to notice young women. He had remembered other meetings with her after that: infrequent, contrived meetings, not all of them in the cove. But it was in the cove he had kissed her for the first time. By that time, he had been at university and had learned enough about kissing — and about more than kissing — to become quite blasé about the whole business. But one touch of Moira's lips had sent his temperature soaring.

He had not reacted to her, though, as he had to the few Oxford barmaids with whom he had had dealings. It had not been an entirely physical thing — or so he had told himself, perhaps to assuage the guilt of having arranged a private meeting with a lady and of having stolen a kiss from her. He had fallen in love with her.

And then, while memory was still rampant in him, while he was still feeling rather sad for that long-ago idealistic, romantic boy, Nelson had found her just beyond the cove. And despite her drab gray cloak and bonnet, she had looked again for a few minutes like the Moira of old — her cheeks and nose flushed rosy with the cold, her eyes wide with alarm, her whole body rigid with terror and then with anger at Nelson and him and at herself for showing such weakness, he suspected. He had had sleepless moments since then over the memory that he had almost stepped close enough to take her into his arms to comfort her and assure her that Nelson would never harm her.

And yet he would have her at least within the circle of his arms during one set of waltzes at the ball. The thought was a disquieting one. As was the thought of dodging Miss Wishart and the concerted efforts of a number of his relatives and hers to throw them together.

On the whole, he thought ruefully, he might have done considerably better to have stayed in London to enjoy the Christmas festivities with Eden and Nat. He should not have made such a momentous decision while too foxed to think straight. They were doubtless enjoying themselves without a care in the world.

For a while on the day of the ball Moira had hopes of avoiding it after all. First there was the letter that arrived for Sir Edwin Baillie from the eldest of his sisters. She wrote to congratulate her brother on his betrothal and to express the pleasure she and her mama and sisters felt at the prospect of welcoming Miss Hayes as a far closer relative than she had been before. She wrote to wish her brother and his betrothed — and Lady Hayes, of course — the compliments of the season. And *she* wrote rather than her mama because Mama was feeling slightly under the weather, having still not quite shaken the chill that had threatened when dear Edwin left. But he was not to feel alarmed. Christobel was confident that another day or two of quiet rest would restore her mother to full health once more.

Sir Edwin was beside himself with anxiety. His mother must be very sick indeed if she found herself unable even to write a letter to her son and her soon-to-be daughter-in-law — if Miss Hayes would pardon such a familiar reference to herself. It was inexpressibly kind of Lady Hayes to try comforting him with the assurance that his sister would surely inform him of any serious decline in his mother's health, but he knew how tenderhearted his sisters were and how stout hearted his mother was. None of them would wish to drag him unnecessarily from the felicity of basking in the happiness of the early days of his betrothal.

He must return home without delay, he decided at one moment. He would have his bags packed and have his carriage prepared. Indeed, he would not even wait for his bags to be packed. But the next moment he decided that he must remain for at least one more day. He could not possibly disappoint

Miss Hayes and Lady Hayes by being unavailable to escort them to Dunbarton in the coming evening. And if he could not escort them, then who would? They would be doomed to remain at home. Besides — and perhaps of more importance when he remembered to set personal inclinations aside — he could not possibly disappoint his lordship, the Earl of Haverford, who had forgiven the Hayes family and himself as head of that family, albeit he bore a different name, and who would be eager to demonstrate the generosity of his restored friendship for all his family and neighbors to behold.

Moira reminded him that Lady Hayes had decided not to attend the ball and assured him that for her part, she would prefer to see him relieve his anxieties by returning home to his mother. Besides, she was not a girl to crave the pleasure of a mere ball.

For which hopeful little speech she was rewarded by having both her hands seized in a fierce clasp. Such generosity of spirit in Miss Hayes, such selfless concern for the health of her future mother-in-law, such tender concern for his own sensibilities, such a willingness to be deprived of a treat left him speechless indeed. How could he respond to such gentle devotion except by demonstrating a matching selflessness? He would escort Miss Hayes to the ball, he would make merry there just as if his heart were not heavy within him, and he would postpone his return home until tomorrow.

Moira smiled and thanked him.

But hope was not entirely dead. Christmas Day had been a cloudy, gloomy day. The clouds seemed even lower and grayer on the morning of the ball, and before noon thin flakes of snow began to float downward, enough to powder the dry ground and the grass and raise Moira's hopes. If it thickened and fell more heavily, travel could become difficult and dangerous, perhaps quite impossible. The ball would have to be canceled or at least confined to a mere dance for the houseguests at Dunbarton.

But the snow stopped altogether soon after noon and did not resume even though Moira paced frequently to the window to peer outward and upward and will the clouds to drop their heavy load. It seemed that she was doomed to attend a grand ball. And to waltz at it with the Earl of Haverford.

And so she dressed later in a new peach-colored evening gown, its sheer muslin overdress revealing the sheen of satin beneath. It was not a remarkably fussy dress.

She was six-and-twenty after all. The hem was simply ruched and there were no ruffles. The high waist was caught beneath her bosom with a silk sash. The neckline was low but certainly not as low as fashion allowed. The sleeves were short and puffed. She had her hair dressed in curls and ringlets but would allow nothing too elaborate. She chose not to wear either a turban or plumes. She had always valued simplicity in dress.

"You look very well, dear," her mother said before she left her dressing room.

"The color is not too bright?" Moira asked somewhat anxiously. They had only recently left off their mourning for her father. Her eyes had become attuned to black and gray. "I do not look too girlish, Mama?"

"You look like the beautiful woman you are," her mother said.

Moira smiled and hugged her. It was an exaggeration, of course. She had never been beautiful, even as a girl. But she *felt* good and she felt in an almost festive mood despite her dashed hopes earlier in the day. Would he think she looked beautiful or at least well enough? Would he think that she dressed too brightly or too girlishly? Would he look at her with admiration? With scorn? Or with no interest at all?

"I am sure Sir Edwin will be very pleased indeed," Lady Hayes said.

Moira's eyes widened. Sir Edwin? Yes, of course, Sir Edwin. It was he she had been thinking of. Of course it was he she had meant. Some of her exhilaration disappeared.

"He has a good heart, Moira," her mother said. "He means well."

"Yes," Moira said, smiling cheerfully. "I am fully sensible of my good fortune, Mama."

Her mother's smile was rather rueful — and warm with affection.

The ballroom at Dunbarton Hall, though rather small in comparison with some of the grander ballrooms that entertained the *ton* during the Season in London, was nevertheless splendidly decorated with gold leaf and paintings and chandeliers, and its size had been artfully enhanced by a coved ceiling and by huge mirrors along one long wall.

For the Christmas ball it had been festively decked out with holly and ivy and pine boughs, and with bells and red silk ribbons and bows. An orchestra had been hired at great expense, and the earl's cook, with extra hired help from Tawmouth, had succeeded in preparing a veritable banquet to fill one anteroom for the whole of the evening and the dining room for supper. Almost everyone who had been invited, neighbors from miles around, had accepted their invitations.

The ballroom would be filled, Kenneth thought, surveying the empty room while most of the ladies were still abovestairs putting the finishing touches to their toilettes and most of the gentlemen were in the drawing room fortifying themselves for the ordeal ahead with the earl's brandy or port. He was tempted to join them there. But the orchestra members came upstairs from the kitchen, where they had been eating their dinner, and he spent some time discussing with their leader the evening's program. And then footmen and maids were bringing up the food and the punch bowls for the anteroom, and he strolled inside to observe the effects of their work. But his presence was not needed. His butler was supervising with cool competence.

In spite of himself he found that he was looking forward to the evening. It was not every day one had the chance to host a grand ball for one's family, friends, and neighbors. He was becoming fond of them all. He was beginning to enjoy his position.

Life as it had been lived for the past eight years was beginning to recede into memory.

And then his mother, looking magnificently regal in a purple silk gown with a matching plumed turban, appeared in the ballroom to announce that the first of the guests were approaching along the driveway, and Helen and Ainsleigh were not far behind her with several of the other house-guests. They had come, Kenneth guessed, so that they might be on hand to observe each new arrival. These first guests were early.

Kenneth took up his position outside the ballroom doors with his mother and waited for the guests to appear on the staircase. They were Sir Edwin Baillie and Moira Hayes. He felt his mother stiffen and wished that they had not been the first to arrive. Later, they might have blended more easily with other guests.

She was looking quite beautiful, he thought unwillingly. Her peach-colored gown looked stunning with her dark hair and eyes, and she had had the good sense to allow simplicity to state its own case. Most of the ladies already in the ballroom — including Juliana Wishart — seemed almost to be in competition with one another to see who could deck themselves out in the most frills and bows and ruffles and curls and ringlets. Moira Hayes was also quite noticeably — and unashamedly, it seemed — taller than her escort.

Lady Hayes sent her regrets, Sir Edwin explained after bowing over Lady Haverford's hand and congratulating himself on being a close neighbor and — dared he be so familiar? — friend of her son. Lady Hayes was too recently out of mourning for the late Sir Basil Hayes to feel easy about partaking of such enjoyment as she felt convinced the evening's entertainment would offer. She hoped that she might call upon her ladyship in the near future.

Lady Hayes, Kenneth thought even before glancing at Moira's face, had doubtless expressed no such hope, and his mother's marble expression was discouraging, to say the least. She made no verbal reply, but merely inclined her head graciously. Sir Edwin appeared not to notice anything amiss. He thanked her profusely.

Moira Hayes curtsied to Lady Haverford. She kept her chin up as she did so and her expression bland. His mother, Kenneth noticed, though she nodded again, did not acknowledge her guest in words or look directly into her face. The feud was not over, as far as she was concerned — or as far as Lady Hayes was concerned, apparently. It was an awkward moment, smoothed over by the good manners of both ladies.

"Miss Hayes." Kenneth took her gloved hand in his and raised it to his lips. It was the first time he had touched her in longer than eight years. He did not, as he half expected, feel currents of awareness sizzle along his arm to lodge in his heart. He merely had a sudden and quite unwelcome image of Baillie touching her — in bed. He wondered if the man would make a speech as he bedded her for the first time but could draw no real amusement from the conviction that the answer was surely yes.

"My lord," she said, and her eyes traveled all along her arm to his lips and up to his eyes. In any other woman he would have called it a practiced and coquettish look. But her eyes were cool and very direct on his. There was not even a suggestion of fluttering eyelids. There never had been. Moira had never been a flirt.

"I trust, Miss Hayes," he said, "that you will remember you are to waltz with me?"

"Thank you, my lord," she said.

And since no other guest had yet arrived, he strolled into the ballroom with her and Baillie to walk about the room with them, introducing them to his houseguests. Although he offered his own arm, he noticed that she took Baillie's even before that gentleman offered it. He half smiled. Ah, but she would waltz with him.

He was surprised by the satisfaction that came with the thought. An almost vengeful satisfaction.

6

A few of Kenneth's closer relatives raised
their eyebrows when Moira's name was
mentioned, but all were polite. None lived
close enough to have ever been personally
involved in the feud. There was certainly no
lack of conversation with Sir Edwin Baillie
only too eager to inform everyone that he
was the baronet of Penwith Manor, they
were to understand, only three miles distant
from Dunbarton, and he might feel disgrun-
tled at being outranked by so close a neighbor — he smiled about each group so that
everyone might realize that he was having
his little joke — were that neighbor not also
a friend.

Somehow, Kenneth discovered, before
they had completed the circle of the room
and before the arrival of any other guest
had necessitated his return to his duties at
the door, he had become escort to Juliana
Wishart, who desired to promenade about

the room, one of his aunts informed him in that young lady's blushing hearing, but could persuade no other lady to accompany her. He had bowed and responded with the obvious gallantry, of course. His aunt had looked charmed.

And then they came to his sister, who had her back to them as they approached.

"Helen? Michael?" he said. "May I present Miss Moira Hayes and Sir Edwin Baillie? Sir Edwin has inherited Penwith Manor. My sister and brother-in-law, Viscount and Viscountess Ainsleigh," he added for the benefit of his guests.

Sir Edwin bowed low and launched into speech while Moira curtsied and Ainsleigh smiled. Helen, disdain in her face, focused her gaze upon Juliana.

"My dear Miss Wishart," she said, cutting off Sir Edwin in the middle of a sentence, "how ravishingly elegant you look this evening. You must tell me who your modiste is. It is so difficult to find one these days worthy of one's patronage. Of course, you are so exquisitely small. I do so admire ladies of small stature. Will you take a turn about the room with me? The air is stuffy in here, I do declare."

And she took Juliana's arm and made off with her, commenting quite distinctly as she went that she also much admired Juliana's blond hair and blue eyes. "I truly pity *dark* women," she said. "Blond women are so much more delicate and feminine."

Sir Edwin picked up his sentence where he had left it off, and Ainsleigh, after looking somewhat startled, smiled more charmingly and drew Moira into the conversation as soon as he was able.

Kenneth reflected with some chagrin that his sister had reacted as his mother had but with lamentably worse manners. It was remarkably unfair of Helen to take out her bitterness on Moira, he thought. It would make more sense for her to turn it against him. But Moira had the misfortune to be Sean Hayes's sister. He had learned one thing already this evening, though, even if he had not understood it before the invitations were sent out. It would be as well to keep his distance from the family at Penwith, at least while his mother and sister were at Dunbarton. And it would suit him admirably to do so, after this evening. This evening he owed Moira Hayes the courtesy of a host.

A glance at the doorway showed him that more guests were arriving. He excused himself and hurried in the direction of the ballroom doors.

Moira had never before attended a ball for which a whole orchestra had been engaged. And she had never before attended one in surroundings more splendid than the rather austere Tawmouth assembly rooms. She had never before been at a ball when more than ten couples at a time could take to the floor.

The Dunbarton ball was undoubtedly the most glittering entertainment she had ever attended or would ever attend. She did not lack for partners since Sir Edwin led her into the opening set, Viscount Ainsleigh had asked for the second, and various neighbors were as gallant as they usually were at the assemblies and made sure that she did not have to sit out a single set.

She wished she were anywhere else on earth but where she actually was. She had never in her life felt more acutely uncomfortable. She might have coped with the embarrassment of being in company with Sir Edwin both during the long stretch of time between their almost indecently early arrival and the beginning of the dancing and between each set — he was not evil, after all, and not quite vulgar. And being in company with him, both in public and in private, was something to which she was going to have to accustom herself. It was something that required a little fortitude and a great deal of a sense of the ridiculous. But it was far more difficult to disregard the well-bred snub the Countess of Haverford had dealt her or the open and quite ill-bred one given her by Helen.

Helen had once fancied herself in love with Sean. Perhaps she really had been. But her plans to elope with him had been thwarted; she had been hurt and embarrassed and disgraced, even if not publicly. And so, hatred for the Hayes family had become a personal thing with her. Or so it seemed to Moira. She had not seen Helen since it all happened. She did not even know if Helen had ended up hating Sean.

Sir Edwin soon had an explanation for Viscountess Ainsleigh's unmannerly cutting of their acquaintance. He observed with a knowing smirk that his host led out the Honorable Miss Juliana Wishart into the opening set.

"It is as I suspected as soon as we were presented to Lord and Lady Hockingsford and the Honorable Miss Wishart, my dear Miss Hayes," he said. "A match is being arranged between Miss Wishart and the Earl of Haverford — mark my words. An eminently eligible match, if I may make so bold as to say so — and I *shall* say so to his lordship in the capacity of a neighbor and friend as soon as I have the opportunity to do so in confidence. Lady Ainsleigh's preference for the young lady is perfectly well explained now that I have realized that they are to be closely related. You would do well to cultivate Miss Wishart's acquaintance too, Miss Hayes, since it seems very likely that you will be neighbors. It is desirable that you be friends too. As Mama always says, when two families are neighbors, it is strongly to be desired that they be friends also. And you are very nearly of an equality in rank with Miss Wishart, though marriage to his lordship will elevate her, of course. As marriage with me will elevate you."

Yes, Miss Wishart surely would suit him admirably, Moira thought. She was very young and wide-eyed and innocent. Doubtless she would be easily dominated. The top of her head did not quite reach his shoulder.

He was looking quite intimidatingly handsome and elegant this evening. He wore a black tailed coat and knee breeches with a silver embroidered waistcoat and white linen and lace. All her neighbors had exclaimed with mingled admiration and surprise at the somberness of the colors, but

Sir Edwin had assured them all that his lordship was dressed in the very height of fashion. Any other gentleman might have looked dull in such clothes, Moira thought, but the Earl of Haverford, with his superior height, his splendid physique, and his very blond hair, looked nothing short of stunning.

It disturbed Moira to have to admit as much. But he always had been handsome. It would be childish to deny the truth, to try to find fault with his appearance. There was no fault there.

She wished she had not agreed to waltz with him. If she had not done so, she could somehow have kept Sir Edwin within the sphere of her neighbors and friends and she might have ignored the nasty embarrassment of the evening's beginning. But she had agreed, and he had reminded her of the promised waltz on her arrival. And when the time came, he was at her side before anyone else had gone out onto the floor and was bowing over her hand. Harriet Lincoln and Mrs. Meeson gazed at her in some shock and some envy, and every eye in the ballroom, it seemed, gazed on her when he led her out to the middle of the empty floor. It was the first waltz. There was more hesitation about performing it than there had been to participate in the country dance, the quadrille, and the minuet that had preceded it.

"I trust, Miss Hayes," he said before the music began, "that you are enjoying yourself."

"Thank you, yes, my lord," she said. He was the first partner of hers tonight, she thought, at whom she had had to look up. She wondered if Helen had realized how much her remark to Miss Wishart about height had hurt.

And then all observations and all stiff and meaningless attempts at polite conversation vanished as the orchestra began to play and he took her hand in one of his and rested his other firmly at the back of her waist. She touched his shoulder and was aware, for all the lightness of her touch, of its hard-muscled breadth. She was aware of *him:* of his height, of his body heat, of his cologne, of his eyes on hers. Her abdominal muscles clenched involuntarily and all memory of the steps of the waltz vanished. She almost stumbled over the first of them.

"The steps are easy," he said. "You merely have to relax and follow my lead."

It was a veiled and well-bred reproof for her clumsiness. She looked coolly into his eyes. "I shall not disgrace you, my lord," she said. "I shall not tread all over your feet or — worse for your self-esteem — contrive to get my feet beneath yours."

"I believe," he said, "I have a little too much skill than to allow that to happen."

She had remembered the steps and picked up the rhythm of the music and felt the guidance of his lead. They twirled about the dance floor and she lost her awareness of everything but the exhilaration and the wonder of the dance. And of the man, tall and solid and graceful, who danced it with her. It was sheer magic as she had always known it would be, she thought, though the thought was not fully conscious. It was a time for feeling more than for thought. She abandoned herself to feeling.

It was a long time before she came back to herself and was once more aware that she was in the ballroom at Dunbarton, waltzing with the Earl of Haverford. Smiling with sheer pleasure into his unsmiling eyes. She sobered and saw people and red bows and mirrors and candles — and him. How naive he must think her, to be transported to another world by a mere dance.

"Moira," he said, his voice sounding strained, almost harsh, "you cannot possibly *wish* to marry him, surely?"

"Sir Edwin?" she said, her eyes widening.

"He is a pompous bore," he said. "He will drive you insane within a month."

The spell had been utterly shattered. "I believe, my lord," she said, "that my betrothal and my future marriage are my concern. As well as my feelings for Sir Edwin Baillie."

"You have accepted his offer because you feel you have no alternative?" he asked. "Would you be quite destitute if you declined? Would he turn you and your mother out?"

"Perhaps you should ask him that final question," she said. "He is, after all, your neighbor and friend, is he not? I am neither, even if by some unhappy chance I happen to live three miles from here. Your questions are impertinent, my lord."

"The waltz is ending," he said after gazing at her quite expressionlessly for several moments. He took a step back from her and then bowed to her and offered her his arm. "And your temper is frayed. Allow me to escort you to the refreshment room, where you may recover it in some privacy."

She wondered if it was the waltz that had prompted him to speak so rashly. But then, he had asked her on the beach why she walked alone. Perhaps he felt that his position as Earl of Haverford gave him the right

to probe into the lives of his inferior neighbors. How dared he! But her nerves *were*
jangling and she dreaded returning to Sir
Edwin just to hear yet again what an honor
had been accorded both her and himself
during the past half hour. She took the offered arm.

"You waltz gracefully," the earl said, leading her to the anteroom where drinks and
other refreshments had been set out for
those who could not wait until supper time.
"It is a novel and rather pleasing experience
to dance it with someone who is at least
close to my own height."

Yes, she thought unwillingly. Oh, yes, it
had felt very good indeed to dance with a
man taller than herself. Why had he had to
spoil it? It had been one of those magical
experiences of her life, one she would long
remember.

Having caught herself in that thought, she
assured herself that it was as well he had
spoiled it. Magical memories involving
Kenneth, of all people, were not what she
wished to take forward into the marriage
she would soon contract.

He had been very indiscreet. He was host
of this ball and was very aware of the fact
that much attention had been focused upon

him all evening. It was understandable, of course. He was newly returned from the wars against Napoleon Bonaparte, newly returned to Dunbarton Hall. Although his father had been dead for seven years and he had borne the title since then, even it was in a sense new, at least for the relatives who were guests in his home and for the people who lived close to Dunbarton. Of course he was the focus of attention.

If one added to those facts the interest that had been aroused over the presence of Juliana Wishart in his home and the attention he had somehow been forced into paying her, then one must expect even more that eyes would follow him about. And when he had claimed his waltz with Moira Hayes, then a different form of curiosity drew attention on him. For he and Moira Hayes, to the knowledge of anyone present except perhaps his mother and Helen, had never had any dealings with each other until very recently, although they had lived only three miles apart during their growing years.

It had been a time to be very careful indeed. He was a man dancing with a neighbor from whose family his own had been estranged for several generations. Their families had been newly reconciled by the efforts of its new head, her betrothed. It was a set the Earl of Haverford should have danced with careful attention to what would appear correct.

What had he done instead? He appeared to have lost twenty minutes or so of his life. It was rather a ridiculous notion. He had not lost those minutes. But he had been caught up in a magic, an exhilaration, a *romance* that had seemed alarmingly beyond his control. After the first stumbling steps, she had proved herself to be an accomplished and graceful partner, one who fit into his hold as if she had been made to fit there.

If he had thought at all during those twenty minutes, it had been to remember her as a girl — as a young woman, after he had become aware of her. It had been her delight to escape from chaperones and maids set to watching after her safety. And when she had escaped, the resulting freedom had been total. Shoes and stockings had frequently gone flying; hairpins had been stuffed into a pocket and hair shaken loose. Ah, that hair: thick and shining and almost as black as coal. She had run and twirled and climbed and laughed, and more than once she had allowed him to kiss her.

She had become that girl again — that girl who had dazzled and enslaved him —

as they danced. He was alarmed at how totally he had lost touch with reality during those twenty minutes. And even when he pulled himself back to reality, he had ended up offending her by being unpardonably impertinent. She had been quite right to use that word.

"May I fill a plate for you?" he asked as he led her through to the anteroom, which was fortunately not overcrowded with people.

"No, thank you." She removed her arm from his. "A drink will be sufficient." She went to stand near a closed side door while he crossed to one of the punch bowls and filled two glasses without waiting for a footman to serve him.

He must converse with her on some trivial topic for a few minutes, he thought as he made his way back toward her, and then return her to Baillie and her own group of friends. He would then forget her presence at his ball. But one of his young cousins, who with a group of other young people was talking rather too loudly and laughing rather too heartily, chose that particular moment to call across the room to him.

"I say, Haverford," he called, "have you seen where she is standing?"

There were a few feminine giggles, some

hearty male laughter.

"Of course he has seen," another distant cousin said just as loudly. "Why do you think he is hurrying?"

"To it, man," a third voice said and the laughter resumed.

Moira looked with raised eyebrows at the group while Kenneth's eyes looked up and found the inevitable sprig of mistletoe in the middle of the doorframe, directly above her head. Alerted, she also looked up and saw it — and blushed hotly and would have moved away if he had not been standing directly in her path, his arms open to either side, a glass in each hand.

Since he had kissed every female in the house during the past two days, it would appear strange indeed to his delighted young relatives and a few older ones who were also in the room if he did not do the gallant thing on this occasion too. He leaned forward, lowering his head only a little, and touched her lips with his. Hers were trembling uncontrollably. By sheer instinct he parted his own over them to steady them. He lifted his head after enough time had elapsed that he would not be accused of trying to escape with a mere peck but before he could be accused of taking liberties that even mistletoe would not excuse.

"The conventions must be observed," he said, looking into Moira Hayes's wide, shocked eyes, shielding them with his body from the view of their cheering, applauding audience. "If you must stand there, ma'am, then you must suffer the consequences."

He handed her one of the glasses. But her hand, when she reached for it, was trembling. She returned it to her side and looked up at him.

"I am not thirsty after all," she said.

"Steady, Moira," he said. "It is Christmas, and I have some relatives who derive enormous amusement from other people's embarrassment. I have spent two whole days doing nothing but kiss aunts and cousins and any other lady who is unfortunate enough to alight under one of these abominations when I am within striking distance. The relatives laugh and cheer and applaud every time. One wonders what they will do for entertainment once the holiday is over and the mistletoe comes down. Doubtless something will crop up. They seem almost alarmingly easy to please. One is left questioning the state of their intellect."

He talked until the startled look went from her eyes. She recovered herself rather quickly and took the glass from his hand when he offered it again. She drank determinedly from it.

"I came tonight because Sir Edwin was set on it," she said. "But he is planning to return home tomorrow and to stay there until he comes back for our wedding in the spring. I hope that between now and then you will not feel obliged to continue the connection with Penwith."

"I imagine," he said, "that my great-grandfather sentenced yours because he did not wish to have his own connection with the trade exposed. I imagine that guilt and the contempt of those in the know was almost as great a punishment to him as transportation was to his victim. Is my family still to feel the guilt and yours to feel the shame?"

"You know very well," she said scornfully, "that what is between your family and mine now, my lord, has nothing whatsoever to do with that old feud. Perhaps an eight-year absence has helped you to trivialize and even forget what —"

But she broke off abruptly, smiled brightly, and sipped from her glass again. Kenneth looked over his shoulder to find Sir Edwin Baillie approaching.

"I cannot find words to describe the full extent of my gratification at such a marked degree of civility, my lord," he said. "To ne it would take my carriage to travel t[o] [P]enwith Manor. I am afraid in my heart tha[t] [th]e snow will impede travel before many [m]ore hours have passed."

"Then I shall come with you to you[r] [h]ome," she said, "and his lordship will send [w]ord to Mama."

But Sir Edwin, despite his deep gratitude — and he would make so bold as to asser[t] [th]at he spoke for his mother and his sisters [to] — for Miss Hayes's concern over he[r] [fu]ture mother-in-law, was not so lost to all [pr]opriety as to assent to her making such a [lo]ng journey alone with him.

"I shall, of course, see to it that Miss [H]ayes is escorted home when the ball is [ov]er," Kenneth said.

For which assurance he was forced to [st]and listening to a lengthy speech of grati-[tu]de from Sir Edwin, who declared that he [ha]d not one moment to spare. Though he [di]d afterward spare several more moments [in] escorting his betrothed into the ballroom [..] where her particular friend, Mrs. Lin-[c]oln, was standing in a group with her [h]usband and several other people.

Kenneth saw him on his way less than half [an] hour later and assured him yet again that [h]e would see to it that Miss Hayes was [de]livered home safe and sound. The snow

single out my affianced bride by leading her into a set at the Dunbarton ball when there are so many other distinguished ladies who might be so honored is a gesture of true neighborliness. To lead her to the refreshment table afterward is a mark, if I may make so bold as to suggest it, of sincere friendship. This is a felicitous start to the new amity between Dunbarton Hall and Penwith Manor."

And doubtless, Kenneth thought, the man would have gone into raptures and counted it as a compliment to himself if he had seen the Earl of Haverford kiss his betrothed beneath the mistletoe. He inclined his head.

But having delivered himself of this speech, Sir Edwin proceeded to look decidedly anxious. "Word has it," he said, "that it is beginning to snow outside, my lord. Your servants have confirmed the fact though they assure me that the fall is light."

"And we are safe and warm inside, sir," Kenneth said with a smile. "But I should be seeing to my guests in the ballroom. Please do join Miss Hayes with a glass of punch."

Sir Edwin felt obliged to express effusive thanks, but he was not prepared to drop the matter of the snow. It appeared that he was fearful it would fall thickly enough during the night to prevent his leaving for home on the morrow. And with his mother dangerously ill — Miss Hayes, he added, might object that his sister's letter, which had arrived just this morning, had made no such assertion, but his lordship must pardon him for having sufficient knowledge of his sisters, especially of Christobel, the eldest, to be able to read between the lines of a letter as well as on them. Had his mother not been quite seriously indisposed, then Christobel would not have mentioned her health at all. Had his mother not been dangerously ill, then she would have written herself to assure her son that he might enjoy the felicity of his betrothed's company — he bowed to Moira — without having to spare any anxious thoughts for her or for his sisters.

"And yet, sir," Kenneth said soothingly, "your mother and your sister surely understand your concerns and would have summoned you if matters were so serious."

But Sir Edwin, though profuse in his thanks for his lordship's concern, was not to be consoled. There was a certain intuition about the heart, it seemed, when the health of loved ones was in peril. His lordship had a mother and a sister and even the special felicity of a nephew and niece and must know of what Sir Edwin spoke. He had a favor to ask of his lordship and was embold-

ened to request it only because his l[...] had already shown that he was [...] neighbor and friend.

Kenneth raised his eyebrows an[...] dered if he would be able to bear [...] only three miles from this man for [...] of his life.

"I must return home without del[...] Edwin said. "I would consider it an [...] donable dereliction of my duty as a [...] delayed one moment longer. It matt[...] that I do not have either my vale[...] bags with me. It matters only that [...] to the bosom of my family before [...] late to clasp my mother in my ar[...] more. I would ask, my lord, that you [...] a carriage and the escort of a [...] convey my betrothed, Miss Hayes, [...] Penwith Manor at the end of the ev[...]

Moira Hayes rushed into speech. [...] return home with you now, Sir Edw[...] said. "I am sure that under the [...] stances, the Earl of Haverford wil[...] us for leaving early."

"It would distress me to leave y[...] without my escort, Miss Hayes, we [...] for the fact that you are in the ho[...] neighbor and friend," he said, "a[...] rounded by other neighbors and f[...] would not delay my journey ever[...]

single out my affianced bride by leading her into a set at the Dunbarton ball when there are so many other distinguished ladies who might be so honored is a gesture of true neighborliness. To lead her to the refreshment table afterward is a mark, if I may make so bold as to suggest it, of sincere friendship. This is a felicitous start to the new amity between Dunbarton Hall and Penwith Manor."

And doubtless, Kenneth thought, the man would have gone into raptures and counted it as a compliment to himself if he had seen the Earl of Haverford kiss his betrothed beneath the mistletoe. He inclined his head.

But having delivered himself of this speech, Sir Edwin proceeded to look decidedly anxious. "Word has it," he said, "that it is beginning to snow outside, my lord. Your servants have confirmed the fact though they assure me that the fall is light."

"And we are safe and warm inside, sir," Kenneth said with a smile. "But I should be seeing to my guests in the ballroom. Please do join Miss Hayes with a glass of punch."

Sir Edwin felt obliged to express effusive thanks, but he was not prepared to drop the matter of the snow. It appeared that he was fearful it would fall thickly enough during the night to prevent his leaving for home on the morrow. And with his mother dangerously ill — Miss Hayes, he added, might object that his sister's letter, which had arrived just this morning, had made no such assertion, but his lordship must pardon him for having sufficient knowledge of his sisters, especially of Christobel, the eldest, to be able to read between the lines of a letter as well as on them. Had his mother not been quite seriously indisposed, then Christobel would not have mentioned her health at all. Had his mother not been dangerously ill, then she would have written herself to assure her son that he might enjoy the felicity of his betrothed's company — he bowed to Moira — without having to spare any anxious thoughts for her or for his sisters.

"And yet, sir," Kenneth said soothingly, "your mother and your sister surely understand your concerns and would have summoned you if matters were so serious."

But Sir Edwin, though profuse in his thanks for his lordship's concern, was not to be consoled. There was a certain intuition about the heart, it seemed, when the health of loved ones was in peril. His lordship had a mother and a sister and even the special felicity of a nephew and niece and must know of what Sir Edwin spoke. He had a favor to ask of his lordship and was emboldened to request it only because his lordship had already shown that he was a true neighbor and friend.

Kenneth raised his eyebrows and wondered if he would be able to bear to live only three miles from this man for the rest of his life.

"I must return home without delay," Sir Edwin said. "I would consider it an unpardonable dereliction of my duty as a son if I delayed one moment longer. It matters little that I do not have either my valet or my bags with me. It matters only that I return to the bosom of my family before it is too late to clasp my mother in my arms once more. I would ask, my lord, that you provide a carriage and the escort of a maid to convey my betrothed, Miss Hayes, home to Penwith Manor at the end of the evening."

Moira Hayes rushed into speech. "I shall return home with you now, Sir Edwin," she said. "I am sure that under the circumstances, the Earl of Haverford will excuse us for leaving early."

"It would distress me to leave you here without my escort, Miss Hayes, were it not for the fact that you are in the home of a neighbor and friend," he said, "and surrounded by other neighbors and friends. I would not delay my journey even by the time it would take my carriage to travel to Penwith Manor. I am afraid in my heart that the snow will impede travel before many more hours have passed."

"Then I shall come with you to your home," she said, "and his lordship will send word to Mama."

But Sir Edwin, despite his deep gratitude — and he would make so bold as to assert that he spoke for his mother and his sisters too — for Miss Hayes's concern over her future mother-in-law, was not so lost to all propriety as to assent to her making such a long journey alone with him.

"I shall, of course, see to it that Miss Hayes is escorted home when the ball is over," Kenneth said.

For which assurance he was forced to stand listening to a lengthy speech of gratitude from Sir Edwin, who declared that he had not one moment to spare. Though he did afterward spare several more moments in escorting his betrothed into the ballroom to where her particular friend, Mrs. Lincoln, was standing in a group with her husband and several other people.

Kenneth saw him on his way less than half an hour later and assured him yet again that he would see to it that Miss Hayes was delivered home safe and sound. The snow was coming down no more heavily than it had earlier in the day, he noticed. There was no need to alert his outside guests to any need to return home before they found it impossible to do so. The chances were good that the snow would stop altogether within the hour.

7

Moira almost enjoyed the ball after Sir
Edwin Baillie had taken his leave. She felt
guilty admitting to herself that it was more
comfortable being with her neighbors and
friends without him, but it was nevertheless
true. And now that the waltz with the Earl
of Haverford was behind her, she no longer
had to feel the tension of knowing that there
was that yet to face. She danced with gentlemen she had known for years or else sat and
talked with their wives and daughters. It
was easy enough to avoid both the countess
and Viscountess Ainsleigh since they were
quite as determined to avoid her.

She would have enjoyed herself completely, she felt, if it were not for the embarrassment of knowing that at the end of the
evening she must be beholden to the earl,
that he was going to have to call out his own
carriage in order to send her home. She
tried at first to think of a neighbor who

would be willing to offer her carriage room, but there was no one who would not have to go considerably out of his way in order to take her along the valley to Penwith. Everyone else except her was going either to Tawmouth or to somewhere on this side of the valley or to somewhere on the other side. And the only road to the other side of the valley went through the village. There was no alternative, it seemed, but to impose upon a man to whom she wished to owe no debt.

But it was to be even worse than she expected — far worse. In the great pleasure of the evening with its restoration of the old tradition of the Dunbarton ball, no one had noticed that the snow was coming down in earnest outside. It was after supper and only an hour before midnight, and Miss Pitt was beginning to comment on the lateness of the hour to listeners who did not particularly wish to hear it when the Earl of Haverford was seen to confer with Mr. Meeson and Mr. Penallen and those gentlemen conferred with others and word reached the ladies that the snow was settling and it would be wise for them to leave without further delay.

Miss Pitt commented that the hour was quite late enough, anyway, and that none on them wished to outstay their welcome and perhaps persuade his lordship not to repeat the ball next year. Everyone, now that there was no choice in the matter, cheerfully agreed with her.

Moira watched with growing embarrassment as her neighbors and friends left the ballroom and only the houseguests remained. Most of them, although she had been presented to them at the start of the evening, seemed like strangers to her, though two elderly ladies were obliging enough to engage her in conversation. She did not know if she should leave the room, too, and go in search of the earl, who was probably downstairs taking his leave of his guests. Perhaps he had forgotten about her. Perhaps she should have gone with Harriet. She could have stayed the night at her friend's house and walked home in the morning. She wished she had thought of doing that now that it was perhaps too late. For a moment her eyes met those of the countess, who looked rather surprised and somewhat disdainful. Moira looked away hastily, got to her feet, and excused herself.

She met the earl on the landing outside the ballroom. He was coming up from downstairs. Everyone had left, then. It really was too late to make her suggestion to Harriet. She felt decidedly uncomfortable.

"I am sorry to have put you to this trouble, my lord," she said. "Is the carriage ready? There is really no need to send a maid with me, you know. I shall be quite safe alone in the carriage."

"I should have acted sooner," he said. "But I hated to spoil everyone's enjoyment before it became necessary. It is hard to judge the weather from the house here." The hollow and the woodland of the park surrounding Dunbarton Hall offered considerable shelter from sea winds. "I walked up to the road and I am afraid conditions are not good. The road to Tawmouth should be perfectly safe for the next hour or so at least, but I fear that the steeper road down to Penwith might be quite dangerous for a carriage. I would not risk your safety. You will remain here tonight as my guest. Tomorrow we will see how we may best get you home."

"Absolutely not, my lord," she said, her eyes widening in alarm. "If it is too dangerous for a carriage and horses, then I shall walk. I am perfectly well accustomed to walking. Three miles is no distance at all."

"But tonight you will stay here," he said. "I must insist upon it. I will hear no further arguments, Moira."

She guessed that he was not used to hearing further argument when he used that tone of voice and bore that chilling look. She guessed that as a cavalry officer he had never suffered from discipline problems among his men. But she was not one of his men.

"I have no wish to stay here," she said. "I wish to go home. Besides, my mother will be worried if I do not return."

"I have sent a groom to inform Lady Hayes that you will be remaining here for the night," he said.

"Oh." She raised her eyebrows. "It is perfectly safe for a groom to walk to Penwith but not for me to do so?"

"Try not to be tiresome, Moira," he said.

Her nostrils flared. "I do not remember, my lord," she said, her tone as icy as his, "granting you permission to use my given name."

"Try not to be tiresome, *Miss Hayes*," he said. He offered his arm to her and made her a half bow. "Allow me to return you to the ballroom. Our numbers are depleted, but my guess is that the festivities will continue for an hour or so yet. I shall have you shown to a room later and will make sure that you have everything you need there."

She felt trapped and utterly uncomfortable. If she really must stay at Dunbarton, then she would a hundred times rather be shown to that room immediately than have to return to a roomful of virtual strangers, almost all of whom were related to him in some way. But saying so would have been to reveal her discomfort to him. She would not do so for worlds. She set her arm along the top of his.

He danced with her again. It was not a waltz, she was thankful to find, but only a vigorous country dance. Even so, she was mortified that his relatives should see him distinguish her for such an unnecessary favor. He had danced with no other lady more than once — even Miss Wishart, who had been in his company several times between sets. She felt the strength of his hands in hers as he twirled her down the set and wished he were not so tall or so obviously strong. She felt diminished, vanquished. She felt like a helpless woman. She *was* a helpless woman. She was being forced into marrying someone she could not even like because she was a woman and quite unable to support herself and her mother. But she did not need further reminders from the Earl of Haverford of all people. It was his fault and Sir Edwin's — *men!* — that she was in this predicament.

He would have escorted her to join a group of youngish people when the set was ended, but she drew her arm from his.

"I shall sit with your aunts," she said, indicating the two ladies who had been kind to her earlier. They were deep in conversation with each other.

"Very well," he said, bowing to her and making no attempt to accompany her.

She was glad of it. She felt as conspicuous as the proverbial sore thumb and quite as uncomfortable. Drat Sir Edwin Baillie and his fussy concern for his mother's health, she thought. He had had no right to leave her alone here. But the realization that even if he had stayed, they might not have been able to return to Penwith that night had her feeling sudden gratitude that he was not there. She dreaded to think of the speech he would have felt obliged to deliver if the Earl of Haverford had offered his hospitality to both of them.

She did not wish to break into the conversation the two ladies were so obviously enjoying. Perhaps they had been glad to see her go, glad to be alone together so that they could discuss whatever it was that was engrossing their attention. She turned direction and slipped into the refreshment room. It was deserted now so soon after supper, though there were still two footmen there and still punch in the bowls. She shook her head when one of the servants made to pick up a glass and a ladle, and stood close to the door, looking out of the window onto a white world beyond. Even in the darkness she could see the snow. What if it continued to fall all night? What if she was unable to go home tomorrow? The very thought made her squirm with discomfort.

And then, above the hum of conversation in the ballroom, she heard two distinct voices. Their owners must be standing close to the anteroom door.

"I have given directions for a room to be made up for her," the Earl of Haverford said. "You will not need to exert yourself in any way, Mama."

"She should have been sent to Tawmouth in one of the carriages," the countess's voice said. "She has acquaintances enough there. I do not like having her beneath my roof, Kenneth."

"Pardon me." The earl's voice was suddenly both chilly and haughty. "Miss Hayes is to spend the night beneath *my* roof, Mama. She will be accorded all the proper courtesies here."

"Kenneth —" It was Viscountess Ainsleigh's voice this time, sounding breathless as if she had just rushed up to him. "Why is Moira Hayes still at the ball? Am I to understand —"

But the sound of her voice was suddenly cut off by the click of a closing door. One of the footmen on duty at the punch bowls smiled apologetically at Moira when she turned her head.

"Pardon me, ma'am," he said, "but there was a nasty draft. I shall be pleased to open the door for you when you wish to leave."

"Thank you," she said, looking away from his acutely embarrassed face. *When you wish to leave.* She wanted to leave now. It was insufferable that she was being forced to stay where she was hated. And they did hate her, she thought, Lady Haverford and Helen. Because she was a member of the family they had always thought of as the enemy. More specifically, because she was Sean Hayes's sister. She wondered fleetingly if they had known about her and Kenneth, if he had ever told them anything about her. He had said once that he loved her, but he had never said more than that. It had been hopeless, of course, even before Sean. . . .

It did not matter now, Moira thought, putting the memories firmly from her and leaning forward to rest her forehead against the glass of the window. Nothing mattered now except the present. Sean was dead and Helen was married to a man her parents had approved of. She herself was soon to marry Sir Edwin Baillie, and Kenneth — well, she did not care what became of the Earl of Haverford. She could only hope that he would not settle permanently at Dunbarton, though he probably would if he married the very pretty Miss Wishart.

She sighed. How could she possibly have landed herself in this predicament? Though none of it was her fault, she reminded herself. She had not even wanted to attend the ball. She had not chosen to be left here while her betrothed tried to outrun a snowstorm. And she certainly had not invited herself to stay here when it became obvious that the roads were becoming difficult.

The road down to Penwith would perhaps be dangerous for a carriage, he had said. He would not allow her to walk home. He had sent a groom, presumably on foot, to inform her mother that she would spend the night at Dunbarton. Her head snapped up suddenly. *He would not allow her to walk home?* It was merely his lordly command that kept her from doing so. There was no other reason in the world why she should not. He did not have to call out his carriage and horses for her to walk home, after all.

She had all the equipment needed: legs and feet. And she was not afraid of a little snow or a little cold or of a three-mile walk in darkness.

She smiled at the footman as he opened the door. She strolled about the perimeter of the ballroom, resisting the urge to stride across it in open defiance of its owner. She guessed that he was quite capable of restraining her by force if he knew of her intent. She left the ballroom quietly. Anyone seeing her go, she thought, would assume she was going to the ladies' withdrawing room. She *did* go there in order to retrieve her cloak and gloves. She was glad she had worn her warmest outdoor clothes despite the fact that Sir Edwin had loaded the carriage down with blankets and hot bricks. And she was glad he had even insisted that she wear her half boots for the journey when she had been intending to wear only her dancing slippers.

She carried the garments downstairs with her and was relieved to find that she passed no one on the way. She dressed calmly and purposefully in the hall, turned to the footman on duty there, handed him a generous vail as he opened the door for her, looking dubious as he did so, and bade him a cheerful good night as she stepped outside.

It was not at all bad, she thought at first. There was snow on the ground and more coming down, but the night was not particularly cold or particularly dark. She strode out of the shelter of the courtyard to the slightly lesser shelter of the driveway and revised her opinion only a little. She set off along the driveway, which sloped gradually upward until it joined the road along the top of the valley.

The wind and blowing snow hit her with full force as she stepped out of the hollow and beyond the range of the park's woodland. For a moment she was alarmed at the realization that there was an actual storm raging and considered turning back. She was chilly already despite her warm clothes. But she could not bear to go back and have her foolishness exposed. Besides, she could be home in a little more than an hour if she moved briskly.

She moved briskly.

At first, Kenneth thought she had merely gone for a few minutes to the ladies' withdrawing room or to the anteroom for a drink. Then he thought she must be hiding out in one or other of those places. But the refreshment room, when he looked there, was deserted apart from one very young couple who were hovering in the vicinity of the mistletoe sprig. And a great-aunt informed him when he asked that Miss Hayes was not in the withdrawing room.

Then he thought that she must have found her way to the bedchamber allotted her and blamed himself for not making sure that she had congenial company in the ballroom now that her neighbors and friends had left. But his butler assured him that he had not given Miss Hayes directions to her room, and when the butler went belowstairs to inquire of the housekeeper, it was to be told that she had not given that information either. And when Mrs. Whiteman went herself to discover if the room was occupied, she found that it was not.

Moira Hayes had chosen somewhere else to hide, Kenneth thought in some annoyance, and he spent a while going from one darkened room to another, a branch of candles held high in one hand. She would be cold. Most of these rooms were without fires. But he was interrupted in his search by the reappearance of his butler, who brought the news that Miss Hayes had left the house alone and on foot half an hour before. The footman on duty in the hall visibly quaked and grew pale when his lordship demanded to know why in thunder he had allowed her to go, but there was no real issue to be made of the matter. It was not a mere footman's task to question the actions of his superiors.

"Fetch a lantern," Kenneth told him curtly as he himself strode in the direction of the stairs. "And a heavy blanket."

She would probably be at home almost before he could set off in pursuit of her, he thought as he changed quickly, without the aid of his valet, into warmer clothes and pulled on his top boots, his greatcoat, his beaver hat, and a thick scarf. He selected his warmest leather gloves. He would go into Penwith Manor after her before she had a chance to retire and shake the living daylights out of her, he thought grimly as he strode from his room and back down the stairs. He *hoped* she was almost home, he thought anxiously as he tucked the blanket beneath one arm and took up the lantern, whose cover would perhaps prevent the flame from being extinguished by the wind. He hoped she would be there to shake when he arrived. His knees felt somewhat weak when he imagined arriving at Penwith to discover that she was not there. What would he do then?

He turned sharply in the direction of the stables and disappeared inside. He emerged only moments later with a wildly joyful Nelson, who pranced and cavorted with exuberance at the unexpected treat of a night walk and appeared quite undismayed by the snow.

Kenneth tried to persuade himself that the storm had abated somewhat since he was last out and that the snow was falling less thickly. But even before he reached the road and left behind the shelter of the hollow and the trees, he knew that he was deceiving himself. The wind whipped cruelly at him and took his breath away with it as he clutched at his hat with one hand and turned the lantern into the shelter of his body with the other. The snow was deep and all but obliterated the road. And it was still falling and swirling so thickly that he could see no more than a few feet in front of him.

He felt real fear. Not for himself. He had become hardened to personal danger, and he was accustomed to being outdoors for days on end in all sorts of weather. Spain had been a country of extremes. He was afraid for Moira, a woman alone in a storm like this. He was too afraid to feel fury. He made his way along the road, noting with a sinking heart that her footprints — if indeed she had come this way — had already been obliterated. Nelson bounded along at his side, woofing with delight at the adventure.

The road to the valley descended steeply from the hilltop about a mile and a half from the end of Dunbarton's driveway. It was impossible to know how far he had come or how far he had to go, Kenneth thought after wading onward for endless minutes. And he was not even sure that the road would be visible. He seriously doubted that it would be passable. If she had had a half-hour head start on him, would she have passed here before the storm became this severe or the snow this deep?

Was she safely at home or at least in the greater shelter of the valley? She would have about a mile to go once she reached the valley floor. But the chances were good, he knew, that the snow would be in deep drifts in the valley and that the wind would be howling along it as through a funnel. Besides, there was the bridge to cross. She would not be safe even when she was down off the slope. *If* she was down off the slope.

He found the road down only because by good fortune he stopped to catch his breath at the very top of it and Nelson went prancing forward and did not fall over a precipice. Had she found it too? He was quite chilled from exposure to the storm, but even so, he felt the sweat clammy on his back. Should he have organized a search party? It had not even occurred to him to do so. And had she come this way at all? Perhaps she had made for Tawmouth. But the village was almost as far from Dunbarton as Penwith was.

She had definitely come this way. After he had waded downward a short distance, trying to move a little faster than caution advised, Nelson stopped to snuffle in the snow and emerged with a snow-encrusted object between his teeth. It was a black glove — a woman's glove.

Oh God! Kenneth looked around him fearfully for unexplainable mounds in the snow, lifting the lantern high and shielding it from the wind as best he could.

"Find her, Nelson," he said, shaking the snow from the glove, opening it back at the wrist, and holding it close to his dog's nose. How had she come to lose a glove? And where was she now?

"Moira!" he yelled in the voice Nat Gascoigne had always teased him about. He had missed his true vocation, Nat had said. He should have been a sergeant. "Find her, Nelson. *Moi-ra!"*

With every step, he realized the near impossibility of going farther. She would never have made it safely home, even with the half-hour head start she had had on him. How much farther had she gone? Had she stopped? Fallen? Strayed from the road?

"Moira!" He could hear the fear in his voice.

And then Nelson veered sharply to the right, leaving the road and half bounding, half wading across the steep slope of the hill. He was whining excitedly.

Kenneth knew just exactly where his dog was going, even though he would not have known they were close and had not thought of it for himself. Was Nelson right? But his dog had no knowledge of the old hermit's hut and no reason to move so purposefully in a new direction if he had not picked up a human scent. Kenneth followed, scarcely daring to hope.

The granite hut had been built and inhabited in earlier centuries when Cornwall had been full of holy men. It was sometimes known as the baptistry because of its steep roof and pointed window and doorway and because it was built above a particularly pretty part of the river, where it flowed beneath a stone bridge before spilling over a short but steep waterfall. But if it had been a baptistry, it had been built impractically high on the hill. More likely, local legend admitted, it had been a mere hermitage. It was still used by the occasional hunter and wayfarer. Kenneth had played there a few times with Sean Hayes. He had met Moira there once.

Nelson barked enthusiastically at the closed door. After Kenneth had turned the handle with some difficulty and pushed the door inward, his dog bounded inside, still barking. He was obviously not sure yet whether he had been sent in pursuit of friend or foe.

8

Moira stood pressed against the wall opposite the door, her palms flat against it on
either side of her body, fingers spread as if
she thought to be able to push the wall
outward and effect an escape. In the lantern
light her face looked deathly pale.

"Nelson," Kenneth commanded sharply,
"sit!"

Nelson sat and panted.

She did not move a muscle. She did not
speak.

"I should take a horse whip to you," he
said. Fear had converted to fury as soon as
he set eyes on her.

Her eyes moved from his dog to him as he
stepped inside, shut the door firmly behind
him, and set the lantern down on the
window ledge.

"How Gothic of you," she said scornfully.

He looked her over from head to toe. She
wore a cloak and hood that he supposed

passed for suitable winter wear for ladies but were about as much use on a night like this as a fan would be in hell. Her half boots might have sufficed to keep out snow up to one inch or so deep. She was wearing one glove.

"What the devil made you decide to try to walk home," he asked her, "when you had been given specific instructions to stay and sufficient reasons for obeying?"

"I did not wish to stay at Dunbarton," she said.

"And so you risked your life," he said, "because you did not wish to stay at Dunbarton." He mimicked her voice.

"It is my life to risk," she said. "And I am not one of your men to be mindlessly obeying *specific instructions.*"

"For which fact you may be eternally grateful," he said.

She lifted her chin and glared. He disdained to show his anger in anything more than a cold stare.

"This," he said, taking her glove from his pocket, "is yours, I believe? You removed it because you were too warm?"

She reached for it and took it from his hand. "The button of my hood came undone," she said, "and I could not fasten it again with my gloves on. I could not find the one in the snow afterward. It was absurd. I knew it had to be there, but I could not find it."

"Your carelessness has proved your salvation," he said. "Nelson took your scent from it."

She looked warily at his dog.

"He is not about to tear out your throat," he said. "He has saved your life tonight. If it *is* saved. We have several hours of cold to survive before daylight will make it a little safer to leave here. Do you see now where foolish defiance leads, Moira?"

"You need not suffer the cold," she said, her nostrils flaring. "You may go home again. I am sure you will find your way. I shall be quite comfortable here on my own, as I was before you came."

He came to stand directly in front of her. "Sometimes, Moira," he said, "you can be very childish. There is no wood or kindling in here, I see. A pity. We will have to do without a fire. This will help for the moment, but only for the moment." He drew from his pocket the flask of brandy he had thought to bring with him. He unscrewed the cap and held it out to her. "Drink."

"Thank you," she said, "but I do not."

"Moira," he said, looking steadily into her eyes, "you may drink voluntarily or by force.

The choice is yours. It makes little difference to me. But you *will* drink."

"By force?" Her eyes widened and her
teeth chattered. She snatched the flask from
his hand and set it to her lips. She tipped
her head back almost vengefully. The next
moment she was coughing and sputtering
and clutching her throat.

"At least I know," he said dryly when she
had caught her breath again, "that you did
not defy me by merely pretending to drink."
He took the flask from her hand and drank
from it himself. There was the satisfying
sensation of heat coursing down through
his throat into his stomach.

"Apart from the brandy," he said, looking
about the hut, "we have our clothes and one
blanket and the combined body heat of the
three of us. It could be worse, I suppose."

"You may have the blanket," she said
angrily. "I shall have the cot."

It was rather narrow. It was covered with
a straw-filled mattress that looked old and
lumpy and anything but comfortable. It was
better than the dirt floor.

He laughed. "I do not believe you understand," he said. "We are not talking about
dignity or propriety now, Moira. We are talking about survival. It is cold. Cold enough
to cause severe illness. Cold enough even to

kill. People do die of cold and exposure, I assure you. I have seen men frozen and quite dead on the picket line after a cold night."

He saw momentary fear in her eyes. But she was made of stern stuff. She had not changed in that way. She had still not accepted the inevitable.

"Nonsense," she said. Her teeth chattered.

"We are going to share everything," he said. "Including body heat, Moira. And if you are embarrassed or repulsed or outraged, good. Any emotion is better than no emotion at all. Presumably death deprives one of emotions."

She had nothing further to say. He could tell from the slight slump of her shoulders that she had realized the wisdom of what he had said. He started to undo the buttons of his greatcoat. She watched him warily.

"Open your cloak," he said.

"Why?" Her eyes flew up to his.

"We are going to share body heat," he said. "We are not going to dilute it with layers of clothing between us when that clothing could better be used about us. Your cloak, my greatcoat, my coat, my waistcoat we will wrap about the two of us as best we can. But inside them all, we are going to be *close*. This is no time for maidenly modesty

155

or even for family feuds. We will share the blanket. Lie down on the cot before I extinguish the light in the lantern. We do not wish to risk being burned to death. It would be ironic, would it not?"

"Kenneth —" she said, her voice wavering slightly. She swallowed. "My lord —"

But he had turned away from her to see to the lantern. How many hours were there until daylight broke? he wondered. He had no idea what time it was. And would they be able to leave the hut even when it was light outside? But it was unwise to look ahead. In any situation of crisis the present moment was everything. He had learned that over the years. Handle the present situation and let the future — whether the next hour or the next day or the next year — look after itself.

He put out the light of the lantern and turned toward the cot.

Her first feeling was one of utter mortification. If she had not been so dreadfully foolish — and that was a mild way of describing her behavior — she would be at Dunbarton now. She would be hating it, but at least she would be warm and safe behind a closed door — and alone. She lay on the cot and backed as far in as she could until she was pressed against the wall. As soon as the light went out, she reluctantly opened the buttons of her cloak and was horribly aware of the flimsiness of her gown. It was flimsier than any of her nightgowns.

Her second feeling was one of acute embarrassment. He lay down beside her and almost on top of her — it really was a rather narrow cot, intended for only one sleeper — opened back her cloak with firm, quite matter-of-fact hands, slid one arm beneath her neck, and hauled her very firmly indeed against him. From forehead to toes she was welded to him, only her thin evening gown — it felt even thinner now — and his shirt and pantaloons between them. He was very solid and felt and smelled alarmingly masculine. He arranged their garments about them like some sort of cocoon and then somehow arranged the blanket on top of all. Then he spoke, but not to her.

"Nelson," he said, "up."

And the dog crashed down on top of them, breathed noisily in their faces, and proceeded to twist and turn until he found a comfortable position across their legs.

Her third feeling was one of relief. There was definite warmth. His greatcoat was heavy. So was the blanket. The dog was heavy and warm. Kenneth's body was

157

warm. Of course he had arranged matters so that she had the best of it. He had pressed her head down beneath his chin and covered her almost completely. Her hands were spread on his chest as on a warm stove. She could hear his heart beating, strongly and steadily. She had not realized quite how cold she had been until warmth began to replace it.

It was a matter of survival, he had said. She concentrated on that thought and tried to hold all other thoughts at bay. His shocking proximity, for example. The musky smell of his cologne, for example. Tomorrow, for example.

"Relax and try to sleep," he said, his breath warm against her ear.

How would she be able to look him in the eye tomorrow? For the rest of her life? How would she look Sir Edwin in the eye? Gracious heaven, Sir Edwin! Would he construe this as neighborliness too? As friendship? She was alarmed by the nervous giggle that she only just succeeded in suppressing. This was no time for hilarity. She felt anything but amused. He had been quite right to call her childish.

"How ridiculous even to consider sleep as a possibility," she said into his neckcloth.

"All things are possible," he said. "Believe me."

And she must indeed have dozed, she thought suddenly and in some surprise. She was cold again but had not noticed getting cold. Their clothes and the blanket no longer seemed so deliciously heavy, and the dog had moved down to their feet. She could feel herself trembling with the chill and although she clamped her jaws together, she could not quite stop her teeth from chattering. She tried to huddle closer, but there was no closer to go. Or so she supposed.

"It *is* confoundedly cold," he said, and the quietness and closeness of his voice were somehow reassuring — until he continued. "There is only one other way that I know of to get warmer. We are going to have to share bodies as well as body heat."

She did not even for a moment misunderstand him. His words were plain enough, heaven knew. But she did lie still for a moment, waiting for the alarm and the outrage that would surely follow such a suggestion. *Share bodies?* She felt nothing except the discomfort of the cold. It was a matter of survival, he had said. People died of the cold. She was not sure their situation was as drastic as that, but she was not convinced otherwise either. Would it bring them warmth? He should know, she supposed.

"Yes," she said and wondered if she had given the matter enough consideration. But she did not withdraw her acquiescence. And already it was too late to do so.

His hand was between them doing something to his own clothing and then pulling up her dress and disposing of her undergarments as if it was something he was well accustomed to doing — as she had no doubt it was. She already felt warmer, she thought foolishly — much warmer. And agitated. What had she agreed to? She needed time to think. But she was too cold — and heated — to think.

She was on her back then and he was lying heavy on top of her, his legs pushing hers apart. He covered them carefully with her cloak and the blanket.

"Just relax," he said quietly against her ear. "Enjoy it if you possibly can after the initial pain is past. Enjoying this is the best way to build heat."

She already felt rather as if she were on fire. Her mind knew one moment of appalling clarity as she felt his hardness push against her and begin to enter her. The future — tomorrow, the rest of her life — flashed before her eyes just as the past is said to flash before those of a dying person. But then her mind recognized the irreversible nature of what was happening — and the appalling carnality of it — and closed in on itself again. He was inside her, stretching her to the point of alarming discomfort. He was going to hurt her. And then he *did* hurt her and came even more deeply in. It was too late to think now. She could not stop thinking.

Sharing bodies certainly did bring heat with it. It was a very, very intimate thing. It was painful. No, it was not. It had been painful for a moment. She was no longer cold. How could she be? The weight of his body was a very effective blanket. Where had Nelson gone? Poor Nelson — he would be cold down on the floor. She was not cold. Her mind tried to focus on such trivial thoughts. They were *not* trivial. She was doing this for *survival,* not for any other reason. And then the most appalling thought of all came. He was *Kenneth.* Oh, dear God, he was Kenneth and he was inside her body. She pushed the thought aside.

"Let yourself relax," he said. "We will make this last as long as possible. We will have you warm again by the time it is over."

This? It? They would make *what* last as long as possible? She was incredibly naive,

161

she thought over the coming minutes. She had thought the uniting of bodies was all. At the elderly age of six-and-twenty she had congratulated herself on not being subject to maidenly ignorance. She had known exactly what to expect in the marriage bed. She had known *nothing.* And he obviously knew *everything.* What a foolish thought. Of course he did. He was a man and she did not doubt that he was very experienced indeed. A man like Kenneth would be. He was moving slowly, firmly, rhythmically in her, pumping into her until the uncomfortable friction of dryness gave place to smooth comfort.

His hands moved inward then to her breasts and he did something with his fingers through the flimsy fabric of her gown to cause a raw sensation that was not quite pain down into her abdomen and up into her throat. His mouth came to hers, open, blessedly warm.

"Try to feel pleasure," he murmured. "It will bring more heat. Open your mouth." And when she did so, blindly obedient to his command, he slid his tongue deeply inside and simulated there what he was doing elsewhere.

She was on fire again, so warm that she could scarcely stand the heat. On fire with pleasure and with amazement that anything so very physical could also be so pleasurable. Somewhere sanity and shame waited to be grasped. Deliberately, she did not reach out. She did not want to *think*.

It went on for a very long time before his movements deepened and he held still. There was an even more intense warmth inside for a moment. Somehow it seemed the most intimate, the most pleasurable moment of all, even though she wanted the pleasure to continue. His weight was heavier on her. He was breathing in gasps against her ear. She was aware of his heartbeat again. She was wonderfully warm.

He moved off her after a while, but only far enough to make it easier for her to breathe. He still half covered her. He did not lower their clothing between them. They lay flesh to flesh.

"That will keep us warm for a while," he said. "We will do it again later if we must. Nelson — here." He patted his thigh and the dog jumped up to lie across their legs again.

His voice was cool and matter-of-fact, Moira thought, just as if they had decided to generate warmth by taking a swallow from his flask again or rearranging their clothing and the blanket. His voice had been like that from the beginning and during what they had done together. As if what had happened was nothing momentous at all. What did she expect? That he would speak in a lover's velvet voice? They were not lovers. They had not made love. They had merely done what was necessary for survival. And very effective it had been, for the time being at least. His shoulder through his shirt was very warm against her cheek.

But his voice had reminded her. He had spoken in the voice of the Earl of Haverford. In Kenneth's voice. He was the Earl of Haverford, she thought very deliberately at last, and she pictured him behind her closed eyelids as he had appeared at the ball: splendidly groomed, tall, elegant, handsome, aristocratic, haughty. He was *Kenneth,* the boy she had worshiped from afar, the young man she had loved and contrived to meet whenever she could until he had caught her . . . and until all that dreadful nastiness with Sean. Until she had seen him for what he really was and had understood where his loyalties really lay. Until she had learned that the love he had protested for her was worth nothing at all. Until she had come to hate him with an intensity equal to the love that had preceded it.

She was lying here in the hermit's hut with

Kenneth, Earl of Haverford. They had just — no, they had not. That was a quite inappropriate term for what had just happened. They had just coupled. Without love, without commitment, without even affection or respect. For the sole purpose of survival. A fate worse than death . . . She half smiled at the thought. The instinct for survival was, after all, stronger than any other, it seemed.

The morning, she thought, dreading the coming of daylight, was going to be quite unbearable. The horrible embarrassment . . . Her mind shied away from dealing with the far more significant issues than embarrassment she would have to deal with tomorrow. And it was all her fault. All of it. How could she have been so foolish, foolish, *foolish*?

The snow had stopped during the night and the wind had abated. In the gray of early dawn it even looked as if the sun was going to shine later. Kenneth stood in the open doorway of the hermit's hut, stamping his feet, thumping his gloved hands together, anxious to get moving so that he could be warm again. Behind him, Moira folded the blanket and buttoned her hood beneath her chin. They had not spoken since she had commented that it was light outside. He had been sleeping.

Running, he thought. Running on the spot. Legs and arms pumping. Forcing up the pace. Keeping up the pace. Ignoring groans of protest and complaints of tiredness. He had done it several times in Spain. He had forced his men to it, bellowing at them, cursing them, standing with them, fitting himself into their ranks, *running* with them so that they would know he was not being merely sadistic. He would lose men to enemy guns if he had to, he had always told them. He would be damned before he would lose even one to the cold. He had never done so.

He could think of it now this morning when it was several hours too late for the thought to be of any use. His mind had not even touched upon it last night. Running on the spot would have kept her alive — and furious, no doubt. She would have survived her fury.

His mind looked grimly ahead. But there was no point in thinking about the future. It was fixed and immutable. He turned impatiently to see if she was ready to go.

"There is something that must be said before we leave here," she said.

He had decided that they would leave even though the snow was deep, and find-

166

ing a safe way down to the valley would not be an easy thing. Not that she would fight against the decision, of course. Against the dark gray of her hood her face looked pale and set and quite calm. Her eyes did not avoid his as he might have expected them to do. But, of course, she was Moira.

"I do not believe there is anything that needs to be put into words at this moment, Moira," he said. "We are both adults. We both know the rules. We need to get moving."

"Oh yes, the rules," she said. "I suppose you will escort me home and have a few words with Mama. You will, of course, take all the blame upon your own shoulders. I suppose you will then write to Sir Edwin Baillie and be discreet and tactful — and take all the blame yourself. I suppose you will then make me a private and formal offer and pretend that marriage with me is the dearest wish of your heart."

"I believe that last detail might be dispensed with," he said, goaded to irritation. Did she imagine that he welcomed the thought of what must now happen? That he was overjoyed by the turn of events that had just set his life on its head?

"It will *all* be dispensed with," she said. "I do not want you trying to make any explanations, trying to shield me from blame. I do not want you making me an offer. I will refuse it if you do."

"You are being childish again," he said curtly. He had had her twice during the night. She had been undeniably virgin — as he had expected. Neither of them had any choice in what must happen now. "There is nothing to discuss."

"In refusing to marry someone I dislike and someone who dislikes me, I am being childish?" she said. "It would seem childish to me to marry merely because circumstances forced us into —" Her chin came up and she glared at him.

"Having carnal knowledge of each other?" he said. "It is what husbands and wives do together, Moira. Or what two people do together before they inevitably become husband and wife."

"Was I your first woman, then?" she asked. "Why has the inevitable not happened to you before now?"

He frowned and spoke irritably and perhaps unwisely. "My first *lady,*" he said. "You are not a whore, Moira."

Her eyes widened, but she laughed. "Mama will be told that I spent the night at Dunbarton," she said. "She already believes it to be the truth. At Dunbarton they can

168

be told that you spent the night at Penwith. No one need know where or how we really spent the night."

"Not even Sir Edwin Baillie?" he asked, looking at her with raised eyebrows.

"No," she said.

"Will he not be a trifle surprised on your wedding night?" he asked.

She looked at him scornfully. "I will, of course, be ending my betrothal," she said. "But I will *not* marry you. You will only cause unnecessary complications if you come asking."

For some reason he was furiously angry. He should be elated, but all he could see was the scorn in her eyes and all he could remember was the way she had huddled close to him during the night and how she had grown hot beneath him when he had had her mounted. By God, she had *enjoyed* it. But what had he expected this morning? he wondered. That she would look at him with the soft eyes of love? He would have abhorred such a thing.

"And I am not blaming you for anything," she said, her nostrils flaring with a matching anger. Her eyes blazed at him. "Do you think I do not realize how very foolish I was to leave Dunbarton last night? Do you think I do not know that you risked your life in coming after me? Or that you saved my life last night? You did, you know. I am not sure I would have survived the night here alone. Do you think I do not know how much in your debt I am?"

"You owe me nothing," he said.

"And do you think I am to repay that debt every day of my life?" she said. "Trying to please you and reconcile you to a marriage you were forced into much against your will? I would rather die. I will *not* marry you."

"I will not ask you, then," he said curtly. "Have it your way. But you may be forced to change your mind, Moira. You must do the asking if there is need. We will see how you like that."

He could see from the slight flush in her cheeks that she understood his meaning. They glared at each other for a few moments longer before he took a step toward her, pulled the scarf from about his neck and wrapped it firmly about hers, and turned and stepped out into the snow. It was knee deep. He turned back to take her arm, and after an initial jerking away from his grasp she accepted her need of his help — with tightly compressed lips and ill grace.

Nelson bounded happily ahead of them.

9

During the week following Christmas, Kenneth kept himself determinedly busy. While the snow lasted, he spent several hours of each day out of doors, sledding, building snowmen, playing snowballs. His younger cousins called him a jolly good sport, his nephew and niece and the other children climbed all over him and begged for more of whatever activity they happened to be involved in at that moment, and even some of the adults accompanied him outside and assured him that he was being an extraordinarily gracious host. Juliana Wishart, her mother persuaded him, had a great love of the outdoors.

When the snow had melted sufficiently for the roads to be safe again, he played escort to an array of aunts and cousins and took them visiting people they had met during the ball and felt constrained to call upon before they returned home. Regrettably they could not, he assured two of his aunts quite firmly, call upon Miss Hayes as the road down to Penwith Manor was still impassable. Perhaps next week — but of course they were both leaving before even this week was out. Juliana Wishart and her mama accompanied Kenneth and the countess on a drive into Tawmouth to look at the shops and to view the harbor from above the seawall. Lady Hockingsford hinted and the countess suggested that he take Miss Wishart down onto the beach for a stroll, but fortunately, that young lady was afraid of heights and almost dissolved into tears at the prospect of having to descend the steep stone steps, even though his lordship would hold her arm and not let her fall, her mother assured her.

At home there were card games to organize and billiard games and spillikins for the children and a few more energetic games, such as hide-and-seek. There were impromptu concerts to organize and games of charades and even one evening of informal dancing. There were aunts to run and fetch for, uncles to converse with, cousins to aid and abet or at the very least to turn a blind eye to as they paired off with other young people of opposite gender and sought out secluded nooks, especially those that sported mistletoe. There were letters to write and a few business matters to be dealt with.

There was his mother to quarrel with.

"You escorted Miss Hayes home?" she said with a frown after he had returned to Dunbarton the morning after his ball and made his explanations to everyone who was present in the breakfast parlor. She had taken him aside after the meal was finished so that they could speak privately. "Alone, Kenneth? In the middle of the night? I am relieved that she did not after all have to stay here, of course, but was it necessary for you to accompany her yourself? Surely one of the grooms would have done very well."

"She was my guest, Mama," he said curtly, "and wished to return home to Lady Hayes. I had given my word to Sir Edwin Baillie that I would see her safely home. That is what I did." *Safely* home? She had been a virgin when she left Dunbarton.

"You went without a word to anyone," his mother said, still frowning. "It was quite unmannerly, Kenneth. And it is impossible now to hide the truth. You might have done so, you know, instead of speaking out for all to hear. Was there really no way of avoiding having to spend the night at Penwith? You will be fortunate indeed if the woman and her mother do not squawk loudly about honor and contrive to win themselves a far more dazzling provider than Sir Edwin Baillie."

He felt angry — and not solely on his own behalf. "The woman and her mother are Miss Hayes and Lady Hayes, Mama," he said. "They are our neighbors. We have exchanged visits. Miss Hayes was my invited guest here last evening. I saw her safely home. I do not believe she is deserving of your scorn."

His mother had gone very still. She looked at him intently. "Kenneth," she said, "you do not *fancy* this woman, do you?"

Fancy? He thought of how she had dozed in his arms and of how, despite the chill of the air and the discomfort of the narrow bed, he had felt desire for her. It was the desire that had clouded his judgment. There must have been a dozen ways to ensure their survival. When she had woken up, trembling with the cold, he had been able to think of only one. Oh, yes, he had fancied her, all right. He had felt pure lust for her. And he had had her — slowly and thoroughly — twice.

"She is my neighbor, Mama," he said. "And she is betrothed." Though not for much longer, it was true.

His mother continued to look at him as if she would read his mind. "And you should be betrothed too," she said. "You are thirty years old and have neither a son nor a brother to whom to pass all that is yours. You owe it to your position to marry. You owe it to your papa and to me. You cannot do better than Juliana Wishart."

"She is a child, Mama," he protested.

"She is seventeen years old," she said. "She has the sort of character that can be controlled and molded by a strong man. She will be capable of breeding for a number of years. Her background is impeccable. So are her manners and her education. She is very pretty. What more could you possibly ask for?"

Someone closer to his own age, perhaps, Someone who could offer companionship, even perhaps friendship. Was it too much to expect of a woman? Someone capable of arousing some passion in him. Someone with the sort of character that was not easily controlled or molded by a strong man. Someone who would fight his mastery every inch of the way until in the end there would be mutual victory, mutual conquest. But then, he had not tried to verbalize, even in his mind before now, the ideal he looked for in a mate. Surely he did not want a woman he could not master.

"Nothing," he said in answer to his mother's question.

She looked satisfied at last. "Well, then," she said, "you must get up your courage, Kenneth. You have spent too long with the military and too little time in society. You have become mute and awkward. Yesterday would have been the perfect time, but today will do just as well. I shall ask Lord Hockingsford to wait upon you in the library after luncheon."

"Thank you, Mama," he said, "but I shall choose my own time and my own place. And my own bride too. I am not at all sure she will be Miss Wishart."

"But neither are you sure she will not," she said firmly. "Thinking about it will only make the whole thing seem more difficult than it is. You must do it before you have time to think. You will not be sorry. Juliana will make an excellent countess."

He refused to commit himself further, and she was forced to be content to bring him together with the girl as often as possible during the coming week. He realized that by the end of the week he might well find himself in an awkward situation indeed, one from which it might be difficult to extricate himself as a free man.

Perhaps he should just go ahead and do it, he thought sometimes. Marry the girl and be done with it. Beget his heirs on her and proceed to live his own life as well as he could despite her. He might even grow fond of her. She certainly was a sweet and biddable young lady.

But he could not enter into a marriage so cold-bloodedly, either for his sake or hers. He was uncomfortably aware that for all her youth and timidity and biddability, Juliana Wishart was also a person — probably a person with dreams of love and romance and happily-ever-afters. She would find none of those things with him. For one thing, he was too old for her.

And he could not enter into any marriage just yet. Not until he knew that he was free to do so, not until he knew that those hours spent in the hermit's hut had had no consequences. The very thought horrified him, but it was a very real possibility nonetheless. Twice he had spilled his seed in her. He could not betroth himself to any other woman before he knew that he was not going to be compelled to marry Moira Hayes.

Moira Hayes! He could blanch at the very thought. She was everything that was most contemptible in a woman: brazenly scornful of convention and propriety, a liar, a criminal, a smuggler! She was every bit as bad as her brother had been — or her great-grandfather. And she had almost snared him just as Sean had almost snared his sister. Though she had rejected him too — with furious bitterness. He did not care to remember that final quarrel. She had been like a tigress. . . .

Perhaps she had mellowed with age or with the loss of her accomplice, but she still wandered about unchaperoned, and she still defied any advice that might be construed as a command. She still went her own headstrong way. She still had no regard for propriety. She should have chosen death over a surrender of her virtue. But no, that was both ridiculous and unfair. No, he would not blame her for that, at least.

But she had refused to listen to his marriage offer *even before he had made it.* It was so typical of Moira to do that. How could she refuse? He had had her virginity. She had lost her virtue and with it all hope of marriage to anyone but him. What would be left for her and her mother after she had ended her betrothal to Baillie? Had she thought of that? It probably would make no difference to her decision. She would scorn to marry him merely because she had lost her virtue to him — *merely!*

All week he kept himself busy. And all week his mind was plagued with memories of that night and memories of her refusal even to listen to his marriage offer. All week he dreaded that she would change her mind or that events would force her into doing so. And all week he was irritated — no, furious with her. She could not refuse him. He could not accept her refusal. It just would not do.

There was to be a ball at the assembly rooms in Tawmouth in honor of the new year. A number of his houseguests had already left, but a few of those who remained decided that the assembly might be amusing even if it could not possibly surpass the Christmas ball at Dunbarton. There was one young man, for example, who remembered the pretty Miss Penallen, and there were two young ladies who made some giggling references to the young Meeson sons. Ainsleigh and Helen were keen to go. Juliana really should see the inside of the assembly rooms, the countess told Lady Hockingsford in Kenneth's hearing. They were quite tastefully designed even if somewhat austere.

Moira would be there, Kenneth thought. She would surely be there. But then, the assembly was not to be avoided on that account. He had been half expecting all week to run into her at the homes of people they visited in the streets of Tawmouth. She could not be avoided forever. And he had no wish to avoid her. Quite the contrary. There was some unfinished business between them, and he intended to see it properly finished. She would not be allowed to defy him.

The very thought of seeing her, of talking with her, irritated him.

Miss Wishart would travel in his carriage with Helen, Ainsleigh, and himself, it was arranged. Two other carriages were to be filled with those of his remaining guests who wished to attend. There was a mood of distinct gaiety as the carriages filled up and set off on their way to Tawmouth.

For the week following Christmas, Lady Hayes was convinced that her daughter had taken a chill during the walk home from Dunbarton Hall the morning after the ball.

"I really do not know what his lordship was thinking of to allow such a thing," she said, "when the snow was too deep to allow of his carriage being called out. The weather is far too cold to be out walking. And the snow is too deep for your boots. At least you had that nice warm scarf to wrap about your face, but it was not nearly enough."

"But I would not hear of staying any longer at Dunbarton, Mama," Moira said. She smiled. "And you know how stubborn I can be when my mind is made up."

"It was obliging of him to escort you in person at least," Lady Hayes said. "But I cannot believe that Sir Edwin would have allowed your stubbornness to persuade him into condoning anything so foolish."

"I was uncomfortable at Dunbarton," Moira said. "Everyone else who was left there is a houseguest. Most of them are members of the earl's family. I know none of them. I had to come home."

Her mother looked at her in some sympathy. "I can understand that, dear," she said, "but you do look unusually pale. I hope you have not taken a chill."

"The walk was brisk and invigorating," Moira said. She hated the lies and half-truths and outright deception she was being forced into. It might so easily come out at some later date that she had left Dunbarton before the end of the ball. It might so easily come out that Kenneth had not spent the night at Penwith. She did indeed *feel* ill, both on that day and on the days succeeding it, but not because she had taken a chill.

She could not write to Sir Edwin. At first

the roads were impassable and no letter could be sent. She found anyway, though, that whenever she sat down to prepare the letter — and she tried a number of times — there was no easy or satisfactory way to express herself. No way at all, in fact. She never succeeded in getting beyond the first few stilted words of greeting. What exactly should she say? What reason could she give for what must be done? It was such a very shocking thing to do, to break off an engagement once it had been formally entered into. Doing so would expose Sir Edwin to ridicule and herself to scandal. She did not care about herself, but he did not deserve ridicule.

And then, when the roads did clear, a letter arrived with the first post informing her, in Sir Edwin's usual flowery manner, that his mother was indeed very ill and that his great anxiety for her health was eased only by the assurance he was confident of feeling that Miss Hayes was kind enough to suffer a similar anxiety for her future mother-in-law. His sisters were similarly reassured.

It was clearly not the time to write her letter, Moira decided. It would be cruel to do so just now. She would wait a week or two until his mother was in better health. She knew that she was being cowardly, that she was making excuses, that no time would be a good time for such an announcement. The realization of her own cowardice only made her feel more ill, though it could not goad her into action. She seemed paralyzed by a massive lethargy.

The events of that night seemed unreal and nightmarish in retrospect, but she knew perfectly well that they had really happened. She was the one entirely to blame. It would have helped, she thought ruefully, if she could have heaped some of the blame upon him, but she could not do so. He had offered the hospitality of his home, despite the disapproval of his mother and sister, and she had spurned it. He had come out after her into the storm, purely out of concern for her safety, risking his own. When he had found her, he had done everything in his power to ensure her survival. She might have thought that the idea of *not* surviving a cold night was absurd if she had not experienced that particular night for herself.

He had not *wanted* to be intimate with her. He had been very practical and dispassionate about the whole thing. He had been merely keeping her — and himself — warm. She could burn with embarrassment and shame at the memory, especially over the fact that she had enjoyed what happened. She had done so on his instructions, of course, but since when had she done anything merely because he had suggested it? She even had a suspicion, which she tried to deny to herself, that she had enjoyed it *because it had happened with Kenneth*. She could not quite imagine that with Sir Edwin . . . She shook off the thought with some horror at herself.

No, she could not blame Kenneth. He had even been prepared afterward to marry her. She hated not being able to blame him or despise him or fault him in any way at all.

She did not take a chill from the night's adventures, but she felt quite ill, nevertheless. There was no one to confide in. The loneliness was perhaps worst of all, and it was compounded by two facts: the weather remained chilly and the snow was slow to melt. When it began to do so and turned to slush, going out was even more difficult. Taking a carriage into Tawmouth was out of the question. Normally, she would have scorned to remain at home just because of a little slush and would have walked to the village, but this week she felt too ill, too lethargic to do so. And there was that other fact that kept her away from Tawmouth and the homes of her friends and neighbors too.

She was terrified of running into Kenneth — into the Earl of Haverford somewhere. She would never again be able to look him in the eye. How could she possibly do so without remembering . . . Even the thought of it could bring a hot flush to her cheeks.

She despised her cowardice.

And she hated him for causing it.

"Perhaps we should stay at home, Moira," Lady Hayes suggested on the day of the assembly in Tawmouth. They had both planned to attend the New Year's ball as they did every year. They had both looked forward to it with some eagerness. "You have still not recovered from that long walk from Dunbarton, and I daresay you are missing Sir Edwin, though we are both agreed that his conversation is sometimes a trial to the patience. I still believe we should summon Mr. Ryder and get him to have a look at you." Mr. Ryder was a physician who had retired from a fashionable practice in London in order to set up a smaller one in Tawmouth three years before.

"I do not need a physician, Mama," Moira said. "But I do need the assembly. We both do. The weather has kept us cooped up here for the best part of a week and has plunged us both into the dismals. An evening of dancing and conversing with our neighbors

185

will be just the thing." It would, too. She could not bear the thought of staying at home any longer. And the New Year assembly was one of her mother's favorite occasions of the year. If Moira stayed at home, then her mother would stay too. It would be most unfair.

"Well, if you are quite sure, dear," Lady Hayes said, sounding quite noticeably cheered. "I am rather eager, I will not hesitate to confess, to discover from Mrs. Trevellas if her daughter-in-law's confinement has been brought to a happy conclusion yet. It is her first, you know."

And so they went to the assembly in the evening. The assemblies were not grand affairs when judged by Dunbarton standards. The rooms were plainly decorated and the music was provided by Miss Pitt on the pianoforte, sometimes with the accompaniment of Mr. Ryder on the violin. One very seldom saw any new faces at the assemblies and the program was quite predictable, as was the food served at supper. One did not approach the Tawmouth assemblies in anticipation of any great excitement, but it was pleasant to be in company with all one's neighbors at once and to be able to dance. It was always a good way to begin a new year.

Moira felt quite comfortable about going to the assembly. The cook at Penwith had heard from the butcher's boy, who had heard from the butcher's wife, who had heard from one of the servants at Dunbarton that the guests there had begun to leave. Those who remained would doubtless be entertained royally to their own New Year celebrations. A mere village assembly would be quite beneath the notice of the Earl of Haverford and any other member of the Woodfall family. None of them had ever attended a ball in Tawmouth.

She sat beside Harriet Lincoln after seeing her mother settled between Mrs. Trevellas and Mrs. Finley-Evans, and proceeded happily with the business of catching up on the week's news. The Meesons' eldest son danced the opening set with her and Mr. Lincoln the second. She shook off the gloom of the preceding week and the dreadful burden that still hung over her, the knowledge that soon — tomorrow — she must write her letter to Sir Edwin. She would think of it tomorrow. Tomorrow was not only a new day, after all, but a new year. Tonight she would simply enjoy herself.

And then, just after she had seated herself beside Harriet again, there was a stir about the doors, which had opened to admit new

187

arrivals. Both she and Harriet looked up in some curiosity. Everyone who had been expected had already arrived. Moira felt a dreadful premonition even before her mind started to work properly or her brain accepted the message her eyes had sent it.

"Well, this is a very pleasant surprise," Harriet said quietly while the whole room seemed to buzz with increased animation. "More young people to make those already in attendance ecstatic. And Viscount Ainsleigh and his wife. And the earl himself, Moira. How very gratifying. Will they find one of our humble assemblies to their taste, do you suppose?"

"I do not know," Moira said lamely. She looked at him aghast, and felt her mouth go dry and her stomach turn queasy. He looked tall, elegant, handsome, aristocratic — remote. He looked like a stranger from a world far above hers. *And he had been inside her body.*

"He is quite sinfully handsome," Harriet murmured, unfurling her fan and waving it in front of her face, even though the room was not overwarm. The new arrivals were being made much of by a self-appointed welcoming committee. There was a great deal of hearty laughter. "More handsome than I expected, though I had been warned."

Harriet had come to Tawmouth only six years before on her marriage to Mr. Lincoln. "Do you not admire his looks exceedingly, Moira? Will he marry Miss Wishart, do you think? He has been paying her marked attention since she came to Dunbarton with her mama and papa. It was quite noticeable at the Christmas ball. And he was showing her the shops and the harbor two days ago — with his mama and hers as chaperones, of course. They make a quite handsome couple, do they not?"

"Yes," Moira said.

Harriet looked at her sharply and laid a hand on her arm. "Oh, poor Moira," she said. "It must be quite distressing to see young love when you are being forced by circumstances into a marriage that is less than palatable to you. You will pardon my plain speaking, but friends speak plainly to each other."

Moira frowned. "I have never said —" she began.

"I know you have not," Harriet said quickly, squeezing her arm. "And I ought not to have mentioned it. Sir Edwin Baillie, I am sure, has his good qualities. It will be an eminently respectable marriage for you. And if one is to be quite truthful and perfectly *spiteful,* one might remark that

Miss Wishart is too young for our earl and will doubtless bore him to death within a month. There, that should make you feel better." She laughed.

Moira forced a smile. And then her eyes met the Earl of Haverford's across the room. It was a dreadful moment, quite as bad as she might have imagined. He regarded her coldly, unsmilingly, and for her part she could not seem to withdraw her gaze even though that queasiness gripped her stomach again and she could feel the blood draining from her head. Her breath felt cold in her nostrils. She felt that she was about to faint.

He looked away, said something to Miss Wishart, and smiled at her.

Self-contempt saved Moira from ignominy. The sight of a man had almost made her faint? The sight of *Kenneth*? Never! Never on this earth. She found herself doing what Harriet had done a minute or two before. She spread her fan and cooled her face with it. She suddenly felt as hot as she had felt cold a few moments before.

10

Kenneth's young relatives were in remarkably high spirits. The young ladies giggled; the young gentlemen talked rather too loudly and laughed rather too heartily. Ainsleigh, the self-proclaimed elder statesman of the group, had undertaken to chaperone the youngsters with his wife. Both were clearly prepared to enjoy the evening and the company of people Helen had known during her youth. Juliana Wishart was sweet and shy and smiling. The people of Tawmouth and its surrounding properties seemed genuinely delighted to have their numbers so unexpectedly augmented — especially by so many young people, Mr. Penallen assured them, smacking his hands together and rubbing them as if he washed them. And of course they were *especially* honored to have the Earl of Haverford in their midst for their humble assembly, the Reverend Finley-Evans was hasty to add.

Kenneth inclined his head graciously to the people who had gathered about to greet them, but only half heard the impromptu speeches of welcome. His heart was thumping uncomfortably against his rib cage and made him short of breath. He felt far more nervous than he would have expected. Indeed, he had not considered nervousness as a possibility — he associated nervousness with the imminence of battle. His palms felt clammy. He knew almost immediately that she really was at the assembly — he saw Lady Hayes sitting close by, beside Mrs. Trevellas.

And then he saw Moira Hayes herself across the room, and his eyes met and held hers. Her deep blue dress was far more demure than the one she had worn to his ball. Her hair was dressed more severely. She looked like a perfectly genteel member of this particular society. She blended into her world just as if she had never stood watch on the clifftop in the dead of night, pointing a pistol at his heart, while below her on the beach, smugglers plied their trade. Just as if she had never lain in the hermit's hut on the hill and traded her virginity for survival. Just as if she had never thumbed her nose at convention by refusing to take the consequences of that night's deeds.

She held her chin high and would not look away from him. If he held her gaze any longer, he knew, people would begin to notice and remark upon it. She was pale. Even across the room and in candlelight she looked noticeably pale. He looked away and down at Juliana Wishart. He forced himself to smile at her.

"Would you do me the honor of dancing with me?" he asked.

She smiled her acquiescence and he wondered why he had not fallen in love with her. He had not been blind to the looks of wistful admiration some of his young cousins had directed at her. But of course none of them had even tried to engage her interest. She was perceived as being his property. Poor Juliana — she might have had a more enjoyable Christmas if his mother and hers had been less meddlesome.

It was a minuet, the music played on the pianoforte rather more slowly than it was intended to be played. He was able to converse a little, and did so to distract his mind from the sight of Moira Hayes dancing with Deverall, one of the wealthier landowners from the other side of the valley. Kenneth kept his eyes on Juliana.

"You will be spending the Season in town?" he asked.

"Yes," she said. "I believe Papa intends to take us there, my lord."

"You will take the *ton* by storm," he said, smiling kindly at her. "You will be the envy of every other young lady. You will have all the gentlemen falling over their feet in a race with one another to pay their respects to you." He had finally verbalized in his mind his feelings for her. They were avuncular.

She blushed and smiled. "Thank you," she said.

He might as well make clear to her what she must already suspect, he decided. "I have no doubt," he said, "that before the Season ends one of those fortunate gentlemen will have won both your hand and your heart. He is to be envied."

He could see from her eyes that she understood. She looked — grateful? "Thank you," she said again.

He suspected something suddenly. "Has he already been identified?" he asked. "Is there already someone special?"

"My lord —" Her blush deepened and she looked anxiously about her for a moment. But her mother was not present to dictate to her how to speak and how to behave.

"There is someone," he said. "I suspected it. I should force his name from you and challenge him to pistols at dawn." He spoke with a twinkle in his eye so that she would know that he teased — and also that he was not nursing a broken heart. "I will wish you joy instead. And the approval of your parents."

"Thank you." Her voice came on a whisper and for the first time she smiled at him with unaffected charm. She laughed and the sound was delightful. "Thank you, my lord."

And that, he thought with enormous relief and perhaps a little twinge of guilt, was that. Moira Hayes was dancing with her usual grace and with a look of bright animation on her face. Not once during the whole set did she glance his way. Not once did he glance her way. He wondered if she was as aware of him as he was of her. He did not like the feeling at all. And he had no intention whatsoever of nursing it all evening.

When the minuet was finished and Ainsleigh had solicited Miss Wishart's hand for the next set — Helen was talking with a group of ladies from Tawmouth — Kenneth strode determinedly across the room and made his bow to Moira Hayes and Mrs. Lincoln. The latter had watched his coming with a smile of gratified surprise. Moira had talked to her, pretending that she had not noticed his approach. She had willed him to change direction, he knew. He exchanged a few civilities with Mrs. Lincoln before turning his eyes on Moira.

"Sets are forming for the quadrille," he said. "Will you honor me by partnering me, Miss Hayes?"

For a silent and awkward moment he thought she was going to refuse. He was aware of Mrs. Lincoln turning her head sharply to look in some surprise at her friend. But she did not refuse. "Thank you," she said, sounding perfectly composed. She got to her feet and set her hand on his.

"You look unwell," he said as they took their places in the set. Her face really was pale. There were faint shadows beneath her eyes. "Did you take a chill?"

"No," she said. He half expected that her eyes would not quite meet his at this oblique reference to their night together, but she looked directly at him. "And I am quite well, thank you."

He had annoyed her, he could see, by singling her out and asking her first, ahead of all the other ladies of Tawmouth, to dance with him. He had annoyed her by asking her to dance at all. "Smile," he commanded her quietly.

She smiled.

He watched her as they danced. There was very little opportunity for conversation, and they did not avail themselves of even what little there was. When she smiled, she showed one of her best assets, her white and even teeth. They had always looked startlingly attractive with her very dark hair and eyes. This was the woman who had lain with him less than a week before, he thought — and the thought seemed unreal to him — the woman who had lain beneath him, warming to his intimate touch. They had been anything but passionate encounters, and yet heat had flared in her both times. She had not known what to do with it and he had not taught her, but it had been there.

He had been right, he thought, to be afraid to touch her. There really was a great deal of latent passion in the very respectable Miss Moira Hayes. She had not changed a great deal in eight years, despite outer appearances. Now, more than ever, he feared it. And yet he did not quite understand his own fear. He had come here to talk to her, to confront her, to assert himself. But perhaps that was the problem. He felt not quite in control in his dealings with Moira. And the knowledge irritated him and disturbed him. He was not accustomed to having his will thwarted.

Supper was announced at the end of the set, before he could return his partner to her seat beside her friend. He had not realized that it was the supper dance for which he had solicited her hand. But then, of course, his party had arrived rather late, and country assemblies often ended early by London standards. He looked at Moira with raised eyebrows and offered his arm.

"Shall we?" he said.

Her lips thinned. "I would rather not," she said.

"But you will." He bent his head closer to hers, his irritation further aggravated. Would she make a fool of him and make herself appear ill-mannered? "People are watching."

She set her arm along his.

He would take advantage of this very opportune moment, he thought. If they must sit and eat together, then they would really talk. They would settle something between them, something more satisfactory than the nonsettlement of the morning after the ball. Most of the square tables in the supper room were set for four. Two tables beneath the windows were set for two. He led her toward one of them and seated her. He left her there in order to fill two plates. Someone had poured the tea by the time he returned.

"I have not heard during the week," he said, not wasting even a moment on small talk, "of your broken engagement."

"Have you not?" she said.

He waited for more, but she said nothing.

"You are not going to marry the poor devil, are you?" he asked.

"No, I am not." There were bright spots of color in her cheeks, and her eyes sparked for a moment until she remembered where she was and forced her expression to blandness again. "Credit me with some sense of decency, my lord. May we now discuss the weather?"

"No, we may not," he said curtly. "We will discuss the necessity of our marrying."

"Why?" she asked. "You have no wish to marry me, and I have no wish to marry you. Why is it necessary that we do something so abhorrent to both of us?"

"Because, Moira," he said, and he deliberately refrained from mincing his words, "I have been inside your body, where only a husband has any right to be. Because I left my seed there and it might even now be bearing fruit. Because even apart from that possibility, it is the proper and the honorable thing to do."

"And propriety and honor," she said, "are

of more importance than inclination? Either mine or your own?"

"Why is the prospect of marrying me so repulsive to you?" he asked, goaded. "You were prepared to marry Baillie, who is an ass by even the kindest estimation."

Her nostrils flared. "I will thank you to watch your language in my presence, my lord," she said. "And the answer should be perfectly obvious to you. Sir Edwin Baillie is not responsible for my brother's death."

He sucked in his breath. "You blame me for Sean's death?" he asked her.

"He would not have been at the Battle of Toulouse if you had not betrayed him," she said. "And if you had not at the same time betrayed me."

"I betrayed you?" He would have liked to reach across the table, take her by the shoulders, and shake her. But he was forced to remember where he was. Besides, the question of who had betrayed whom was not the main point at issue. "No, I suppose I must concede that he would not have been there. He might have been hanging from a rope long before the Battle of Toulouse. Or he might now be living at the other side of the world, chained to a gang of other convicts like himself. At the very best he might have been living somewhere in pov-

erty and disgrace with my sister — and in wretched unhappiness, I do assure you. Such a life would not have suited your brother. I did what had to be done."

"Who made you God?" she asked bitterly.

He sighed and picked up his teacup. "We have strayed from the point," he said. "The point is that we have been together, Moira, that we have had carnal knowledge of each other. Our motives for doing so, our feelings for each other, are of no significance at all now. The point is that we must take the consequences."

"As a criminal must take the consequences for his crimes," she said quietly. "You make marriage sound so very *inviting,* Kenneth. To tell you the truth, I would rather marry anyone on earth than you — and that includes Sir Edwin Baillie. I would rather remain a spinster for life — which is what I will do. I would rather live in destitution — which might be only a slight exaggeration of what will in fact happen to me. I would rather kill myself. Is there anything else I can add to convince you that you can take your sense of honor and toss it into the sea?"

He would have liked to retaliate in kind. He was furiously angry — at her defiance, at her accusations, at her scorn of him. *I would rather kill myself.* Her instinct for survival had been somewhat stronger when put to the test a few nights ago. She had not chosen death then. He would like to have flung that fact in her face. But he did not have quite the freedom she had to show his scorn of her. He raised his eyebrows and regarded her coolly. "No," he said. "I believe you have been more than adequately eloquent on the subject. You will, of course, have to eat humble pie if you discover that you are increasing."

Her eyes wavered from his for only a moment. "I would rather live with the disgrace," she said.

"But I would not allow it," he said. "No child of mine will ever be a bastard, Moira. If the situation arises, it will be pointless to try to set your will against mine. You will not win." And on that point at least she would not shift him.

"Arrogance suits you," she said. "You have the looks for it and of course the rank for it. You must have made a wonderfully effective officer."

"My men learned that obedience to my commands was the best way to deal with me," he said.

She smiled and even succeeded in looking amused. "Oh, but I am not one of your men, Kenneth," she said.

He had a startling memory of just how much she was unlike any of his men. But he did not want to remember how he had desired her as he warmed her — and even before that. That memory could only complicate the issue. "I will grant you your wish," he said, "since a week of reflection appears not to have brought you to your senses. I will grant it because it suits my inclination as well as yours. But only if there are no consequences to our coupling, Moira. If there are, you are to send for me — without delay. I will hear your agreement to this."

"You are so very Gothic, Kenneth," she said. "This and the horse whip. Would I be expected to snap to attention every time you cracked it?"

Unexpectedly and quite alarmingly he felt amused. So much so that he sat back in his chair and smiled slowly at her. "I doubt I would need a whip," he said and immediately felt the doubt he had just denied.

"Oh, famous." She rolled her eyes ceilingward. "Please do not complete that thought — I have just eaten. You are about to tell me that you would master me with your charm."

He laughed outright. But he leaned toward her again before getting to his feet and offering his escort back into the ballroom. "You will marry me if there is a child, Moira," he said. "For the child's sake even if not for your own. And, by God, you will know something of the force of my anger if you try to do otherwise."

She did not stand up. Even on the minor point of his escort she was determined to set her will against his. "I shall join Harriet Lincoln," she said, nodding in the direction of a table nearby. "Thank you for escorting me to supper, my lord, and giving me the pleasure of your company. It has been a great honor."

He made her his most formal bow. "The pleasure has been all mine, Miss Hayes," he said, and made his way back into the adjoining room, smiling and nodding at people as he went, his pulse hammering audibly in his ears. He wanted to commit murder, he thought. Failing that, he wanted to give someone two black eyes and a broken nose and smashed teeth. Since neither option was appropriate to the occasion, he went to ask the very young Miss Penallen to dance.

Moira drew some steadying breaths. She hoped it had not been obvious to anyone else in the room that they had been doing anything more than engaging in light social chitchat. Whenever she had thought to do so, she had smiled. He had smiled most of the time. It had been rather disconcerting to quarrel with a smiling man.

She would rather marry a toad, she thought, but the uncharitable and rather silly thought succeeded only in raising her irritability level again. She smiled determinedly preparatory to getting up and joining Harriet and Mr. Meeson at their table nearby. But someone sat down swiftly in the place the Earl of Haverford had just vacated. Someone who was also smiling.

"Stay away from him," the Viscountess Ainsleigh said breathlessly.

Moira raised her eyebrows.

"You have done very well for yourself," Helen said. "With Papa dead, you have contrived to be on visiting terms with my brother no more than a few weeks after his return here. Of course, that happy effect had nothing to do with you, did it? It was all the doing of Sir Edwin Baillie. Doubtless you did nothing whatsoever to encourage him." There was sarcasm in her voice.

"Sir Edwin Baillie is now the owner of Penwith," Moira said steadily, "and exercises his authority as he sees fit. But you were once prepared to defy that old feud, Helen. I would have expected you to be glad enough that it is over."

Helen glared for a moment, but she remembered to smile again. "How opportune it was for you," she said, "that Sir Edwin decided, quite without any prompting from you, of course, that he must leave for home in the middle of Kenneth's ball, and that Kenneth insisted upon dancing with you for a second time and then escorting you home personally when you were too concerned for your mother to accept his hospitality at Dunbarton. How opportune that he could not return but was forced to remain at Penwith for the night. One might almost think it had all been *planned.*"

"You believe I planned the snowstorm?" Moira asked scornfully. She had not expected either Helen's hostility at the Dunbarton ball or her controlled fury now.

"I suppose next," Helen said, "we will be hearing of the unfortunate ending of your betrothal. I wonder who will end it. It would be humiliating for you if Sir Edwin did it but shameful for you if you did. You have a difficult decision to make, *Miss Hayes.* Of course, all will be worthwhile if you can win the greater prize. My brother is temptingly eligible, is he not?"

Moira frowned and looked down to rearrange her napkin next to her plate. She could not quite understand this tirade. Unlike their brothers, she and Lady Helen Woodfall had had few dealings with each other as children. They had obediently avoided each other.

"Are you bitter over what happened with Sean?" she asked.

"Bitter?" Helen leaned forward in her chair. "Because he loved me and would have married me and was forcibly prevented from doing so? You may say if you wish that it was my father and my brother who did the preventing, but do not imagine for one moment that I do not know who betrayed us. Whom did you tell? Kenneth? Were you trying to win his favor even in those days? I have always suspected that you were. But you were not very successful, were you?"

"I thought he would be pleased," Moira said. "I thought he would try to help. I . . ." She had been very naive. She had believed Kenneth when he told her he loved her. She had thought he meant to marry her, to fight his father and her own to win her hand. She had thought he would be pleased to know that Sean and Helen would join their fight. It had not occurred to her that the prospect of Sean's *marrying* Helen would prompt Kenneth into such actions as he had taken and such lies as he had told. Even thinking about it now made her feel ill again.

Helen was smiling and watching her. "I expected you to be more quick-witted," she said disdainfully. "I expected you to have a dozen denials and explanations and excuses at your fingertips. Perhaps you have a conscience, after all. Stay away from Kenneth. He is to marry Juliana Wishart, and his family is *very* happy about it."

"You have nothing to fear from me, then, do you?" Moira said sharply. She was feeling very angry again. Had she thought to lift her spirits by coming to this assembly? She thought suddenly of that afternoon early in December — less than a month ago — when she had stolen an hour to herself and gone up to the hollow on the cliffs. She had looked forward during that hour with calm good sense to the changes that were about to be wrought in her life. And then Kenneth had appeared on the skyline. How much had happened since then! Her life had been permanently ruined since then.

All because he had broken a promise and come home.

"Stay away from him," Helen said again, and she smiled once more, rose to her feet, and disappeared through the doorway into the ballroom.

And Kenneth, Earl of Haverford, wished

her to marry him? Moira thought. To make Helen into her sister-in-law and the countess into her mother-in-law? The very thought was frankly terrifying.

She wished suddenly that she had not eaten. *Had* she eaten? There was still food on her plate, she found when she looked down at it, but perhaps less than there had been. How foolish that she could not remember whether she had eaten or not. She had drunk half her tea. She felt thoroughly nauseated — and then felt blank terror when she thought of the implications of nausea.

She was being utterly foolish, she thought, giving herself a firm mental shake. She got to her feet and crossed to Harriet's table, smiling and ignoring the feeling of queasiness.

11

Sunshine beyond the morning room window promised well for the new day and the new year. The snow had all disappeared, leaving the grass somewhat pale. It would be at least a month before the first shoots of spring pushed through the soil. The bare branches of the trees were spread against a blue sky.

Moira gazed through the window, one elbow resting on the top of the small escritoire at which she had been writing, her chin in her hand. A completed letter lay on the desk in front of her, the ink drying. *The* letter — the most difficult one she had written in her life. It was fitting, perhaps, that it should be written on the first day of the new year.

What would become of her? she wondered. What would become of her mother? Sir Basil Hayes had been able to leave them very little in his will. They were almost entirely at the mercy of Sir Edwin Baillie. Yet how could they expect any great generosity from him now when she had humiliated him by ending her betrothal to him? It was something that was just not done. It was enough, if they moved in higher circles, to have her ostracized for life. Even here in Tawmouth she would find it difficult for a while to hold up her head and be sure of her welcome at the homes of their friends.

She folded the letter carefully. She would not fall into self-pity. She had no one but herself to blame for the predicament in which she now found herself. She got to her feet. It was time to send the letter. She would walk into Tawmouth. The exercise would do her good. She still felt queasy this morning. The feeling would go once she had done what needed to be done. It was the indecision, the guilt that had made her feel ill for a whole week. As soon as she returned home, she would speak with Mama.

But her mother came hurrying into the room before she could reach the door. Lady Hayes was carrying an open letter in one hand.

"Oh, my dear Moira," she said, "here is a letter from Christobel Baillie and it appears that we have been doing Sir Edwin an injustice. We have thought him oversolicitous for his mother's health. But she is on her deathbed. They are Christobel's own words. You may read for yourself. The physician has warned them all that her demise is imminent. Poor Sir Edwin is distraught with anxiety and grief and is quite unable to write himself."

Moira took the letter from her mother's hand and read it. It was quite true, it seemed. Mrs. Baillie was dying. Perhaps she had already passed on.

"It is only the assurance my brother feels that you, ma'am, and his dearly betrothed are as anguished as we are," Christobel had written, "that will sustain him through the coming days. We will all have a dear mother to take the place of the dearest of mothers, Edwin tells us, and a new sister too. There is light beyond the darkness, as of course there always is."

Moira bit her upper lip hard and was surprised to find that the page had blurred before her vision. *You were prepared to marry Baillie, who is an ass by even the kindest estimation.* And so a man had been callously dismissed last evening. And she had wronged him in one of the worst imaginable ways. Yet he was a man who loved his mother and his sisters and who, in his own way, perhaps, even loved her and her

212

mother. Was that so very asinine?

"Yes, dear." Her own tears had provoked her mother's too. "We will dry our eyes and drink a cup of tea and then each write a letter. I shall write to Christobel and her sisters. I think it would not be amiss if you wrote to Sir Edwin. It will be quite proper under the circumstances, especially as he is your betrothed." Only then did she notice the folded paper in her daughter's free hand. "But you have written already?"

Moira crumpled the page into a ball. "But it is not appropriate now," she said. "I shall write another, Mama. Poor Sir Edwin. I was inclined to make light of his anxiety, but it has proved to be well-founded. I feel very guilty."

"I am just as guilty, Moira," her mother said, pulling on the bell rope to order the tea tray. "We must learn to value that young man. He is fussy in his ways and a little tedious in his conversation, but I have come to believe that he will make an excellent and a loyal husband and son-in-law." She smiled and dabbed firmly at her eyes with her handkerchief. "Poor Cousin Gertrude."

She should have written six days ago, Moira thought. As soon as the Earl of Haverford had taken his leave the morning after the ball and as soon as she had washed and changed and had a hot drink, she should have written instead of making excuses. Now it was more difficult to send such a letter. It was almost impossible to do so, in fact — and would become even more so if and when news arrived that Mrs. Baillie had died. She would have to wait a suitable interval. How long? A week? A month? Longer? Sir Edwin would wish to postpone the wedding, of course, she realized suddenly, perhaps for a whole year of mourning. It felt like a reprieve — or a license for further procrastination.

She sat down hastily on the nearest chair, bowed her head, closed her eyes, and swallowed repeatedly. By a sheer effort of will she kept herself from vomiting. What if — ? But she quelled the feeling of blank terror that threatened to wash over her. It was guilt pure and simple that was making her feel ill. Oh, how she *wished* she had written that letter five days ago.

By the end of January, Kenneth was alone at Dunbarton again. His mother had been the last to leave. She had gone to spend a month or two with her sister before returning to Norfolk.

It felt good to be alone. He was able to concentrate on work. He knew very little about farming and the running of a large estate, he had realized over Christmas. But it was knowledge he was determined to acquire, and so he threw himself into weeks of intensive study, both indoors while he pored over the books and outdoors while he tramped about fields and meadows and spoke endlessly with farmers and consulted with his steward. Spring would be coming soon and he wished to be able to make most of the decisions concerning his own farms for himself.

The temptation to go away was not entirely absent. Although he was well received by his neighbors and never lacked for invitations to dine or to join an evening of cards or to go out shooting, he became aware, too, that he could not expect to make any close friends here. He was too well regarded, too highly respected. Perhaps he would not have felt the need of close peer friendships if he had not known them during his years with the cavalry — but he had known them.

Nat and Eden were both going to Stratton Park in Kent to spend some time with Rex. Both had run into trouble — entirely predictable — in town over Christmas. Eden had had the misfortune to be caught in bed with a married woman — by her husband, of whose existence he had not known. Nat had felt the noose tighten about his neck after he had kissed a certain young lady beneath the mistletoe and raised expectations in her family. Kenneth could relate to that situation, at least. So both had decided to rusticate for a while as the wisest course — and along with Rex, they wanted Kenneth to join them at Stratton.

The temptation to do so was strong. It would undoubtedly be good to see the three of them again. But he knew very well what would happen after the first few days. He would feel restless and idle again. Besides . . .

Besides, he thought with a certain gritting of the teeth a few days after his mother's departure, a feud had been ended more than a month before, and the two families concerned had put themselves on visiting terms once more. Yet he had not been near Penwith Manor since the morning after his ball. And he had seen neither Lady Hayes nor Moira since the New Year's assembly. He owed them a call — unpalatable as the thought was to him and unwelcome as the visit doubtless would be to them. Besides, he had learned something during a visit from the Reverend Finley-Evans the day before that made the courtesy of a visit quite necessary.

He rode down to Penwith the following afternoon, Nelson loping along beside his horse. It was a particularly sunny, deceptively springlike day. Perhaps, he thought, the weather had taken the ladies from home. He almost hoped it was so until he realized that he would only have to do this all over again tomorrow.

Lady Hayes was at home; Miss Hayes had walked into Tawmouth, the servant who answered the door informed him. He felt a certain relief, but it was short-lived. He spent an awkward fifteen minutes conversing with Lady Hayes, expressing his condolences on the recent death of Sir Edwin Baillie's mother. She did not say a great deal and was easily as uncomfortable as he was, but she did make one significant comment. Sir Edwin had thought it only proper to postpone his nuptials until at least the autumn, perhaps for the full year of his mourning.

Moira Hayes had still not ended the betrothal, then.

He took his leave after declining the invitation to take tea and rode slowly back along the valley. He was trying to make up his mind whether to cross the bridge above the falls when he came to it and take the road to the hilltop on the other side or whether to ride right down the valley to Tawmouth. Even then he might miss her. And what purpose would be served by seeing her? He had left a message of sympathy for her with her mother. And if she chose to marry Baillie despite everything, who was he to interfere? He doubted Baillie had a great deal of sexual experience. Perhaps he would not even notice that he had a less-than-virgin bride. Perhaps she would get away with her deception.

He would not even try to see her, he decided when he reached the bridge. He turned his horse onto it and whistled to Nelson, who had run ahead. And yet he found himself stopping and dismounting when he came to the middle of the bridge. It really was a beautiful day. One might even imagine that there was warmth in the sun. The sunlight was sparkling off the water as it fell over the short waterfall and continued on its way to the sea. This was surely one of the most beautiful spots in all England. Heavy ferns overhung the banks on either side of the river. The baptistry was up on the hill above the trees, overlooking it all. He turned his head and looked up at it after leaning his arms along the mossy stone wall of the bridge.

He could not remember how many times

he had met her in all, after that first un-
planned encounter in the cove when he was
a boy. Ten times? A dozen? Certainly not
many more than that. It was not easy for
gently bred young ladies to get away on
their own, to escape from the close chaper-
onage of mothers and maids and govern-
esses. And he had had a strong conscience
— stronger than hers. She had used to laugh
at him when he became nervous about what
would happen to her if she was caught. She
had used to pull the pins from her hair and
shake it free. If they were on the beach, she
would pull off her shoes and stockings and
toss them aside before running barefoot
over the sand. In her naïveté she had not
realized, perhaps, how such actions had
inflamed his passion for her. But in all es-
sential ways he had been a proper young
gentleman. A few stolen kisses . . .

Nelson was barking joyfully and racing
down the wrong bank of the river — racing
to meet someone. She was wearing the gray
cloak and bonnet he had seen before. She
was quite alone. He drew breath to bellow
at Nelson, but his dog had recognized her
and had clearly abandoned any idea of her
as a possible enemy. His tail was waving
gleefully. She stood very still for a moment,
but she dropped her hand to pat the dog's

head when he halted in front of her and nudged his nose at her in greeting. She looked up and ahead to the bridge.

He did not go to meet her as she walked closer. He stayed where he was and watched her. She moved with her customary grace. She also, he thought as she reached the end of the bridge and stopped, looked very pale. Quite ill, in fact.

"Hello, Moira," he said.

"My lord." She regarded him with steady, unsmiling eyes.

"I have been calling on Lady Hayes," he said.

She raised her eyebrows but did not reply.

"With my condolences," he said. "I understand that Sir Edwin Baillie lost his mother less than a week ago."

"She had been ill since before Christmas," she said, "severely so since just after. But despite the fact that Sir Edwin was expecting this outcome, it has been a severe blow to him. He is very close to his family."

"And you," he said. "Are you still planning to marry him?"

"That is my concern, my lord," she said, "and his."

He was still leaning on the wall of the bridge, looking at her sideways. Even her lips were pale. "You have been ill," he said.

"Not ill so much as housebound by the inclement weather for most of this month," she said. "Fortunately, spring is coming."

His eyes had been moving assessingly down her body. But if anything, she was slimmer than usual. He asked the question anyway. "Are you with child, Moira?" he asked.

Her chin jerked up a notch. "Of course not," she said. "What a ridiculous notion."

"Ridiculous?" he said. "Have you never been told about the birds and the bees?"

"If you still worry that you will be called upon to make the supreme sacrifice," she said, "allow me to reassure you. I am not increasing. You are under no obligation to me. You are quite free to go in pursuit of Miss Wishart and make her your offer. I suppose that I have delayed it. Delay no longer. Spring is said to be a good time for a wedding."

"I will remember that," he said. "And it is enormously comforting to know that I have your blessing."

They stood looking at each other while Nelson ambled across the bridge and joined his horse, which was cropping the grass beside the bank.

"Good day to you, my lord," she said at last.

"Good day," he said, "Miss Hayes."

He looked down into the water again as she walked on. He waited for the feeling of relief, which was going to be quite overwhelming when it came. The suspense, the fear, had been there at the back of his mind all month. He could feel nothing. He had always — almost always — tried to do what was right and proper. He had befriended Sean against his father's orders, of course, but he had shunned the friendship when Sean had grown older and wilder. He had kept trysts with Moira despite the fact that she was a young lady and a Hayes in addition. But he had never tried to coax her to any intimacy beyond relatively chaste kisses, and he had fully intended to put his love for her to the test, to bring it into the open, to assert his firm intention of marrying her. For the sake of an old friendship he had turned a blind eye to Sean's criminal activities, persuading himself that smuggling in the area of Tawmouth was not a very serious business, anyway. Only when he had learned that Sean was dallying with Helen had he acted. Perhaps wrongly. Who knew? Who could ever know? He had gone with his conscience, and in the process he had discovered things about Moira he would rather not have known. He had broken his own heart.

He could not feel the relief he should have felt in the knowledge that he had not impregnated Moira on the night of his ball. *You are under no obligation to me.* Her voice had been quite steady when she had said it. She had meant it. But he could not believe it, much as he might wish to do so. He had ruined her, but she would not allow him to salve his conscience.

Foolishly he wished — and how he wished it! — that he had not gone down onto the beach and into the cove on that long-ago day of his youth to sit and think. If they had not met on that day, the whole course of his life might have been different.

He laughed rather harshly as he pushed himself upright at last and turned toward the bank and his horse. What a ridiculous notion. *What a ridiculous notion.* She had spoken just those words a few minutes ago. Making light of what had happened. As if it was quite impossible for his seed to take root in her.

He wondered how he was going to cope with the burden of guilt in the weeks and months ahead.

Why had she denied it? Moira asked herself as she walked on up the valley. The perfect

223

opportunity had presented itself, and she had rejected it.

Are you with child, Moira?

Of course not. What a ridiculous notion.

Did she imagine that by continuing to deny it, the whole thing would just go away? Mama had been wanting to send for Mr. Ryder, and she had kept assuring Mama that she was feeling indisposed merely because the weather had been consistently dreary since the beginning of the month. In the past week, of course, since news of the death of Mrs. Baillie had reached them, Mama had not questioned her lack of color or appetite. Moira had looked at her own symptoms, even to the absence of her monthly flow, and had given herself a dozen explanations — a dozen over and above the one her mind had skirted around.

She had known for some time, of course — perhaps in some strange way even from the start — why she was feeling constantly off color.

She would have to tell him.

He had just asked right out without any circumlocution. And she had denied it.

She would have to write to Sir Edwin.

His mother had just died, and he had written her a long letter full of pomposities and absurdities and raw grief.

She would have to tell Mama.

Tomorrow.

"Tomorrow and tomorrow and tomorrow," she muttered aloud. That was a quotation. Pope? Shakespeare? Milton? Her mind would not function. It was not important, anyway.

Tomorrow she would do it all — speak to Mama, write to Sir Edwin, send for Kenneth.

But tomorrow she had promised to accompany Harriet on a visit to the ailing Miss Pitt.

Lord Pelham and Mr. Gascoigne came down to Cornwall in March to spend some time with their friend. Rex Adams, Viscount Rawleigh, had not come with them though the three of them had been together for some time, first at Stratton Park and then at Bodley House in Derbyshire, home of Rex's twin brother.

"We left there in something of a hurry," Lord Pelham explained with a chuckle as the three friends talked at Dunbarton on their first evening together. They were still at the dining table, drinking their port, though they had been there for several hours and the food had long ago been borne away. "The predictable reason."

"A woman?" Kenneth raised his eyebrows.

"A woman," Mr. Gascoigne said. "A real looker, Ken. And a widow to boot. Unfortunately, she was the only looker in the whole of Derbyshire, as far as we could see."

"I take it," Kenneth said with a grin, "that she was not looking at you, then, Nat? She fancied Eden or Rex more than you?"

"None of us, actually," Mr. Gascoigne said with mock gloom.

"Though to be fair to our handsome and charming selves," Lord Pelham said, "it should be added that Nat and I were not given the chance to try our charms on her. Rex fancied her and warned us off before we could put in our own claims. We believe she gave him his royal comeuppance."

"Rex?" Kenneth was still grinning. It felt enormously pleasurable to be with his friends again. "That must have been an insufferable blow to his pride. It is rare for a woman to thumb her nose at him."

"He left Bodley with scarce a moment's notice," Mr. Gascoigne said, "dragging us along with him. Mrs. Adams, his brother's wife, you know, must have had an apoplexy when she found Rex gone. She has a marriageable sister and had definite designs on his person."

"He would not come here with us,

though," Lord Pelham said. "He was going home to Stratton bearing a distinct resemblance to a whipped cur eager to lick its wounds. I would give a king's ransom to have been able to eavesdrop on his final conversation with the delectable — and doubtless virtuous — Mrs. Winters."

They all laughed heartily, though not out of callousness for their friend. For eight years they had supported one another, laughed at and with one another, fought alongside one another, helped one another bear the burdens of a difficult and dangerous life. All of them at varying times during those years had had dealings with women, usually wildly successful, occasionally not. They had never allowed one another to become despondent over the failures. They had teased and insulted until the loser came out of his doldrums if only to hit back.

"It was a good thing he did go home," Lord Pelham said. "He was like a bear tied to a stake. He has a serious case of lustsickness. He was not scintillating company, was he, Nat?"

"I will have to coax him down here," Kenneth said before the conversation turned his way and his friends demanded an account of his escapades since he came into the country. They flatly refused to believe that there had been none and when none were forthcoming, they invented their own outrageous ones for him until all three of them were roaring with laughter.

"But imagination aside," Lord Pelham said at last, "what do you have here for our entertainment, Ken? Apart from scenery and riding and shooting and a decent wine pantry? What do you do for company?"

"Preferably young and pretty and female," Mr. Gascoigne added. "That was what he meant, Ken."

"There are the usual country families," Kenneth said with a shrug, "with about the usual number of unmarried daughters."

"By Jove," Lord Pelham said, "that sounds like manna in the desert, Ken, after our weeks at Bodley."

"They and their mamas will be ecstatic when news reaches them of your arrival," Kenneth said. "How long have you been here? Four hours? Five? Doubtless everyone within a ten-mile radius of Dunbarton knows of it by now, then. Invitations will double in number."

"Splendid," Mr. Gascoigne said. "But you have found no one to your particular liking, Ken? Is he lying, do you suppose, Ede?"

"He is lying, I suppose, Nat," Lord Pelham said. "But we will ferret out the truth.

We will watch for the one lady who brings the stars to his eyes."

"And the one lady he will not allow us near," Mr. Gascoigne added. "She is sure to be the prettiest. I am feeling out of temper already, Ede."

Lord Pelham grinned. "Have another glass of port," he said.

12

Moira had seen very little of Kenneth in the almost two months since she had come upon him while walking home from Tawmouth one afternoon. They had nodded to each other at church a few times, had exchanged civilities on the street one day when she was with Harriet, had discussed the weather for all of one minute at the Meesons' one afternoon when she was ending a visit and he was beginning one, and had both changed direction while walking along the cliff top so that they would pass far enough distant from each other that only a nod of recognition was necessary.

She was finally less fortunate on the evening of a gathering at Mr. Trevellas's home that Lady Hayes particularly wished to attend. It was not until they arrived there that they heard the news with which Tawmouth had been abuzz all day. The Earl of Haverford had two new houseguests at

Dunbarton, and both were young gentlemen of fortune. One of them was even a *baron,* Mrs. Trevellas explained to Lady Hayes, though it was said that the other gentleman, who had no title, was just as well connected and just as wealthy.

Mr. Trevellas, the only one present at the evening gathering to have seen the two guests during the day, had failed to notice if they were handsome gentlemen, but as Miss Pitt remarked — and other ladies nodded as if to commend her on the good sense of her words — if they were young and fashionable gentlemen and if they were friends of Lord Haverford's, then she dared say they were at the very least passably handsome.

"They have been invited here to join the gathering," Harriet Lincoln said to Moira with a smile, taking her arm and leading her toward a couple of chairs away from the crowd clustered about a clearly triumphant Mr. Trevellas, "and have accepted. Are we not all to be merry this evening? What a blessing it is that the Grimshaws have arrived home after a four-month absence and have brought their four daughters with them. I do believe Mrs. Grimshaw is already planning a double wedding. Doubtless she dreams of a *triple* wedding, but the tone of her voice when she speaks of our earl betrays a certain awe. I believe she considers him above her touch." She laughed.

"The eldest Miss Grimshaw has grown into a tolerably handsome girl," Moira said. "And she has pleasing manners."

"I expect a most diverting evening," Harriet said. "Especially as Edgar Meeson, who has grown into a very fine young man, clearly has eyes for the eldest Miss Grimshaw. We will sit here and observe and have a merry laugh at everyone's expense but our own. It is to be hoped that they are handsome gentlemen, of course, but provided they behave agreeably and show some interest in the young daughters of Tawmouth, they will be declared the handsomest of men tomorrow morning. Mark my words."

"I suppose," Moira said, "the Earl of Haverford will be coming too?"

"Oh, assuredly," Harriet said. "But we will not mind *him,* Moira, beyond enjoying a private gaze at his beauty. He is altogether too highly connected to be considered a matrimonial prize possible of attainment in this part of the world. I daresay he will take himself off to London one of these years and bring himself back a countess who will have us all as speechless with awe as his mama had us at Christmastime."

"Perhaps Miss Wishart," Moira said.

"Oh, I think not," Harriet said. "He did not show quite enough interest in her, you know. Why, he danced with you at the Dunbarton ball and at the assembly as much as he danced with her. Will there be dancing here this evening, do you think? I do not doubt someone will suggest it. How could the company of handsome young men be wasted on an evening devoid of dancing, after all? But you and I will sit here like sober matrons, Moira, and watch. You will not dance, will you? You really have suffered a severe decline since Christmas. Mr. Lincoln declared that he scarcely recognized you at church last Sunday."

"I feel better now that spring has come," Moira said.

"Ah," Harriet said. "The excitement begins. Here they are."

A hundred times or more during the past two months Moira had determined to act, to *do* something about her situation. She would write to Sir Edwin, she would talk with her mother, she would call upon Kenneth — always the same three things to be done. And yet it seemed that the more determined she became, the more often she delayed. And the more often she delayed, the more impossible it became to do anything at all. Just as if her problem would go away if she just stayed inactive long enough.

She had not known one day of good health in three months. Her mother, she knew, was worried about her, and Mr. Ryder, who had finally been summoned to Penwith, had appeared puzzled by the symptoms she had shared with him — he had not dreamed of drawing the obvious conclusions, of course — and had given her a tonic. But she knew that she would be better as soon as she had finally unburdened herself to the three people most nearly concerned. And delay was so very foolish. If she delayed much longer, she would not need to say anything. The thought of any of the three of them learning the truth *that* way was horrifying.

But she had still done nothing.

"Oh, Moira," Harriet murmured, moving her head closer to her friend's, "this grows more and more interesting. Have you ever in your life seen three more handsome gentlemen in company together? Our earl has the advantage of height and that glorious blond hair, but one of those gentlemen has the bluest eyes — I never could resist blue eyes — and the other one has a smile to turn even this matron's knees weak."

Moira had not noticed the other two gentlemen. She had seen only Kenneth, handsome and distinguished in his dark evening clothes. And she had felt only the total impossibility of talking with him. She felt dull and ugly and old — and hated herself for feeling inferior. She would never be able to call on him, to wait for him in the salon at Dunbarton where she had once waited with Sir Edwin, and to tell him. She would not be able to do it. It could not be done. She could no longer believe in the reality of that night at the baptistry, which was a foolish thought in light of her physical condition.

He was talking with Mrs. Trevellas while Mr. Trevellas took his two friends about, presenting them to his neighbors. Kenneth was looking about him as he talked. Moira watched his eyes rest on her mother for a moment and then move on. They passed over her and then came back to her. He frowned briefly before looking away.

She ought not to have worn her mulberry-colored gown, Moira thought. It was the dullest of garments. She had thought so ever since the bolt of cloth had been made up. She had worn it only three or four times, always at home. But it had suited her mood when she had dressed this evening. She knew she looked very far from her best. But then, why should she care?

Mr. Trevellas had stopped before her and Harriet and was presenting Lord Pelham, the gentleman with the very blue eyes, and Mr. Gascoigne, the gentleman with the very attractive smile. Yes, Moira thought a little bitterly as they turned away after a brief exchange of civilities, they were worthy friends for Kenneth. His good looks did not completely overshadow them.

"I believe Mr. Gascoigne must be a kind gentleman and Lord Pelham must be a rogue with the ladies," Harriet said when they had passed on. "Would you not agree, Moira?"

"But perhaps a kind smile may be quite as seductive as blue eyes," Moira said. And blond hair and light gray eyes most seductive of all.

Harriet had guessed quite correctly. Mr. and Mrs. Trevellas would have been quite happy to settle all their guests to cards or conversation until suppertime, but the young people had other ideas, and it was the second-youngest Grimshaw daughter who was finally bold enough to ask for a jig to be played on the pianoforte and who grasped the hand of young Henry Meeson and pulled him to his feet to add weight to her demand.

"Miss Pitt, do play for us," she begged

with a bright smile. "I shall die if we do not dance."

But Miss Pitt was still frail after a lengthy indisposition that had kept her in her bed for the whole of one month. Moira got to her feet. She would be quite content to withdraw to the far side of the drawing room and hide away there for the rest of the evening.

"I will be happy to play," she said. "Do stay by the fire and enjoy the dancing, Miss Pitt."

"Oh, dear Miss Hayes, how very kind of you," Miss Pitt said. "But very well. You will not wish to dance yourself this evening, of course, in the absence of dear Sir Edwin Baillie."

The eldest Miss Grimshaw and Miss Penallen had drawn the coveted partners for this particular jig, Moira noticed as she seated herself at the instrument and began to play a lively jig. They danced with the houseguests from Dunbarton. Kenneth himself did not dance but stood and watched, the Reverend Finley-Evans at his side, until Moira became aware of the vicar bending over Miss Pitt's chair and looked sharply about, almost allowing her fingers to trip over themselves as she did so.

Kenneth had crossed the room toward the

pianoforte and stood a short distance away watching her, his face unsmiling. He was quite alone.

Moira returned her attention to the music she played. He was close enough to speak to. They were far enough removed from the rest of the room's occupants that they might hold a low conversation without any fear of being overheard. If he stood there until the end of the jig, she might speak to him before the dancers were ready for something else with new partners. What she had to say would take very little time. Just enough for the utterance of one sentence — that was all.

She would do it, she decided. Without giving the matter further consideration. Before she lost her courage. The music was almost at an end.

She felt clammy with fear.

He was appalled at the sight of her. He had seen her a few times in the past two months and had even spoken briefly with her once or twice. She had appeared pale and out of spirits on each of those occasions, but tonight, when he had a chance to take a good look at her, he was amazed by the change in her. She was almost unrecognizable. When he had looked about the room for her after seeing that her mother was present, he had at first looked right past her.

Her hair was dressed severely and did nothing to soften her face, which was colorless except for the lavender shadows beneath her eyes. Her cheeks were hollow and made her face look longer and thinner than usual. Her dreadfully dull gown sapped her of what little color she might have had. She had completely lost her looks. If he had not known her, if he had been seeing her for the first time tonight, he might have thought her ugly and a good deal older than her six-and-twenty years.

She had always been slender. She was thin now, he thought when she got to her feet and crossed the room to the pianoforte. She looked gaunt. He had been sociable since his arrival. He had conversed with his host and with a group of ladies. It had been quite unnecessary to see to Nat and Eden's entertainment, of course. They had been whisked off — quite willingly — to amuse the young ladies, among whom were four sisters Kenneth had not seen himself until this evening. But though he talked and smiled and even listened with half an ear, he could not take his mind off Moira Hayes. He had not done so in three months, he thought ruefully, but now, this evening, all

239

the guilt, all the frustration were back in full force. He must speak with her.

She played very well, he noticed as he approached the pianoforte and stood close to it, watching her, his back to the rest of the room. It seemed strange that he had never heard her play before, though he could remember that as a girl she had spoken about her love of music. She played from memory. There was no music propped on the stand before her.

He waited for the jig to end. There was a great deal of laughter and excited chatter behind him when it did so. Moira looked up at him. Her jaw was set in a hard, stubborn line he recognized. She opened her mouth and drew breath.

No, he would not allow her to send him away.

"Is this what I have done to you, Moira?" he asked her very quietly.

She froze into immobility and did not say what she had been about to say.

"You escaped the worst consequences of that night," he said. "You told me so at the end of January. But you have not been able to put the guilt of it from your mind, have you? It has ruined your life."

How unfair life was to women, he thought. He doubted that even if he tried he would be able to remember exactly how many women in all he had bedded. And yet for a woman, for a lady, even one man outside wedlock could change the whole course of her life for the worse. Yet in her stubbornness Moira would not marry him — merely because she hated him.

For once she had nothing to say. She looked back at him with troubled eyes and a very slight frown.

"You would not wish to dance tonight because Sir Edwin Baillie is not here," he said, repeating what Miss Pitt had said to her earlier. "You are still betrothed to him, then, Moira? I did not understand, perhaps, that you really wish to marry him. I beg your forgiveness for anything I might have said about him that hurt your sensibilities."

Her frown deepened.

"It seems to me very probable, you know," he said, "that he would not realize the truth after he had married you. And it would not perhaps be utterly deceitful to marry him without first confessing all to him. You were not really unfaithful to him after all, were you? Not in your heart. And he will never hear of it from me. No one will. Unless you have confided in anyone — and my guess is that you have not — then we are the only two people in the world who know."

She opened her mouth to speak again, but merely passed the tip of her tongue across her upper lip.

"You do not need to suffer like this," he said. "It was really nothing so very dreadful, Moira. Nothing to put you into a decline like this. It is time you put it behind you, forgot it. I forgot it long ago."

Her smile did not reach her eyes. "Did you, my lord?" she said. "But to what do you refer? What is it you have forgotten? I cannot remember, I must confess. I took a chill during the winter and have not yet fully recovered my health. I expect to do so rapidly now that the weather has turned warmer."

He should not have pretended to have forgotten. It was a gauche and foolish thing to have said. He could hear the anger behind the sweetness of her voice. But he felt angry too. If only she knew how to behave, she would have married him almost three months ago and he would not have had to live with the gnawing guilt ever since then — only with Moira and her eternal presence in his life.

"I beg your pardon, ma'am," he said, making her a stiff bow and turning back to the rest of the room. At the same moment the dancers, who had formed a double line, the

ladies facing the gentlemen, were demand-
ing that Miss Hayes play a country dance.

"I had forgotten," Mr. Gascoigne said, "how
merry a country entertainment can be. And
how pretty and sprightly country girls can
be, by Jove."

"The eldest Miss Grimshaw was by far
the handsomest girl there," Lord Pelham
said. "Did you form the impression, though,
Nat, that the copper-haired young gentleman wished to put a bullet between our eyes
every time we led her into a dance or drew
her into a discussion on bonnets?"

"Miss Sarah Grimshaw was more amiable," Mr. Gascoigne said. "And a bold little
chit, too. Do you really intend to give a ball
at Dunbarton, Ken?"

Kenneth shrugged. "I agreed to it when
she asked," he said. "I shall honor my
promise, I suppose."

Mr. Gascoigne sat back on the carriage
seat and regarded his friend in silence for a
moment. "You were giving nothing away,
Ken," he said. "Do you really fancy none of
the young ladies? Or were you trying to
throw us off the scent by ignoring the one
you favor?"

"He was throwing us off the scent, Nat,"
Lord Pelham said. "Though one must

remember that Ken *lives* here and has to be careful of showing too much gallantry or too much partiality to one lady. He might find himself with a leg shackle in no time at all."

Mr. Gascoigne chuckled. "He was being very careful tonight, then, Ede," he said. "Instead of dancing with one of the young girls, he followed the pianoforte player across the room and stood listening to her music. Now, if she had been young and pretty, we might have made something of it."

"The pale scarecrow?" Lord Pelham said. "We might still do it, Nat. My theory is that she is the very one. Our Ken has conceived a passion for an older woman, for a colorless cadaver. Perhaps he finds youth and plump beauty tedious after so long an acquaintance with them."

"You are being unkind, Ede," Mr. Gascoigne said. "I daresay the lady is consumptive."

"Ah, then perhaps our Ken has conceived a passion —" Lord Pelham began.

"And perhaps," Kenneth said, "you would care to keep your mouth shut, Eden, unless you have sense to utter."

Lord Pelham winced theatrically. "I sense a challenge on the way, Nat," he said. "I have caught Ken on the raw. He definitely has conceived a passion for the scarecrow. But she has spurned him. She is holding out for a duke."

"I believe, Ede," Mr. Gascoigne said, "that Ken is offended by the way you are talking about one of his neighbors. And I will wager the lady really *is* consumptive. She cannot help her age or her thinness or her lack of looks."

"I say," Lord Pelham said, sitting upright, his tone of levity suddenly gone, "I meant no offense, Ken. I do beg your pardon."

Kenneth smiled. "I understand," he said, "that the Misses Grimshaw wish to show the two of you the beach and the quay. I suppose you will not want my company. Without me, you will have two each, one for each arm."

"As for myself, Ken," Lord Pelham said, "I would just as soon have one lady on one arm — if the beach and the quay have any coves or caves or secluded nooks, that is."

"One can only hope," Mr. Gascoigne added, "that the sun will shine tomorrow."

"Tomorrow," Kenneth said, "I must write to Rex. If he has bruised pride to nurse, he might as well do it here."

But the idea of coaxing Viscount Rawleigh

down to Cornwall died a swift death. Only a little more than a week after the arrival of his friends and before a reply to his own letter could reasonably be expected, Kenneth received a letter addressed to all of them. Rex had returned to Derbyshire after less than one full day at Stratton and was to marry Mrs. Winters within the week. He was intending to take his bride back to Stratton and hoped that his friends would call upon him there.

His friends each read the letter in turn. They looked at one another, stunned. Rex about to be married? Indeed, he probably was married by now. To a woman who had very recently rejected all his advances and sent him scurrying home to Stratton?

"Thereby hangs a mystery," Kenneth said. "An intriguing one."

"The devil!" Lord Pelham said. "He must have ruined her and been forced to go back and do the decent thing. At Claude's insistence, if I am not much mistaken. Claude is rather more respectable than his twin."

"Claude won't like it above half," Mr. Gascoigne said.

"Neither will Rex," Lord Pelham said dryly. "I was not under the impression that he had matrimony in mind when he was pursuing the lady."

"And neither," Mr. Gascoigne added, "will Mrs. Winters like it, at a guess. She is probably no longer Mrs. Winters, of course, but the Viscountess Rawleigh. Deuce take it. Old Rex married."

"If you are right, Eden," Kenneth said quietly, "and honor has forced him into it, he will not be a happy man. But better that, perhaps, than have her refuse to allow him to do the decent thing. At least he has retrieved his honor."

"I could not see any woman refusing a man who had ruined her," Lord Pelham said. "His honor was never in much danger of being permanently lost, I daresay. Are we going to Stratton?"

"So soon?" Mr. Gascoigne asked. "We have scarcely arrived here. And Ken's ball is tentatively set for next week."

"It can be postponed. And there is such a thing as curiosity," Kenneth said. "I have not even seen the lady."

"And none of us knows the real story behind the hasty marriage," Lord Pelham said.

"Besides," Mr. Gascoigne added, grimacing, "Rex may need our moral support. Are we going to let him down?"

And so they went. Kenneth went out of curiosity and out of a genuine desire to see his newly married friend and wish him happiness — if happiness were possible in a marriage that seemed to have had an inauspicious beginning. He went because all the hard work he had engaged in and all the social engagements he had honored and even the eventful week he had just spent with his friends had not been able to lift his spirits or erase his sense of guilt.

Or his anger. He was angry with her. If she was making such a deal of her own sense of guilt, then why did she not simply marry him? If she was determined not to do so, if she was set upon marrying Baillie, then why did she not fight free of the unpleasant memories? It was unlike Moira not to fight. He resented the guilt her obvious loss of health aroused in him. He had *tried* to do the decent, honorable thing, and she had refused to allow him to do it. He could almost envy Rex.

He went because his absence would perhaps set her free. She could not marry Baillie during his period of mourning, perhaps, but she could begin planning her future, shaking off the memory and effects of the unfortunate incident that had clouded her happiness. But how could she be *happy* about marrying such an ass as Baillie? It was not his concern. If he went away — and stayed away — perhaps he could do her some good and shake off some of his own damnable guilt.

He had not believed it possible to resent or hate anyone as much as he resented and hated Moira Hayes. And even his resentment and his hatred weighed heavily on his conscience.

13

A letter had arrived at Penwith expressing Sir Edwin Baillie's fond wish that Lady Hayes and Miss Hayes would honor him and his dear sisters by spending a couple of weeks with them at Easter. He had hoped for a far more joyful event to brighten the spring, but that was now, of course, out of the question. Even so . . . The letter continued at some length and ended with an assurance that Sir Edwin would send his own carriage and several stout servants to fetch the ladies to his humble home, where he and his sisters would await their arrival with as much eager anticipation as the melancholy circumstances of their lives permitted.

"It is very civil of them to be willing to entertain us at such a time," Lady Hayes said to her daughter. "But understandable, of course. I do believe Sir Edwin is genuinely fond of you, Moira. And his sisters must really be curious to meet you, especially since you are a distant cousin."

"It is a kind invitation," Moira agreed.

But her mother frowned at her. "Shall we go, then?" she asked. "You have still not recovered your health, Moira, despite the tonic Mr. Ryder prescribed for you. I fear that a journey of thirty miles will be too much for you."

Moira hesitated on the brink of assuring her mother that a change of scene and the company of new acquaintances were all that she needed to recover her spirits. The time for lies and evasion was fast disappearing. And Sir Edwin's home was the last place she could go. She did think fleetingly that perhaps it would be best to go and speak with him face-to-face, but she knew it was an idea that could not be given serious consideration. She smiled and took the letter from her mother's hand.

"With your permission, Mama," she said, "I will answer Sir Edwin's letter myself. You may read it and give it your approval before it is sent." Her stomach churned at the thought. But the time had definitely come.

The time had come, in fact, for more than one letter to be written. Clearly she did not have the courage to say *anything* face-to-face. She must write, then. She sat at the

251

escritoire in the morning room and wrote them both. She stared at the clock in disbelief when she was finished. Had it taken her two hours to write two short letters? It took her another twenty minutes to summon the courage to get to her feet and go in search of her mother.

Lady Hayes had just come in from the outdoors with an armful of spring flowers for the vases. She smiled at her daughter. "This lovely spring is making up for a miserable winter," she said. "Are you going to walk to Tawmouth to post the letter? I believe the exercise will do you good."

"Mama," Moira said, "sit down."

Her mother looked at her, seemed alerted to the fact that something was amiss, and sat. She took the letter for Sir Edwin from Moira's hand and directed her attention to it.

"Oh," she said, looking up after a few moments, "you have declined the invitation. Perhaps that is a wise decision, dear. But I do hope Sir Edwin will not be hurt or offended. Have you explained that you are not in the best of health? I am sure he would be the first to urge you to remain at home if he knew that."

"Read on," Moira said.

Her mother read in silence to the end of

the letter. She set it down in her lap and took a few moments to gather her thoughts.

"Is this wise, Moira?" she asked. "What will become of us?"

"I do not know," Moira said. She had gone to stand by the window, though she did not really see the prettiness of the garden beyond it.

"But that was a purely selfish thought and quite unworthy of me," Lady Hayes said. "My own future is of no significance. I have never deceived myself into believing that this marriage would bring you any degree of happiness. But I did persuade myself that it would be a respectable match and would secure your future: You are six-and-twenty years old, after all."

"An old maid," Moira said and then bit her lip. She should have chosen to call herself a spinster.

"One ought to consider the possibility that this may be your last chance for matrimony," Lady Hayes said. "You have had other chances, Moira, and have rejected them all. This may very well be the last. Would it perhaps be wise at least to go to Sir Edwin's home and see him again? And meet his sisters? Perhaps you will find after all that marriage with him is preferable to no marriage and no prospects."

"I cannot, Mama," Moira said quietly. She held the other letter in her hand. She would deliver it personally after posting the one to Sir Edwin. She would perhaps have a reply tomorrow or even this evening. But even so, she could not force herself to say anything else to her mother. She would not have believed before all this sorry mess started that she could be capable of such cowardice as she had shown during the past three months.

Lady Hayes sighed. "It can bring on dreadful disgrace, Moira," she said, "to break a formal engagement."

"Yes," Moira said.

"We may find that we are not so well received by our neighbors in future," her mother said.

We. Mama would be caught up in the disgrace, of course. That was the worst of it. If the consequences of sin could be confined solely to the sinner, they would be very much easier to bear, Moira thought. But she would not be the only one to suffer. There were Sir Edwin, his sisters, Mama.

"I will be sorry for it, Mama," Moira said. "More sorry for your sake than I can possibly say. But I cannot marry Sir Edwin."

Half an hour later, she was on her way to Tawmouth along the valley, which had become lushly green with spring. The river wound its sparkling way to the sea and the hills were loud with birdsong. But Moira could not enjoy her surroundings. Soon both letters would be out of her hands and a whole cycle of events would begin that she should have set in motion a long time ago. But there had been Sir Edwin's bereavement — a poor excuse for such a long delay — and the continued presence of Lady Haverford at Dunbarton — an even poorer excuse. Anyway, she had left more than two weeks ago. But other visitors had followed closely on her heels.

That was certainly no excuse. It was perhaps the arrival of his friends that had brought Kenneth to Mr. Trevellas's a week ago. She had had the perfect opportunity there. She had steeled herself to speak. She had opened her mouth and drawn breath.

But he had spoken first. He had been cold, angry at the fact that she was making a great to-do about nothing. Angry that just the sight of her was reminding him of his own guilt.

You escaped the worst consequences of that night. You told me at the end of January.

It was really nothing so very dreadful, Moira. Nothing to put you into a decline like this. It is time you put it behind you, forgot it. I forgot it long ago.

Moira winced again at the pain his words had aroused and felt again the anger that had provoked her unwise response and had sent him away before she had said what she had planned to say.

So today what she had to say must be stated in a letter. Today she must ignore the fact that there were visitors at Dunbarton. Their presence was no excuse at all to avoid going there. If she came face-to-face with them, it did not matter. She only hoped she would not come face-to-face with *him* — not today, not before he had read her letter. She could, of course, have had one of the servants from Penwith deliver it to Dunbarton for her, but it seemed somehow important to her to do it herself.

It was a long walk, first into Tawmouth, then up the hill to the cliff top, and then along the road above the valley to Dunbarton Hall. The sun was high in the sky when she reached it and there was surprising warmth for the time of year. How different the sloping, shaded driveway looked now from the way it had looked the last time she saw it, Moira thought — and shivered.

His lordship was from home, the footman who answered her knock at the door informed her. Moira explained that she had come merely to deliver a letter for the Earl of Haverford.

"Will you see that it is given to him?" she asked, holding it out with one hand. Her heart was beating so loudly that she wondered the servant could not hear it. Once the letter was taken from her hand . . .

But the butler had appeared in the hall, and the footman stepped to one side.

"Is it an invitation, ma'am?" the butler asked after making her a stiff half bow and looking with disapproval beyond her shoulder to note the absence of an accompanying maid. "If it is, I beg leave to inform you that his lordship will be unable to accept. He is from home."

"From home?" she said. An afternoon outing would hardly prevent him from accepting all invitations.

"His lordship left this morning to go into Kent for an undetermined length of time, ma'am," the butler said. "I do not expect his early return."

Moira stood looking at him, her hand still outstretched. *This morning. I do not expect his early return.* She felt the beginnings of an all-too-familiar coldness in the head.

"Would you care to sit down for a while, ma'am?" the butler asked, peering at her in some concern.

"No." She returned her hand to her side and smiled at him. "No, thank you. I must be continuing on my way." She hurried off back through the courtyard and scarcely slackened her pace all the way home. When she was descending the steep road to the valley, she determinedly did not look right to where the picturesque stone baptistry overlooked the valley and the little waterfall.

More than a week passed before she returned to Dunbarton and asked to speak with the Earl of Haverford's steward. She had to wait almost half an hour while he was fetched from somewhere out of doors, and he was clearly surprised both by her appearance at Dunbarton and by her request. But he did agree to enclose her letter with the report he would be sending his lordship within the week.

It was all done, she thought as she made her way home, raising an umbrella to shield herself from the light drizzle. Everything was out of her hands now — for the moment at least, though she had still not told Mama.

Kenneth had found just the medicine he needed — or so he persuaded himself. He got quickly caught up in someone else's problems. Viscount Rawleigh was at Stratton with his bride the morning his three friends arrived from Cornwall. In fact, he was outdoors with her and standing on a bridge the earl's carriage must drive over. Kenneth leaned forward and rapped on the front panel to signal the driver to stop, and then he sat back while Lord Pelham and Mr. Gascoigne jumped out to a great deal of loud talk and laughter and excited barking from a small dog. He was eager to see Rex again and to meet his bride.

But he made an immediate and horrible mistake. He jumped out of the carriage, hugged Rex, greeted him, clapped a hand on his shoulder, and turned to see the bride, who was laughing with Nat and Eden. But as soon as his eyes alighted on her, he recognized her. He had seen her in London six years before when he had been sent home to recuperate from his wounds. He had even danced with her once or twice at *ton* balls. She was Paxton's daughter — the Earl of Paxton.

"Why, Lady Catherine," he said before he could notice the dawning shock and dismay in her eyes. Half a second later, he saw shock also in the eyes of his three friends — a look that was quickly veiled in Rex's. And he remembered. Eden and Nat had called her Mrs. Winters, a widow. They had said nothing about her being Paxton's daughter, Lady Catherine Winsmore. Winters, Winsmore — very similar. Had she been married? Had she been a widow? What had she been doing in Derbyshire? Had she been living there incognito? Did his friends — *and even Rex* — not know her true identity?

The noise, the hearty laughter resumed, but Kenneth knew that damage had been done. And his fears were confirmed when he was finally alone with Nat and Eden some time later. No, indeed they had not known, they assured him, and it seemed a reasonable assumption, given his quickly controlled reaction, that Rex had not known either. He had married a woman without knowing her true identity? He had married her without knowing that six years ago she had been totally disgraced in an association with London's worst blackguard and rake? Gossip had even had it that she had been with child and certain it was that she had suddenly disappeared. Kenneth had by now remembered those facts — far too late.

"Rex heard what I called her, I suppose?" he asked half hopefully.

"He heard," Lord Pelham told him.

"And it came as a surprise to him." He did not have to frame the words as a question.

"Rex could never tread the boards," Mr. Gascoigne said. "He is not a good enough actor."

And yet he acted well enough for the rest of the day, smiling and welcoming and solicitous of his wife's comfort. She was a beauty, too, as his friends had told Kenneth and as he remembered himself from six years ago. She was dark-haired and hazel-eyed.

But they could not stay at Stratton. Despite Rex's near-perfect acting, they agreed that there was an almost unbearable tension between Rex and his wife. The best they could do was to leave them alone, pretend that they had come merely for a day or two on their way to London.

And so to London they went the day following the next, even though Lord Rawleigh took them aside first of all and assured them that he knew his wife's story — that he had always known it. She had told him some time yesterday, then, they had understood. Kenneth almost forgot his own troubles in the terrible embarrassment of his faux pas. He was dreadfully afraid that he had wrecked a marriage that had probably had a shaky start, anyway. But how could Lady Catherine have married Rex without telling him about her disgrace? And how would

Rex react to discovering the truth now when he was already married to her? It was none of his business, of course, Kenneth tried to tell himself.

But it became his business a little more than a week later. Viscount Rawleigh and his wife had appeared unexpectedly in town only a couple of days after his own arrival, and now Rex had asked his three friends if they would be sure to attend the Mindell ball, to which he had determined to take Lady Rawleigh, even though the chances were strong that the *ton* would cut her acquaintance. He wanted as much moral support — and enough dancing partners for his wife — as he could gather about him.

The ball took on even more significance when another guest arrived late — Sir Howard Copley, the very man who had ruined Lady Rawleigh six years before. The lady herself did not see him as she was dancing when he arrived, and he disappeared to the card room on catching sight of her. But a quick conference among the four friends determined a plan of action. Kenneth was the one elected to dance the following quadrille with Lady Rawleigh while the other three left the ballroom. After the set was over, Lord Pelham told him the expected news: The duel was to take place early on the morning after next. Eden was Rex's official second, but Nat and Kenneth would go too, of course.

Dunbarton and Kenneth's own frustrations had been pushed from his conscious mind. They had become only a nagging heaviness to cause him considerable sleeplessness at night and troubled dreams when he did sleep. Rex's problems were so much more real than his own. One thing had become very clear during the past week: Rex was obviously desperately in love with his wife, and if Kenneth's guess was not far from the mark, she returned the feeling. It was a happy realization — if Rex lived. He had escaped death a thousand times during the wars, of course, and was an expert marksman — the duel was to be fought with pistols. But one could be sure of nothing in a duel, especially with a blackguard like Copley as the opponent. It was said, probably quite correctly, that Lady Rawleigh had not been his only victim.

The following day — the one before the duel — was endless. Lady Rawleigh had invited her husband's three friends to dinner, and they sat over it and in the drawing room afterward, talking and laughing and reminiscing — at her request. She wanted to know about their years together, she insisted. It was by all appearances a jolly evening, but Kenneth was thoroughly weary and worried by the time he arrived home. If he had been the one facing tomorrow's duel, he would have felt sick and nervous and terrified. But they would at least have been familiar feelings. He had felt them before every battle he had fought, and would defy any soldier to boast that he had not shared those feelings. But he would have known, too, that once the danger became real and was to be faced, a cold concentration would take the place of all the negative feelings and his right arm would be as steady as a rock. But he was not the one facing the duel. It was harder to know that one would have to stand helplessly to one side and watch a man take aim at the heart of one's closest friend.

He almost did not open the package that had arrived from Dunbarton during the day, addressed in the neat hand of his steward. It could wait. He would not be able to concentrate on business matters tonight. But neither would he be able to sleep, he realized. His mind was agitated. Perhaps reading a few dull reports would calm him. Perhaps — forlorn hope — they would even lull him to sleep. He opened the package to find the expected contents — and a sealed letter addressed in a different hand. A female hand, if he was not mistaken. Curiosity made him open it before he read anything else.

"My lord," she had written, "I have ended my betrothal to Sir Edwin Baillie. I am three months with child. This is not a plea for help. I have, however, come to the conclusion that you have a right to know. Your obedient servant, Moira Hayes."

He stared at the letter for several minutes before folding it carefully into its original creases and then crumpling it hard in one hand and hurling it across the room. Three months. The damned woman. The bitch! *Three bloody months?* His hand clenched into a hard fist and he closed his eyes tightly.

When had he asked her about her condition? It had been in the valley at the end of January. Two months ago — longer. She must have known already then. He had asked her right out. *Of course not,* she had said. *What a ridiculous notion.* He could see now the look of proud disdain on her face. And yet she must have known even then. And at Trevellas's, only a week before he left Dunbarton, she had said *nothing.* He had spoken to her, tried to be kind to her, tried to free her from her guilt, and all she had done was look defiant and pretend to have forgotten the incident. She had been almost three months with child.

The damned — bitch!

She had waited until he went away to inform him coolly and curtly that she was three months with child and to assure him that she was making no plea for help. She had signed herself very formally as his obedient servant.

"Obedient." He had said the word aloud through clenched teeth. "Obedient indeed, Miss Moira Hayes. For the rest of your wretched life, I swear. You may thank providence that you are not within reach of my hands at this moment. You may pray that my temper will have cooled by the time I reach Cornwall."

A license, he thought. He would need a special license. He would get one as soon as possible in the morning and be on his way. But Rex was to fight a duel early tomorrow morning. Perhaps he would not survive it. There would be a funeral. . . .

He surged to his feet and dragged the fingers of both hands through his hair. "God damn it to hell!" he said aloud. He swore even more profanely. There would be no passion lacking in his marriage, anyway, he thought grimly and laughed aloud. It would be the passion of intense hatred.

His marriage. *His marriage!* He was going to be a married man. He was going to be a father in six months' time. And Moira Hayes was making no plea for his help.

"God damn you," he whispered. "Damn you, Moira."

Rex Adams, Viscount Rawleigh, survived the duel he fought against Sir Howard Copley. Sir Howard did not — and did not deserve to, for in addition to his past sins, which were legion, he broke the rules of the duel and fired his pistol prematurely, before the signal was given. He wounded Lord Rawleigh in the right arm but did not incapacitate him. He was then forced to stand and wait while his opponent took slow and careful aim, paused as if considering whether he should shoot to kill or merely to wound, and proceeded to kill him.

Mr. Gascoigne had aimed another gun at Copley after he had fired and the shocking red stain of blood had spread on the viscount's shirtsleeve. Kenneth and Lord Pelham had stood frozen. They had not known how severe the wound was.

But after it was all over, Rex came striding toward them, his expression grim, and began to dress without a glance at the surgeon and what he and Copley's second were doing over the body. He did have to turn sharply away before his coat was on to vomit into the grass, but it was a reaction to a battle just fought that was familiar to all of them. One never became quite hardened either to facing death or to meting it out.

"Breakfast," he said, his face ashen and resolute when he was dressed again. "At White's?"

"At White's." Mr. Gascoigne slapped a friendly hand on his left shoulder. "He would not have lived, anyway, Rex. I would have done it if you had not."

"Perhaps my house instead of White's," Lord Pelham said. "A little more privacy and all that."

Kenneth drew in a deep breath. "I have to leave immediately," he said. "I have to return to Dunbarton."

He would have avoided this if he could, but of course it was impossible. They all turned and looked at him in some surprise.

"To Dunbarton?" Lord Rawleigh said, frowning. "Now, Ken? This morning? Even before breakfast? I thought you were here for the rest of the Season."

It was suddenly starkly real, now that he had to put it into words. "There was a letter waiting for me when I arrived home last evening," he said. He tried to smile but realized the impossibility of hiding his true feelings from these men who knew him almost as well as he knew himself. "It appears that I am to be a father in six months' time."

There was a strange stillness, considering the fact that there were four of them standing there and that a duel had just been fought. The surgeon was still kneeling beside Sir Howard Copley's body.

"Who?" Lord Pelham asked at last. "Anyone we met when we were there, Ken? A *lady*?"

"No one you met," Kenneth said grimly. "A lady, yes. I have to go home to marry her."

"Dare I comment on the fact that you do not appear thrilled?" Mr. Gascoigne said, frowning. All of them were looking at him with the same puzzled concern in their eyes.

He laughed. "Her family and mine have been enemies for as long as I can remember," he said. "I do not believe I have ever disliked a woman more than I dislike her. And she is with child by me. I must marry her. Wish me joy." He laughed again and felt intensely disloyal. He had had no business saying that, even to his closest friends.

"Ken," Lord Rawleigh said, "what are we missing?"

But he had said enough. Too much. She was to be his wife, and he had told them how much he disliked her. And Eden had called her a pale scarecrow and a colorless cadaver. "Nothing that I care to divulge," he said. "I have to be going. I am glad things turned out as they did this morning, Rex. Have that arm seen to before you leave here. I am glad you did not shoot into the air. I feared you would. Rapists do not deserve to live."

He strode away in the direction of his horse. He did not look back. There was a license to be purchased. It should not take long. Then there was a long journey to be made in as much haste as he could muster.

And at the end of the journey there was a woman to confront. Moira Hayes. His future wife. The mother of his child. God help her — and him.

14

Sir Edwin Baillie had replied at some length to Moira's letter. He commended Miss Hayes on being a woman of more than usual sensibilities. She must have realized, he wrote, that he had regretted the impulsiveness with which he had sought his own felicity at a time when his dear mother had been gravely ill. Miss Hayes must have realized the guilt that his own gratified affections had aroused in his bosom when he had three orphaned sisters under his protection and guidance. And so Miss Hayes had had the courage and the selflessness and the kindness to release him from his commitment. She and her esteemed mama would do him the honor of considering Penwith Manor their home, at least until he felt free to renew his addresses — perhaps in a year or two's time. He remained their humble and obedient servant.

"It is a remarkably civil letter," Lady

Hayes said when she had read it. "And so we may relax here for another year or two, Moira."

"Yes," her daughter said.

"And you can feel that a burden has now been lifted from your shoulders," her mother said. "Do not imagine, Moira, that I have not realized that guilt and worry have sent you into this decline. Now, finally, you may recover your health. Have you been taking the tonic Mr. Ryder prescribed?"

Moira smiled noncommittally. She would give the Earl of Haverford two weeks, she had decided. After that, there could be no more delay. Her mother at least would have to know. Indeed, if such a thing were not so completely unthinkable, she would doubtless already suspect. Despite an overall loss of weight, Moira's abdomen was softly swelling beneath her fashionably loose-fitting, high-waisted dresses.

She had seen the anxiety in her mother's eyes. She knew that her mother feared for her and tried to convince herself that the spring air and the tonic — and now the release from stress that Sir Edwin's letter had brought — would bring back the bloom of good health. It was unfair of her to allow Mama to fear that she was dying when she might have explained the true cause of her indisposition.

She had come to despise herself.

It was a particularly wet afternoon in early April when he came. There was no possibility of going out and no chance that visitors would venture all the way to Penwith. Besides, Moira was not sure how ready their neighbors were to call on them, even in the best of weather. She had told Harriet that her betrothal had been ended, by mutual consent, and had permitted her friend to pass on the news. Doubtless everyone knew by now. Moira sat with her mother in the sitting room embroidering while the rain beat so hard against the window that it was impossible even to gaze out into the garden.

She raised her head and listened for a moment. A carriage? But they were at the back of the house and the rain was loud. It would have been next to impossible to hear a carriage. Besides, it would be a risky business to try to bring a carriage along the valley. She lowered her head and plied her needle again, only to jerk her head up once more when there was the unmistakable sound of the knocker banging against the front door.

"Why, who can be visiting on a day like today?" Lady Hayes said, brightening considerably. She threaded her needle through her own work, set it aside, and rose to her feet just before the maid opened the sitting room door.

"The Earl of Haverford, ma'am," she said and stood aside.

There was no time for any reaction. He strode into the sitting room on the girl's heels. He looked tall, elegant, virile, and coldly angry, Moira thought, sucking in her breath and holding it.

"Lady Hayes?" He clicked his booted heels together and made her a stiff bow. "Miss Hayes?"

Her mother looked quite startled, Moira saw. "Why, Lord Haverford," she said, "this is a dreadful afternoon on which to be out, though we are delighted to see you, of course. Please have a seat."

"Thank you, ma'am," he said. "Perhaps you would allow me to have a few moments alone with Miss Hayes. Either here or in another room."

Lady Hayes looked even more bewildered. "With my daughter, sir?" she said. "Alone?"

But Moira had got to her feet. "It is quite all right, Mama," she said. "I will take his lordship into Papa's book room."

She did not give her mother a chance to protest but moved swiftly across the room to the door, her skirts brushing against the Earl of Haverford as she passed. But he was before her to the door. He opened it for her.

"Thank you, ma'am," he said to her mother before following Moira across the hall to the book room where her father had spent much of his time while he lived. "I do not anticipate keeping her long away from you."

Moira hurried into the book room, leaving the door open behind her, and took up her stand before the window. She could scarcely see the grove of trees that always made such a pleasant walk on a warm day. The door clicked shut behind her and for a few seconds there was an almost unbearable silence.

"I understand" — his voice was icily cold and almost frighteningly quiet — "that you make no plea for my help."

She drew breath slowly. "No," she said.

"But you thought I had a right to know," he said.

"Yes."

"I must thank you for your thoughtfulness," he said.

She licked her lips. She did not know where he was going with this conversation.

"A man *does* like to know when his bastard is within six months of being born," he said.

One hand clenched about the edge of the

windowsill. "You will not use that word in my hearing," she said.

"Oh, will I not?" he said. His voice was ominously pleasant. "What, then? A by-blow? You doubtless find that word equally offensive. A love child, then? But he will hardly be that, will he? It was not a love encounter in which he was begotten."

It was an unexpectedly hurtful remark. "No," she said. "I have long been aware that you are incapable of love. And there was not even a pretense of it on that night."

"Why the *devil*," he asked, and for the first time he allowed some of his anger into his voice, "did you lie to me, Moira?"

"I did not —" she began, but it was pointless to add lie upon lie.

"I know why you did it."

She gripped the windowsill with both hands and only just stopped herself from jumping with alarm. His voice had come from just behind her shoulder.

"It was because I told you quite categorically at the Tawmouth assembly that you would marry me if there was a child. It was because I directed you to send for me without delay if you found yourself with child. It was because you would do anything in the world to defy me."

"Yes." Her temper was up and, unwise at

it was with him standing so close, she spun to face him. "I have disliked and despised you for many years, *my lord.* And if hatred became muted over the years, it has flared back into existence during the past four months. The thought of being in any way dependent upon you is abhorrent to me. The thought of doing anything merely because you have said I must is — is . . ."

"Abhorrent to you?" he suggested, his eyebrows raised. "Has your eloquence deserted you, Moira? A pity. You were doing remarkably well. And so your stubbornness and your childishness have put us both into a deeply embarrassing predicament. The truth cannot be hidden now, you know."

She laughed rather harshly.

"And so our child will always have the stigma of near-illegitimacy hanging over his head," he said.

"Complete illegitimacy," she said, knowing how foolish she was to give in even now to the temptation to defy him. "He or she will be illegitimate. I do not care. I —"

"Stop being childish," he said so coldly that she was left standing with her mouth open for a moment. "We will be married tomorrow morning."

"Never," she said, knowing it was an argument she could not — and really did not want to — win. Rationality always seemed to desert her when she was confronted with Kenneth. All she could feel was a consuming hatred. "The banns —"

"I have brought a special license with me, of course," he said. "We will marry tomorrow. You will reconcile your mind to it, Moira. Somehow you will learn to control your abhorrence of me. It will not be insurmountably difficult, perhaps. I cannot imagine that I will wish to be much in your company. And you will learn to be obedient to me. That will not be as dreadful as it doubtless sounds. I will be sure to remember that you are my wife and not one of the men of my regiment. I suggest we return to your mother. Does she know?"

"No," she said. "And not tomorrow. It is too soon. I need time."

"Time," he said coldly, "is something you do not have, Moira. You have already allowed far too much of it to pass. You will be the Countess of Haverford by this time tomorrow. You will be living at Dunbarton. I suggest that you inform your maid so that she may —"

But she heard no more. Ice came knifing through her nostrils and a high-pitched bell shrieked in her ears and the carpet beneath her feet came rushing at her face.

"Just keep your head down," a voice was saying to her from some distance away, a voice that was quietly assured, a voice she instinctively trusted, "and allow the blood to flow back into it. Breathe deeply." A firm, reassuring hand was against the back of her head. She was sitting down. The bell that had been ringing without ceasing was growing fainter, to be replaced by a slight fuzziness. Her cold, clammy hands were finding comfort in one large warm one.

Consciousness was returning. She had fainted. She was in the book room — with the Earl of Haverford. She breathed deeply and evenly and kept her head down almost on her knees and her eyes closed.

He was down on one knee in front of the chair on which he had placed her, his one hand pressing her head downward, his other holding both of hers, trying to warm them. He was filled with alarm and shame. He had quelled his first instinct, which had been to pull the door open and call for Lady Hayes. Lady Hayes did not know, Moira had just said. There were perhaps less alarming ways for her to find out.

"Are you going to be all right?" he asked. "Shall I send for your mother?"

"No," she said faintly. He understood that

it was his second question she answered.

He had noticed from his first sight of her how ill she looked. She had looked thin, even slightly stooped. Her hair beneath her cap had lost its luster. Her face had been more than pale — it had been tinged with gray. Even her lips had been quite bloodless. She had looked haggard, unlovely, older than her years. Worse even than she had looked at the Trevellases'.

Somehow, the sight of her thus had only inflamed the fury that had driven him homeward with scarcely a stop for either food or rest. She had looked the epitome of the suffering woman abandoned by her man. He had felt little short of murderous. How dared she do this to him.

She was ill. Perhaps she had brought it on herself by harboring secrets unnecessarily, by stubbornly refusing to send for him so that he might release her from at least one major burden. But she was unmistakably ill. It had not been the time to rip up at her. She must be badly in need of a shoulder to lean upon, though he knew that in a thousand years she would not admit it.

She was ill. She was bearing his child, and she was ill.

He took his hand from her head and chafed her hands with both of his. "You looked unwell at the assembly," he said. "You looked unwell when we met in the valley. You looked downright ill at Mr. Trevellas's. You looked ill when I arrived this afternoon, before we came in here to talk. Have you been constantly ill?"

"It comes with the condition, I believe," she said.

"I think not." He touched the back of one hand to her cheek. It was still unnaturally cool. "I will have the physician — Ryder, is it? — examine you at Dunbarton the day after tomorrow. He had a reputable practice in London before coming here, I believe. If we have no proper satisfaction from him, I will take you to London and have you see a physician there. This will not do, Moira. You should have sought help sooner." *Don't scold her,* he told himself.

"I do not need help." She lifted her head, though she directed her eyes at their hands rather than at his face. "I am having a child. It is something I have to do alone."

"Without the help of your mother or of a physician or of your child's father," he said, struggling against a return of anger. "Independence of spirit is to be commended, even in a woman. Stubbornness of will is not. Tomorrow you will be giving up much of your independence. You would do well to

281

reconcile yourself to giving up your stubbornness too, if you hope for any compatibility in our marriage."

"I have no choice about marrying you, Kenneth," she said, raising her eyes to his at last. "Of course I do not. But be very clear on one point. I will marry you because I must. I do not expect to find that we are or can become compatible. I shall make no effort to fit my ways to yours. I despise you and your ways."

He fought anger and was surprised by the realization that he felt as much hurt as angry. They had a mutual problem, one that could be solved in only one way. Did she hate him so much that she would court lifelong unhappiness for herself rather than try to make the best of a bad situation?

"You do not know either me or my ways, Moira," he said. "We had a dozen or so encounters when we were very young. We had no dealings at all for longer than eight years. We were not even living in the same country. In the four months since my return, we have had a few brief encounters and the unfortunately more lengthy one in the hermit's hut. We do not know each other at all. Yet tomorrow we will become man and wife. Can we not agree to make tomorrow a start of something wholly new? Can we not make an effort at least to tolerate and respect each other?"

She seemed to be considering the question. "No," she said finally. "I cannot so easily forget the past."

He released her hands and got to his feet. "Perhaps you are more honest than I am," he said. "I cannot so easily forget, either, that you stood in the hollow on the cliff top one night and held a pistol pointed at my heart and told me to go off home and mind my own business when you had kissed me in that same hollow just the day before and smiled when I told you I loved you."

"I should have laughed rather than smiled," she said, "at hearing such a lie."

He strode over to the door and pulled it open. But there was no one in the hallway. He strode across it and tapped on the door of the sitting room where he had been received earlier. Lady Hayes's voice bade him enter.

"If you would be so good as to step across to the book room, ma'am," he said with a bow.

She looked as surprised now as she had earlier, but she came without further prompting and preceded him back across the hall.

"Moira?" she said, hurrying inside. "What

283

is the matter? Have you taken another turn? She has been in poor health for most of the winter, my lord," she explained, turning her head toward where he stood just inside the door, his hands clasped at his back. "I do hope —"

"Miss Hayes has just consented to marry me tomorrow morning, ma'am," he said.

She looked at him in blank amazement.

"I am more than three months with child, Mama," Moira said, looking into her mother's widening eyes. "I did not spend the night of the Christmas ball at Dunbarton Hall. I foolishly tried to walk home through the storm. Lord Haverford came after me and found me taking shelter in the baptistry. We were forced to spend the rest of the night together there."

Lady Hayes was fortunately close to a chair. She sat hurriedly down on it. She looked at Kenneth and her lips thinned.

"Lord Haverford offered me marriage the very next morning," Moira said quickly. It was not strictly true, of course. She had not allowed him to make the offer. "He offered several times after that. He even tried to insist. I would not have him. I wrote to him the same morning I wrote to Sir Edwin. But I found when I took the letter to Dunbarton that he had left for Kent a few hours before.

He came as soon as it had been sent on to him. None of this is his fault."

He half smiled. Moira was defending him?

"I should, ma'am," he said, "have spoken to you when I escorted Miss Hayes home that morning. I should have written to Sir Edwin Baillie myself that same morning. A great deal of anguish would have been avoided if I had not made grave errors of judgment. I blame myself. But there is little to be gained now from castigating myself for past actions or inaction. I am in possession of a special license and Miss Hayes and I will be married tomorrow. The day after, I will see to it that she is properly attended by a physician."

Lady Hayes had both hands to her cheeks. "I can only be thankful, my lord," she said, "that neither your father nor my husband lived to see this day." She turned her head to look at her daughter. "Moira, why did you not tell me? Oh, why did you not *tell* me?"

"I suppose," Moira said, "I thought that if only I did not speak of it or even think of it, the whole nasty nightmare would go away. It seems I have been nothing but foolish since Christmas." She looked at Kenneth. "It will never go away, of course. It is with me for a lifetime."

He strode in the direction of the bellpull. "With your permission, ma'am," he said, "I will summon your maid. I believe both you and Moira would be better for a cup of tea."

"Moira?" Lady Hayes said, and frowned.

She had not failed to notice the familiarity with which he had referred to her daughter. Well, it did not matter now. Miss Moira Hayes would be his wife within one day. Tomorrow she would be Moira Woodfall, Countess of Haverford — for whom the nightmare of the present was to last a lifetime.

He jerked grimly on the bell rope.

The church in Tawmouth was almost empty when the Earl of Haverford married Miss Moira Hayes. Apart from the two principals and the Reverend Finley-Evans, the only people in attendance were Lady Hayes, Mrs. Finley-Evans, a hastily summoned Harriet Lincoln with Mr. Lincoln, and his lordship's steward.

It was nothing like the wedding she had dreamed of in the long-ago days of her youth, Moira thought. Nothing like it in more ways than the absence of guests. There was no groom to be gazed at adoringly. Only Kenneth. He looked knee-weakeningly handsome, of course, dressed as immaculately as if he were on his way to court to make his bow to the king — or to the prince regent. He was wearing shades of pale blue and white, which looked quite glorious with his blond hair. He looked like the prince of fairy tales. Although she wore a favorite white gown she had almost chosen to wear to the Dunbarton ball at Christmas, she knew she was not by any means in good looks. His own handsome appearance served only to make her feel uglier.

And she felt so very ill that for a few minutes after she had got out of bed in the morning she had considered sending a message to inform him that she must postpone the wedding. It had not been possible, of course. As he had pointed out and as she had realized for herself, she had allowed far too much time to pass as it was. But she felt ill in almost every possible way: Her head ached; she felt faint and nauseated; she was cold and lethargic. And she hated her symptoms, her self-pity. She wanted to break loose and run and run and run. She wanted an impossibility. Perhaps, she thought with grim humor, she was indulging a death wish.

It was not the wedding any woman would have dreamed of. And yet it was startlingly real. It was not, after all, just a nasty necessity that had to be lived through in order that decency be restored to her life. It was a wedding. It was something that was joining her fate to Kenneth's for the rest of their lives. Perhaps because the ceremony was a physical ordeal for her, it also took on a stark reality. She listened to every word the Reverend Finley-Evans spoke and every word seemed something new, as if she had never heard the wedding service before. She listened to Kenneth's voice, low and pleasant and very masculine, and heard the words he spoke. He told her he worshiped her with his body. She listened to her own voice and what it said. She promised to love him and to obey him. She felt the shining gold ring surprisingly warm against her finger. She watched him ease it over her knuckle and slide it into place. She heard a hastily suppressed sob behind her: Mama? Harriet? She felt his kiss, warm, firm, his lips ever so slightly parted, his breath warm on her cheek.

Kenneth. She looked into his eyes as he lifted his head. They looked steadily back but told her nothing. They were absent of all expression. *Kenneth. I loved you so very much. You were every dream I ever dreamed. You were every breath I breathed.*

"Please," he murmured, leaning closer as

the Reverend Finley-Evans began to speak again, "stop yourself from crying. Don't do this to me."

He had misunderstood. He thought that her tears were ones of revulsion. They were tears of regret for youthful dreams and ideals. Once, she had believed in heroes and in perfection and in romantic love — all of them embodied in Kenneth. When she had woken up to reality, everything had come crashing down. If she had not loved him, she thought now, perhaps she would never have hated him either.

But she could not imagine reacting to Kenneth without passion of some sort. She could never be simply indifferent to him — unfortunately.

Her mother hugged her and kissed her; Harriet and Mrs. Finley-Evans, both looking puzzled and curious, kissed her cheek; the Reverend Finley-Evans, Mr. Lincoln, and Dunbarton's Mr. Watkins bowed to her and kissed her hand. And suddenly and strangely, anticlimactically, it was all over. She was leaving the church on her husband's arm, and he was handing her into his carriage. Everyone else was to come to Dunbarton for breakfast in two other carriages.

It felt even more real when they were

alone together, sitting side by side, not quite touching, looking out of opposite windows of the carriage.

"If you are feeling too ill to sit through breakfast," he said as his carriage labored up the steep hill beyond the village, "you must retire to your rooms. If you feel able to sit with our guests, I would be grateful if you would force a smile or two."

"Yes," she said, "I will smile."

"At the very least," he said, "try not to weep."

"I shall smile," she said. "It is your first command to me, my lord, and I will obey it."

"Sarcasm is unnecessary," he said.

She laughed softly and blinked her eyes determinedly, her head turned away from him. He would never again see her tears. He would never again see her vulnerable.

Kenneth. She felt a fiercely nostalgic longing for the man she had loved — just as if he were not the same man as the one who sat beside her now, his shoulder almost touching her own. Her husband. Father of the child she carried inside her.

15

The drawing room was too large for two people, Kenneth decided. In future they would have to find some other, smaller room in which to spend their evenings except when they were entertaining. The coved and painted and gilded ceiling, the massive doorframes, the marble fireplace, and the huge, framed paintings all succeeded in dwarfing his wife as she sat near the fire, her head bent to her embroidery.

His wife! Only now, on the evening of his wedding day, with their guests gone, did he have the leisure to comprehend the reality of the past week — not even a week. Despite his earlier resolve to make Dunbarton his home, he had been intending after all to stay in London to enjoy the Season with Nat and Eden. He had been quite prepared to participate to the full in all the frivolities and excesses and debaucheries that town had to offer.

Being at Dunbarton, near Penwith, near her, had become insupportable to him. He had hated her and loved her. He had resented her and wanted her. He had despised her and admired her. At the time, perhaps, he had not recognized the duality of his feelings. But he had felt his helplessness. She had rejected him. He now knew that she had even gone to the lengths of lying to him in order to be rid of him.

She looked up from her embroidery and met his eyes across the room. Her hand, holding the needle and silken thread, remained poised above her work. Pale and out of looks as she was, there was still a natural grace about her. But she was thin. Her cheeks were hollow. The evening dress into which she had changed for dinner hung loosely on her. After more than three months, should not the opposite be happening?

They had looked at each other long enough in silence. "You are tired," he said. "Shall I escort you to your room?"

"Not yet," she said.

She had been in a state of near-collapse by the time her mother, the last of their guests, had left. But she had refused to miss dinner — though scarcely a mouthful of food had passed her lips — and she had

292

insisted on coming to the drawing room afterward only because he had suggested both times that she retire to her own apartments, he suspected. Had he told her, in a brisk tone of command, that he expected her to bear him company at dinner, she would probably have stayed upstairs and dared him to go to fetch her down.

"What are you doing?" she asked.

He looked down at the paper on the desktop before him and at the quill pen he held in his hand. "I am writing to my mother," he said, "and to my sister."

She had lowered her needle though she was not stitching. "They will be thrilled," she said.

"Their feelings are immaterial," he said. "You are my wife. We are to have a child in less than six months' time. They will have no choice but to accept those facts cheerfully."

"Cheerfully." She smiled. "They almost had an apoplexy apiece when they expected that I would be spending one night here after the Christmas ball."

"You exaggerate," he said. "Had they been consulted on the matter, they would have been pleased to insist that you stay rather than endanger yourself by returning home."

She continued to smile. "I decided to

endanger myself, Kenneth," she said, "after overhearing each of them in turn express to you her objection to my continued presence at Dunbarton."

Was it possible? He supposed it must be if she said it. They had both been outraged, after all. *That* was why she had so recklessly walked off into the storm.

"I beg your pardon," he said. "Doubtless they did not intend you to hear."

"Eavesdroppers rarely hear good of themselves," she said. "Or so it is said. When they read your letters and make some calculations, perhaps they will wish they had urged me to stay. One night at Dunbarton and they would have been rid of me forever."

"Their wishes are of no significance," he said. "And you may rest assured that they will behave toward you with perfect good breeding."

She smiled at him once more before plying her needle again. He watched her for a few minutes before returning his attention to his difficult letter. They would be horrified, of course: at the identity of his bride, at the manner of his wedding, at the circumstances that had dictated its haste. But they would accept her. By God, they would, if they expected to have any further dealings with him.

He finished the first letter and began the second before looking up again. When he did, she was sitting with her embroidery in her lap and her eyes closed.

"What is it?" He got to his feet and hurried toward her.

"Nothing." She picked up her needle.

"Put your work away," he said. "I am taking you to bed."

"Another command?" she asked.

He gritted his teeth. "If you wish," he said. "If you choose to make this marriage intolerable to both yourself and me by forcing me to issue commands and to insist upon obedience to them, then so be it. If you wish to make some sort of game of our marriage in which I am always the oppressor and you the victim, then I cannot stop you. But at this moment you are tired and unwell and need to be in your bed. I am going to take you there. You may stand and take my arm if you will. If you will not, I shall lift you from your chair and carry you upstairs. I leave you a choice, you see."

She took her time about threading her needle through the cloth and folding it with the silks inside and setting it aside before getting to her feet. She leaned so heavily on his arm as he led her slowly upstairs that he knew she must be weary indeed.

"I will send for Ryder tomorrow morning," he said. "We will see what he can do for you, Moira. You cannot go on like this."

She would not even argue with the truth of his final statement. Her head slumped sideways against his shoulder, alarming him. He sat her down on a chair in her dressing room, pulled the bell rope to summon her maid, and went down on his haunches before her chair to take her hands in his.

"I have done this to you," he said. "Men escape lightly in such matters, do they not? But I will take every burden except this off your shoulders, Moira. I will try to be a good husband. Perhaps we can learn to rub along well enough together if we try."

"Perhaps." Her eyes were on his. It was the first concession she had made.

He raised her hands one at a time to his lips and then released them and got to his feet as her maid arrived.

"Good night," he said to his wife. He went back downstairs to finish the letter to Helen, but he did not stay up late. He undressed in his dressing room, donned a dressing robe over his nightshirt, and proceeded to stand at the window of his darkened bedchamber well into the night.

It was not the sort of wedding night a man dreamed of. It was not the sort of *marriage* a man dreamed of. And yet it was real enough. And one thing had been alarmingly clear to him during his wedding. As he had spoken his part of the marriage service, he had meant every word. He had heard it said that the nuptial service was a pious farce, that bride and groom were forced to utter solemn and ridiculous vows that neither had any intention whatsoever of honoring. He feared that he would have no choice but to honor his.

It was not a happy thought. He felt that he had doomed himself today to perpetual unhappiness.

And yet at one time happiness and Moira had seemed synonymous terms. She had seemed made for happiness: lithe and bursting with health and energy and high spirits. She had scorned the feud that should have kept them apart and the social restrictions that should have kept her always within view of a chaperone. She had scorned the rules of ladylike propriety that would have kept her hair pinned up and her shoes and stockings on her feet and her pace at a sedate walk. He could see her now running across the hill above the waterfall, his hat in her hands, while he chased after her to retrieve it, and twirling about on the beach, her arms outstretched, her face turned up to the sun, and sitting in the hollow on the cliff top, hugging her knees, gazing out to sea, wondering what life in other countries must be like. Talking, smiling, laughing — so often laughing. And kissing him with warm ardor and smiling at his protestations of love.

It was hard — almost impossible — to believe that she was the same woman as the one he had left sitting on a chair in the dressing room next to his own. Except that the soreness about his heart told him that she was indeed the same and that he was responsible for the differences.

"Moira," he whispered, but the sound of his own voice startled and somewhat embarrassed him. He closed his eyes and set his forehead against the glass of the window.

It was a strange room in a strange house — large, high-ceilinged, warm. The bed was large and comfortable. Everything was far superior to her room at home — at what had been her home. But she could not sleep.

She wondered where he was, where his own rooms were. Close to her own? As far away as they could be?

She had been perfectly horrid all day. She had not quite understood herself. He had made an effort to be civil, even amiable. She had twisted everything, thwarted him at every turn. She had behaved like a spoiled child. She had not seemed able to stop herself. But they were married. She could not continue like this for the rest of their lives.

She touched her thumb to the smooth gold ring on her finger. They were *married* — she and Kenneth. She had reached the summit of her girlhood dreams. He was surely the most handsome man in the whole world, she had once thought — and still thought.

Tomorrow she must try to do better. Tomorrow she must be civil. No marriage could be so bad that a little effort at civility could not make it bearable, unless the man was abusive or had some uncontrollable addiction. Neither applied to this marriage. Tomorrow she would try.

She could not sleep. The room tilted beyond her closed eyelids, bringing on the too-familiar nausea; her head pounded, and the muscles in her abdomen were clenching involuntarily and causing discomfort and even pain. She wondered if her confinement would take a more normal course now that all the anxiety and uncertainty and secrecy and guilt were at an end. She wondered if Mr. Ryder would be able to suggest something to make her feel well again. It would be so *embarrassing* to have to admit the truth to Mr. Ryder, to have him examine her. She wondered if Harriet had suspected the truth — and Mrs. Finley-Evans. She did not know how they could not have done so. She was so very tired. She would sleep for a week if she could but nod off, she was sure.

And then she was waking up, clawing her way out of a nightmare that had left her hot and sweating, gasping her way free of claws that had clamped onto her and were knifing into her flesh. She lay staring at the canopy over her bed, breathing loudly through her mouth. And she knew that only a part of what had happened had been a dream. She lay very still, closed her eyes, tried to relax. She had almost succeeded before it happened again.

There was a bell rope beside her bed. There was another in her dressing room. She forgot about both. She stumbled barefoot to the door of her bedchamber and flung it open. But she did not know where he was. The house was strange. Everything was strange.

"Kenneth," she said. She filled her lungs with air. *"Kenneth!"*

A door opened somewhere close as she clung to the doorframe, and then two hands were on her arms, drawing her to rest against the silken warmth of a night robe. She buried her face against him and tried to draw sanity from him.

"What is it?" he was asking her. "What is wrong?"

"I do not know," she said. But it was starting to happen again and she clawed at him, moaning as she did so. "Kenneth —"

"My God." He had swept her up into his arms and was setting her back down on the bed. But she clung to his neck, in a panic.

"Don't leave me," she begged him. "Please. Please."

He wrapped his arms about her, kept his head close to hers, talked to her. "Moira," he said over and over again. "My love. Moira."

He must have pulled on the bell rope. There was someone else in the room, someone with a candle. He was instructing whoever it was to send for the doctor immediately and to inform him that it was an extreme emergency. He was using the voice he must have used on the battlefield, she thought. And then the pain gripped her again.

She did not know how long a time passed before Mr. Ryder came. But she knew what was happening long before he arrived. There was the waking nightmare of recurring and tearing pain without the sustaining expectation of joy waiting at the end of it all. Her maid was in her room. So was the housekeeper. So was *he,* talking to her, smoothing his hand over her head, bathing her face with a cool cloth. Eventually, she heard another man's voice — Mr. Ryder's — telling him to leave, but he did not go.

He did not go until it was all over and she had heard Mr. Ryder tell him — she did not think he had intended her to hear — that he did not believe her ladyship's life was in danger. But he would return in the morning, early.

"Moira?" Kenneth's voice. She opened her eyes. "Your maid will stay here with you. She will come for me if you have need of me. You must not hesitate to ask. Sleep now. Ryder has given you a draught that will help you." His face was a cold, impassive mask.

She closed her eyes again. She heard someone laugh very weakly. "What a wonderful irony," someone said — was it her? "One day too late."

"Sleep," he said, and the coldness was in his voice, too, now.

He felt deeply bereaved and was surprised by the feeling. Apart from the fact that Moira's pregnancy had forced them into

302

marriage and that her illness resulting from her condition had caused him concern, he had not had a chance really to think about a child being born — his child. A person. A part of himself and her. A son or a daughter. Now there was to be no child, and he grieved for his own loss — and for Moira's.

Especially for Moira's. And he still feared for her health, for her life. When he went back into her bedchamber early in the morning after dressing, she was lying still and quiet on the bed, turned onto her side facing away from him. But he could see when he walked closer that her eyes were open. She was staring straight ahead. He raised his eyebrows at her maid, and the girl bobbed a curtsy and left the room.

"Have you slept at all?" he asked. He clasped his hands at his back. He could not bring himself to touch her this morning.

"I suppose so," she said after a lengthy silence.

"You will feel better after you have rested for a few days," he said. He could hear the stiffness of his own voice. "There will be other chances for — for children."

He closed his eyes. What stupid, *stupid* things to say. Why had he not simply grieved with her? But he felt he had no right to his grief. He had done none of the suffering that had led to the miscarriage of his child. All he had done was keep her warm on a cold night. She would not appreciate his trying to share her grief.

"If this child had only had the good sense to die one day sooner," she said, her voice a dull monotone, "we would not find ourselves this morning facing a life sentence, my lord."

The words were more brutal than any whip could be. He winced from the pain. He stood where he was, trying to think of something to say. There was nothing. No possible words to be spoken.

"Yes, I will feel better after a few days," she said. "How could I not? I am the Countess of Haverford, mistress of Dunbarton Hall. Who would have expected it of a mere baronet's daughter? And a Hayes into the bargain?"

"We will make the best of it," he said. "There is nothing else for us to do. People marry all the time for reasons that have nothing to do with love or affection. Women miscarry. Children die. People live on. They get on with their lives. They make the best of them." He tried desperately to convince himself with his own words. *How* did people get on with lives that had been dragged down into the deepest gloom?

But she had turned over on the bed and was gazing up at him with hostile eyes. "Women miscarry," she said. "I do not *care* that women miscarry. *I* have miscarried. I do not *care* that children die. *My* child has died. It cannot possibly matter after only three months, of course. It was not a real baby. It was nothing at all. Of course I must just get on with my life. Of course I must make the best of it. How foolish of me to be very slightly despondent this morning."

He opened and closed his hands behind his back. "Moira —" he said.

"Get out of here," she said. "If there is any decency in you, get out of here. The fact that it was *your* child should perhaps have made it abhorrent to me. But it could not help its paternity. I *loved* my child."

"Moira —" He could feel his control slipping. He blinked his eyes.

"Get out of my sight," she said. "You are cold, cold to the very center of your heart. You always have been. I wish I might never have to set eyes on you again. Oh, how I wish it."

Cold through to the center of his heart, he stood looking at her; then he turned on his heel and strode from the room. He closed the door quietly behind him, spread both hands over his face, and gasped for breath. Last night's ordeal had made her distraught, he thought. He must not believe that she would speak thus or think thus once she had had time to recover her health and her spirits. He should not have gone to her so early. He should have waited for the doctor's arrival. He should have — oh, devil take it, he should have chosen his words with far greater care.

But no words he might have spoken would have comforted her. She was seething with a hatred of him that was very real, even if it seemed somewhat in excess of the facts. There seemed now no way of making anything of their marriage. She had consented to it with the greatest reluctance only because of her pregnancy. And now, that pregnancy had been terminated less than twenty-four hours after the wedding. An irony indeed, as she had observed last night. The reason for the marriage — at least in her eyes — had been taken away, but the marriage had been solemnized and was quite indissoluble.

He strode back into his dressing room to don outdoor clothes, and within a few minutes was on his way, on foot, toward the cliffs, an exuberant Nelson bounding on ahead of him. He had not even waited for the doctor's visit, he realized half an hour later.

Moira was in the small, cozy sitting room that was part of her own apartments, reclining on a chaise longue. She was neither reading nor sewing. She had not done much of either during the past week. But her lethargy was beginning to be irksome to her. She doubted she would be able to follow the doctor's orders to remain in her own rooms for another week. She was not supposed to go outside for a whole month. She would be out long before that.

Her mother had left an hour ago, Harriet just five minutes ago. Poor Harriet. She had accepted at least outwardly the myth that Moira's chill, which had lasted from Christmas almost to the present time, had finally culminated the day after her wedding in a serious but short illness, from which she was finally recuperating. The truth had not been spoken, yet Moira was sure Harriet knew it but could not understand how it could possibly be. Other ladies who had called on her during the past two days had looked puzzled and curious but had been too polite to pose any probing questions about either her marriage so soon after the ending of her betrothal to Sir Edwin or her illness. Conversation in the drawing rooms of Tawmouth must be lively indeed these days, Moira thought ruefully.

She had scarcely seen her husband all week. Ever since the morning after her wedding — and her miscarriage — he had appeared only once a day at her sitting room door to inquire after her health, to make his bow to her, and to take his leave.

She tried not to think about her husband or about her marriage — or about her miscarriage. But it was hard not to think.

Moira. My love. Don't die. I'll not let you die. My love. Ah, my love. Please, please don't die. Don't leave me. Ah, Moira. My love.

She had heard it all that night — or thought she had. She had seen anguish in his ashen face, even tears — or thought she had.

It was strange how the mind and the memory could play tricks on one. It was the way she had preserved her sanity, perhaps. The fact that she was losing her baby had been beyond denial. And so she had comforted herself with imaginary words, imaginary looks. Could she have imagined such things?

If she had not, then he had not meant them. Against all reason, against her better judgment, against her very heart, she had waited for him to come back, to look at her that way again, to say some of those words again. She had waited to feel his hand on her head again. She had waited for him to say something about their lost baby. Something to comfort her and dull the raw pain of grief.

There will be other chances for children. His voice stiff and cold, as if accusing her of making a fuss over nothing at all. *Women miscarry. Children die. People live on.*

She had wanted to *love* him again. She realized it now, to her shame. At her wedding she had wanted to love him. She had resisted the need for the rest of the day — she understood now that was why she had been so horrid to him. But she had wanted to be convinced. Before he had left her dressing room, she had finally admitted that perhaps they could make something of this marriage. And then, somehow, despite all the horror of her miscarriage . . .

She had wanted to love him.

She could only hate him now with a renewed passion. Unfeeling man. How could he be so very callous?

There was a knock at her dressing room door, a knock she had come to recognize. He never walked into her room. She must give him that, she supposed.

"Come in," she called.

He bowed to her, his face cold and impassive. "How do you do today?" he asked.

"Well, thank you," she said.

"The doctor seems to believe you are out of all danger," he said. "You are looking better. I must ask you a question, ma'am." He had not used her name for a week.

She raised her eyebrows.

"A week ago," he said, "you told me that you wished you need never see me again. You were not quite yourself at the time, perhaps. Do you still feel as you did then? Do you still wish it?"

Kenneth. Had life really brought them to this moment? Why had he come back to Dunbarton? Why — ? Pointless questions, pointless thoughts.

"Yes, I do," she said.

He made her another bow, more elegant, more formal than the last. "Then you shall have your wish, ma'am," he said. "I shall leave for London tomorrow morning early. I will not disturb you before I leave. My steward will know where I may be reached at any time you have need of me. Goodbye."

It was an unreal moment. She had married a week ago. She had been more than three months with child. Now she had no child — and no husband. Yet she was locked forever into a barren marriage.

"Good-bye, my lord," she said.

She stood staring at the door for a long time after it had closed behind him.

16

"Brighton for me, I do believe," Lord Pelham said. "Prinny and all the fashionable world will be there. One cannot help remembering that this time last year we were about to face the Battle of Waterloo. There is much of life still to be celebrated in a world that is finally at peace. I intend to celebrate."

"I will go home, perhaps," Mr. Gascoigne said. "My father has been ailing, and there comes a time . . ." He shrugged.

They were riding in Hyde Park quite early one morning in late May. They were discussing what they would do when the Season was over.

"And you, Ken?" Lord Pelham asked.

"Me?" Kenneth laughed. "Sorry, I was woolgathering. Or rather I was admiring the ankles of the maidservant walking the dogs over there. No, you may not go either to greet them or to terrorize them, Nelson.

There is no point in gazing at me so soulfully. What will I do? Follow the fashionable world to Brighton with Eden, I suppose. Or go to Paris, perhaps. Yes, I fancy Paris — or Vienna or Rome. Even America. The world is out there to be enjoyed, and there is insufficient time, alas, to enjoy it all even during a lifetime."

"You will not be, ah, going home?" Mr. Gascoigne asked.

"Home?" Kenneth laughed again. "Not a chance, Nat. There are more congenial things to do than incarcerate myself in Cornwall. Pursue the delectable Miss Wilcox, for example. Did you know that when she danced the supper dance with me at Pickard's last evening she broke a commitment to dance it with Pickard's eldest? I thought for one moment that he was about to slap a glove in my face. She will be in Brighton for the summer — a definite argument against Paris, would you not agree? I could keep Paris for the autumn, of course."

"The woman is an incurable flirt," Lord Pelham said, "and of questionable character, Ken."

"Else she would scarcely be dangling after me, would she?" his friend said. "Jealous, are you, Eden?"

"I would have thought you would wish to

be at least in England during the autumn, Ken," Mr. Gascoigne said. "Lady Hav—"

"You thought wrongly." Kenneth spurred his horse into a canter and looked about at the lawns and trees, at the handful of other riders, at the few pedestrians. Nelson raced joyfully at his side. He was enjoying himself enormously. There were more entertainments to choose among in London than there were hours in the day. There were enough gentlemen to talk with, enough ladies to flirt with that one had no time left in which to think or to brood. Whenever he did find himself alone, it was usually so late at night or so early in the morning that he fell immediately into an exhausted sleep.

His mother had been in town for the past few weeks, as had Helen and Ainsleigh. He had informed them of his marriage but had made no explanation either of the event itself or of the fact that he was living separate from his wife. He had not sent the letters he had written on his wedding day. To their questions of shock and outrage he had merely answered that he had nothing further to add but that if they found themselves with anything else insulting to say about the new Countess of Haverford, perhaps they would be well advised to say it out of his hearing.

To Nat and Rex and Eden he had merely announced his marriage. Being close friends of his, they had understood instinctively, it seemed, that he would say no more on the subject and had steered clear of it — almost. There were, of course, the occasional prompts and hints as there had been a few minutes ago.

He did not know what he would do during the summer, Kenneth thought. But he must decide soon. There was only a little longer than a month of the Season left, and then London would be empty of society. The world was his for the traveling and enjoying — an exhilarating thought. There was only one place on earth he could not go, but it was a quiet backwater of a place that could excite no one's interest beyond a fleeting moment of admiration for its beauties.

It was a place that haunted him night and day.

She had recovered her health, Watkins had informed him. She had not written to him herself. But then, neither had he written to her.

A week ago you told me that you wished you need never see me again. Do you still wish it?

Yes, I do.

Eden and Nat were chuckling over something.

"One somehow cannot imagine Rex setting up a nursery," Mr. Gascoigne said. "But he looked mightily pleased with himself when explaining that Brighton was not the best place for Lady Rawleigh's health and that he would be taking her home at the end of June. His meaning could not have been clearer."

"We are in grave danger of becoming very ordinary family men, Nat," Lord Pelham said. "Two out of four. Are we two going to fight on alone to preserve the freedom that had us all rejoicing less than a year ago? While the other two are increasing the population and accomplishing something as dull and respectable as securing their lines?"

"You have already decided that both will be boys, then?" Mr. Gascoigne said. "Ken, what —"

But Kenneth spurred his horse into a gallop and rode on ahead of them.

It was much later the same day that everything came finally into the open. Mr. Gascoigne and the Earl of Haverford had shared a carriage to a ball — their friend had escorted an aunt and a cousin in his own carriage — and agreed on the way home that they would not look for any further entertainment that night. But Mr. Gascoigne had accepted the invitation to come inside the Earl of Haverford's house on Grosvenor Square for a drink before walking home.

"Miss Wilcox really has set her cap for you," he said, seating himself, glass in hand. "She danced three sets with you. Was I mistaken or did *she* ask *you* the third time?"

"Can I help it if I am irresistible?" Kenneth asked with a grin.

"She wants to bed you," Mr. Gascoigne said. "It is common knowledge that you would not be the first, Ken. But it might be well to remember that fast though she be, she is also a lady of the *ton* and there might be some awkwardness."

"Yes, Mother." Kenneth raised his glass — and one eyebrow.

"It would not be wise," Mr. Gascoigne said.

"But I can hardly be trapped into marriage, can I?" Kenneth said.

His friend sat back in his chair and regarded him broodingly. "This is very hard to accept, Ken," he said. "You have been the gayest blade in town for the past two months. You have made Ede and me look and feel like a couple of maiden aunts in comparison. You have been like a keg of

317

powder waiting for a spark before exploding into a million pieces. We are worried about you. Rex too. He says that an unexpected and difficult marriage cannot be made to work if one does not keep one's bride firmly at one's side. He should know."

"Rex can mind his own damned business," Kenneth said. "So can you and Eden."

"Is she so — impossible?" Mr. Gascoigne asked.

Kenneth sat forward and set down his glass on the table beside him with an audible click. "Leave it, Nat," he said. "My wife is not for discussion."

His friend swirled the brandy in his glass and gazed down into it. "Will your son or your daughter grow up a stranger to you, then?" he asked.

Kenneth sat back again and breathed in slowly.

"You were always — wild," Mr. Gascoigne said. "We all were. But never irresponsible. It has always seemed to me that we are basically decent men and that when the time should come to settle down . . ." But he had looked up from his glass and stopped talking. He sat very still.

Kenneth was gripping the arms of his chair very tightly.

His eyes were closed. "There is to be no child, Nat," he said. "We lost the child on our wedding night." Why had he said *we*? The loss had been all hers. And it had not really been a child. She had been increasing for only a little over three months. But he realized something suddenly, something that explained Nat's stunned silence. He was weeping.

He surged to his feet and half stumbled toward the window so that he might stand with his back to the room.

"Ken," Mr. Gascoigne said after a while, "you might have told us, old chap. We might have offered some comfort."

"Why should I need comforting?" he asked. "It was conceived during a one-night encounter with a woman I did not like. I did not know of its existence until a week before my marriage. She miscarried it the very night of my marriage. I need no comforting."

"I have never seen you cry before tonight," Mr. Gascoigne said.

"And never will again, I can assure you quite fervently." He was acutely embarrassed. "Damn it. God damn it, Nat, do you not have the decency to leave?"

There was a lengthy silence. "I remember that time," Mr. Gascoigne said at last, "when I went under the surgeon's knife and was terrified I would scream or faint or otherwise disgrace myself before he ferreted out the bullet. I begged you — I swore at you — to leave, to return to the regiment. You stood there beside the table the whole time. I swore at you afterward too. I never told you how much it meant to me just to have you there. Friends share pain as well as pleasure, Ken. Tell me about her."

What was there to tell about Moira Hayes — about Moira Woodfall, Countess of Haverford? He had hardly noticed her through his childhood when she had been frequently with Sean and had been set aside to amuse herself while the two boys played and fought. She had been a thin child, dark, unpretty, uninteresting. She had been just a girl, after all. But, ah, the transformation in her and in his perception of her when he saw her again after an absence of years at school. Tall, lithe, beautiful, fascinating Moira — forbidden to him both because of the feud between their families and because she was gently born. And therefore tempting beyond his powers to resist.

He had arranged meetings with her as often as was possible — not nearly often enough. He had talked with her, laughed with her, loved her — though their physical relationship had never gone beyond hand-holding and a few relatively chaste kisses. He had declared his love for her. She, perhaps more aware of the impossibility of it all than he, had always only smiled in return. Not knowing, not being sure of her feelings had driven him to distraction. He had been intending to defy his father and hers and the whole world if necessary to marry her. He had thought life would not be possible without her.

"But your father won?" Mr. Gascoigne asked. "And hers? That is why you bought your commission, Ken?"

His friendship with Sean Hayes had deteriorated through the years of their youth until there was only enmity left. He might have excused, even if he could not condone, Sean's wild ways even though his gaming debts must have put a strain on his father's purse and his promiscuous liaisons were apt to give him the pox. But it was harder — impossible — to excuse the way he began to cheat at cards and dice to recoup some of his losses and the way he would take the favors of any woman he fancied by force if they were not freely given. Kenneth might have excused some minor dabbling in smuggling. It was no longer a major or a lucrative business in the area of Tawmouth. But

he could not excuse the way Sean had attempted to build the business by gathering
about him a band of thugs and by consort-
ing to bullying and intimidation and vio-
lence. Sean had been clever enough to keep
the center of his activities away from Tawmouth itself most of the time.

"You broke with the sister because of the
brother?" Mr. Gascoigne asked.

He had got wind of two things: first that
Sean planned a landing in the cove at Tawmouth, and second that Sean had been dallying with Helen's affections. Moira herself
had told him of the latter matter, though
she had not called it dalliance. She had been
pleased. She had thought *he* would be
pleased. She had perhaps thought that
together the four of them could blast apart
a family estrangement that had continued
far too long.

He had thought to deal with the matter
himself. He had thought to witness Sean in
the act of smuggling and to issue an ultima-
tum the next day. He would expose Sean as
a smuggler or Sean would renounce his sudden interest in Helen's fortune. Blackmail?
Oh, yes, it would have been blackmail pure
and simple. But when he had appeared on
the cliff above the cove that night, he had
run into someone on guard, someone who

322

had pointed a pistol right at his heart. Moira.

"She was one of them, Nat," he said. "One of those ruthless thugs and bullies. She had a *gun.* Had it been anyone but me, she would doubtless have fired."

"Can you be sure?" Nat asked. "Perhaps she was —"

"She told me to go home and forget what I had seen," Kenneth said, "or she would kill me. Or have me killed."

He had gone home and told his father about both Sean's smuggling and his secret dalliance with Helen. The latter had turned out to be far more serious than he had realized. There had been an elopement planned. Sean, it seemed, had guessed that the Earl of Haverford, Helen's father, would never consent to the marriage but would perhaps release her dowry after the fact, if only to avoid the worst of the scandal. The earl had acted with some restraint. He had given Sean a choice between prosecution as a smuggler and enlistment in the army. Sean had chosen enlistment, though Sir Basil Hayes had made his fate a little easier by purchasing a commission for him with a foot regiment. He had been killed at the Battle of Toulouse.

"And I bought my commission," Kenneth

said. "I could not forgive Moira, and she could not forgive me. She was not the woman I had thought her to be. I swore never to go back to Dunbarton. But I did go back. And now she is my wife."

"You betrayed her trust," Mr. Gascoigne said. "And she would protect her brother, even against you. Nasty."

"*He* was nasty," Kenneth said. "He was not the sort of man a woman would protect — unless she was as ruthless and as evil as he."

"He was her brother, Ken," Mr. Gascoigne said. "Do you still love her?"

Kenneth laughed. "I would have thought the answer to that has been obvious enough during the past two months," he said.

"Actually, yes," Mr. Gascoigne said. "A great deal has been explained in the past half hour. It has been rather obvious during these two months — Rex even suggested it to us — that indeed you still do love her."

"Leaving her one week after we were wed, planning never to go home to her is proof that I love her?" Kenneth said, turning from the window and staring at his friend with raised eyebrows.

Mr. Gascoigne got to his feet and set down his empty glass. "It is time I went home," he said. "It has seemed to us that it is unlike you, Ken, to abandon a wife for whom you felt mere indifference. And love and hate — well, you know what is said of them. Might I suggest that men do not cry over a child that is miscarried after only a few months unless they have powerful feelings for the woman who did the miscarrying? Hatred or love?"

"I felt responsible," Kenneth said. "She suffered dreadfully, Nat. She told me she wished she need never set eyes on me again. I allowed for the fact that she spoke only hours after her ordeal. I gave her a week. When I asked her again, she said the same thing. So if you are imagining that I have cruelly abandoned a wife who is pining for me, you may revise the image."

"And she said this one week after miscarrying," Mr. Gascoigne said. "*One week, Ken*? And you *believed* her?"

"Since when have you become an authority on women?" Kenneth asked.

"Since having five sisters and a resident female cousin," Mr. Gascoigne said. "They never say what they really mean when their emotions are up, Ken. They are just like men in that respect. I am leaving. It was quite all right, you know, for me to deny my pain after I had been under the knife that time and to curse you for offering me soothing words and laudanum — I recovered faster. I am not at all convinced that you will recover at all if you deny your pain. On which words of priceless wisdom, I really do take my leave. I'll see you at White's in the morning?"

Kenneth went to bed after seeing his friend on his way. But an hour later, as dawn broke, he was still awake and staring upward. He diverted himself for a while with images of having Nat Gascoigne tied up hand and foot and of visiting exquisite torture on his person. But since it was impossible after all to contemplate the pain of a friend with any degree of pleasure, he got up from bed, pulled on a night robe, and went downstairs to the library, where he wrote a letter.

He set it on the tray in the hall to go out with the morning post before he went back to bed — and to sleep.

Moira had indeed recovered her health, and boundless energy to go with it, it seemed. Although Penwith was not a large manor and her mother had always been the one to see to its smooth running, Moira set about the daunting task of teaching herself to be mistress of Dunbarton despite the rather disapproving references the housekeeper occasionally made to the way the Countess of Haverford had always done things. Moira had reminded Mrs. Whiteman — and herself — that *she* was now the Countess of Haverford.

She spent a great deal of time out of doors, consulting with the head gardener, making suggestions for changes in the courtyard and in the park. Soon the fountain in the courtyard, which for years had been merely ornamental, was again spouting water, and the empty lawns surrounding it sported colorful flower beds.

She visited or entertained almost daily, refusing to cower away out of sight for fear of what was being said about her among her friends and neighbors. What they believed about her broken engagement to Sir Edwin Baillie, about her hasty marriage, about her illness, about the fact that she now lived alone, she did not know. She made no explanation and all her acquaintance — even Harriet — were far too well-bred to ask. But of course she was accepted. After all, everything was respectable and even more than respectable in her life. She soon learned that the difference between being Miss Moira Hayes and being the Countess of Haverford was like the difference between night and day. Her company was eagerly sought after, as were her invitations.

She walked out a great deal, alone almost always. Large as the park about Dunbarton was, it was not large enough for her energy. She walked along the cliff tops, across the beach, along the tops of the hills, through the valley. She watched spring pass by and summer begin to take its place.

She was very fortunate, she convinced herself. She had been saved from a marriage of convenience that had been only a little less than abhorrent to her. She had been saved from the alternative of impoverishment. She had a home as magnificent as any in England, she dared say, and enough pin money with which to buy everything she could possibly need. Indeed, when she had had new clothes made after recovering her health, she had waited for the bill to come that she might pay it, but when she had finally asked Mr. Watkins about it, he had looked surprised and assured her that his lordship had already taken care of it. She had security for a lifetime — and so did her mother. If and when Sir Edwin decided that Mama must leave Penwith, then she would move to Dunbarton.

It was all more than Moira could possibly have dreamed of just a few months before.

And she need never fear that the happy routine of her days would be upset. He had gone forever. He would never come back. She was happy that it was all finally over. She even consoled herself for her miscarriage with the thought that now there would not be even the birth of a child to bring him home. She was far better off without him. She truly did not want ever to see him again.

It was strange, then, perhaps, that she should react as she did when the butler handed her the post on her return from an early walk to the cliffs one morning and she thumbed through the pile as she stood in the hall, paused at one letter, turned pale, swayed on her feet, and then went racing off up the stairs and into her private sitting room to stand with her back against the door, her eyes closed, as if she thought to keep an army at bay.

It would be a formal inquiry after her health, she thought. It would be a scolding over her extravagance with the dressmaker. It would be a reprimand about the unnecessary expense of repairing the fountain and making the flower beds. It would be . . . She opened her eyes and looked down at the letter. Her hand, she saw, was trembling. Why? What was wrong with her that she should react thus to a letter from *him*?

She sat down on the chaise longue and opened the letter. It was very short, she saw. A mere business letter, then. What had she expected? Something personal? He had signed himself boldly at the end — *Haverford.*

"Ma'am," he had written, "it would please me if you would set out for London within two days of your receipt of this. My steward will take care of all the details. There will be a few weeks of the Season to be enjoyed after your arrival here. Your servant, Haverford."

She stared at it for a long time. It was a summons, she thought. *It would please me . . . Your servant . . .* They were meaningless courtesies. It was an imperious summons, a command. But why? Why would it please him? Why should he care that she enjoy a few weeks of the Season? Why did he wish to see her again?

She would not go. She would write just as short, just as curt a letter informing him that it would not please *her* to travel to town and that she would derive no enjoyment from the London Season.

She could go to *London*. She had been once to Bath when she was sixteen. She had been nowhere else in her whole life. She could go to London during the *Season.* There would be balls and routs and concerts and the theater and Vauxhall Gardens and Hyde Park. She had heard about them all, dreamed about them, but had never expected to see them or experience them for herself.

She could go — the day after tomorrow.

She could see *him* again. There was such a stabbing of pain in her lower abdomen that she bent her head down and lifted the letter to her face. She could see him again. She could see him again.

She could punish herself yet again and once more disturb the quiet peace of her days.

She sat up once more and stared way off into space. He had summoned her. He had given Mr. Watkins commands. She had vowed to obey him. Very well, she would obey him now.

She would go to London.

She would see him again.

17

For longer than a week, Kenneth had been performing mental calculations, always with the same results. If his messenger had taken the least amount of time possible to ride to Dunbarton, and if Watkins had been able to make the necessary arrangements in the two days allotted him, and if his carriage made the best time possible on the way to London, then he might expect her tomorrow — tomorrow at the very earliest. Most likely it would be the day after or perhaps the day after that, especially if rain should hinder travel. He would try not to expect her tomorrow.

He would be wise not to expect her at all. It had taken him an hour to write and rewrite his short letter. He had been careful not to command her to come but merely to inform her that it would please him if she did so. A command might have had less effect than a request with Moira. If she did not wish to come, or if she felt that defiance was worth any cost, then she simply would not come.

And what would he do then? Go after her? He knew he would not. If she refused to come, then he would end the matter right there — forget about Dunbarton, forget that he was a married man. He would travel all over the world. Perhaps he would employ a mistress and take her with him. He would put something of a life together. He would not mope over a wife who did not want him. As for begetting a son and heir — well, to the devil with it.

The very earliest he could expect her was tomorrow.

He knew that if he stayed at home he would be like a caged bear. And so he went off to a garden party in Richmond and spent an agreeable afternoon mingling with the other guests, strolling with Lady Rawleigh, talking with Miss Wishart and her newly betrothed, an earnest young man for whom she obviously felt a deep affection, playing a game of croquet with Mrs. Herrington, a bold widow, who had told him just the week before that she was in search of a new lover and favored large blond men, and avoiding Miss Wilcox.

He went off to White's afterward and

dined with a group of acquaintances, including Nat and Eden. He decided not to go to the theater afterward or to Mrs. Somerton's soirée. Perhaps he would look in at Almack's later, he told a group who were off to the opera.

"You look like a bear in a cage, Ken," Lord Pelham said.

Kenneth smiled and stopped drumming his fingernails on the tabletop.

"I suppose," Lord Pelham said, "you are considering whether to accept the widow's proposition. She told me about it, you see, when she thought I was about to make her one of my own."

"Was she right, Ede?" Mr. Gascoigne asked, chuckling. "*Were* you about to?"

"You have just set up your little dancer," Kenneth said.

Lord Pelham grinned. "And a fine and vigorous performance she gives, too," he said, "both on and off the stage. I was merely being gallant to Mrs. Herrington."

"Ha," Mr. Gascoigne said.

"She would make a fascinating armful, though, Ken," Lord Pelham said. "She told me that blond men drive her — *wild* was the word she used, especially when they come equipped with tall military bearing and cold silver eyes. God's truth." He held up his right hand while his two friends roared with laughter. He joined them.

"I am not at present in the market for a mistress," Kenneth said, getting to his feet. "Come to Haverford House for port? Almack's later? Do you fancy it?"

"We had better not be one second later than eleven, then," Mr. Gascoigne said, "or the dragons will not let us past the doors — even if we put you in front, Ken, to charm them with your blond hair and tall military bearing and chilly silver eyes."

They all laughed again as they left the dining room.

They were still laughing when they arrived at Haverford House on Grosvenor Square. They were reenacting the Battle of Waterloo, avoiding the bloodbath it had been by organizing a bout of single combat between a French champion and a British champion who would slay his foe with his blond good looks and his tall military bearing and his silver eyes cold as ice and sharp as lance points. The ability to laugh and to focus on the absurd had stood them in good stead during the years when there had been little in life that was amusing.

"Have port and brandy sent up to the drawing room," Kenneth instructed his butler.

"Yes, m'lord," the man said. "M'lord —"

"We could have sent Ede along with you as your squire," Mr. Gascoigne said. "His blue eyes have been known to wreak havoc upon certain persons who have the misfortune to gaze into them."

"Now, if old Boney could only have been prevailed upon to send out a *female* as his champion . . ." Lord Pelham said with a loud sigh.

"She would probably have turned out to favor dark Latin lovers," Kenneth said, "with black oiled hair and curled, waxed mustaches and teeth." They were all laughing as he opened the drawing room door and led the way inside.

He stopped short a few paces inside the door. A woman was rising from a chair beside the fireplace, all tall grace and willowy curves. She wore a stylish gown of pale blue, elegant in its simplicity. Her hair, dark and shining, was curled softly about her face, piled high behind. Her long oval face was again like that of a Renaissance Madonna. There was a flush on her cheeks, a light in her eyes. She looked in perfect health. She looked beautiful.

He was aware of silence in the room and took a few hurried steps forward before stopping and making her a bow. She curt-

336

sied, her dark eyes remaining on his.

"Ma'am," he said, "you have made excellent time. I trust you are well?"

"Very well, thank you, my lord," she said.

"And I trust your journey was comfortable and not too exhausting?" he asked.

"It was very pleasant, thank you," she said.

He felt so breathless he could scarcely speak. It seemed so very unreal to have her — to have Moira here in London. She had come. She had not defied him. He took two more steps forward.

"May I have the honor of presenting my friends to you?" he asked. "Mr. Gascoigne. Lord Pelham." He turned and indicated them, noted their polite, curious glances. "The Countess of Haverford, gentlemen."

"Mr. Gascoigne. Lord Pelham." She curtsied.

"My lady."

"Ma'am."

They bowed.

It was all stiffly, embarrassingly formal.

"But of course," he said, "you have met before."

Recognition dawned in Nat's eyes first. "When we were staying at Dunbarton," he said. "You played the pianoforte for the dancing one evening. It is a pleasure to meet you again, ma'am."

Eden's face was a blank mask that hid horrified embarrassment, if Kenneth's guess was not very wide of the mark. "You displayed remarkable talent, ma'am," he said.

She smiled.

"Please do sit down again, my dear," Kenneth said, and then cursed himself for deciding upon the endearment, which sounded hopelessly unnatural. "I have asked for port to be sent up. Shall I order the tea tray too?"

"Yes, please." She sat down on the chair she had vacated at their entrance and smiled at his guests while he pulled on the bell rope and went to stand beside her chair.

"My wife has come up from Cornwall to join me for the last few weeks of the Season," he explained. It would have been very much easier if he had told them he was expecting her. But he had been afraid of appearing weak and foolish to his friends if she had refused to come.

"You will find town busier than usual, ma'am," Lord Pelham said, "with numbers swelled by former officer types like us."

"I have never been to London before, my lord," she said. "I have never been beyond Cornwall except for one visit to Bath when I was a girl."

Kenneth looked at her in some astonishment. He had not known that. He had assumed that Hayes must have brought her to town for at least one Season.

"Then you must prepare yourself to be amazed and impressed, ma'am," Mr. Gascoigne said. "Being in town during the Season is an experience not to be missed."

"I am looking forward to it, sir," she said, smiling. "Did you know my husband in the army?"

He had seen her, Kenneth realized suddenly, only stiffly uncomfortable in the company of Sir Edwin Baillie and angry and defiant and hostile in her dealings with himself both before and after their fateful indiscretion. He stood beside her chair now, feeling that in some ways he was seeing her for the first time. She was warm and charming, interested and interesting. He watched, fascinated, as his friends relaxed and fell under her spell during the half hour before Nat, closely followed by Eden, got determinedly to his feet, made his bow, and took his leave.

"We will see ourselves out, Ken," Lord Pelham said, lifting a staying hand as Kenneth would have accompanied them from the room. "Lady Haverford? It has been an honor and a pleasure to make your acquaintance, ma'am."

Kenneth stood looking at the closed door for several silent moments after they had left. "Well, ma'am," he said finally, turning to look at her. She was standing before the fireplace. Some of the light and the warmth had gone from her face, but the flush of color remained in her cheeks. He could hardly believe how she had changed for the better in two months. She certainly showed no visible signs of having pined for him — ridiculous thought.

"Well, my lord," she said quietly and she resumed her seat. Her spine did not touch the back of the chair, he noticed, and yet she sat with an easy grace.

He walked toward the empty fireplace and set one hand on the high mantel and one foot on the hearth. He gazed at the unlit coals. He felt all the awkwardness of being alone with her and for a moment cursed his impulsiveness in having sent for her.

"I was not sure whether to expect you or not," he said. "I thought you might not come."

"When I married you," she said, "I vowed to obey you, my lord."

He turned his head to look at her for a moment before directing his gaze back at the coals. He almost smiled. He did not at all believe in such meekness. "You are in good looks," he said.

"Thank you." She made no effort to carry the conversation now as she had done while his friends were still present. She showed no visible pleasure in the compliment he had paid her. There was a lengthy silence.

"Why did you come?" he asked. "Apart from the fact that you felt obedience necessary."

"I wished to come," she said. "I wished to see London. I wished to see it during the Season. I wished to participate in some of its entertainments. I would have had to be inhuman not to wish to come."

"You had no wish to see me again?" he asked.

She smiled very slightly but did not answer him. It had been a foolish question to ask. The silence stretched again.

"The fact is," he said at last, "that we are married."

"Yes."

"Neither of us wished for it," he said. "And we did not even have the good fortune of being indifferent to each other when we were forced into it. There has been a dislike, even a hostility, between us for so long that it has been difficult for us to be in company with each other and remain civil."

"Yes," she said.

"You told me two months ago," he said, "on two separate occasions that you would as soon never set eyes on me again. I complied with your wishes since they so nearly matched my own. But it has occurred to me since that we were both thinking with our emotions at that time, so soon after your miscarriage. It has occurred to me that now we have distanced ourselves somewhat from that unhappy event, we should perhaps rethink the decision to spend our lives apart."

"Yes," she said.

It seemed strange to be talking to a Moira who was not arguing. Was she being coldly obedient? Coolly indifferent? Or had she done her own thinking and come to similar conclusions? Did she find the present state of her life insupportable as he did his — or as he had since that night when Nat had chipped away the ice about his heart and actually reduced him to the ignominy of tears?

"As the Countess of Haverford," he said, "it is right that you should be presented to the *ton*. And there is a great deal of enjoyment to be had from the activities of the Season. They will increase in both number and quality during these last few weeks, I would guess. You cannot be blamed for coming here to participate in them, even if you came for no other reason. Perhaps you will do me the honor of allowing me to escort you to some of the entertainments and to present you as my countess."

"That seems reasonable enough," she said.

"And perhaps at the same time," he said, "we can both be deciding whether there is anything to be made of our marriage."

There was a lengthy pause. But when he turned his head to look at her again, it was to find her looking back at him, perfectly composed. "That sounds reasonable too," she said.

"I will give no commands at the end of the Season," he said. "We will each make the decision. Neither of us knows yet if a marriage lived out in close proximity to each other can ever be tolerable. It is to be hoped that we will come to the same decision. If we do not, we must hope that at least we can come to some sort of amicable agreement. If living together even occasionally proves to be quite out of the question, you may return to Dunbarton and live out your life there. I shall make a home of the rest of the world. And there will be no further commands to join me. Though I did not frame it as a command, Moira, but as a request." He heard the resentment in his own voice

343

and hoped she had not noticed it.

She half smiled. "Is not a request from a husband the same thing as a command?" she asked him.

"No," he said curtly. "Not from this husband. And this husband is the only one you have. I will not have you picking quarrels with me at every turn as you did in Cornwall, Moira. I would have you treat me with the civility of common courtesy."

"Is that a command, my lord?" she asked.

He opened and closed his hand on the mantel. "You agreed a few minutes ago to give this thing a chance," he said. "I have been at pains to explain that I will give you an equal say in solving this problem we have. Are you still willing to try?"

"Yes," she said, "I suppose so. Yes, I am willing to spend these weeks with you or part of them at least. You have your friends here and doubtless will wish to spend time with them. It would be intolerable for us to spend every moment of every day together, would it not? But perhaps some of the time."

Her eyes had darted to his at the word *day*. It was something he had been quite undecided about. He was still undecided — and should perhaps keep silent until he knew at least what he wished. But the word seemed to hang in the air between them, together with an awareness that it was evening and that they were alone in this house together, apart from the servants. And that they were man and wife.

"One thing more," he said. "And the choice is yours. Do you wish to have marital relations with me during these weeks? Tell me what your preference is."

For the first time, she looked discomposed. Her cheeks flamed. But she did not move or dip her head. "It would be unwise," she said.

"Unwise?" He felt as if much of the air had been somehow sucked from the room.

"It is for love," she said quietly. "And there is no love."

"There is frequently no love in marriage," he said. "Sometimes it is simply for pleasure. Sometimes it is for other reasons."

"There would be no pleasure," she said. "We have agreed to find out during the coming two weeks or so if there is any chance at all that we can live together, at least occasionally. I am aware that we must try to find that chance. You are a man of wealth and property and will wish for an heir of your own body to succeed you. But at the moment, my lord, there is nothing between us except the will to try and a thinly veiled hostility that has broken into irritation more than once just this evening."

He might have trusted Moira to be brutally honest. Was he disappointed? He wanted her — he would admit that to himself. And if he did not have Moira, then he would have no one — at least not until after they had made a final decision never to live together again. But was it perhaps better not to have the emotional entanglement that a physical relationship would inevitably bring with it? He was not convinced that it was — or that it was not.

"Is that your final answer, then?" he asked. "There will be no marital relations between us?"

She paused to think. "No," she said, "it is not a final answer. I am here so that we may spend some time together, so that we may enjoy some of the entertainments of the Season together, so that we may come to a decision about the future. For now, for tonight, it is an answer."

"I may ask you again, then?" he said.

"Yes." She looked steadily at him. "But I cannot promise that my answer will change."

He nodded. "That is fair," he said. He *was* disappointed. It was all startlingly real suddenly, the fact that she was his wife. And that she was here at Haverford House, poised and elegant and beautiful. And that she was Moira.

"You must be tired," he said, looking at the clock over the mantel. "It is quite late. What time did you arrive?"

"In time for a late dinner," she said. "We started early this morning so that we would not have to spend another night on the road."

"You must allow me to escort you to your room, then," he said, pushing himself away from the mantel and taking the few paces to her chair.

"Thank you." She got to her feet and set her hand on his wrist. He was reminded of her height and pleased by it. He was so mortally tired, he realized, of dancing and walking with ladies who did not even reach to his shoulder — Miss Wilcox and Mrs. Herrington, for example.

They ascended the stairs and walked along the corridor to her dressing room in silence. He could see a band of light beneath the door. Her maid must be in there unpacking her things, waiting for her to come to prepare for bed.

"I will do myself the honor of staying at home tomorrow morning," he said, "so that I may be at your service. You must not feel compelled to get up before you are fully

347

rested, though."

"Thank you," she said.

He bowed over her hand and kissed it before opening the door for her. "Good night," he said. "I am pleased to see you again and to see that you have recovered your health."

"Good night." She half smiled at him, but she did not return the compliment. It was a well-remembered reaction of Moira's. She had never said anything to him merely because he had first said it to her. When she was a girl he had told her — more than once — that he loved her. She had never said those words to him.

He drew a slow breath as he closed the door again after she had stepped through it. It was not going to be easy having her here, seeing her daily, and not touching her. But perhaps she had made the right decision. What was wrong in their marriage could not be put right with a bedding. It could perhaps only be complicated — especially if he were to impregnate her again.

But, by God, this was not going to be easy.

Moira stood at the window of her bedchamber, playing absently with the heavy braid she had draped over one shoulder and gazing out onto the square. There were lights in the house on the opposite side and two carriages outside the door. The coachmen were sitting on the carriage steps, out of sight of the house, talking and laughing. Moira could hear the sounds. London, she concluded, was a busy and a noisy place.

She wondered if she would sleep, tired as she felt. Everything was so very new. Entering London had been like entering another world. And seeing Kenneth again . . .

She did not know if any of the decisions she had made in the past week or so had been good ones. Decisions would be so much easier to make, she thought, if one always knew what was right and what was wrong, or if one could at least know the consequences of each. Had she been right to come to London? Her life had been peaceful and productive since she had recovered her health. And, as he had said earlier, his letter had not been a command, but a request. She could have said no.

Had she been right to agree to allow him to escort her to *ton* entertainments for the rest of the Season? To try to enjoy the Season with him? But what would have been the point in coming if she was not willing to try at least that much? Had she been right to agree that they try to make something of their marriage? How could they when their mutual hostility ran so deep and went back so far? Yet how could they not? They would be married for the rest of their lives, even if they never saw each other again after these weeks were over.

Had she been right to refuse to allow marital relations? Surely if they were to give their marriage a try, they must treat it as a proper marriage. But how could she have said yes? She could not have. She could not make a sane decision about their marriage, about their future, if she allowed him into her bed. She had known that as soon as she saw him this evening, long before he had put the question to her.

She had seen him striding into the room ahead of his friends, laughing, unaware that she was there, and she had been almost overwhelmed by emotion. She would not call it love — she did not love him. Quite the opposite, in fact. She would not call it lust either, though she had felt a deep, almost frightening desire for him. She was not sure what to call it. But she did know that her experiences of almost nine years ago and those of a few months ago had revealed him to her as a man she could never fully trust or like or respect. She did not believe — though she would try to keep an open mind — that the events of the next two weeks or so could change her opinion of him enough to make a difference. But she did know — she felt it instinctively — that if she allowed him the sort of intimacies that husbands enjoyed with their wives, the sort of intimacy they had shared on that dreadful night of the storm, she might never be able to make a rational decision. She would lose her self-respect.

She feared — she greatly feared — that it would be very easy to be in love with Kenneth. Not to love him, but to be *in* love with him. And if she was in love with him, she might decide that she wished to stay with him, even though the saner part of herself would know very well that she could never find happiness with him.

"Kenneth," she whispered. She wondered if he had any inkling of how much she had desired him as he had stood by the fireplace, one foot on the hearth, one hand on the mantel, in a posture of masculine ease, looking handsome and elegant and somewhat remote. She desired him still.

She drew a deep breath and let it out slowly.

I am pleased to see you again.

Oh, yes. And she, God help her, had been pleased to see him again too.

18

It felt strange waking and getting up and knowing that his *wife* was in town — in the rooms adjoining his own, in fact. She had come and she had listened quietly to what he had said and had agreed with him. She had agreed to enjoy the pleasures of what remained of the Season with him. She had agreed to give their marriage a trial — except for the one aspect. It surprised him, when he thought about it, that he had slept remarkably well all night.

He felt absurdly nervous. He did not know quite how he would face her today, how he would treat her, what he would talk about. But he was not given long to consider the matter. She was up early, despite the fact that she had traveled long hours for several days and everything here in town was strange to her. But he might have known she would keep country hours. She was dressed elegantly and stylishly even if not in the first stare of fashion. She looked as beautiful to his eyes as she had looked the evening before.

"Perhaps," he said, having seated her at the breakfast table and waited until the attendant footman had filled her plate according to her directions, "you would like to see some of the shops this morning? And take out a subscription at the library?"

"That does not sound like the sort of amusement a gentleman would crave," she said. "Do you plan to escort me, my lord?"

"It would be my pleasure, ma'am," he said, one of his hands playing absently with a fork beside his plate. She seemed like a stranger to him this morning — a stranger he somehow wished to please. It *would* be a pleasure, he thought. He did not crave his usual morning ride with his friends or the leisurely hour or two he usually spent at White's, reading the papers and conversing with acquaintances.

She smiled at him. She was not being herself either, he thought. She was playing a part: the gracious and charming lady living up to her end of a commitment. They were like a couple of polite strangers this morning, but perhaps that was no bad thing.

"Then I would like it of all things," she said. "I daresay the shops in London quite put those at Tawmouth in the shade."

"I am surprised," he said, "that your father did not bring you to town for a Season."

"A Season in town is costly, my lord," she said. "There was Sean's . . ." She speared a piece of sausage with her fork and popped it into her mouth without completing the sentence.

There had been Sean's commission to purchase and the uniform and sword and other gear to go with it. The expenses would have put a severe strain on the resources of Penwith — already hugely depleted by Sean's debts. But he had hoped to avoid all reference to the past during these few weeks together. Nothing could change the past. And therefore nothing could save the future, perhaps. But they must try to see what could be done.

"The pleasure of acquainting you with London and its shops and sights and entertainments will be all mine, then," he said. "I am selfishly glad it will be all new to you."

"Thank you." She smiled again.

Perhaps, he thought later as they strolled along Oxford Street, it really was as well that they had somehow become strangers. They had conversed politely, even if a little stiffly, all morning without a hint of a quarrel. And he was enjoying having her on his arm, watching heads turn to take a second glance at her. People must wonder who it was the Earl of Haverford was escorting. She was unmistakably no ladybird, but no one would know who exactly she was — until he presented her as his countess. He was exhilarated by her company.

He took her inside a milliner's shop when she admired the bonnets in the window, and soon had her trying on a dozen different creations.

"But I do not need any more, my lord," she said, turning from the oval glass on the counter to reveal more fully to his admiring eyes an extremely fetching straw bonnet, trimmed with flowers about the crown and with a wide blue ribbon that tied in a bow beneath the chin. "I already have plenty."

But he knew that she loved it and wanted it.

"We will take it," he said to the milliner's assistant.

"My lord," she said, but she blushed and laughed and made no further protest.

At another shop he bought her a pair of fine straw-colored gloves to match the bonnet. They were such an extravagance, she told him, but she thanked him. He found that he was enjoying himself enormously.

"Oh, what beautiful fans," she said on

Bond Street, stopping to gaze into another shop window. "Do look at the paintings on them, my lord. They are works of art. Quite exquisite."

He stood beside her looking at them — and at her.

"Which one do you like best?"

"The naked Cupid shooting his arrow at the fleeing nymph, I do believe," he said. "She might as well stand still. She does not have a chance of escaping."

"But I, too, would wish to escape from such a silly-looking shepherd," she said, laughing. She looked youthful and happy, he thought. "I like that one — the one with the lady sitting on a mossy bank while a gentleman leans across the stile to admire her. It is a romantic scene."

Despite her alarmed protests, he went inside the shop and bought her that particular fan.

"I will be afraid to express a liking for anything else," she said to him when he came out again, "for fear that you will buy it for me. You do not need to, my lord. You make me a very generous allowance and I have everything I could possibly need."

"Perhaps, ma'am," he said, "it pleases me to buy you pretty things."

She half frowned and her eyes clouded for

a moment, but she smiled again. "Thank you, then," she said.

She kept determinedly silent as they stood before a jeweler's window even though he drew her attention to a display of bracelets and tried to play the same game as she had played with the fans. She would not be drawn.

"Come inside," he said, "so that we may see them without the barrier of the glass. Jewels should be seen with the naked eye."

She was very quiet in the shop. She agreed with the jeweler that all the bracelets were very lovely, but she insisted that she did not have a favorite.

"That one," Kenneth said at last, indicating the most lovely — and most costly — of all, a delicate bracelet encrusted with diamonds. "Wrap it, if you please."

Moira stayed at the counter while he went to the back of the shop to pay for the bracelet and take possession of it. It would be like a wedding gift, he thought — a belated one. He had given her nothing on their marriage except her gold wedding ring. Now he would give her diamonds to wear.

She did not return his smile when he rejoined her at the front of the shop. She turned quietly and preceded him out onto the pavement. Her eyes, he saw when she looked up at him, were troubled.

"It must have cost a *fortune,*" she said. "You do not need to do this. You do not have to buy my — my favors."

"Good Lord," he said, lowering his head to peer beneath the brim of her elegant brown bonnet. "Is that what you think I am doing? You are my bride of fewer than three months, ma'am. I have bought you baubles because it pleases me to do so. I have bought you diamonds because I have yet given you no wedding gift."

"A wedding gift?" she said. "But what if we do not remain together?"

He did not want to think of that possibility this morning. "That will not alter the fact that there was a wedding," he said. "And a gift is just that. The bracelet is yours to keep, no matter what happens between us. Perhaps if nothing else, it will remind you of a — pleasant morning."

"Very well, then," she said quietly. "Thank you."

But somehow some of the joy and exuberance of the morning had gone. He had been planning to take her for an ice. But if he did that, they would have to sit at a table together and make conversation. What would they talk about? Had he made an idiot of himself, buying her gifts as if he were an infatuated youth? He had better take her straight to the library, he decided, and then home.

But even as he offered her his arm, his attention was taken by another couple, who had stopped close to them.

"Ken?" a familiar voice said, and he turned to greet Viscount Rawleigh and to bow to Lady Rawleigh. "I met Nat in the park this morning. Will you do me the honor of presenting us?"

Kenneth made the introductions and watched Rex look curiously at Moira while she smiled and talked with the same charm she had shown the evening before.

"Mr. Gascoigne told my husband that you had arrived in town," Lady Rawleigh said to Moira. "We were planning to call upon you this afternoon, were we not, Rex? Mr. Gascoigne said this is your first visit to London."

"Please come anyway," Moira said. "We will be delighted."

"But I have a better idea," Lady Rawleigh said. "Are you to attend Lady Algerton's ball this evening?"

Moira looked inquiringly at Kenneth.

"We are indeed," he said.

"Then you must come first to us for dinner," Lady Rawleigh said. "Will that not be splendid, Rex?"

"I shall certainly look forward to making Lady Haverford's closer acquaintance, my love," the viscount said. He grinned. "And to chatting with you too, of course, Ken. Perhaps you would be so good as to reserve the second set of dances this evening for me, ma'am." He smiled at Moira.

"They seem very pleasant," she said when the two couples had gone their separate ways a few minutes later. "Lord Rawleigh was another of your friends in the cavalry, my lord?"

"There were the four of us," he said. "We were as close as any brothers could be, I believe. Will you like to go to Rawleigh's for dinner?"

"Yes," she said. "It is why I have come, is it not? To meet people, especially those connected with you? Did Lady Rawleigh travel with her husband? Follow the drum, I believe the term is."

"They are only recently wed," he said. "No more than a few weeks longer than us, in fact."

"Oh," she said. "They seem fond of each other."

"Yes," he said, "I believe they are." And the silence stretched between them until they reached the library and had a good excuse not to speak aloud. He would not tell her that Rex's marriage had been quite as sudden and quite as reluctantly entered into as his own. It would only be more obvious to her, as it was to him, that those two had worked on their differences and overcome them while he and Moira had not. Not yet. This morning he had been hopeful. But now there was something between them again — something negative. That damned bracelet. He should have walked past the jeweler's and taken her for an ice.

Moira would have liked to relax during the afternoon, perhaps by walking in Hyde Park. She longed to see it — it was so very famous. She would have liked to relax and look forward to the evening. Viscount Rawleigh had seemed amiable and his wife warmly charming. It would feel good to have a friendly acquaintance of her own gender in London. Her husband would not wish to spend the whole of every day with her, after all. And she would have liked to feel a pleasurable anticipation of the evening's ball — a real *ton* ball, one of the Season's famous squeezes. She was eager to build up memories to take home with her in a few weeks' time — pleasant memories.

The morning had not been a success. And the fault was largely hers, she admitted. Life at Penwith had been lived so very frugally for years past. There had been no room in her life for impulsive extravagance. The straw bonnet this morning had seemed just that, as had the gloves. But her husband was wealthy, she had realized, and they were in London during the Season, and she had done nothing really to hide her longing for the bonnet. She would have been delighted with just those gifts. They would have made an already exciting morning perfect.

But then there had been the fan. And finally the bracelet, which she was quite sure had cost more than she and her mother had spent in a year. She did not want extravagance or gifts, she had thought. She wanted — oh, something of more human value. Friendship, perhaps, even affection. She had thought that was what she had agreed to — to try to build some sort of amicable feeling between them that would perhaps help them to make something workable of their marriage. She had not agreed to have her affections bought or to encourage him in the belief that lavishing money and gifts on her was an acceptable substitute for affection.

But she had felt his change of mood after they had stepped out of the jeweler's. And she had realized her own mistake. He had been enjoying himself. He had bought her the gifts because he had *wanted* to. And she had spurned him. She would simply have to try again and try harder. She had not expected this to be easy, after all. And so she hoped for a walk in the park, for a simple pleasure that would enable them to talk to each other, perhaps, without this morning's stiffness of manner.

But the afternoon was not to be either a pleasant or a relaxing one — not by any means. Her husband told her during luncheon that he would be taking her to call upon his sister. And when her stomach had already taken a plunge at that announcement, he added that his mother was staying at Viscount Ainsleigh's too.

"No," she said firmly. "Oh, no, my lord. I will not call upon them." She had not agreed to this. She had agreed to a pleasurable few weeks seeing London and participating in *ton* events. She had not agreed to be trapped into following his less pleasant agenda. She had nothing to say to his mother or his sister.

"Yes," he said with an answering firmness, "you will. You are my wife. I must present you to them."

"But I will not be your wife in a few weeks' time," she said. "Not in anything but name. And they both made their sentiments toward me quite clear at Christmastime. I have no wish to have any dealings with them."

"At Christmastime," he said, "you were not my wife or even my betrothed. We will make the call, Moira. There are certain civilities that must be observed. This is one."

"It is a command, then," she said, tight-lipped. "I am being given no choice in the matter."

His eyes were cold. He was the old Kenneth again. "It is a command," he said. "One that would not need to be given if you knew what was what."

It was an accusation that rankled. "So this is what the diamond bracelet and the bonnet and fan were all about this morning," she said. "And the gloves."

"You are being childish," he said.

"We always return to that, do we not?" she said. "We have a disagreement, and I am childish. And you, my lord, are a boorish tyrant. I was foolish to come, and foolish to agree to try to make things different between us. Nothing will ever change."

"Not unless we decide that it will," he said.

"There is no *we* in any of this," she said. "Only you and I: you giving orders, me obeying them."

He was drumming his fingertips against the tabletop. "You refuse to observe the proper civilities by calling on my mother this afternoon, then?" he asked.

She got to her feet, forcing him to his, though there was still food on his plate. No, he would not do this to her. He would not accuse her of the failure of their experiment before even a single day had passed.

"I shall be ready," she said, "when it pleases you to send for me, my lord."

He stood where he was as she left the room.

She let anger sustain her through the next hour and through the silent carriage ride that followed it. How dared he force her to call upon his mother, who had all but driven her from Dunbarton on the night of the Christmas ball, and on his sister, who had treated her with such disdain and dislike on the evening of the assembly in Tawmouth. But then, he would dare anything. There had never been any real human compassion in Kenneth.

She turned to him as the carriage slowed outside Viscount Ainsleigh's town house. "Do they *know*?" she asked him. "Do they know why we married?" His answer would make all the difference to how she would behave.

"I offered them no explanation," he said. "None was necessary. But if you would care to change that look on your face, ma'am, we may make it easier on ourselves by having it appear that it was a love match."

"We were so deeply in love," she retorted, "that we separated after one week and lived apart for two whole months? They will not believe it for a moment."

"I thought you did not care for my family," he said. "Do you care what they believe?"

"No," she said.

"Well, then," he said, "it does not matter if we fail to deceive them, does it? But if you will smile at me, ma'am, I will smile at you." He did so, giving her the full force of his not inconsiderable charm.

"But of course," she said, "you care for them, do you not? And you care what they believe."

"If I admit to that, Moira," he said, "then I will merely be ensuring that you scowl at me throughout the coming hour."

"You deserve to be scowled at," she said.

"Quite so," he said so agreeably that she was left wondering if they had been bickering or joking. Perhaps this was all a joke to him, but it was very serious to her. She would rather be doing anything on earth other than what she was actually doing. She was being handed down the steps of the carriage.

The Dowager Countess of Haverford and Viscountess Ainsleigh had clearly not been warned of this visit, though both were at home to visitors. Two ladies and one gentleman sat with them and Viscount Ainsleigh in the drawing room. Perhaps it was as well, Moira thought. Although the faces of both her mother-in-law and her sister-in-law were studies in frozen surprise when she and Kenneth followed the butler's announcement into the room, good breeding demanded that they treat her with the strictest courtesy. Lady Haverford even seated Moira beside her on a sofa and poured her tea.

"I trust you left Lady Hayes in good health," she said.

"Yes, thank you," Moira said. "She was quite well."

"And I trust you had a comfortable journey to town."

"Yes, thank you," Moira said. "My hus— Kenneth had his steward send several servants with me for safety and had them reserve the best rooms in the best inns. It was a very pleasant and interesting journey. Everything was new to me, of course."

"You have not been to town before?"

Helen asked. "You must find it all very strange and different from country living."

Moira chose not to read disdain and condescension in the words. "I arrived only last evening," she said. "But I certainly found the shops very exciting. Kenneth took me along Oxford Street and Bond Street this morning."

"And are you to attend Lady Algerton's ball this evening, Lady Haverford?" one of the lady guests asked.

Yes," Moira said, "and I look forward to it with some eagerness." She must appear quite rustic to these people, but she would not try to pretend to a sophistication and an ennui that would merely make her look ridiculous. She smiled.

"Kenneth will be dancing the opening set with you, doubtless," Viscount Ainsleigh said. "Will you reserve the second for me — Moira? May I call you that since we are brother and sister?"

"I should like that." She smiled more warmly. She had liked the viscount from her first meeting with him at the Dunbarton ball, when he had tried to cover up for his wife's rudeness to her and Sir Edwin Baillie. "But I am afraid the second set is promised to Viscount Rawleigh, sir."

"Michael," he said. "Then we will make it

the third — if that is not reserved too?"

"Thank you, Michael," she said.

Kenneth was standing beside the sofa, slightly behind her. He rested one hand lightly on her shoulder and without pausing to think, she lifted her hand to touch her fingers to his. It was a gesture that she knew was not lost on her in-laws or on their guests — a not-strictly-proper gesture that was nevertheless perhaps excusable in newlyweds who were much in love with each other. That was not the case at all, of course. He had thought, perhaps, to offer her some moral support. She had felt the need to accept it. But it did not matter. Perhaps, as he had suggested in the carriage, it would be easier to have it thought that theirs was a love match. She turned her head to look up at him and, when he smiled at her, she smiled back.

"You will, of course, bring your wife to my side when you arrive this evening, Kenneth," the dowager countess said when they were leaving a short while later. She accepted his arm to descend the stairs with them. "I shall see that she is presented to all the people with whom the Countess of Haverford ought to have an acquaintance."

"As you wish, Mama," he said, inclining his head.

"Thank you, ma'am," Moira said.

Her mother-in-law looked at her with unsmiling eyes. "It is as well," she said, "that you miscarried. A new countess who lacks both town bronze and a recognizable name does not need the added gossip that would arise from a confinement a mere six months after the nuptials."

He had *lied* to her. He *had* told them. All the while, when she had been sitting with them in the drawing room, they had *known*. Moira's chin went up.

"I suppose you have been in correspondence with Mrs. Whiteman at Dunbarton," Kenneth said. "I must have a word with her about misplaced loyalties. It has taken Moira all this time to recover her health and spirits, Mama. But we can find no real consolation for the loss of the child that would have been ours. I would be grateful if you would not mention this to anyone else."

"I would be hardly likely to," she said. "So you have won yourself wealth and position and security, Moira. I can do nothing to change that. I can only hope that you will live up to what is expected of you — and offer to help you move smoothly into the life that must be yours."

It was a grudging offer. There was no warmth behind it, no offer of affection. But it was an offer, nonetheless. An offer of some sort of acceptance. If she was to stay with Kenneth, Moira thought — *if* — then she would be foolish to reject it.

"Thank you, ma'am," she said.

"You had better call me Mother," the dowager countess said. "I have guests in the drawing room. I must return to them."

Kenneth bowed to her. Moira curtsied.

And then they were back in the carriage, sitting stiffly side by side.

"I am sorry," he said when they were in motion. "I did not realize that she knew. Mrs. Whiteman will, of course, be dismissed from her post at Dunbarton. I will not tolerate a housekeeper whose loyalty to my mother is stronger than her loyalty to you. What my mother said must have hurt you."

"Yes," she said. But what *he* had said had unexpectedly touched her. He had spoken as if the loss had been his as well as hers — *we can find no real consolation for the loss of the child. . . .* And he was prepared to dismiss the housekeeper for going over her head and reporting to her former mistress. *Oh, Kenneth,* she thought, *don't confuse me.*

"Was the visit quite as bad as you expected?" he asked.

"No." She fixed her eyes on her hands in her lap. "If we had not called this afternoon,

371

we would have met them this evening, would we not? It would have been intolerably awkward."

"Yes," he said.

"And you thought of that." She foolishly had not. "Yes, it was better than I expected. At least no one showed me the door when I went in."

"They would not dare," he said. "You are my wife."

She smiled at her hands.

"Am I forgiven, then," he asked, "for issuing the command?"

"It is your right to command me," she said.

"That is a dangerously meek reply," he said, looking at her sidelong.

She shrugged her shoulders and changed the subject. "I like Viscount Ainsleigh — Michael," she said. "He is a true gentleman." She was surprised that she liked him. Sean had loved Helen and should have married her. And would have if . . .

"Helen was fortunate," he said. But when she turned her head sharply to glare at him, he forestalled her. "Leave it, Moira. Let us have these two weeks or so. We have done moderately well this morning and this afternoon, have we not?"

"*Moderately* well," she agreed.

"But then, we did not expect to fall instantly in love with each other and find that everything about the other was perfection itself, did we?" he asked her.

"Heaven forbid," she said fervently.

"I would expire from boredom in a week," he said.

"I believe I would do it," she said, "in six days."

Neither of them laughed. They did not even look at each other. But somehow they were back to the near amity they had shared this morning up until the moment he had bought her the fan.

19

"Well, Ken." Lady Rawleigh had taken Moira to the drawing room for tea following dinner, leaving the two men to enjoy a glass of port together. The viscount had just filled their glasses. "You and I have come to a sorry end very soon after regaining our freedom."

"Sorry?" Kenneth said. "Is that what it is?"

His friend smiled and sat back in his chair. "We are both in marriages not of our own choosing," he said. "I was seen slinking out of Catherine's cottage at the dead of night — after she had roundly repulsed my less-than-honorable advances, I might add — and set a villageful of tongues to wagging and my twin to threatening death or worse if I refused to do the honorable thing. I did the honorable thing — poor Catherine. I understand your situation was not vastly different?"

Kenneth was not about to describe a certain snowstorm — even to one of his closest friends. "And yet," he said, "you both seem reasonably contented, Rex."

"Then we are remarkably good actors, Catherine and I," Viscount Rawleigh said. "We are far more than *reasonably* contented."

"Why do you tell me this?" Kenneth asked. "Merely as a boast?"

His friend laughed. "That too," he admitted. "One feels exceedingly clever to have discovered love in one's own life — in one's own marriage. And one feels constrained to share one's wisdom with others. Lady Haverford is a very charming lady, Ken. And extremely handsome too, if I may be permitted to say so. She and Catherine appear to have taken well to each other."

Kenneth sipped from his glass and then pursed his lips. "Correct me if I am wrong, Rex," he said, "but do I detect a *scold* coming? Or is it merely a lecture?"

"It seems to be an inescapable fact that you abandoned the lady for three months following a certain, ah, event," Lord Rawleigh said, "and then hurried home, married her, and rushed back to town. Now, two months later, you have brought her here for a couple of weeks of entertainment. Will you pack her off home again afterward while you go to Brighton? Eden is going there, I gather. Or to one of the other spas? Or to Paris?"

"I would be obliged to you," Kenneth said, "if you would mind your own damned business, Rawleigh."

"But I am your friend," the viscount said, sounding quite uncontrite. "And I know you rather well. I know your conscience. It used to puzzle and even annoy the rest of us at times. You have not had a woman since your marriage, have you?" He held up a hand. "No answer needed or expected. Nat and Eden have been merrily sowing their oats with a wide array of willing beauties — though Ede has a cozy nest now with his little dancer, of course — while you have been abstaining. But you need a woman. You were always quite as red-blooded as the rest of us."

"I am a married man," Kenneth said, almost in a growl.

"Precisely." Rex raised his eyebrows. "Even I have realized that marriage vows lay a great obligation on the conscience, and I was never much of a one for conscience where women were concerned, was I? You are doomed to a celibate life, Ken, if you do not remain with Lady Haverford."

"Rubbish," Kenneth said.

"I would wager a fortune on it," his friend said. "And an unhappy life too. And it seems a distinct possibility, Ken. You have sat here tonight being amiable to me and charming to Catherine. Lady Haverford has smiled and been charming to both Catherine and me. And you have both behaved as if the other was not even in the room."

"The devil!" Kenneth said.

"Perhaps I have misread all the signs," Lord Rawleigh said, lifting one hand in a gesture of helplessness. "Perhaps —"

"Perhaps," Kenneth said through his teeth, "unlike Lady Rawleigh, Moira refused to allow me to do the honorable thing after the *certain event*, as you so euphemistically describe it. Perhaps she refused several times, even to the point of lying about her condition. Perhaps after she was eventually forced to marry me, she sent me packing, declaring she never wanted to see me again. Perhaps I have invited her to town in the hope that we can piece together something of a marriage after all. Perhaps I do not need my *friends* poking their noses where they do not belong. And perhaps we should have joined the ladies ten minutes ago."

"And perhaps" — Viscount Rawleigh was smiling — "you have married the very woman for you, Ken. Has she really treated you so shabbily? Not the other way around? I have seen women by the score use every wile imaginable to lure you into matrimony or even simply into bed. I have never — no, I really have not — met one who gave you your marching orders. Until today, that is. Yes, do let us join the ladies, Ken. I want to take an even closer look at the lady who clearly has you rattled. This is far more interesting than I ever realized." He got to his feet and gestured toward the door.

His mother was going to take Moira under her wing, Kenneth thought irritably as he pushed back his chair. Lady Rawleigh was going to befriend her. Rex was going to take a closer look at her. Nat and Eden, after dismissing her as a pale cadaver and a consumptive at Tawmouth, were now going to fall under her spell. Ainsleigh and Rex and doubtless half the male population of London were going to dance with her this evening. Was ever an attempted reconciliation conducted so much in the public eye? He had been a fool. He should have taken himself off to Dunbarton instead of bringing her here.

He wanted to dance with her himself this evening. Every set. Instead of which, he would be fortunate to have the two dances

378

with her that proper decorum allowed.

"If you scowl like that, Ken," Viscount Rawleigh said, slapping a hand on his shoulder, "you will be frightening Catherine and inviting your wife to abandon you for another two months or so."

"The devil!" Kenneth muttered while his friend chuckled.

"Oh, we will certainly stay until the end of the Season," Lady Rawleigh said in answer to a question Moira had asked. "I must confess that I am enjoying it. I shall enjoy it even more now that you have come. We must go walking together and shopping and visiting together. You know very few people here, I suppose."

"None except Kenneth," Moira said, "and his mother and sister."

"They will all help you feel more at home, of course," Catherine said. "But it is important to have friends — of one's own gender. Rex does not enjoy looking in the shops. I do." She laughed. "I am so glad you have come to town at last. We have been very curious."

She smiled and Moira smiled back. There was an awkward little silence.

"We will spend the summer at Stratton," Catherine said. "In Kent, you know. We will probably stay there for the autumn and winter too. I am increasing, you see, and Rex is afraid to allow me to travel more than necessary, though I have never felt so well in my life."

"You must be very happy," Moira said with a stabbing of envy — and fear.

"Yes," Catherine said softly. "I had long expected that I would never marry. I had accepted my spinsterhood quite cheerfully and had learned to lavish most of my affections on Toby." She glanced affectionately at the little terrier who had frightened Moira earlier with his barking but who was now stretched out fast asleep before the hearth. "And then Rex came along. How I hated him for upsetting the quiet contentment of my days." She laughed. "And upset it he certainly did. But it is wonderful to be married when one expected never to be, Lady Haverford, and to have a deep affection for one's husband when one expected to dislike him intensely — and to be increasing when one had expected to be childless."

But her smile faded suddenly as she looked into Moira's face. "Oh, I do beg your pardon," she said. "You *lost* a child, did you not? It is the worst feeling in all the world."

"Yes," Moira said.

"We did not even know of it until very

recently," Catherine said. "Your husband kept it all bottled up inside, poor man, and hid the truth even from his closest friends. Mr. Gascoigne told Rex that Lord Haverford actually cried when he finally mentioned it. Which only proves how fond of you he is. We were puzzled by his leaving you in Cornwall so soon after your marriage, but all was explained then. The pain was too intense for him, and he must have felt quite helpless to ease yours."

"Miscarriage is very common," Moira said. "It is foolish, perhaps, to feel it as such a grievous loss."

"I once lost a child," Catherine said, "a few hours after his birth. It was a number of years ago. Perhaps your husband mentioned to you the duel Rex fought just a few months ago against the father, my seducer? I should have been glad to lose that child when there had been so much ugliness and so much ruin surrounding his conception. I was not glad, Lady Haverford. I hope never again to have to face the nightmare of grief I lived through for a long time after he was gone, my son."

"But you are happily risking it all again?" Moira asked, frowning.

Catherine smiled. "The desire to bear life is far stronger than fear," she said. "Especially when the man is very dear to one. And one cannot allow fear to rule one's life, can one? Not unless one wishes to be endlessly unhappy — and lonely. Do you not feel the need to try again too? Or is it a little soon yet? Am I embarrassing you? But you will, I am sure, Lady Hav— oh, *may* I call you Moira? I am Catherine."

"I felt wretched the whole time," Moira said. "But perhaps that was because . . ." She bit her lip.

"Yes, I am sure it was," Catherine said. "I was very ill that other time too. And miserable. And unwilling and unable to eat or to rest. This time I am fit to bursting with good health. But this time I am happy."

Moira smiled.

There was no chance to continue the conversation. The drawing room door opened to admit the two men, and in the half hour before they left for the ball, Moira's attention was taken by Lord Rawleigh, who sat beside her, instructed her to tell him all about Cornwall, and focused the whole of his attention on her answers. Kenneth accompanied Catherine to the pianoforte at the other end of the room and stood beside the instrument, watching her play.

One cannot allow fear to rule one's life. . . .

Not unless one wishes to be endlessly un-
happy — and lonely.

The words repeated themselves at the
back of Moira's mind all the time she spoke
and smiled. But she was not afraid, was she?
Of conceiving again, perhaps. But not of
anything else. Not of — loving. Not of loving Kenneth. One could not be afraid of
something one was in no danger of doing.

. . . endlessly unhappy — and lonely.

Kenneth experienced both the success and
frustration of his hopes in the course of the
Algerton ball. It was a large squeeze of an
affair, as most entertainments were at this
stage of the Season. It was a fitting setting
for what was, in effect, Moira's debut into
society. And she certainly looked lovely
enough for the occasion, dressed as she was
with her usual elegant simplicity in pale
gold. The only glittering detail of her appearance, in fact, was her diamond bracelet,
which she wore over her long glove.

He enjoyed the interest and curiosity with
which the *ton* looked at his wife when she
first entered the ballroom on his arm. News
traveled faster than lightning in London, of
course. He would wager that everyone present knew her identity after the first five
minutes. And he would wager, too, that for

the past two months there had been a great deal of avid curiosity about the mysteriously absent Countess of Haverford.

He danced the first set of country dances with her and watched her dance with skill and grace — and with open enjoyment. He would waltz with her too, he decided. But later, perhaps after supper. He would not dance with her again too soon and know that he could not dance with her any more for the whole evening. That would be too dreary.

But once the first set was over, it seemed that control of the evening was taken from his hands. His mother, true to her word, took her daughter-in-law under her wing and moved about the ballroom with her, presenting her to all the female dragons whose every word was law in London society. Moira, he could see, was acquitting herself well. She was behaving with quiet poise, though she was not mute. He resisted the temptation to follow her about. This was women's business, and she did not need him. He did not know if she enjoyed being with his mother, but she appeared to have accepted her sponsorship with quiet good sense. He was very pleased with the development.

And of course she danced — every set.

Rex danced the second with her and Ainsleigh the third. Nat and Eden both danced with her, of course, as did Lord Algerton and Viscount Perry, Lady Rawleigh's young brother. She danced the supper waltz with Claude Adams, Rex's twin brother, who was in town with his wife, and of course went off to supper on his arm afterward.

After supper, her evening did not lose momentum at all. She danced with gentlemen to whom his mother had presented her, most of them the highly ranked, highly respected husbands of the dragons. It might be said, Kenneth thought, watching her with mingled pride and jealousy, that the *ton* had taken the Countess of Haverford to its bosom at her first appearance in its midst.

"She is really rather handsome," a lady's voice said from behind his shoulder, and he turned to find Mrs. Herrington standing there, languidly fanning her face, "if one likes unusually tall women who are as dark as Spaniards. Some officers, I have heard, my lord, grew tired of Spanish beauties from too long a familiarity with them."

"Did they, indeed?" he said, fingering the handle of his quizzing glass, though he did not raise it to his eye. "How extraordinary."

"Of course," she said, smiling at him over the top of her fan, "some men grow tired of their wives for the same reason. If such should be your fate, my lord, there is consolation close at hand, I do assure you."

"Sometimes, ma'am," he said, lifting his glass to his eye and watching his wife smile and converse and perform the rather intricate steps of the dance all at the same time, "one can be fervently thankful that one is neither *some officers* nor *some men.*"

She sighed and then laughed. "There are other tall, broad men," she said. "There are other men who have been officers. There are other blond men. But none have all those attributes so splendidly united as they are in you, my lord. I must regret your wife's timing in arriving in town just now. But I shall renew my search. Perhaps the next time I am between lovers, or the time after that, you will be in a different frame of mind." She touched him on the shoulder with her closed fan and was gone.

She was amazingly brazen, he thought, and found himself chuckling.

But he was not chuckling after he had approached his wife and his mother at the end of the set and discovered that Moira could not dance the next waltz with him, as it was already promised to someone else. And indeed every set for what remained of the evening was already taken.

"So you need not worry about me, Kenneth," she said. Her cheeks were flushed and her eyes were shining — not at his arrival at her side, he suspected, but at the excitement of the ball and her own success.

"I never for a moment doubted, ma'am," he said, bowing to her, "that you would have more partners than there are sets to be danced. Enjoy yourself." He took himself off to dance with Lady Baird, Rex's sister.

And so their first day together was over, he thought when the ball had ended and he handed his wife into the carriage. It had not been quite what he had anticipated. When he had suggested to her that they simply enjoy what remained of the Season and put all else from their minds, he had pictured them together, carefree, laughing, talking — perhaps a little as they had been when they were very young. He had forgotten that the whole idea of the Season was that people mingle and enjoy themselves with *one another.* He had forgotten that husbands and wives rarely spent more than a few minutes of each day in company with only each other when they were in town.

It had not been a total disaster of a day, he thought as he settled onto the carriage seat beside his wife. It had not been a total success either, but then, he had not expected miracles. Perhaps tomorrow would be better.

"Lady Rawleigh — Catherine — has asked me to walk in the park with her tomorrow morning," Moira said, turning her head to look at him in the darkness, "while Lord Rawleigh spends a few hours at White's. I thought you would wish to go there too."

"I am pleased," he said, "that you have made a female friend."

"I believe Lady Baird is coming too," she said. "She is Lord Rawleigh's sister, you know. Your mother wishes me to make some calls with her during the afternoon. I thought it wise to say yes. She was kind to me this evening. And making afternoon calls is the thing to do here, I understand, just as it is at home. Does this meet with your approval, my lord?"

It did not. She might as well have slapped him in the face. She was not going to have need of him all day? "You are asking for *my* approval?" he asked. "Dare I give it? If I do, you will be sure to think you have done something drastically wrong and will change all your plans. I most certainly do *not* approve, ma'am." He looked at her sidelong and had the same impression he had had fleetingly during the afternoon when they had been returning from Ainsleigh's. He felt almost as if they had teased and understood and amused each other.

Perhaps, he thought, this was the best they could expect of the coming weeks — a few fleeting moments of amity. Not nearly enough to become a working basis for a marriage. They lapsed into silence.

Moira was tired and footsore. She was also excited and exhilarated. She had been to her first *ton* ball, and it had been wonderful. She could still hear the music and smell the flowers and see the swirling colors of silks and satins and the sparkle of jewels. She was also disappointed. She had danced the opening set with Kenneth, but after that he had not come near her even once or spoken a single word to her except when he had wanted to waltz with her after supper. She had wanted so badly to waltz with him. She had remembered their waltz at the Dunbarton ball. She had expected that they would be together much more than they had been.

She felt rather dreary about the coming day. She looked forward to the walk in the park with Catherine and Lady Baird, but she had agreed to it before her mother-in-law had suggested the afternoon calls. She knew that ladies spent very little of their time, especially during the day, with their husbands. Even at home in Cornwall it was so. But her situation with Kenneth was not an ordinary one. Somehow, last evening, when he had suggested that they enjoy the Season together, she had pictured them *being* together, all day and all evening.

But the train of her thoughts surprised her. Did she *want* to spend all her time with him? Could she not better enjoy London and the Season with the new friends she was already making? But how would she know within a mere two weeks or so if she wished to remain with Kenneth or if she wished at least to see him occasionally?

A few things puzzled her. Why had he brought her to London? Why had he even thought to try to make something of their marriage? He was an extraordinarily handsome and attractive man. She had seen the way other women had looked at him, both on Oxford Street and Bond Street during the morning and at the ball during the evening. He did not need her for any of the obvious reasons.

And there were her memories of that most dreadful of all nights, when she had miscarried. Memories of his ashen face, even of tears, and of his voice saying the same things over and over again: *Moira, my love, don't die. I won't let you die, my love.* She had dismissed them all afterward as products of her imagination, quite at odds with the coldness of his behavior during the morning and week following her ordeal.

But — *Mr. Gascoigne told Rex that Lord Haverford actually cried when he finally mentioned it.* Kenneth had not told his friends for a long time. And when he had, he had cried. Why? Because he was fond of her, Catherine had suggested.

There was one part of each day when husbands and wives could be alone together without the press of other company, she thought.

She pushed the thought away.

One cannot allow fear to rule one's life. Not unless one wishes to be endlessly unhappy — and lonely.

"Kenneth?" She turned her head to look at him and found that he was sitting across the corner of the carriage seat, looking silently at her in the darkness.

"Yes?" he said.

One cannot allow fear . . . "You asked me last evening," she said, and she could hear the breathlessness in her voice, "if you might ask again."

Clearly he knew just what she was talking about. "Yes," he said quietly.

"And I said yes."

"Yes."

They stared at each other. They must be almost home.

"Do you wish us to have marital relations?" he asked her.

"I think we ought," she said. "I think we must if we wish to make a — a sensible decision. It is not a friendship we are putting to the test, after all, is it? Or even a courtship? It is a marriage."

"Yes," he said. "I may come to your bed, then? Tonight? Are you too tired?"

"I am not too tired," she said.

The carriage lurched slightly on its springs and came to a halt. They both turned their eyes to the door, which would soon open.

She felt as if she had run home rather than ridden in the carriage. She had to force herself not to pant out loud. What had she done? She had not really considered the matter, pondered it, looked at it from all possible angles to know if it was wise.

She remembered that there had been something rather frightening about what happened. Not so much the pain — there had been less than she had expected — but the dreadful intimacy, the sense of violation, the giving up of oneself, even of one's body, to the control of a man.

There had also been something exciting about it. His weight, his size, the heat and pleasure his movements had aroused.

That time he had got her with child.

Perhaps it would happen again tonight. For a moment she felt blind panic. She clutched her new fan until she could feel the sticks digging painfully into her fingers.

One cannot allow fear to rule one's life.

The door opened, and her husband vaulted out and turned to hand her down. She looked at his hand for a moment before setting her own in it. It was large and strong and warm. Frightening. And exciting.

20

She did not know whether to leave her hair loose or braid it as she usually did at night. She left it loose. She did not know whether to wear a dressing robe over her nightgown or leave it off. She left it off. She did not know whether to get into bed or stand somewhere in the room — at the window or beside the fireplace. She got into bed after imagining herself walking across the room to climb into it — with his eyes upon her. She did not know whether to prop her pillow behind her or lie flat. She lay flat — on her back, and then on her side. She noticed that she had left all the candles burning. She should have blown out all except the one beside the bed.

But it was too late to do anything about that. There was a tap on the door, and it opened even before she could call an answer. She despised her nervousness. She was acting like a skittish and virgin bride. She hoped fervently that the color in her cheeks did not match the heat she felt in them.

He was wearing a long brocaded dressing robe of dark green. She could see the white of his nightshirt at his neck. She was shocked by the stabbing of pure lust she felt for him — she would not dignify it even in her mind by a softer word. It was certainly not love. She did not love him.

He snuffed the candles she had remembered too late and strolled toward the bed, where a single candle still burned. "It might be as well to remember," he said, "that this is not the first time, that you know what happens, and that tonight there will be no pain."

The color in her cheeks *did* match the heat, then. She felt them burn hotter. "I am not nervous," she said. "How foolish. Are you going to blow out the candle?" He had removed his robe and was drawing back the bedcovers.

"I think not," he said. "I wish to see that it is with you I do this, Moira. I wish you to see that you do it with me. It is important that we accept the truth."

"Are you suggesting that in fantasy I might make you into someone else?" she asked, shocked.

"It is not an impossibility," he said. "I am

Kenneth, the boy you loved, though you never put your feelings into words; the man you hated and perhaps still hate; your husband."

Her mind had been trying to focus on just the last of those identities. Did he have to remind her at this particular moment of what they had agreed to forget for these weeks?

"And you are Moira," he said, "the girl I adored; the woman who threatened to shoot me through the heart and almost did succeed in killing me; my wife."

Yes, she thought, looking into his face and feeling one of his hands working on the button at her neck, perhaps he had been right about fantasy. Perhaps without the candle, without his words, she would have pictured him only as the very handsome, elegant stranger with whom she had spent much of the day, the man with whom she had wanted to waltz earlier.

"Yes," she said. "This is very serious, is it not?" She was not even quite sure what she meant by the words.

He kissed her.

She had never really thought of a kiss as a sexual act. She had kissed any number of people in her life as a gesture of affection. Even as a girl, when Kenneth had kissed her, it had been a romantic thing, not really anything deeply physical. But she remembered now how he had kissed her in the hermit's hut — entirely as a way to raise her temperature. It had not been an affectionate gesture. He did it again now, opening her mouth wide with his own, reaching deep inside with his tongue, tickling surfaces with its tip, moving it rhythmically in and out until she felt a rush of sensation in that other part of herself where he would soon do something very similar.

She became aware of the total helplessness of her inexperience. While her whole attention had been focused on her mouth, her nightgown had been unbuttoned and folded back so that she was to all intents and purposes naked to below the waist. The hand that was not about her shoulders was smoothing lightly over her breasts. His thumb was pulsing against one of her nipples and making it both hard and tender, almost sore. And then he slid his hand down over her stomach and abdomen and down between her legs. His fingers probed with shocking intimacy. She was *wet.* She jerked at the embarrassing realization.

"No, no," he said, his voice low against her ear. "This is as it should be. I would cause you discomfort if you were dry. Your body has been warned of what is to come and has prepared itself."

She hated her ignorance and inexperience. She felt quite helpless in his so obviously very experienced hands. She wondered how many women there had been in the last two months and shut down the thought with an inward shudder.

It was all very different without the layers of heavy winter clothing, without the bone-chilling cold. His body now was not just a heavy bulk that promised warmth. It was magnificently hard and masculine — and naked. She could not remember when he had removed his nightshirt. There was not this time the necessity to remain covered, the uncomfortable, narrow confines of the lumpy cot. When he bared her, ready for union, he lifted her nightgown to her waist, threw back the covers, and settled himself between her thighs, pressing them wide. She had not remembered its being quite as physical as it was tonight.

But she remembered what came next. She remembered the mounting — the hardness and the size of him, the stretching sensation, the momentary fear that she could not contain such deep penetration. But tonight there was no pain. And tonight she could hold herself wide so that she could feel it all. She slid her legs up the outside of his, braced her feet flat on the mattress, dropped her knees outward. And she tilted her hips so that she could draw him deeper. It was surely the most rawly physical sensation in the world — the union of man and woman. She realized that his weight had been lifted away from her chest and opened her eyes. He was bracing himself on his elbows and looking down into her face.

"Yes, it is very serious," he said. He withdrew almost completely from her and paused on the brink of her while her eyes fluttered closed again in anticipation of what this time she knew was coming. She had not known that first time. He came back into her slowly, smoothly, deeply.

"Ah," she said with a satisfied sigh, feeling the pleasure of the moment, anticipating the pleasure yet to come. It *had* been pleasant. There had been so many other things that night and the following morning to cloud the pleasure. But it had been a wonderful feeling while it had lasted — and not only because it had brought her warmth.

He lowered himself onto her, though she knew that she did not bear his whole weight. And the pleasure began, the slow and rhythmic pumping, which she could enjoy so much more consciously tonight because she was warm and comfortable and could feel him with the whole of her body, and not just there, where they were joined. And he was able to move more freely in the warm room and on the wide bed. His inward thrusts were firmer, deeper than they had been on that other occasion. He was more comfortably centered between her hips, in the cradle of her thighs.

But her mind did not long hold to the comparisons or to any other moment than the present. It was such a very physical thing, the marriage act, that thought was unnecessary and indeed impossible after the first minutes. She became centered upon sensation, upon the ache between her thighs and up inside where he worked her. The ache spread upward in waves, through her womb, into her breasts, into her throat and up behind her nostrils, out to her fingertips. She lay very still so that she would not miss one moment, one pulse of it.

She did not want it to end. She could hear herself make little protesting noises when his rhythm finally changed, quickening and deepening even further so that she knew it was ending. It could go on all night as far as she was concerned. But then memory was back as he strained against her, held still and deep, and sighed almost soundlessly against the side of her head. The rush of heat at her core was familiar. He had given her his seed.

He was Kenneth, she thought as his full weight relaxed down onto her. She did not open her eyes, but she did not need to. She did not need the candle. She had known with every mindless moment of what had just happened that he was Kenneth, that he could be no one else. That there *could be* no one else.

They must do this, she had told him earlier in the carriage, if they were to make a sensible decision. How could she make a sensible decision now? For what had happened had only succeeded in exposing to her conscious mind what she must block from it if she was to make any rational decision about her future. It was really quite immaterial that she loved him, that she always had and always would. Love was not blind, despite what the poets said. Or if it was, then it ought not to be. There were other considerations of far more importance in a workable relationship — liking, respect, trust, for example. It did not matter that she loved him. But she feared that after tonight she would no longer be able to put that fact far enough to the back of her mind. She sighed.

"I beg your pardon. I must be very heavy."
He moved off her and she felt suddenly cool
and damp — and a little bereft. He pushed
her nightgown down and pulled the bedcovers up about her. He lay beside her,
propped on one elbow. "I believe you were
right," he said. "We must use this dimen-
sion of our marriage as well as others to
help us work out our future. You will learn
in time — if we decide to give ourselves
enough time — to come to full pleasure.
You have much to learn — and doubtless
just as much to teach. But it is very late. It
must be almost dawn. Do not worry about
rising early. We are invited to the Adamses'
for dinner, did you know? And to the theater
afterward. I will see you in time to escort
you to dinner."

"Yes," she said. "Thank you." She would
not see him again until evening? She waited
for him to lie down properly. She felt chilly
with his body removed from her own. She
wanted to touch him, sleep with her body
against his, as they had slept in the baptistry.

But he got out of bed and pulled on his
nightshirt and his robe unhurriedly, without
any apparent embarrassment. But why
should he feel any? They had passed the
point of physical embarrassment with each
other. Besides, he was perfectly beautiful.

Even the numerous scars of old wounds did not detract from that.

"Good night," he said, turning to look at her before he left the room. "I am glad you came, Moira."

"Good night," she said. He waited for a moment, but she could not bring herself to say that she was glad too. She was not sure she was — or rather, she was not sure she ought to be.

She had not expected to be left alone, she thought after he had gone. She was chilly — she buttoned up her nightgown — and she was a little sore. No, not really sore. She still felt the pulsing ache he had aroused in her. And she felt lonely — and alarmed by the thought. She might well be spending the rest of her life alone — she did not wish to start thinking of aloneness as loneliness.

You will learn in time to come to full pleasure. What had he meant? Did he not know how much pleasure she had felt? There could not possibly be more. There could be nothing more pleasurable in the whole world. *You have much to learn.* She felt shamed, humiliated. He had found her wanting. Of course he had. She knew nothing. She had thought it the most wonderful experience in her life, and he had thought that she had much to learn.

She sighed hugely and turned onto her side to punch her pillow. The whole day — and almost the whole night — had been nothing but turmoil. It was a day and a night that seemed to have been a month long. She was not sure she could endure two weeks or more of this.

But then, she was not sure she would be able to endure the quiet tedium of life alone at Dunbarton after even this one day. She lifted her head and punched her pillow into shape once more, though with rather more vengeful force than was strictly necessary.

She wished — oh, how she wished! — she had not brought into the open her deepest, darkest secret. She wished she had not admitted to herself that she loved him. And she wished she had not lain with him. She wished he had stayed and kept his arms about her and his body half covering hers as he had done that other time.

Perhaps she was with child again.

She wrapped the pillow about her head and addressed herself determinedly to sleep.

Kenneth spent a congenial morning with his friends. Although he had had only a few hours of sleep, he felt full of energy as he rode in the park with them. He even welcomed the blustery chill of a cloudy morning.

Lord Pelham spent a few minutes apologizing abjectly and with obvious embarrassment. "That will teach me to be witty and cruel at the expense of strangers I do not even know," he said. "I did not realize at the time that she was anything more to you, Ken, than a neighbor. But even if she had not been, it was unkind to make fun of her behind her back."

"Better that than to her face, I suppose, Ede," Mr. Gascoigne said.

"Never tell me," Lord Rawleigh said, grimacing, "that you exercised your sharp wit at Lady Haverford's expense, Eden. This was before you knew of her connection to Ken? You were extremely fortunate not to have been called out, old chap."

"She was increasing at the time, had not admitted the truth to me, and was still betrothed to someone else," Kenneth said. "That time has passed. Forget it, Eden."

"Betrothed to someone else?" Lord Rawleigh said. "Ouch! But whatever she might have looked like then, she is in remarkably good looks now. Catherine and Daphne are bringing her into the park later this morning. It would be strange indeed if they did not then proceed to go shopping. You will be a lucky man, Ken, not to have your fortune eaten up during the coming weeks and to see your wife often enough to bid her a good morning and a good night."

"Are you complaining, Rex?" Mr. Gascoigne was laughing.

"I am complaining," the viscount said. "Not that I have an extravagant wife. She has been too accustomed to frugality. But the conventions of society and the entertainments of the Season conspire together to keep a man and his wife apart too often. I shall be quite happy to retire to Stratton for the summer — and for the autumn and winter too, I daresay."

"Nelson!" Kenneth roared as his dog spotted a couple of children out walking with their nurse and began to gallop in their direction, barking joyfully. He reduced speed to a reluctant lope and then stopped altogether. But the smaller child, a girl, had to leave her nurse's side and come to pat Nelson's head, which was on a level with her own, and pronounce him a nice doggie. She giggled and scrunched up her face as Nelson licked it.

"The killer hound," Mr. Gascoigne said in mock disgust. "By Jove, it is difficult now to realize that he really is."

"As are we all, Nat," Lord Pelham said.

"Not hounds, perhaps, but certainly killers. I cannot say I am sorry that chapter of our lives is closed."

But Kenneth was thinking about Viscount Rawleigh's last words. It was true that London during the Season was not quite the place to spend time with one's wife. He had not realized it when he had invited her here. He, too, would be happy to retire to his home for the summer — but it was not part of their agreement. It was a new point that would have to be negotiated with her. And it was a new idea to him too — Dunbarton during the summer. With Moira.

It was a seductive thought.

He had always enjoyed a morning with his friends. He enjoyed this morning. And he enjoyed the afternoon at the races with Mr. Gascoigne and a few other acquaintances. Lord Rawleigh had been invited with his wife to a picnic and Lord Pelham had arranged to spend the afternoon with his new mistress. But all day he was plagued by the thought that he had only two weeks during which to persuade Moira to remain with him as his wife, and one day was slipping away without his having set eyes on her. And this was not likely to be an untypical day.

He was riding home from the races late in the afternoon when he finally realized the trend of his thoughts: *to persuade Moira to remain with him.* Was this not a mutual experiment they were engaged upon? Were they not both taking these two weeks to decide if they could tolerate each other, if they could make something of their marriage? When had he begun to think in terms of having to persuade her? Was he convinced then of what he wanted?

He thought inevitably of the night before. She had taken him quite by surprise. He had not expected that she would consent to being bedded, especially as the day had had its moments of friction and had not by any means been an unqualified success. But it was something that had given him enormous pleasure — that was a vast understatement. She had enjoyed it too. She had not actively participated, and she had reached no climax, though he had tried to give her as much time as she needed. But she had positioned herself so that she was fully open to him, and she had been relaxed and receptive. He would have known if she had found it unpleasant. She had not.

Was that when he had decided that he wanted her with him for the rest of his life? Was it no more than a sexual thing? But even with the most satisfactory of the mistresses he had ever employed, he had never thought in terms of permanency. A man needed variety in his sexual life, a change of partners now and then. No, he must not be unfair to himself by imagining that his only interest in Moira was sexual. Besides, she was easily the least skilled lover he had ever had.

No, he thought with some reluctance. There was only one reason why a man would wish permanence in a relationship with a woman and would find himself relinquishing his preference for variety and a change of partners. Not lust. Only its opposite. He hated to put it into words. But he had no choice. He might prevent his voice from saying the word, but he could not prevent his mind from thinking it.

It was because he loved her. She could be obnoxious and stubborn and sharp-tongued — and many worse things if he sent his mind back almost nine years. And he loved her.

He found himself striding eagerly into his house a short while later, having handed his horse over to a groom's care. Was she home yet? He had not seen her since he had left her bed a short while before dawn — with the greatest reluctance. But he had not wanted to take advantage of her generosity by remaining to sleep with her. Surely she must be home by now. It was really quite late.

Her ladyship was in the drawing room, his butler told him with a bow. He took the stairs two at a time and then felt foolish when he realized that his servants would be observing him and exchanging knowing smirks.

She was sitting very straight-backed, very elegant beside the fireplace. She set aside her embroidery when he opened the door. He felt foolishly shy. He advanced partway across the room and made her his bow.

"I trust you have had a good day?" he said.

"You are rather late, my lord," she said. "Perhaps you have forgotten that we have a dinner engagement?"

He raised his eyebrows and looked at the clock. "Late, ma'am?" he said. "I think not. Is that the only greeting I may expect? A cold-eyed, tight-lipped scold?" His mood had changed to one of instant irritation. What sort of a child's fairy tale had he been weaving for the past hour or so? *This* was the real Moira. *These* were his real feelings for her.

"I believe it would be discourteous to Mr. and Mrs. Adams," she said, "to be late. And you are *dusty,* my lord. You will need to bathe."

"You may rest assured, ma'am," he said, "that my servants noticed the same thing and that even now hot water is being carried up to my dressing room. My apologies for offending your sensibilities by appearing thus before you."

She made no response. She reached for her embroidery, changed her mind, and returned her hands to her lap.

"What has happened?" he asked. "This has nothing to do with my imagined lateness or my very real dustiness, does it?"

She looked at him consideringly, her eyes hostile. "Did you put her up to it?" she asked. "Was she speaking on your instructions? I deeply resent your deceit in bringing me here under false pretenses."

He went to stand in front of her and clasped his hands at his back. "And I deeply resent your attitude, ma'am," he said. "If I have something to say to you, I will say it. What has my mother said to so upset you?"

"It was insinuations and suggestions all afternoon long," she said, "usually when we were in company with other ladies and she knew very well that I could not retaliate. It seems that I am to work very hard to overcome my roots as a member of the lesser gentry. That will mean keeping my company more exclusive when I return to

Dunbarton by not issuing indiscriminate invitations or accepting every one that is sent to me. I must no longer consider Harriet Lincoln to be my *friend*. I must invite houseguests to Dunbarton for the summer so that I might be seen mingling with people more suited to my position as the Countess of Haverford. I must discourage my mother from being forever in and out of Dunbarton. I must be sure to present you with a son at the earliest possible moment. Shall I continue?"

He was very angry — against his mother, against Moira.

"And you assumed this came from me?" he asked her.

"Why *did* you summon me to London?" she asked.

"I *invited* you here for the very reasons I gave you the evening before last," he said. "My mother speaks for herself. If you find what she says objectionable, ma'am — and if you do not, I most certainly do — then I shall have a word with her. Better yet, *you* must have a word with her. I would remind you that you are the Countess of Haverford and mistress of Dunbarton, not she. You may be as familiar as you wish with our neighbors, Moira, and count as many of them friends as you choose. Lady Hayes is welcome to take up residence at Dunbarton if it is your wish. And as for a son, he — or she, a daughter — will doubtless come without our having to will it if we continue having marital relations. You may deny me your bed anytime you choose. You may rest assured that I will never use force to claim my rights." As he felt at the moment, he had no wish even to continue with their experiment. He would be just as happy if she announced her wish to return to Cornwall. How could she believe that his mother had been speaking for him this afternoon?

"It seems I have done you an injustice," she said stiffly. "I beg your pardon."

But his mood had been ruined. And perhaps it was just as well. There was little point in falling in love with her.

"I trust that your morning at least was enjoyable?" he asked.

"Yes, thank you," she said. "The company was very pleasant. We went shopping after walking in the park."

He half smiled. Rex had been quite right.

"I bought something," she said, turning to fumble on the side table behind her embroidery. "I paid for it with my allowance. You will not be receiving a bill."

"You may have bills sent to me at any time," he said.

"But this is a gift." She held out a small package to him. "A sort of wedding gift, I suppose. You gave me one yesterday."

He took it from her hand and unwrapped a small and exquisitely lacquered snuffbox.

"I have never seen you take snuff," she said. "But it was pretty."

Life would never be tranquil if he remained with Moira, he thought. His mood had swung dizzyingly between two extremes just within the past ten minutes. He wanted to cry. It was not a particularly expensive gift. He had seen snuffboxes of far greater value. And it was true that he did not take snuff and that therefore the box would be useless to him. But it was a wedding gift — his from his wife.

"Perhaps I will have to start taking snuff," he said, "and sneezing all over you."

There was merriment in her eyes for a moment, and he smiled.

"Thank you," he said. "It *is* pretty."

"We are late, my lord," she said, standing up.

"And I am dusty," he said. "Dare I offer my arm to escort you to your dressing room?"

She lifted her arm to take his.

21

The two weeks crawled by and sped by. Sometimes it seemed to Moira that every day was so crammed full with activities that there would never again be time to rest or to relax. Sometimes she longed for the quiet and for the leisurely pace of life in Cornwall. At other times she remembered that these weeks were perhaps the only ones she would ever have in London during the Season and that really there was a great deal of enjoyment to be had there. Sometimes she longed to be away from Kenneth so that she could think straight. Never a day went by that they did not antagonize each other, especially on those days when they spent some time together. At other times she felt the beginnings of panic at the thought that perhaps she would be spending the rest of her life away from him. How would she live without him? Sometimes she was frustrated by the demands of her lady friends and acquaintances and by the demands of his male friends that kept them apart for hours of the day at a time — occasionally for the whole day. At other times she thought that they might be better friends if they saw even less of each other.

There was only a part of each day when they never quarreled or disagreed or were in anything but perfect amity with each other. But a relationship could not rely on *that* alone, wonderful as it was. She wondered how she would be able to do without it if she returned to Dunbarton alone. The same way as she had always lived without it, she supposed. But it would be difficult now that she knew what she would be missing. Not that she knew all or even most, she suspected. Each night it was different — and each night it was glorious.

When they were not about their separate pursuits in the daytime, they went walking or driving together in the park, visiting galleries, on picnics, and to one Venetian breakfast and one wedding at St. George's. They spent their evenings at the theater, at soirées, concerts, balls, a literary evening. They had frequent invitations to dinner and entertained at their own home one evening. There was never a lack of company or of things to do.

There was one memorable encounter during the two weeks. Moira's sister-in-law came face-to-face with her in the park one morning when she was with Lord Ainsleigh's cousin and Moira was with Lady Rawleigh and Lady Baird. They all stopped to exchange civilities, and Moira was surprised to find that when they walked on, the other two ladies took the same direction as theirs and Helen maneuvered matters so that she walked with Moira, a little apart from the others.

"Mama is in high dudgeon," she said after they had exhausted the topic of the weather. "That must have been quite a setdown you gave her."

"I am sorry to have given that impression," Moira said stiffly. "I merely wished her to understand that I am answerable for my behavior only to my husband."

"Oh, Mama will recover," Helen said. "She cannot bear to be out of favor with Kenneth, and he has given her an even mightier setdown, as you must know."

Moira did not. She was curiously pleased.

"The point is," Helen said, "that Michael has no sisters, only brothers. You are my only sister. And of course, I am yours. It would seem sad if we were to go through life as permanent enemies."

"I did not realize until last Christmas that we were supposed to be enemies," Moira said. "You once loved Sean, and so did I."

"Until last Christmas," Helen said, "until I went back to Dunbarton, and until I saw you, I did not realize how deeply wounded I had been by all that business with Sean. I married Michael within a year of it and I have grown truly fond of him. But perhaps it is only natural that one's first love is lodged forever in one's heart. I did love him, Moira. And you betrayed us. You told Kenneth that we were going to elope, and of course, being Kenneth, with his very powerful sense of responsibility, he felt obliged to tell Papa. And that was the end of it all."

"I did not tell him you were going to elope," Moira said, frowning. "I did not even know it myself. I told him only that you loved each other and were determined to wed. I thought he would be pleased. We also loved each other, you see, and I thought — mistakenly, as it turned out — that he meant to marry me too. I thought that together, the four of us would have a better chance persuading your father and mine."

Helen laughed. "Who can know the truth of it now?" she said. "But you were a fool if you thought that, Moira. Our father would never have consented to any match between one of his children and a Hayes. Even apart from the feud, your father was a mere baronet and not a wealthy one at that. And Kenneth would not have lowered himself so."

"Thank you," Moira said curtly.

"I do not know what happened this year," Helen said. "I do not know why Kenneth suddenly rushed home, married you, and returned to London without you. I suspect — but no matter. The point is that we are sisters, Moira, for better or for worse. If you will forgive my rudeness at Christmas, I will forgive you for betraying me. Perhaps I never would have been happy with Sean. I am very comfortable in the society in which I move, you see. Anyway — what do you think?"

"I will forgive your rudeness," Moira said.

"Oh, good." Helen took her arm and squeezed it. "I *do* wish I could have heard what you said to Mama. No one ever stands up to her, you know, except Kenneth, who has always done it in that quiet, frosty way he has so perfected. I would not dare try. I still feel like an infant in leading strings when Mama speaks."

"Doing it almost gave me heart palpitations," Moira admitted. "But Kenneth had instructed me to remember who I am, and I had to do it. I cannot imagine a worse ignominy than having him believe me a coward."

They both laughed with a shared delight.

"He may think it of me whenever he wishes," Helen said. "He has always frankly terrified me. I believe he might have met his match in you, though. I do hope so. Men like Kenneth should not be allowed to go through life having their own way and reducing everyone in their path to jelly. Do you love him?"

"Yes," Moira said after a short pause. She laughed. "But please do not tell him."

Helen squeezed her arm again. "It will be our secret," she said. "I do hope we can be friends in time, Moira. I have always wanted a sister. And I once expected her to be you."

"I will hope so too, then," Moira said. But it would not be easy, she knew. There would be an awkwardness between them for a while. And if she went home to Dunbarton without Kenneth, then all chance of amity between her and her in-laws would be at an end.

But it felt good to have sorted out her relationship with his family to a certain extent. Now, if only she could sort out her relationship with Kenneth himself.

■ ■ ■ ■

Kenneth took his wife to the Egyptian Hall on Piccadilly one afternoon with the sole purpose of showing her the display of Napoleonic relics there, including Bonaparte's bulletproof carriage, which had been captured after Waterloo. The Rawleighs were with them. He and Rex were not particularly eager for reminders of the war, Kenneth thought, but the ladies were. They had both expressed their curiosity at a dinner the evening before. They both wanted to know about their husbands' lives for the past number of years.

They were going to go to Gunter's for ices after they had gazed at the carriage with suitable awe and for a sufficient length of time. It was a sunny afternoon, and they were in a merry mood. But as they came out of the front doors and turned onto the street, Kenneth noticed a couple in very heavy mourning coming in the opposite direction. He bent his head closer to Moira's.

"Do you see who is approaching?" he asked her.

"Oh," she said after she had looked. "Oh, dear. Is there any way of escaping?"

"Too late," he murmured and prepared to be cut cold by Sir Edwin Baillie.

But that gentleman, upon spying them, stopped in his tracks, made them a deep and deferential bow, and begged for the honor of presenting his companion to the Earl and Countess of Haverford. Lord and Lady Rawleigh walked tactfully onward.

Sir Edwin's companion was his eldest sister, a plain and sensible-looking young lady who nevertheless looked quite awed by the honor that was being accorded her. Her brother tried to reassure her by reminding her that her ladyship, the Countess of Haverford and mistress of Dunbarton, the finest estate in Cornwall, was also her cousin and that therefore his lordship, the Earl of Haverford, hero of the wars that had stamped out tyranny from all of Europe and saved their fair England from the threat of invasion, was in a sense her cousin too — if his lordship would pardon the familiarity of such a claim.

His lordship pronounced himself pleased to make Miss Baillie's acquaintance.

"And if you will pardon the further familiarity, my lord," Sir Edwin continued, "as coming from a neighbor and a cousin and — I might make so bold as to say — a friend, might I commend you on the extreme kindness you have shown my dear cousin, Lady Haverford, in taking her as your wife?"

Kenneth pursed his lips and inclined his head. Moira stood very still beside him.

"You knew of my dreadful predicament on the demise of my dear and much lamented mother, my lord," Sir Edwin said. "I had my grief to contend with and my sisters to settle and my affairs to set in order. I was unable to give the attention to my betrothed that any young woman of delicate birth delights in. I take it as the mark of a true friend — yes, I must insist upon the honor of so calling you, my lord — that you stepped in and released me from my predicament by marrying Miss Hayes — Lady Haverford, that is — yourself."

"It was my pleasure, sir," Kenneth murmured. It was a long time, he thought, since he had been so marvelously diverted.

Sir Edwin became suddenly aware of the vulgarity of engaging in a lengthy conversation in the middle of a public thoroughfare. He would not keep his lordship and her ladyship a moment longer. He bowed himself past them after explaining that business had necessitated his coming to town, but that despite the somberness of the occasion and the depth of his grief, he had thought it not quite disrespectful to the dearly departed to take his sister to view the relics of that monster in the defeat of whom his lordship had played such a distinguished part. He hoped his lordship would not accuse them of behaving in a spirit of too much levity so soon after their mama's demise.

His lordship did not accuse them of anything at all.

"Well, Moira," Kenneth said as they walked on to catch up with their friends.

"Oh, dear," she said, "what do you expect me to say?"

"I am in fear and trembling," he said, "lest you tell me you were making comparisons as we stood side by side and decided that you had made the wrong choice."

"I do not believe this is a subject for a joke," she said primly. "Besides, if you will remember, I had no choice."

"Because you walked out into that infernal storm," he said. But he could feel a quarrel coming on and Rex and his lady were not far ahead. Besides, he was feeling in too good a humor to enjoy a quarrel. "Was he not generosity itself, Moira? Commending me on marrying you? Considering it as a compliment to himself?"

"What did you expect him to say?" she asked. "I daresay he has as much pride as any other man."

"What did I expect?" he said. "I am not sure. The man is unique in my experience. But I will tell you what I would have done if the situation had been reversed. I would have popped him a good one. I would have seen to it that his nose was protruding from the wrong side of his head before I bowed myself out of his sight."

She stopped walking and pressed a closed fist to her nose and mouth. She closed her eyes tightly. But she was unable to contain what she tried so valiantly to contain. She exploded with laughter and shook with it, totally helpless, until tears were streaming down her cheeks.

"Dear me," Kenneth said and then joined her.

"Oh, my side," she wailed at last, clutching a hand to it. "Oh, Kenneth, is he not *priceless*?"

"For myself," he said, "I would not disown him as a cousin for all the tea in China, or whatever more convincing cliché you can think of to substitute. And as for Sir Edwin himself, when he finally decides to honor some other young lady with his addresses, he will overpower her with awe by claiming kinship with the Earl of Haverford, master of Dunbarton, et cetera, et cetera."

"And one must not forget," Moira said, "that the late Mrs. Baillie was a Grafton of Hugglesbury." She doubled over in another paroxysm of glee.

"Oh, dear me, no," he said. "And how mortifying, Moira, if he should make boast of that fact before mentioning me." He threw back his head and roared with laughter.

There was a delicate cough from nearby. "Do you intend to stand there for the rest of the afternoon, guffawing and making a spectacle of yourself, Ken?" Viscount Rawleigh asked.

"You should have stayed to be introduced," Kenneth told him. "Sir Edwin Baillie would have been speechless with wonder and *that* would have been something to behold. Sir Edwin is Moira's cousin with a couple of seconds or thirds and a few removes to make the relationship more palatable to her. And I tell you, Rex, he is positively my favorite cousin-in-law. Is he not, Moira?"

She was dabbing at her eyes with a handkerchief and looking embarrassed and self-conscious. But he grinned at her as he offered his arm. It was the first time in years that they had laughed together and been silly together. It felt wonderful to laugh and be silly with Moira.

The Season had all but ended. Many people had already left town for their country estates or one of the spas. Most of those of the beau monde who remained would follow them within the next week or so. Nothing had been said between Moira and Kenneth about leaving — for obvious reasons. She would return to Dunbarton, of course. The only detail to be decided upon was the day of her departure. But would she go alone? It was a question of such significance that both of them avoided it and the setting of any date. But it would be soon.

It was a question they would face and answer after the night at Vauxhall. That night had been arranged well in advance, and it had been assumed among the members of the group that were to go that it would be the final celebration of the Season. Lord and Lady Rawleigh were to leave for Stratton Park the morning after, and Mr. and Mrs. Adams were to return to Derbyshire. Lord Pelham was going to Brighton the day after that. Moira suspected that he was taking a mistress with him, since there had been a loud silence when she had asked if Mr. Gascoigne was to accompany him.

Mr. Gascoigne, it seemed, was to go home, as his father was ailing and there was still a sizable family to be managed.

Within three or four days of the Vauxhall evening, all their closest friends were going to be gone, Moira thought. Helen and Michael and her mother-in-law had already left. She would have to leave too. But first they must make a decision. She did not welcome the thought. She did not know what she wanted to do. But it was a problem she would put aside until after Vauxhall. Nothing must spoil that evening.

She had looked forward to all the entertainments of the Season and to seeing all the famous sights of London. But the best had been kept until last. Vauxhall, she had heard, was a magical place, especially at night when the pavilion was lit with numerous lamps and candles, and colored lamps swayed from the tree branches along the paths that the patrons strolled. There were boxes at the pavilion where one could sit and eat while listening to the musical entertainment. There was dancing there. And often there was a fireworks display.

Only the weather could spoil the evening. Moira watched it anxiously all through a heavily clouded morning and a partly cloudy afternoon. But the sky cleared with the coming of evening and the air seemed to grow warmer just at the time when one might have expected it to cool off.

"You look very lovely," her husband said when she joined him in the hall.

"Thank you." She smiled at him. She was wearing the only gown she had bought in London, an extravagance in lace and pale green satin that Catherine and Daphne between them had persuaded her into purchasing — not that she had needed much persuasion, it was true.

"The gown is new?" he asked, taking her warm shawl from her arm and wrapping it about her shoulders. "Have I received the bill for it yet?"

"I paid for it myself," she said.

"You will present me with the bill tomorrow, then," he said, handing her into the carriage and climbing in beside her. "Your allowance is for personal expenses, Moira. I will clothe you."

She did not reply. It would be senseless to argue. And foolish. She should be delighted — the gown had been very costly. But she hated to be dependent upon a man. *I will clothe you.* There was something mortifying in the thought. She had been dependent upon a man all her life, of course — on her father, and more lately, on Sir Edwin Baillie.

But this seemed different.

"It will always be so, ma'am," he said, reading her thoughts, his voice rather cold, as it so frequently was. "There is no point in looking mulish. Even if you never see me again after this week, you will always be my wife."

"My possession," she said quietly. "You might as well say it aloud."

"You will always be my possession," he said curtly.

They were quarreling over his generosity. Was she mad? *Even if you never see me again after this week.* Panic threatened.

"There will be dancing tonight," he said abruptly, changing the subject after a short, resentful silence. "Everyone will wish to dance with you — Rex and his brother, Baird, Nat, Eden. But I would waltz with you, Moira. The first after supper. You will reserve it for me."

"That is a command, my lord?" she asked.

"Yes, by God, is it a command," he said, sounding thoroughly irritated, but he looked at her sidelong as she was looking at him. It was something that had been happening between them occasionally — flashes of irritation deflected by a shared sense of humor.

"Then I need not agree to save it," she

said. "I have no choice anyway."

"You are learning," he said.

"Yes, my lord," she replied meekly.

He continued to look at her sidelong without turning his head toward her.

Vauxhall, which they approached by water in company with the other members of their party, was everything Moira had expected and more. The lights from colored lamps shimmered across the surface of the Thames and when they entered the pleasure gardens there was the feeling of entering a fairy tale, of leaving the real world behind.

"Oh, Kenneth," she said, gazing about her, looking upward into the tree branches, "have you ever seen anything lovelier?"

"Yes." He covered her hand on his arm with his free hand. "Moonlight shining in a band across the sea at Tawmouth."

Very daringly she had met him in the hollow above the cliffs after dark one evening and they had watched just the scene he had described, sitting side by side, his arm about her shoulders. He had kissed her, yet she had felt in no danger at all from him. Ah, the sweet innocence of youth.

He might never see Tawmouth again. She might live there alone — with her memories.

It was a warm, only slightly breezy evening.

Vauxhall Gardens was crowded with revelers, perhaps because the end of the Season had arrived and everyone was making much of the last few entertainments available to them. They had done all that people did at Vauxhall: They had strolled along the shady paths in couples before supper, though none of them had walked with their own spouses; they had listened to the orchestra play Handel; they had eaten the thin slices of ham and the strawberries and drunk the champagne for which the Gardens were famous; they had conversed and laughed; they had danced.

There was a feeling almost of desperation about the evening — at least there was for Kenneth. It was not a particularly pleasant prospect that all these friends of theirs would disperse to various parts of the country within the next two days. There was no knowing when they would meet again. But that sadness was nothing in comparison to the greatest uncertainty of all. Would he and Moira also be going their separate ways? He would know soon. They could not postpone the decision much longer. Tomorrow — they must make it tomorrow.

They both knew it. They were both determinedly merry tonight. They had not sat beside each other in the box Sir Clayton

Baird had reserved. They had not walked together or danced together. They had not once looked into each other's eyes. But the orchestra was about to play a waltz — at last. And it was after supper. He stood and fixed his eyes upon her for the first time. She was laughing over something Eden was saying to her, but she sobered immediately and looked up at him.

"This is my waltz, I believe, Moira," he said, holding out a hand for hers.

"Yes." She looked at his hand for a few moments before setting her own in it. She was not smiling when she stood up, as she had smiled all evening. The very air seemed to sizzle with tension. Surely they must all feel it, Kenneth thought. Indeed, it seemed that everyone in the box fell silent and watched the two of them leave together to waltz.

"Well," Mr. Gascoigne said, "what is the verdict on those two?"

"My guess is," Lord Pelham said, "that the lady does not allow herself to be easily dominated. Our Ken would not like that."

"I would have to agree with you, Eden," Viscount Rawleigh said. "He would not like it at all. But I do believe he might be caught by it. Irrevocably caught."

"I would say that she certainly does not like being dominated," Lady Baird said, "and that Lord Haverford, if he is wise, would relax that cold, rather domineering manner of his."

"But he does it so very *handsomely,* Daphne, you must confess," Lady Rawleigh said with a laugh. "And I believe Moira is quite competent to deal with it. Besides, they *love* each other. That is as plain as the nose on my face."

"Ah, a woman's answer," Mr. Adams said. "They *love* each other and all has been said." He smiled affectionately at his sister-in-law.

"It will not be a tranquil marriage," Mr. Gascoigne said.

"Quite frankly, Nat," Lord Rawleigh said, "I do not believe Ken could endure a tranquil marriage."

"They certainly know how to laugh together, anyway," Lady Rawleigh said, exchanging an amused smile with her husband.

"They are sure to live happily ever after, then," Sir Clayton said, getting to his feet. "Come and waltz, Daph?"

22

"You are enjoying yourself?" Kenneth asked Moira after he had led her onto the dancing floor before the pavilion.

"Immensely," she said. "I knew this would be a lovely place and a wonderful evening. I have not been disappointed. And dancing in the outdoors is the most delicious thing to do. I wish I could dance all night. May we dance until dawn, my lord?" She lifted one hand to set lightly on his shoulder and set the other in his.

"I hope not," he said. "I have other plans for what remains of the night after we arrive home."

The music began and she moved smoothly with him into the rhythm of the waltz. They had danced with each other so few times since her arrival in town. This was their first waltz together since the Dunbarton ball. All the doubts ever expressed about the propriety of the waltz were thoroughly well-founded, he thought.

"Ah, yes," she said in response to what he had said a few moments before. "And that will be more enjoyable by far than dancing."

He twirled her about. He could not take his eyes from her. She was again that vivid girl who had scorned convention and had said boldly whatever was in her thoughts. But he could not quite believe the evidence of his own ears on this occasion. She was flirting with him, he realized. Flirting not as other ladies of his acquaintance flirted — with fluttering eyelashes and soulful eyes and parted lips — but as the boldest courtesan might flirt. But then, what else would he have expected of Moira?

"In many ways," he said, "it bears a remarkable resemblance to dancing. In this waltz, you see, you have fit yourself comfortably to my rhythm."

"It is not difficult," she said, "to follow the lead of a man who moves with such confident skill."

"There is nothing," he said, bending his head a little closer to hers, "better designed to bring mutual pleasure to two people than a dance in which they move as one."

"Except," she said, her voice almost a whisper, "that which bears a remarkable resemblance to dancing."

The minx! She was not going to relinquish mastery to him, then. She was not to be disconcerted by risqué conversation. She made outrageous love to him with her eyes and with her words. He had almost forgotten their surroundings. He remembered them now and put a little more distance between them. Their bodies had been almost touching.

"You waltz well, Moira," he said. "A great deal has happened since the first time we waltzed together."

"Yes," she said, and he could see the recklessness fade from her eyes to be replaced by an almost dreamy look. "It was the very first time I had waltzed. It had a reputation in Tawmouth as a scandalous dance."

"A justly deserved notoriety," he said.

"It is the most wonderful dance ever invented," she said. "I thought so then, and I think so now."

They danced the rest of it in silence, moving together with an instinctively shared sense of its rhythm, and with a mutual awareness of the other dance they would perform together in the privacy of their own home before the night was over. The cool evening breeze fanned their hot cheeks. The lamps on the pavilion and in the trees merged into a kaleidoscope of color about the edges of their vision.

It could not be all that far from dawn, Moira thought later as they rode home in the carriage. It had been the last entertainment of the Season. Everyone had been reluctant to see it end. She kept her eyes closed and felt pleasantly sleepy and even more pleasantly aroused for what was to come when they arrived home.

She kept her thoughts firmly away from tomorrow.

"You are not sleeping, by any chance, are you?" her husband asked.

She opened her eyes to smile at him. "I am not," she said. "I am just resting."

"A good idea," he said, a wealth of meaning in the words.

She wondered suddenly why there was a decision yet to make. They had quarreled during the two weeks they had been together, but not all the time. There had been more times when they had not quarreled. She would guess that there were many marriages in which there was more bad feeling between the partners than there was between her and Kenneth. And yet somehow those other married couples succeeded in rubbing along together well enough.

Rubbing along together — she sighed inwardly. That was the whole trouble. Merely rubbing along with a husband could never be enough for her, and she suspected that the same was true of Kenneth. Though it was not entirely true of her, of course. She would have married Sir Edwin Baillie, knowing very well that the marriage could only ever be tolerable at best. But then, that had been a different matter altogether. She had not *loved* Sir Edwin.

It was too complicated a matter to be thought of tonight, she decided, and she had promised herself that she would not do it. Tomorrow would come soon enough. She wished tomorrow would never come. She wished tonight could last forever.

"We are home," a low voice said close to her ear, and her eyes snapped open. Her head was resting very comfortably on a broad, warm shoulder.

"Perhaps," he said, "I should escort you to your room and leave you there to sleep."

"No," she said, sitting up. "I do not want to sleep — yet."

"Ah," he said. "You wish to dance again, ma'am?"

"I told you I wanted to dance all night," she said.

"And your wish is my command," he said.

It was a dance in which they were immediately in harmony. He left all the candles burning, stripped away her nightgown and his nightshirt, kneeled with her on the bed, face-to-face, explored her with lightly seeking hands as she did the like to him, watched her through half-closed lids as she watched him, touched her face lightly with opened mouth and caressing tongue as she touched his.

When he lifted her breasts high with his hands and lowered his head to lick at her nipples, to suck them one at a time into his mouth, she held his head with both hands, her fingers threaded into his hair, and lowered her own head to croon to him, to moan her pleasure.

He was on fire for her almost from the first moment. He had never wanted, he realized, as he wanted tonight. Always before Moira there had been simply a woman's body to give him pleasure, to be pleasured in return. Tonight, more even than for the past two weeks, it was *her* body, and he knew that all his adult life he had lived this moment in fantasy though he had never admitted it to himself until now. Always there had been Moira, as unconsciously a part of his life as the air he breathed.

She knelt with spread thighs and threw her head back as he slid his hand beneath her and teased her with fingers experienced at arousing desire. With his mouth he caressed her throat. Desire was a pain that throbbed in his groin and pounded against his temples and thundered against his eardrums.

Women, he knew from long experience, drew their sexual pleasure far more from foreplay than from penetration. He would have patience if she needed patience. He would wait for her all the rest of the night if necessary. Tonight she would know all the pleasure there was to know if it was within his power to give it to her.

"Does this feel good?" he asked against her mouth. "Do you want more? Do you want me inside? Tell me what you want."

"Come inside me," she whispered.

He put himself between her thighs, lifted her astride him, positioned himself, thrust hard and firm up into her — and waited for her to settle into a more comfortable position and wrap her arms about his shoulders.

"Dance with me now," he said. "Let us share the rhythm and the melody."

"Lead the way, then," she whispered, "and I will follow."

She stayed still for a few moments, as she had always stayed still during his lovemakings, while he began the thrust and withdrawal of love, and then she began tentatively to match his movements. After a while she added the rhythm of inner muscles clenching and unclenching about him and he lost all sense of time or place. Everything became sensation: the sound of labored, sobbing breath, the smell of cologne and sweat and woman, the feel of hot, slick, muscled depths, the instinctive determination to hold back, to prolong pain until he felt his partner first burst into release. Moira. His partner. She was part of the sensation. Not for one moment did his body lose its awareness that she was Moira.

She broke rhythm. She bore down hard on him, clenched hard about him, strained with tautness.

"Yes," he murmured against her ear, holding deep in her, rocking his hips against her. "Yes. Come, then. It is the end of the dance."

Release did not burst from her, as he expected. It came in soft sighing murmurs and in a gradual and total relaxation. It came in peace and incredible beauty. He withdrew slowly and slid deep once more, releasing his pain, his need, into her, sighing against her hair.

"Yes," he said softly when he had finished.

"You were right," she said a long while later. They were still kneeling up, clasped together, joined at their core. "There was more pleasure to be had. I had no idea."

"I am always pleased to be of service to you, ma'am," he said, kissing her nose.

"Pleasure *is* good — for a while at least," she said.

"Very good." He pondered her words: *for a while at least.* It was so easy to believe when one was engaged in sexual activity that sex was all. It was not, of course. Not even nearly all. And he had needed Moira to remind him of that. He lifted her carefully off him and laid her down on the bed, straightening her cramped legs. "And so is sleep when the dancing is at an end."

He got off the bed, covered her, picked up his nightshirt without bothering to pull it on, and smiled down at her. "Good night, Moira. That was a great pleasure indeed."

"Good night, Kenneth," she said. She did not smile back at him. She closed her eyes before he turned away.

And tomorrow we will talk. Neither of them had spoken the words aloud. But they had both heard them quite clearly.

Tomorrow they would talk.

■ ■ ■ ■

Despite the late night, made later by an hour of vigorous lovemaking, they were up and out by the middle of the morning. They walked to Rawleigh House to wave the viscount and viscountess on their way. The sky was a brilliant blue, unmarred by even the smallest of clouds, and the day, already hot, promised to be a scorcher later on.

"It is a reminder," Kenneth said, "that it is time to leave London behind for the opener spaces and cleaner air of the countryside or the seaside."

"Yes," Moira said.

They had been chatting quite amicably since she had joined him at the breakfast table earlier. And yet it had needed only carelessly spoken words like these to silence them. Moira did not doubt that he was as aware as she of the difference between what they had done together in bed the night before and what they had done during the two weeks preceding it. And of course he was as aware as she of the decision they must come to during the next day or two. He had just come perilously close to putting it into words.

They walked the rest of the way in silence.

Viscount Rawleigh and his wife were in good spirits. They were clearly excited at the prospect of returning home to Stratton Park in Kent. Mr. Gascoigne had also come to bid them farewell. Lord Pelham had not.

"He fully intended to, Rex," Mr. Gascoigne said, grinning. "But I daresay he is still abed, fast asleep after — ah, after the late night at Vauxhall."

"I daresay you are right, Nat," the viscount said dryly while Catherine caught Moira's eye, tossed her glance ceilingward, and shook her head.

Lord Pelham, Moira thought, must be thoroughly infatuated with his new mistress.

"Thank you for coming to see us on our way, my dear," Lord Rawleigh said, taking one of Moira's hands in both his own. "We will miss our friends. I asked Ken to bring you to Stratton for a few weeks, but he assures me that you have other plans. Enjoy the summer, then. It has been a delight to meet you." He raised her hand to his lips.

"Moira." Catherine hugged her tightly. "I feel that I have known you all my life instead of just two weeks. I am so glad our friendship will continue because our husbands are friends. I will write to you — at Dunbarton? Is that where you and Lord Haverford are going?"

Moira smiled and nodded.

"You must come and visit us there," Kenneth said from behind Moira before taking Catherine's hand and bowing over it. "Must they not, Moira?"

"Of course." She smiled again. "It is in one of the loveliest parts of the world."

"Perhaps next year," the viscount said with a chuckle. He looked fondly at Catherine. "After a certain event has been brought to a safe conclusion."

She smiled back at him and blushed. Moira, looking at them, felt a stab of envy.

Mr. Gascoigne was kissing Catherine's hand. "And you, sir," she said. "May we expect you at Stratton anytime soon? We would both be very happy to have you. Or is your father seriously ailing?"

"I suspect," he said, grimacing, "that my father's indisposition arises as much as anything from the fact that he has five daughters yet to marry and a niece who has been growing mutinous."

"Oh, dear," Catherine said.

"I believe," he continued, "that he has pleasant mental images of me lining up eligible suitors for my sisters and taking my cousin over my knee and giving her a good walloping. He is wrong on all counts, of course. But I am going, you see."

"If I were you, Nat," Kenneth said, "I would emigrate to America today — or, preferably, yesterday."

"Is there no more distant location?" Rex asked.

Mr. Gascoigne smiled almost apologetically. "I went home just before Waterloo, if you will remember," he said. "I stayed for five days before leaving again in a hurry — so many females, all of them riding roughshod over my poor father, who loves nothing better than to spend his days in his library. But now that I have recovered from the shock of finding the girls all grown up, I must confess to a fondness for them."

"And a desire to line up those eligibles for them," Viscount Rawleigh said, slapping a hand on his shoulder. "To it, then, Nat, old chap. Take Eden with you." He laughed. "We must be on our way, my love."

He handed Catherine into the carriage and within minutes they were on their way, both of them waving from the open window.

"Well," Mr. Gascoigne said, gazing after them, "that was one hastily contracted marriage that appears to have turned out well."

Moira stiffened. Kenneth said nothing.

Mr. Gascoigne swung around to look at them. He winced and grimaced simultaneously. "Oh, I say —" he began.

"Think nothing of it," Kenneth said. "You are quite right. Moira and I are going to stroll back through the park. Would you care to join us?"

"I hope to be on my way later today," Mr. Gascoigne said. "There are numerous things to do first. You will excuse me? Lady Haverford, ma'am —" He took Moira's hand in his. "It has been my great pleasure to make your acquaintance. Ken is a lucky devil, if you will pardon my language."

He shook Kenneth's hand and then the two of them hugged each other impulsively before he strode away, leaving them standing together on the pavement outside Rawleigh House.

"*Shall* we stroll in the park?" Kenneth asked.

Moira nodded and took his arm. She had pictured them talking in the drawing room, deciding their future there. But there was a tension between them as they walked, a silence that was in no way comfortable. It would happen in the park, she guessed. They were walking toward the most crucial moment of their lives.

"We will wait until we are inside the park," he said quietly, as if he had read her thoughts. "We will walk down by the Serpentine, I think."

"Yes," she said.

"Well, Moira." They had not spoken for fifteen minutes or more. But they had strolled across lawns, beneath trees, along by the Serpentine. They had watched a group of children trying to sail a boat on the water, guiding it with a stick so that it would not sail beyond their reach. A nurse had warned them rather weakly to be careful.

Kenneth could hear his wife inhaling slowly.

"Three months ago," he said, "we married because circumstances forced us into it. The morning after and again a week after that you told me you wished never to set eyes on me again. A little over two weeks ago you joined me here because I had — summoned you. You agreed to remain to enjoy what was left of the Season. Have you enjoyed it?"

"Yes," she said.

"And to decide if you still felt as you did three months ago. Do you?"

There was a lengthy silence. "We were *both* to decide," she said at last. "You were as reluctant about the marriage as I. You were as eager to get away from me as I was to see you go. Why you decided that we should rethink that decision I do not quite know, but it was both of us who were to do it. Do *you* still feel the same way?"

It was quite as difficult as he could possibly have imagined. A mutual decision necessitated that either he commit himself first or that she do it. It could not be done simultaneously. And then the other must react. But what if the other had made the opposite decision?

If she still felt as she had done at Dunbarton, though, would she not have said so without any hesitation at all?

But she spoke again before he had framed an answer to her question. "Why did you cry?" she asked hurriedly. "When you told Mr. Gascoigne that I had miscarried, why did you cry?"

"The devil!" he said, horrified. "He told you that?"

"No, not he," she said. "Catherine told me."

Good Lord!

"Why did you cry?" she asked again.

"I lost a child," he said. "One I had only recently learned about, one I had hardly accustomed my mind to expecting. And then it was lost — in pain and anguish. *You* lost a child — my child. A child died that night and with it — two other lives. Or rather, a possibility for a life, a — I do not know what I am trying to say. I believe I wished during the days following that I had died in battle. I — did not particularly wish to live on. Perhaps I still felt the same way when I spoke to Nat. Perhaps I thought that I might have wished to live on if only that had not happened. Perhaps I thought that the wrong person had died on that night. I do not know what I am saying. Am I making any sense?"

"Why did you send for me?" she asked.

"Perhaps to discover if there was anything to live for," he said. "Though I have never thought of it quite that way until this moment."

"And is there?" she asked. "Anything to live for?"

Was there? Somehow one dreamed . . . No, he must say it aloud. "One dreams of perfection," he said, "of happily ever after. Of romantic love that defies time and death and spans eternity. It is hard to accept the very different reality of real life. We could never know perfection, Moira. There could never be a happily ever after for us. We could never truly love each other. Am I willing to settle for less than the dream? Are you?"

"I don't know," she said. "I have tried to

imagine life without you. I have tried to imagine returning to Dunbarton alone, knowing that I would never see you again."

"And?"

"It is an image of peace," she said.

Ah. He had not realized how much he had wanted her to contradict all that he had just said. He felt suddenly shattered. But he could not blame her. It was a mutual decision they were making.

"It is an image of emptiness," she said.

A little boy and his father were trying to get a kite aloft without much success. There was too little wind. But the father patiently tried again, bending over his son and positioning his hands correctly on the string. Kenneth felt a wave of envy and of longing.

"Moira," he asked, "when are your courses due?"

"Now," she said. "Today, yesterday, tomorrow. Soon."

"How would you feel," he asked, "if you found that you were with child again?"

"Terrified," she said. "Excited."

"You know," he said, "that I would not leave a child of mine to grow up without a father."

"I would not expect it," she said.

"Do you hope it is not so?" he asked.

There was a lengthy pause. "No," she said softly.

"Neither do I," he said. "But if it is not so now, it could be so next month or the month after."

"Yes," she said. And he waited for her to make the final decision. He had surely made his own wishes clear. "Kenneth, come home with me."

"For the summer?" he said. "For always?"

"We do not have to make that decision now," she said. "We can say it is for the summer or until Christmas or — whenever. Do you want to come?"

"Yes," he said.

"Then come." She set her free hand near her other on his arm and tipped her head to rest briefly on his shoulder. "You can see the fountain and the flower beds and the other changes I have made. We can walk on the cliffs and sit in the hollow. We can run on the beach. We can —"

"Make love in the baptistry," he said, interrupting her. He smiled at her. She had sounded excited, lighthearted.

"Yes," she said, her voice soft again.

"We will give it a try, then," he said, "for the summer. And if we find that it will not work, and if you are not with child, then we will make different plans when the summer is over."

"Yes."

"But for now, we will not think of that," he said.

"Autumn is a long way away," she said. "Oh, Kenneth, the trees in the park are always so beautiful in the autumn."

"I have almost forgotten what they look like," he said. "This year I will have to see them again."

"Yes," she said. "When will we leave? I can scarcely wait."

"Tomorrow?" he suggested. "Can you be ready that soon?"

"Yes, tomorrow," she said. "By this time next week we will be home at Dunbarton."

Together. They would be home together — for the summer and perhaps the autumn. Perhaps until Christmas. Perhaps, if there was a child, forever.

It would be painful to dream again. But he was dreaming again. And there was pain.

23

Life seemed almost ominously tranquil after they had arrived home in Cornwall. They stopped quarreling. At Dunbarton they resumed their separate duties, which occupied them for much of each day. They visited and entertained their neighbors, often together. They spent a part of each night together in Moira's bed before sleeping separately. It might have seemed that they were slipping into something resembling a happily ever after — or a contentedly ever after, at least.

Except that it seemed to Moira as if she lived with constantly bated breath. Nothing had been settled. They had agreed to extend the trial period of their marriage; that was all. She was with child again, of course. After three weeks there was little doubt of that. But the outcome of that might be no different from the last time, though she felt none of the ill health she had felt then and was eating and sleeping well. If she miscarried this time, would she tell him that she did not wish to see him ever again? Would he be eager enough to take her at her word?

No, she knew she could never again say that to him — not unless she had been severely provoked. But would he go anyway? Had he suggested coming to Cornwall merely because her answers to his questions had shown him the very real possibility that she had conceived again? Sometimes she thought there was more to it than that. *Most* of the time she thought so, but she was afraid to believe too deeply. She tried to guard her heart against future pain.

If she carried her child through to term and if the child lived, he would stay with her. But she did not want his staying to depend upon those facts alone. She did not want him to stay just for the sake of the child. She wanted him to stay because of *her.*

Sometimes she despised herself for having grown so dependent upon him, for having come to love him so unconditionally, so uncritically. Sometimes she fought against her dependence — often in a quite irrational manner.

They were to call upon her mother one afternoon. They had arranged it at breakfast.

Because the weather was glorious after almost a week of gloomy fog and drizzle, they had decided to walk to Penwith Manor in order to make a full afternoon's outing of the visit. There had seemed to be a silent communication between them too. It happened often and had Moira wondering if she imagined it or if their thoughts really did intermingle at times. On this occasion they had both thought of the hermit's hut a short distance from the road down to the valley. They had both thought of stopping there on the way back from Penwith. It was one of the things he had mentioned during that walk by the Serpentine. They would make love in the baptistry, he had said.

They had never made love during the daytime. Apart from that first time, they had never made love anywhere but in Moira's bed. There was something distinctly arousing about the thought of making love on a summer afternoon in the hut, the door left open to the sunshine and the breeze. They would be able to see down into the valley to the river and the waterfall.

But the depth of her feelings for him frightened her. "Perhaps," she said to him during luncheon, "you have other, more important things to do this afternoon than visiting, Kenneth. There is really no need for you to accompany me to Mama's."

"Is there not?" His eyes surveyed her rather lazily. Had his eyes changed? Had they become softer, dreamier of late? Or did she imagine it? "You would prefer to have a private tête-à-tête with her, Moira? Complain to her of all my sins when I am not there to defend myself? I suppose your complaints would fall on fertile ears."

She bristled. "I would imagine that Penwith must be one of the places you least like to visit," she said, "and that Mama must be one of the people you least like having to converse with."

She realized, with some surprise, what she was doing. She was trying to provoke a quarrel with him. It was almost as if she felt safer when they quarreled, as if she was then better able to guard her heart.

He raised his eyebrows and she knew from his suddenly haughty expression that he was accepting the bait. "Indeed?" he said. "You believe that we have identical sentiments about each other's mother, then, Moira?"

"With the difference," she said, "that your mother has been openly unkind to me."

"Oh, I think not," he said with an impatient wave of one hand. "My mother likes to be in control. She has very definite ideas of what is expected of a countess. She merely tried to take you under her wing. She hoped — foolishly — to mold you into being the sort of countess she has always been. She did not mean to be unkind."

"I beg to differ with you," she said. "You say it was a *foolish* hope because I am incapable of being a proper countess?"

"A proper countess," he said curtly, "does not quarrel with every word her husband utters and twist it into a meaning he did not intend merely because she derives perverse enjoyment from irritating him."

"I have irritated you?" she said. "All I intended to do was release you from a potentially tedious afternoon by offering to go to Penwith alone this afternoon."

"And you may do so, ma'am," he said. "As you suggested, I have other, more important things to do than sit with a mother and daughter who would far prefer to be alone together. I shall order the carriage brought around for you."

"I will walk," she said.

"You will, of course," he said, "do as you please. Take your maid with you."

She had no intention of doing so and would have said so except that she realized that she had pushed him far enough. If she expressed this one extra defiance, it would be just like him to insist. How dreary it would be to have to walk all the way to Penwith and back with her maid trailing her. How dreary it was going to be to walk *alone*. Why had she done it? She had so looked forward to the afternoon, and now single-handedly she had spoiled it.

"What will you do?" she asked.

His eyes were no longer soft and dreamy when they looked into hers. "Something far more congenial to me than what I had originally planned, you may be sure, ma'am," he said.

She hated being called *ma'am*. How ridiculous when she was his wife, when they enjoyed such knee-weakening intimacies each night, when she was with child by him. But she would not tell him how she hated it. Then he would never call her anything else.

"Then I am glad I had the foresight to suggest it, my lord," she said, smiling brightly. She was behaving just like a silly child. She had goaded him to irritation and now resented it. She had deliberately ruined her own afternoon and now wanted to indulge in self-pity and throw all the blame upon him.

And it was all for nothing. There was no way, she realized with a flash of uncomfortable insight, of guarding the heart.

■ ■ ■ ■

He went striding off along the top of the valley until he reached the cliffs. He turned to walk along the top of them, his eyes on the jutting rocks and the faded green of the coarse grass rather than on the sea below, sparkling in the sunshine. He felt thoroughly irritated and irritable. Nelson, unaffected by his mood, raced on ahead of him, circled back to trot by his side for a few yards, and went racing on again.

He had been settling quite comfortably into domestic bliss. He had been happy to be back, to be at work again, to be feeling useful again. He had been happy to see that his wife was competent and enthusiastic in the performance of her own duties. He had been enjoying the social life of the neighborhood, limited as it was. He had been contented with the knowledge that there was no further decision to make, that he would be staying at Dunbarton. He had visited his wife's bed every night, including the nights they had spent on the road. It was perfectly clear that she must be increasing.

While their only real personal contact with each other happened in her bed and was entirely sexual in nature, he had felt a closeness between them, the sort of harmony that he expected of a marriage. He had assumed that they would both relax into it and allow all those factors that had driven them apart just to fade away into the past. He had expected that they would never be confronted and that they need never be.

It had been a foolish expectation and a foolish hope. How could one expect peace and tranquillity with Moira? She had created a quarrel out of nothing at luncheon and he, like a puppet on a string, had quarreled. No one had ever been able to manipulate him. He had been known as a stubborn boy and as a man with an iron will. It infuriated him that a *woman* could do what no one else had ever done — and could do it with such ease.

Sometimes he hated her. This afternoon, he hated her.

Two of the Misses Grimshaw were strolling toward him on the arms of two of the Meeson sons. He had to roar at Nelson to sit when the elder sister screamed at his enthusiastic barking, but he realized even as he did so that the scream had been prompted entirely by the golden opportunity Nelson had given the lady to cower close to her escort and engage in a graceful fit of the vapors.

He stood with the two couples for a few minutes, discussing with them the weather and the health of Lady Haverford and the Grimshaw and Meeson parents. He continued on his way even further irritated. All four of them had been patently in awe of him, even frightened by him. Most people were frightened of him, he thought, scowling. It could not be just his title and his property and wealth. It must be something in his manner, something he had deliberately cultivated during his years as a cavalry officer. There were distinct advantages to seeing hardened soldiers almost literally quaking in their boots every time they caught his eyes upon them. It was rather more disconcerting to provoke the same reaction in one's neighbors.

Moira was one of the few people not afraid of him — not one whit. Kenneth scowled. Perhaps he should see to it that she developed a healthy fear of him. But the thoroughly silly thought only had him scowling more ferociously. It would be an impossible thing to accomplish, for one thing. For another, he would not be able to abide having to live with a docile Moira.

He chuckled suddenly and found his good humor unexpectedly restored. A docile Moira — a flat mountain, a hot iceberg, a dry ocean, a flying pig. He amused his thoughts with other combinations of an equal impossibility to a docile Moira as he made his way back to Dunbarton across country.

His wife's maid was in the hall when he went inside. For more than one reason she had no business being there. He rather suspected that the presence on duty of a certain handsome footman explained the matter. He raised his eyebrows as he looked at the bobbing, embarrassed girl.

"Her ladyship is back home already?" he asked her. He knew very well even before she answered that her ladyship was not.

"Oh, no, my lord," her maid said. "Her ladyship has gone to Penwith, my lord."

"Ah," he said. "And whom did she take with her, pray?"

"Her ladyship went alone, my lord," she said.

It was as he had known as soon as he spotted the girl, of course. It was what he should have expected even before he saw her. Had he not instructed Moira to take her maid with her? Had he really expected her to *obey* him? Was he still that naive? She had always wandered alone, of course — when she was a girl and earlier in this year. But she was his *wife* now, and by God she would not be so careless of her own safety merely for the sake of defying him.

"Thank you," he said curtly, and turned to leave the house again. The footman, he saw, was standing near the open door looking like a wooden soldier. He might have felt amused had he not been in such a towering rage. He went back to the stable for Nelson, who greeted him with as much ecstasy as he might have shown if they had been separated for a month.

Moira was walking back home along the valley. Despite the bright sunshine and the heat, despite the lush greenery of trees and grass and ferns and the sparkling blue of the river, and despite the fact that she had had a good visit with her mother, she felt depressed. There would be a strangeness, an awkwardness, a coldness, between her and Kenneth this evening, and she did not know how it was to be dispelled. They had no engagement for this evening. They would be alone together. Should she apologize? But it went so very much against the grain to apologize to Kenneth of all people. Besides, he had made that thoroughly disagreeable remark about her complaints to her mother falling on fertile ears. As if she would ever speak even the whisper of a negative comment about him to Mama. She had more pride than to do any such thing.

And then she stopped dead in her tracks. But the momentary and purely habitual wave of panic immediately gave place to smiles and she stretched out her arms to Nelson, almost inviting him to gallop right up to her, jump up on her, and half bowl her over. She laughed and hugged him and turned her face away.

"Nelson," she said, not for the first time, "you do not have the sweetest breath, you know."

She felt suddenly happy and lighthearted. Where Nelson went, Kenneth could not be far behind. He had come to meet her. She looked eagerly ahead and, sure enough, there he was in the distance, standing in the middle of the bridge. It was just where he had stood that other afternoon in January when he had asked if she was increasing and she had said no. That seemed a lifetime ago. She went hurrying forward, smiling brightly as she went. She was almost running by the time she reached the bridge and turned onto it.

Cold gray eyes watched her from a cold, unsmiling face.

"Doubtless," he said, "you have been walking too fast for your maid to keep up.

Shall we wait for her, ma'am?"

It was instantly clear to her that he knew very well she had come alone. It was equally clear that he had come, not to meet her, but to scold her. He was furiously angry. They could have a glorious quarrel if she so chose — *if* she so chose. It was almost too good an opportunity to miss.

She continued to smile. "Don't scold," she said. "I am deeply, abjectly apologetic. I will never disobey you again."

His nostrils flared and his eyes cooled off several more degrees. "You choose to mock me, ma'am?" he said so quietly that Moira felt a small flicker of alarm.

She tipped her head to one side and assessed her physical danger. Her smile softened and she took the three steps that would bring him within reach. She set the fingertips of one hand against the lapel of his coat. "Don't scold," she said again. "Don't scold."

He was not going to give in easily. "Can you give me one good reason why I should not, ma'am?" he asked.

She shook her head. "None," she said. "I cannot think of one good reason or even one weak reason. Kenneth, don't scold."

She had him puzzled, she could see. She was puzzled herself. She had never before failed to take advantage of a looming quarrel. But she had admitted to herself earlier that the heart was not to be guarded. And her heart was singing — and crying.

"I do not give commands for the sake of exercising power over you, Moira," he said. "Your safety is my concern and my responsibility."

"Is it?" She smiled at him.

"You are in a strange mood," he said, frowning. "When the great guns used to fall silent in battle, our flesh would crawl with fear because we would know that the real attack was about to begin."

"Is your flesh crawling with fear?" she asked.

But he merely continued to frown at her.

She thought of something suddenly and grinned at him. "Oh, Kenneth," she said, "I *must* tell you. You will be *wonderfully* diverted." She laughed at the mere thought of it.

He had one elbow resting on the parapet of the bridge. But she noticed that his other hand covered hers, holding it against his lapel.

"Mama had a letter from Sir Edwin," she said. "Oh, Kenneth, when he was in London he made the acquaintance of a great and gentle heiress — his words — who is going to need a gentleman of wisdom and experience and a man of solid principle and humble worth — I do wish I could remember his exact words. It is quite unsatisfactory merely to paraphrase the words of Sir Edwin. Anyway, she is going to need such a gentleman, presumably as a husband, when she completes her year of mourning for her papa — coincidentally at almost the exact time that Sir Edwin completes his for his mama. It seems, Kenneth — you will be amazed — that Sir Edwin judges himself to be just the man for the task and that he has persuaded his great and gentle heiress of the same happy truth by explaining to her that the Earl of Haverford, master of Dunbarton, one of the finest estates in Cornwall, is his kinsman by marriage and his dear friend besides, and that his mother was a Grafton of Hugglesbury — *in that order, Kenneth.* Are you not vastly relieved?"

"Vastly," he said. "I might have hurled myself from this bridge in mortification had he put it the other way around."

"The outcome of all this," Moira said, "is that it is unlikely Sir Edwin will wish to take up permanent residence at Penwith in the foreseeable future. He will be greatly honored if Mama will continue to live there as — oh, listen to this, Kenneth — as the

469

widow of the late lamented Sir Basil Hayes, and as the mother-in-law of the Earl of Haverford, master of — Do I need to finish?"

"So we are not after all to have him as a neighbor?" Kenneth asked. He was grinning.

"Can you contain your disappointment?" she asked.

"It will not be easy." He threw back his head and laughed. "But life is a series of disappointments to be overcome. I shall try my best."

They laughed together for several moments until the laughter faded and they looked self-consciously at each other.

"Have I teased you out of the mopes?" she asked at last.

"I was not in the *mopes,* Moira," he said. "The very idea! I had good reason to be angry. What you have done is divert my anger. Very clever of you."

She smiled at him. "Why did you come?" she asked.

"To give you a good tongue-lashing," he said. "To blister your ears with my displeasure."

She shook her head. "No," she said softly. "Why did you come?" She had discovered in London, at Vauxhall, that she had a skill she had not even suspected before then. She

470

had the ability to flirt in the most outrageous manner. And she had discovered that flirting could be marvelously exciting when one saw it take effect — and marvelously arousing too. She took a step closer and set her other hand on his other lapel. She looked very directly into his eyes and whispered. "Tell me why you came."

"Minx," he said. "Do you believe I do not know what you are up to? I will not scold you, then. Are you satisfied? My anger is all gone." He drew breath sharply. "You had better not start what you are unprepared to finish, ma'am."

She had found the one spot in the center of his throat that was not covered by his cravat and neckcloth. She had set her lips against it. She could not quite believe that she could be so brazen — in broad daylight in the outdoors when he had not first taken the initiative.

"I am always prepared to finish everything I start," she said, kissing the sensitive spot between his jaw and his earlobe. "And to work thoroughly at every part of the task that comes between start and finish. Everything worth doing is worth doing well, you know. Is that not a piece of marvelous wisdom?"

"Moira," he asked, his voice low to match

her own, "are you making love to me?"

"Am I doing so poorly that you have to ask?" she said. She touched the tip of her tongue to his earlobe and he jerked.

"Minx!" he said again. "I assume you do not intend for this to be taken to its natural conclusion in the middle of a bridge. Might I suggest the baptistry?"

"You might." She drew back her head and smiled at him. "This is why you came to meet me, is it not?"

"*You* started this," he said.

"No." She shook her head. "If you had not been standing here on the bridge, there would have been nothing for me to start, would there? Tell me this is why you came."

"Not to scold you but to love you?" he said. "Have it your way, then."

"I intend to," she said. "Always. For the rest of my life." This, she thought, was what must be meant by burning one's bridges behind one. She was opening herself to rejection and pain. She did not care. There was no way of protecting herself, anyway.

"You are going to have a battle on your hands, then," he said, "for the rest of your life. But not this afternoon. This afternoon I am in accord with you. Come."

He set an arm firmly about her waist so that she had little choice but to do the same to him. She pulled off her bonnet and held it by the strings so that she could rest the side of her head against his shoulder. They walked thus up the steep road toward the hilltop in the shadow of the trees until they left it not far from the top in order to cross the hillside to the hermit's hut.

He stood outside the door with her before they went inside. He drew her against him and kissed her deeply. It was the first time in nine years, she realized, that they had kissed outside of her bed — except beneath the mistletoe and at their wedding. She could feel the warmth of the sun on her head.

"Yes," he said, lifting his head and looking down at her. "This is why I came, Moira. To love you where I loved you first. To set right all that was wrong on that occasion. But to tell you with my body that I am not sorry it happened. To tell you I am *glad* it happened. Come and make love with me, then."

"Yes," she said. And she told him with her eyes and with the one word that what he had said had been spoken for both of them.

"And afterward," he said, reaching behind him for the handle of the door, "we will talk, Moira. About everything. We will *talk*."

"Yes," she said as he opened the door and led her inside.

24

They made love in a band of warm sunshine from the open door of the hut. There was little fear of discovery by a chance wanderer — Nelson sat in the doorway, gazing down into the valley. He would give them ample warning, Kenneth assured her as he lay back on the narrow cot, adjusted his clothing, and raised her dress as he took her astride him. Besides, he said, setting his hands on her hips, positioning her, and bringing her down firmly onto him, almost no one ever wandered in the hills.

"Come," he said, reaching for her shoulders and bringing her down over him. His hands moved in her hair and it all came cascading over her shoulders and about his face. He reached over to set her hairpins on the floor. "Ah, my beautiful Madonna. Ride me, then."

It was not a new position to her. She loved it, as she loved all the positions he had taught her. She loved the freedom to move, to set the pace and the rhythm, to indulge the illusion of mastery. She knew it was only illusion. She had learned — he had taught her and perhaps she had done some of the teaching too — that there was no mastery in a truly satisfying sexual experience, but only mutual giving and taking.

She rode him, but he did not lie passive beneath her. He moved with her, and his thumbs hooked the low neckline of her dress beneath her breasts so that his fingers could work with agonizing skill at her nipples.

A loving was always new. And yet there was a familiarity too by now. She knew that excitement would build until it reached a point of mindless pleasure and pain, beyond which was nothing and everything and perfect bliss. She had learned to sense the moment when the sharp ascent to climax would begin. And eventually, after a long, energetic building of sheer pleasure, she could feel it approaching. Soon, now, there would be the straining and the frenzy. But not just yet. And he knew it too, though she knew that the physical progress to fulfillment was a little different for him. He could read her body's responses as well as she.

He spoke to her just before the moment,

raising his hands to cup her face, holding it so that she gazed down into his eyes. "I love you," he told her. "I love you so much it hurts."

She hovered between thought and physical sensation. He smiled at her. "I love you too," she said. "I have always loved you." She smiled back at him.

But he had not intended an interruption to their lovemaking, only something to heighten and intensify it. His hands came to her hips and held them firm, stopping her movements while he drove up hard into her. Ascent, achievement of the summit, and descent happened all simultaneously in one shattering, terrifying, glorious burst of light and warmth and physical release and love. She was aware of crying out, but she was aware, too, of hearing his cry mingled with her own. She felt heat gush deep inside. She was half aware of Nelson woofing beside the cot before retiring to the door again and lying down there.

Some time later, she turned her head to nestle more comfortably on Kenneth's shoulder while he straightened her legs on either side of his own. She loved it when he did not immediately disengage from her. She loved the feeling of union. She sighed and felt relaxed from the topmost hair on her head to her toenails.

She did not sleep. The feeling of utter well-being was far too precious to be wasted in sleep. Kenneth slept for a while. She reveled in his relaxed warmth, in his quiet, even breathing. He had not said it just as a sexual thing, she thought. It had not been said just because he had been reaching the end of a good bedding. He often spoke to her during lovemaking, sometimes with a question or a request, sometimes with an appreciative comment for what she was doing, sometimes with erotic words that were all part of the process of arousal. He had never spoken of love. Not until this afternoon. And this afternoon the words had been spoken very deliberately and had been planned too. He had chosen the very last moment before everything was lost in sensation. He had chosen that moment so that what they had shared right afterward had been not only sex but also love. Both combined in perfect marital union.

She was glad she had spoken the words back to him. She had never been able to as a girl. She had always been afraid of the final commitment, the full baring of her soul. She was still afraid, but she was learning that fear must not be allowed to rule her life. Someone had told her that recently.

She could not remember who.

"Were you sleeping?" He kissed her forehead.

"No," she said.

There was a companionable silence. His fingers were massaging her head. "Are you feeling well this time?" he asked at last.

"Oh, yes," she said. "I feel full of health and well-being. I feel quite different from last time." It was the first time either of them had referred to her pregnancy.

"Are you afraid?" His lips were against her forehead again.

"Yes," she said.

"I wish I could offer some consolation," he said. "I wish I could assure you that all will be well. I cannot. I am terrified too."

"But I will not give in to fear," she said. "I will live my life boldly. If I have a child, I will consider myself the most fortunate of women. If I have children, I will wonder what I have done to deserve such happiness. If I have none, I will remember all the other blessings of my life — oh, yes, and grieve too. But I will not give in to fear."

He chuckled. "That is a familiar phrase," he said. "It was something of a motto with Rex, Nat, Eden, and me. We had a reputation for madness and recklessness, you know. Someone once called us the Four

Horsemen of the Apocalypse, and the name stuck. But we were not bold because of madness or superior courage or insensitivity. We were bold because we refused to give in to fear. We used to say it in chorus together."

"Well, then," she said, "we will not fear because I am with child, Kenneth."

"Except," he said with a sigh, "that I cannot ride into battle for you, can I? I have to wait and watch you do all the suffering — for a child I have begotten in you. You humble me, Moira, and render me helpless. That should delight you."

She smiled but said nothing for a while. She did not want to win mastery over him any more than she wanted to be mastered by him. "But I need you," she said. "When there is pain, and even more when there is sorrow, there can be terrible loneliness. But if there is someone there . . . Kenneth, when I was miscarrying, you stayed with me even though Mr. Ryder told you to leave. You were pale and you had tears in your eyes. You begged me not to die, not to leave you. You called me your love. I did not imagine it, did I?"

"No," he said. She felt him draw a deep breath. "I would have died for you if it would have helped. Cheerfully."

She swallowed. She had not imagined it, and yet the very next morning she had told him she never wanted to see him again. He had seemed so very cold. Had he merely been unhappy, uncertain, waiting to take his cue from her? Could she have had him for comfort during that dreadful week and the weeks that had followed his leaving? Human communication was a terrible thing; it so often gave off false messages or else broke down altogether.

She lifted herself off him without looking into his face. There was the momentary pang of regret, as there always was, as she felt her body disengage from his, but she did not stop. She pulled up her bodice, straightened her skirt, pushed her feet into her shoes, flicked her hair behind her shoulders, and stepped outside into sunlight and heat. She lifted her face to the sun and closed her eyes. And then she stepped off the slightly worn path to sit on the grass of the hillside and look down into the valley, her arms clasped about her knees. Nelson settled beside her with a satisfied sigh, his head on his paws.

She had another lesson to learn, she realized. She had to learn to be dependent. A marriage was a mutual dependency, not a double independence. She had to learn to accept his love, his care, his need to protect — even if it meant taking a maid with her when she went out without him. She had to learn to sense his fears and his occasional feeling of helplessness — and to watch his tears. She had to learn to accept his love. Love was not something just to give. It had to be received too, even at the expense of some independence.

But she loved him. And he loved her. Oh, God, how she loved him. She lowered her forehead to her knees.

He did not know if he had said something or done something to offend her. He followed her outside half fearfully. But she was seated on the grass close to the hut and she lifted her head from her knees when he sat down beside her, and she smiled at him. It was a soft, warm smile. He set one hand against the nape of her neck. Her hair was warm and silky between his palm and her flesh.

"The decision is made, then, Moira?" he asked. He was no longer fearful of her answer or in any doubt of his own. "We will stay together no matter what? Because we wish to? Because we love each other?"

"And because we are married," she said. "Because marriage is the new challenge of our lives. I do not suppose there is really such a thing as living happily ever after, is there?"

"Fortunately, no," he said. "How boring it would be, Moira. No more quarreling. I do not believe either of us could stand it."

She laughed softly. "No," she said. "It sounds quite horrid. *Yes, my lord* and *no, my lord* or *yes, ma'am* and *no, ma'am.*"

He chuckled with her. "We will stay together and meet the new challenge, then," he said. "Just promise never again to try to kill me."

"Silly," she said. "You must have known that the pistol was not loaded. You knew how I felt about guns. I do not even know how to load one. It is amazing I was even holding it by the right end. *Was* I?"

"I was referring more to the four thugs you sent after me three days later," he said. "They thrashed me within an inch or two of my life, you know. I believe my father's steward came along in the nick of time. But no matter. Doubtless you thought yourself severely enough provoked. And it is all long in the past now."

"Kenneth." She had turned her head to look him very directly in the eyes. Her own were wide. "What thugs? What thrashing? What are you talking about?"

He felt a sudden doubt, one he had never felt before this moment — perhaps because he had never *wanted* to doubt.

"The one I succeeded in felling confessed it," he said, "after we had restored him to consciousness with a pail of water over the head. He said *you* had sent them as punishment for what I had done to Sean."

"But what made you believe I had any power over them?" she asked, all very obvious amazement.

"They were your brother's men," he said. "*Your* men."

"Sean's? Mine?" Her brows had snapped together into a frown. "I did not — I *do* not even know who any of them were," she said. "I doubt even Sean knew. They were all disguised or had their faces blackened that night. Sean went with them that once as a lark, because he could never resist an adventure. And I found out from one of the servants and went after him to try to stop him before he was caught. I took that gun with me. Kenneth, I had *nothing* to do with those men. Sean had very little to do with them. It was his first time, and it all turned out disastrously for him. Because *you* did not wait to talk to us the next day after we had calmed down and could have talked rationally."

"They told me you were part of the gang," he said. "*Sean* told me."

"I do not believe you," she said. But she held up a staying hand. "No, I do believe you. But you must have misunderstood him. He would not have said that. It was not *true.*"

He understood everything with a sudden and sickening clarity. He got to his feet and stood looking down at the waterfall, his back to her. "It was revenge," he said quietly. "By God, it was revenge. I had turned him over to my father and destroyed his plans to elope with Helen and gain her fortune. And so he destroyed what was most precious in my life. He destroyed my love for you." He drew in a deep breath. "He must have persuaded them to say you had set them on me."

"No, Kenneth," she said. "It was someone else, someone who had a grudge against all of us. It was not Sean. He was rather wild and reckless, it is true, but there was no evil in him. He loved me; he was your friend; he was in love with Helen."

He turned his head to look down at her. By God, she believed what she said. It might have been as well, he thought, to leave the past where it was. Somehow they had overcome it and had learned to love again.

She could have been left with her memories of her brother intact. But it was too late now. Their own new love would be damaged if he did not continue — and perhaps if he did.

"Moira," he said, "Sean was the *leader* of that smuggling gang. He had gathered together all the most ruthless cutthroats in this part of Cornwall and was honing them into a dangerous and murderous band of smugglers. I should have spoken up before I did. A memory of friendship held me back — and my fear of losing you." He laughed mirthlessly. "He did not love Helen. He wanted her money. There are children in this part of England who are Sean's. Not all of their mothers went to him willingly. Your father, I believe, had set aside a decent portion for you and your mother. I believe, too, that it was spent in payment of your brother's debts. This information came directly from Sean when there was still some semblance of friendship between us. I betrayed him, Moira. I have never denied that. But he betrayed us all. And he avenged himself on me by ensuring your permanent unhappiness."

She had returned her forehead to her knees. Did she believe him? Was everything now ruined — again? Part of him wished they had never opened this topic. Part of him knew that it had been inevitable. If it had not happened now, it would have happened at some time in the future.

"He was a brave officer," he said. "He was one of those soldiers whose fame extended beyond his own regiment. He asked nothing of his men in the way of bravery or exposure to danger that he was not prepared to share with them. I am surprised I had not heard of his death until you told me. I have no doubt that he was in the thick of battle when it happened, doing his duty."

She kept her head down.

"I am sorry," he said. "I can tell that you believe me. I should have left you with your memories of him intact."

She shook her head and lifted it. She looked rather weary. "No," she said. "I will not stop loving him. One does not, you know. He was my brother. And he *did* die bravely. He went forward into gunfire to drag back a young private soldier who had been wounded. He succeeded before he died. The private survived. Sometimes people really do redeem themselves."

"And us?" he asked fearfully after a pause. "Has this conversation spoiled everything, Moira?"

"No." She shook her head. "You know

now that I was not one of those smugglers. Have you really thought it all these years? And you know that, apart from threatening you with an unloaded pistol — which was not a very nice thing to do, anyway — I never did anything to try to harm you. I said everything that I had to say in that short, screaming quarrel we had the day after Sean was arrested."

"And you know, perhaps," he said, "that I did what had to be done, for any number of anonymous people, for my sister, and even for you. I wanted to release you from that band of smugglers before you were caught and transported. I *did* betray your trust, Moira, for without your having told me, I would not have known about Sean and Helen and would not have gone on to discover for myself that their plans extended to an elopement. I have never quite forgiven myself for betraying you, but I did what I thought I had to do, even knowing that I would lose you. I made a choice — and I believe I would make the same one if it was to be made again and feel the same guilt after making it."

"If only you had *told* me," she said.

"I was not feeling kindly disposed toward you, Moira," he said. "Besides, we did not talk to each other during that one meeting we had. We yelled. We *both* yelled. Neither of us listened."

She got to her feet and came to stand beside him. She took his hand in hers, lacing their fingers together, and rested the side of her head on his shoulder. "What a wonderful sense of release," she said. "Since going to London, since falling in love with you all over again, I have allowed my thoughts to roam over all our dealings together, even back to childhood, when I worshiped you and you were unaware of my existence. But there was always that one series of events that my mind had to skirt around — and always the thought to be suppressed that somehow you were to blame for Sean's death."

He rubbed his cheek against the top of her head.

"I will be able to accept his death better now," she said. "He had a chance to redeem himself when he might as easily have been in transportation — and deservedly so. He was given the chance, and he took it and used it well. Was it you who suggested enlistment rather than transportation to your father?"

"Yes," he said.

She lifted her head and smiled at him. "Thank you," she said. "I love you."

"How I longed to hear those words when we were very young," he said, squeezing her hand. "It is the loveliest thing in the world to be told, Moira."

"And the most frightening thing in the world to say," she said. "One feels that one is giving away a part of oneself and leaving oneself open to pain and rejection."

"And to joy," he said, smiling. "I will never knowingly hurt you, my love, and I will never reject you. I will argue with you and scold you and quarrel with you — and love you all my life."

"Will you?" she asked. "Promise?"

"On all counts?" He grinned at her. "I promise. Faithfully."

"And I," she said. "I promise always to love you."

"And to quarrel with me?" he asked.

"Yes, and that too." She laughed.

"Good," he said. "It is sure to be an interesting life, then."

He wrapped an arm about her waist and drew her closer against his side. They gazed downward over the tops of leaf-laden trees to the bridge and to the river and the waterfall, blue and sparkling in the sunshine. He could not imagine a lovelier place on earth in which to live — with his first and his only love.

They turned their heads at the same moment, smiled at each other, and closed the small distance between their mouths. Nelson heaved a sigh of deep contentment and proceeded to doze.

Dear Reader,

For a number of years many of you have been telling me that you have read and loved *Irresistible,* Book 3 in the Horsemen trilogy, but cannot find the other two books. I know as a reader myself how annoying that can be when a series is involved, but yes, they have been out of print and it has been beyond my power to bring them back. That has now changed, to my great delight, and, almost twenty years after they were first published, all three books will be out again in 2016 with gorgeous new covers. Indeed, when I first saw the cover of *Indiscreet,* Book 1, I loved it so much that I told my editor I wanted to live in the cottage. Both she and my agent said they would join me there for tea and scones. Perhaps you will drop by too and enjoy the three stories, as I know read-ers did in the past.

If you are familiar with my recent Survivors' Club series, you will note the contrast in my treatment of men (and one woman) returning from war. There I chose to concentrate on the wounds, both physical and psychic, that the Napoleonic Wars caused my main characters. In the trilogy, however, I chose to tell the stories of four young cavalry officers (two of them are combined in Book 3) who have returned from war unscathed and eager to enjoy life to the full and forget about responsibility for a while. Life intervenes for them all, of course, and leads them through adversity to romance and the sort of happiness they had not anticipated. I hope you will enjoy reading or rereading their stories in these lovely new editions.

Mary Balogh

ABOUT THE AUTHOR

Mary Balogh grew up in Wales and now lives with her husband, Robert, in Saskatchewan, Canada. She has written more than one hundred historical novels and novellas, more than thirty of which have been *New York Times* bestsellers. They include the Slightly sextet (the Bedwyn saga), the Simply quartet, the Huxtable quintet, and the seven-part Survivors' Club series.